The critics ador

SUNRISE

"Poignant, endearing, tender, and charming."

—Patricia Gaffney

"*Sunrise* has all the elements that make Ms. Jarrett such a popular writer. . . . Jarrett provides her myriad of fans with an enjoyable historical romance."

—*Affaire de Coeur*

"Jarrett . . . draws her protagonists vividly and with charm."

—*Publishers Weekly*

"Lovely. Jarrett's writing is elegant, her voice sure, her characters vital. *Sunrise* is intensely emotional but never overwrought. In all ways an exceptional novel and a joy to read."

—*Contra Costa Times* (CA)

MOONLIGHT

"Five stars! Miranda Jarrett is one of the genre's best. . . . *Moonlight* will only enhance her high esteem with readers. . . . Fast-paced and delightful!"

—*Amazon.com*

"What a touching, heartfelt story! . . . Every detail will keep you wanting more. Beautifully written."

—*Rendezvous*

"Wonderful. . . . The magic of *Moonlight* lies in the characters, and Miranda Jarrett has given her readers a beautiful relationship with lovers who will clearly spend their lives living happily ever after."

—Booksquare.com

WISHING
A Romantic Times "Top Pick" and a "Pick of the Month" for January 1999 by Barnesandnoble.com

"Readers are sure to find themselves swept off their feet by this utterly enchanting and imaginative romance by the mistress of the seafaring love story. Delightfully charming and fun, yet poignant, exciting, and romantic, this is Miranda Jarrett at her finest!

—*Romantic Times*

"Sheer pleasure."

—*Rendezvous*

"Vivid and enjoyable. . . . An engrossing, heartwarming story set in a true historical background."

—*Cape Cod Journal* (MA)

"*Wishing* is a great book to curl up with."

—*Literary Times*

"A winning nautical . . . sure to appeal to all fans of colonial-era romances."

—*Booklist*

"Wonderful. . . . The early eighteenth century come[s] alive for the reader."

—*Under the Covers*

CRANBERRY POINT

Named Amazon.com's #1 Best New Romance Paperback for June 1998 and a "Pick of the Month" for July 1998 by Barnesandnoble.com

"A vivid and exciting portrait of colonial America. . . . A memorable tale of trust and love, of healing and passion, and most of all the magic of romance."

—*Romantic Times*

"[A] passionate love story rich in history and characterization. . . . This is an award-winning saga from a sensational author."

—*Rendezvous*

"Everything Jarrett does is magic."

—*Affaire de Coeur*

"A delightful book, well-crafed and vividly written. I'm enchanted."

—Linda Lael Miller, *New York Times* bestselling author of
The Women of Primrose Creek series

THE CAPTAIN'S BRIDE

"As always, Ms. Jarrett takes the high seas by storm, creating one of her liveliest heroines and a hero to be her match."

—*Romantic Times*

"Fabulous . . . loaded with action and high-seas adventure."

—*Affaire de Coeur*

"Deliciously entertaining . . . a swift, rollicking romance . . . with a richly textured understanding of the seafaring life."

—Mary Jo Putney, *New York Times* bestselling author of
The Wild Child

Books by Miranda Jarrett

The Captain's Bride
Cranberry Point
Wishing
Moonlight
Sunrise
Starlight

Published by Pocket Books

MIRANDA JARRETT

STARLIGHT

SONNET BOOKS
New York London Toronto Sydney Singapore

An *Original* Publication of POCKET BOOKS

A Sonnet Book published by
POCKET BOOKS, a division of Simon & Schuster, Inc.
1230 Avenue of the Americas, New York, NY 10020

Copyright © 2000 by Miranda Jarrett

ISBN: 0-7434-0355-X

First Sonnet Books printing October 2000

10 9 8 7 6 5 4 3 2 1

SONNET BOOKS and colophon are trademarks of Simon & Schuster, Inc.

Front cover illustration by Steven Assel

Printed in the U.S.A.

for Carol Backus
writer and friend
you are missed

The Fairbourne Family

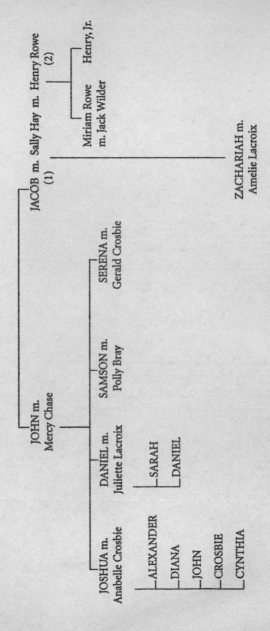

STARLIGHT

1

London
June, 1747

She'd done it again.

On this, the last day they'd likely ever spend alone together, she'd gone and spoiled everything.

Alexander Fairbourne dipped his battered knuckles into the trough of cold water beneath the inn's court-yard pump, and used what tiny bit of self-restraint he still possessed to keep from swearing before his younger sister.

"I told you this morning, Diana," he said through gritted teeth. "I've no desire to challenge every blasted rogue in this city to protect your virtue."

"Oh, bother, Alex, I never intended such a thing," said Diana, sinking down beside him in a rustle of petticoats, heedless of the silk drifting into the mud, and heedless, too, of the curious looks of those around them. "But I could hardly let that wretched fool go unrebuked, not after what he said about my—my person."

"So then he couldn't go by without answering you," said Alex as patiently as he could, "which meant I had to jump into it, too, to save your good name and split my knuckles open in the bargain."

"But I had no choice," argued Diana indignantly. "You heard what he said!"

Alex sighed. He'd heard it, and then he'd seen how Diana had dumped the man's own ale over his head, too, settling the tankard on him like a crown.

"Just because I am from the colonies and not London-born doesn't mean I'm any less of a lady," continued Diana, self-righteousness rising with every word, "and it certainly doesn't mean that I must tolerate the rude advances of a common—"

"Don't explain any further, Diana," said Alex wearily. The only explanation that mattered was simply that Diana was Diana, and always, always, at the center of misadventure and mayhem.

Not that she was any different from the rest of their family. From his father on downward, they all were far too eager to jump into any fight that happened along. Alex had only to look down at his knuckles to know he wasn't any better. For all of them, it was at once a noble blessing and a curse of the worst kind. For why else would Alex be here in London, single-handedly determined to rescue the Fairbourne fortunes from the ruinous hole his father had dug for them?

"No use in hashing it over, Diana," was all he said now. "You and I have been down this road together more times than I care to remember."

She looked up at him, the indignation vanishing from her face as suddenly as it had come. "Oh, Alex," she said softly. "Now we're almost to the end of that road, aren't we?"

"Not an end, Di," said Alex quickly, and with a gallantry that sounded false even to his ears, "but a beginning of great things for you."

"Oh, yes," said Diana half-heartedly. "Great things, indeed."

Alex sighed, wishing he knew what to say next. He understood exactly how Diana felt for he'd been feeling the same way all day. No one had forced her into making this journey with him; Father had been most careful to keep the grim truth about the family's finances from the women, and Alexander doubted his sister had any idea of how perilously close to ruin they were.

True, Diana hadn't found any of the bachelors in Massachusetts to her liking, not with most young men away at war with the French and Spanish, but neither Mother nor Father had suggested she need travel clear to London to search for a husband.

Instead his sister had gleefully concocted the entire scheme for herself with the help of one of their mother's childhood friends here in London. Crossing the ocean in an armed sloop hadn't fazed her, nor had outrunning a French frigate. She was determined to capture the capital by storm, as well as find true love and banish forever that uneasy taint of spinsterhood that was already clinging to her in Appledore. Considering she'd inherited her father's will and her mother's beauty, Alex didn't doubt that she'd succeed.

But now that the final day had arrived before Diana must carry out her plan in earnest alone, the reality of it weighed heavily upon them both. Because she'd wished it, he'd sworn to her he was weary of being her constant champion since childhood, but now he was discovering he wasn't nearly ready to relinquish that responsibility to anyone else.

"You can come back home with me, you know," he

said gruffly, flexing his fingers that now didn't seem to hurt nearly as much. "No one will fault you if you do."

"No one except Father and Mother and every other person in Appledore," she said sadly. "Fairbournes don't quit, Alex, even the female ones. I think Father must have whispered that into our ears while we were still in the cradle, taking care that Mother didn't hear. Why-ever else would we all be so eager for scrapping now?"

She tried to smile, giving her shoulders a small, twitching shrug of resignation. "Besides, if I don't find myself a husband here—and a good one, too, one that will make all those smug, simpering girls back home sick with envy—how else will I be able to find you a worthy wife?"

"A wife, ha," scoffed Alex softly. This was a sign of how upset she was, falling back on teasing him about something so moot. Even a woman like Diana needed a husband to complete her life, to give her children and a home, but he—he was a deep-water captain married to his ship and the sea, and if he married at all, it wouldn't be until he was well past thirty and ready to become a stay-at-home landsman. "I'd rather you found me a banker with deep pockets and no questions."

"You be th' young buck what struck th' scoundrel in th' White Boar?" asked an old woman who'd suddenly appeared at Alex's elbow. "You be him, don't you?"

Alex stood, frowning as he quickly tucked his bat-tered hand behind his back. He'd already slipped the White Boar's keep a few coins to cover any damages that the scuffle might have caused, and he'd been gen-erous, to make sure the man didn't go running to the constable. He wasn't about to pay any more, especially not to this sharp-eyed old beggar-woman.

"The matter is resolved, ma'am," he said, drawing himself up to his considerable captainly height. "I don't believe it needs further discussion."

"Oooh, don't you be the fancy gentleman!" the woman cackled with obvious delight. She was short and squat, her patched petticoats hiked up over unmatched stockings, and in the few yellowed teeth that remained in her head she clenched a stained clay pipe. "You can keep your pride, cap'n, an' your pocketbook, too. I don't mean to take a farthing from you or your pretty sister, but to make you a gift. Aye, I do."

Carefully she set the large wicker basket she'd been carrying on the ground, bending over to untuck the checkered cloth covering it.

But Alex didn't want to wait to see what was inside, nor did he wish to linger in the old woman's company. There was something odd about her that he couldn't quite finger, something that made the hair prickle on the back of his neck.

"Come along, Diana," he said firmly, taking his sister by the arm. "Time we were on our way back to the ship."

"No, Alex, wait," she protested, pulling her arm free. "I want to see what she has."

"Aye, m'lady, well you should," said the old woman, nodding shrewdly as she raised the cloth with a conjurer's flourish. "Now don't that be th' proper reward for a hero's work, eh?"

"Oh, Alex, look!" cried Diana with a gasp of delight that sent another tingle of wariness down Alex's spine.

"Diana, please," he began, again reaching for her arm to pull away. "We shouldn't—"

"Hush, Alex, and just look, *look* at that dear little face!"

Blast and damnation, the old witch was going to try to foist some wretched foundling on them. "Diana, we must—"

"No, *you* must!" She crouched down beside the basket, and though he dreaded what he was going to see, Alex had no choice now but to look into the basket, too.

He looked, and nearly laughed aloud with relief.

The basket was full of kittens.

Seven tiny kittens, barely weaned, he'd guess, their legs still trembling beneath their rounded, pink bellies, their tails irate pointed stalks of bristling fur as they mewed and crawled over one another.

"What beauties, what little loves!" crooned Diana as she reached down to stroke a small, fuzzy head. She was so much like their mother this way, tenderhearted toward any helpless young creature. "Have you ever seen anything so dear, Alex?"

He had, for there'd always been a new litter of kittens in the barn behind their house in Appledore. But now he could also see exactly where this crafty old woman was leading Diana, and it wasn't going to be a comfortable place for him.

"You can't have one, Di," he said firmly, "so don't even ask."

" 'Tis a gift, cap'n," protested the old woman, "and a rare gift, too. These don't be ordinary beasts. These be most special, like living lucky pieces. Seven to th' litter, mind, th' seventh birthed by th' dam, and each born with seven toes to a paw. And there be more, too, m'lady, if you harken."

She crooked a gnarled finger for Diana to come closer, and to Alex's dismay his sister did exactly as she was bid.

"They're special beasts, m'lady, these kits," the woman confided in a whisper still loud enough for Alex to hear. "For with all their sevens and sevens, they've th' power to fetch you your own true love."

He saw how Diana's eyes widened with wonder, marking the end of any common sense she might have possessed, and he knew he'd lost. She'd come to London to find a husband; how could she resist a gift like this that guaranteed that she would?

He sighed, resigned. "Very well, Di. Which kitten will it be? Choose carefully if this is going to be how you find your true love."

"Oh, Alex, I don't know!" she said with anxious indecision as she stroked first one little cat, then another. "They're all so cunning, I don't know how to pick!"

The old woman winked up at him slyly, jabbing the brown-stained stem of her pipe in the air toward Alex for emphasis. "You choose, then, cap'n."

Alex frowned. If he didn't decide on a cat, they'd either be here for another hour while Diana tried to make up her mind, or worse, end up with the entire litter. He peered down into the basket of wriggling, furry bodies, orange, white, or striped like brown tigers.

One little cat, however, seemed to stand apart from the others by choice—brave and bold on his unsteady legs, all midnight black except for a white blaze like a star on his forehead. He gazed up with yellow-green eyes, almost challenging Alex to pick him, then blinked, yawned, and settled back onto his haunches, curling his tail neatly over his oversized front paws.

"This fellow." He scooped the black kitten up with one hand, cradling it in his palms for a moment. The little cat mewed once by way of introduction, and blinked again as Alex stroked the white patch above his eyes. No kitten's purr could be heard over the racket of the street and courtyard around them, but Alex would have sworn he could feel the rumbling vibrations of contentment in his hand as the cat rubbed his tiny jaw against his thumb. A brave little cat like this one would be good company for his sister, he decided, though as he handed the animal to Diana he almost—almost—felt a quick pang of regret, enough to make him smile wryly at himself. It was a well-kept secret, of course, but at heart he knew that he, too, had inherited a goodly share of his mother's tenderness toward strays and other innocents.

"I'll call him Blackie," said Diana happily as she brushed her cheek against the little animal's soft black fur. "Young Master Blackie."

"Young Master Blackie?" repeated Alex, appalled to hear his brave little tom burdened with such a foolish name. "What the hell kind of name is that?"

"A perfect one," said Diana, slipping into the sort of high-pitched mushy voice used by women with infants and animals. "Isn't that so, my little sweet? You're young Master Blackie because except for this funny little white patch, you're black as ink, black as coal, black as midnight itself."

"You'll ruin him, Diana," grumbled Alex as he fished in his pocket for a coin to give the old woman in exchange for the cat. "A week of that nonsense, and he won't be fit for a single useful feline endeavor."

But as Alex turned with the farthing in his hand, he discovered that the old woman and her basket and the other six kittens had vanished as if they'd never been there at all. He frowned, glancing up and down the narrow street as his earlier uneasiness returned. If his sister weren't still holding the black kitten, he'd wonder if he'd dreamed the whole peculiar encounter.

"My own little Blackie," cooed Diana as she nestled the kitten beneath her chin. "You'll lead me to my true love, won't you?"

"To start he can lead us back to the ship," grumbled Alex, cursing his superstition as he settled his hat back on his head. "And the sooner we leave this place, the better for us all."

"Here, Starlight!" called Cora MacGillivray softly, ducking through the murky shadows of Lady Waldegrave's garden. "Here, here, Starlight!"

She knew she shouldn't be alone outside, not this close to dusk. Lady Waldegrave was most adamant about that, and how could Cora argue? In this last year, trust had become a luxury Cora had no right to covet, and she'd learned to measure her every movement against the risk to her freedom.

Freedom: Cora looked wistfully up at the tall brick walls around the garden and the large brick house looming beside her. Each one of those bricks marked the boundaries of her world now, a hemmed-in handkerchief of a world compared to the wild, open moors and heath where she'd been born. But when she remembered the bleak, narrow cell that would be her fate if she wasn't careful, wasn't cautious, this garden beneath the grimy London sky seemed like paradise indeed.

She shivered, tugging her shawl higher over her shoulders. Lady Waldegrave's laughter rippled through the dusk from the open window of the back parlor, echoed by the lower rumbling amusement of a gentleman. There was always at least one gentleman laughing somewhere in the house at this time of the evening, often more than one, before the other ladies arrived. Every chair around the long mahogany table would be full at supper, for widowed Lady Waldegrave craved company and amusement, and couldn't bear to be alone.

It was, Cora suspected sadly, the real reason she herself had been granted this uneasy haven. Even Lady Waldegrave's sense of duty must have its limit. To keep from finding it, Cora always took care to hide her own sorrows, and played instead the ever-cheerful companion, neither a servant nor a poor relation, but hardly an honored guest, either.

Yet when Cora considered how much Lady Waldegrave must be risking for her sake, this exchange seemed more than fair. She'd be unforgivably ungrateful to think otherwise.

But late at night, alone in her dark little chamber up under the eaves, loneliness and grief would eat at her until she wept for all she'd lost, burying her tears in her pillow and wishing that she, too, had died with the others. Which was why, now, it was so important that she find Starlight.

She pushed aside the trailing branches of the beech tree and peered into the shadows beneath. The long, heavy branches reached the ground, making a leafy cave in this corner of the garden that was exactly the kind of place where Starlight would love to hide. Unfortunately, it was also the kind of place that harbored a great many spiders, enough to make Cora hesitate before ducking inside.

"Starlight?" she called, parting the branches like a curtain as she tried to find him in the darkest shadows.

"So help me, if you're hiding in here the better to tease and vex me, why, I'll vow I'll have to—"

"Have to what?" asked a man behind her, and with a frightened gasp she jerked around to face him.

"I didn't mean to startle you," the man continued. "Better for you to hear me, I figured, than to turn about and bump into me outright."

"I beg your pardon, sir," said Cora with automatic, icy formality meant to mask the pounding of her heart. From what she could see of him here in the shadows, he didn't look like a sheriff or magistrate, and he certainly wasn't acting like one, but then that might be his way of toying with her before he made his arrest. "This is a private garden, sir, and intruders are not welcome."

"Oh, aye, but you see I'm here at this house by invitation," he said easily. "Same as you, aren't you? You and whoever it is who's teasing and vexing you."

Whoever *that* might be, thought Cora unhappily, other than himself, blocking her path back to the house like another brick wall. Not that she could fault him for assuming she was another guest. Although her hair had come half unpinned from ducking through the bushes, the castoff silk gown from Lady Waldegrave that she wore was still more than grand enough for a fashionable supper.

He tipped his head back a fraction. "I thought you might need a bit of help, sweetheart, that's all."

"I don't wish for your help, sir." She should never have come out here so late and let herself be caught

alone, even in a place she'd always believed was safe.
"What I wish is for you to leave at once."

"At once, lass?" He shook his head ruefully. "And
here I thought you were going to let me be useful.
Come, let me have a peek at this base scoundrel you've
hidden away in the tree."

He tried to look past her, leaning too close, and she
scuttled backward until her hands brushed the droop-
ing branches. She was trapped now, she thought with
rising panic, trapped between him and the murk full
of spiders.

"You protect your rascal, then?" he asked, shifting
to where the last bit of evening light over the wall
caught his face. "You don't truly wish to see him throt-
tled?"

Swiftly Cora shook her head. Poor little Starlight
would be even more terrified of this great looming
giant than she was herself. The man's voice was deep,
his words accented with a rough, ungentlemanly edge.
Not that Lady Waldegrave would care, not when she
doled out her invitations to supper. She'd overlook a
great deal more than a provincial accent if it came
with a face as handsome as this man's.

And Lord, he *was* handsome. Cora might be frightened half out of her wits, but she wasn't blind. It
wasn't just the firm cut of his jaw with the neat cleft in
the chin or the strong, straight nose and dark brows
that matched his thick, black, unpowdered hair or the
keenest blue eyes she'd ever seen. Such things mattered, of course. Even Cora knew that.

But what set him apart from the other handsome
men who'd come to Lady Waldegrave's house was the
undeniably, unavoidably masculine self-confidence that

went along with those regular features. It wasn't the petulance that so many of the spoiled young blades here in London displayed, nor the aristocratic arrogance of their fathers. This man had the assurance that came from knowing he was capable of doing whatever he wished and not being crossed. In any group of men, he'd be the leader, the one who stood out, the one the others would respect and obey without question, and fear, too, if it came to that.

God knows Cora was more than a little afraid of him herself, and it was taking all her willpower not to run like a coward and abandon poor Starlight.

Poor Starlight, and herself, too, she thought, her heart racing even faster with fear and excitement. For what if this man was the one, the one her father had promised would come? What if he'd come here, now, to help set her lost world back to rights?

What if he were the one?

"What a brave, loyal, little creature you are," he said with a half-smile that showed a single lopsided dimple. "Rare and most admirable, especially in a woman. I hope the rascal you're hiding is worth it."

As frightened as she was, she very nearly smiled back. It had charm, that lopsided dimple of his, enough charm to soften and gentle the harshness of the man's face into something more pleasing than Cora had dreamed possible. When she'd tried to imagine this moment, late at night when she could not sleep, the man had been stern, severe, the way saviors were supposed to be. He certainly hadn't been graced with the kind of grin that likely had been making women smile in return and forgive him every sin since he'd been a babe in the cradle.

Until now, Cora told herself with fierce determination. She had no more use for charm in her life than she had for trust, especially not the charm of dark, handsome men in shadowy gardens. She'd need more than that from him, much more, and he'd have to prove to her that he was capable, just as he'd have to earn her trust with more than a smile.

"What is your reason for being here, sir?" she asked, lifting her chin with what she prayed he'd interpret as boundless confidence.

"Reason?" There was that dimple again. "The drawing room was warm. My hostess was demanding. My sister was shrieking. Do you need any more?"

Cora frowned, wishing he'd offered something more substantial. "You didn't come here specifically to see me?"

"Oh, sweetheart." He frowned. "You're forcing me to be either untruthful or ungallant."

"Truthful, then," she said. "For you couldn't be gallant and lie."

He sighed. "Then the truth it must be. Before I found you here I didn't know you existed, which would have made it damnably hard to come seek you out."

"Ah." She nodded, disappointment sinking like a stone through her breast. She'd expected more from him, but likely she'd just granted the qualities of a hero to him simply because she'd wished it so badly herself and because his eyes were such a bonnie, bonnie blue. "Then perhaps it's better if you leave me. Yes, that would be best."

He flung one arm out by way of apology. "There now, you're punishing me for telling the truth you sought."

"Not to punish you, sir," she said, "but to preserve my reputation. If you do not leave directly, then I shall shout for the manservants to come."

He studied her long enough that she felt herself flush.

"No," he said finally. "You won't."

"Oh, yes, I shall," she said warmly. "You misread my resolve, sir."

"It has nothing to do with resolve, sweetheart. You won't call or shout or scream because you're not supposed to be here, either. Especially not with that cowardly bastard still hiding in the bushes that you—*oww!*" Wincing, he reached up to rub his hand back and forth across the front of his coat, over his heart.

"Are you—are you ill?" she asked uncertainly. The man she needed must be strong, not weak, or else he'd never do. "I can—oh, my, whatever happened to your hand?"

"This?" He glanced down at the back of his hand—the knuckles swollen, the broken skin angry and bruised—with the sort of careless modesty men always affected after scrapes. "Defending a lady's good name, that's how I've come by that, and now I've—blast, that's *enough*." He jerked open the top buttons on his coat and slipped his hand inside.

"Here you go, you little devil," he said, carefully drawing out a small black kitten. "Wishing to pay your respects to this lady is one thing, but clawing me to bits to do so is quite another."

"Starlight!" cried Cora with joy and relief as she reached eagerly for the little cat in the man's hand. "Oh, thank you so much for finding him!"

"But this can't be your Starlight," said the man, as he

protectively lifted the kitten away from Cora's hands. "This kit belongs to my sister, and his name's Blackie."

But he didn't and it wasn't, thought Cora, her desperation growing. He was her Starlight, her own little cat with the white patch on his forehead, the one she'd found not a week before shivering here in this very garden. She'd taken him in, warmed him and fed him and lavished all the love she'd held locked away for two years upon his small furry head. He was a stray like herself, lost and unwanted, and he'd become her charge, her secret, her one single friend who'd listen endlessly to whatever she whispered into his small pointed ear.

"Hey, Starlight, Starlight," she said softly, and the kitten's ears pricked toward her. He mewed, little more than a squeak of greeting, and leaned as far as he dared out of the giant's hand toward her.

"I tell you, lass, he's Blackie, not Starlight," said the man with surprising gentleness in his voice. She liked that gentleness, just as she liked the kindness he'd showed her cat, both qualities that were precious rare in her life now. "I chose him from the litter myself for my sister this very afternoon. I'm sorry if you've lost your kitten, but you're mistaken about this one."

"But I'm not!" cried Cora impatiently. "He's Starlight, and he's mine, not yours, and I'm not going to give him up!"

Before the man could answer she rushed forward and seized the kitten in both hands. Starlight knew her, she could tell, his little body trembling as she cradled him close to her breast, his tail curling against her wrist.

Before the man could grab him back, she turned

and ran, darting through the garden, ducking beneath the branches, and not once looking over her shoulder.

"Come back here, girl!" the man shouted, crashing through the bushes after her. "Come back with my cat!"

But Starlight was hers, and Cora wasn't going to give him up, and what was more, she knew the way through the dark garden and the man didn't. Swiftly she reached the safety of the kitchen, slipping unnoticed through the confusion of Cook preparing supper. She ran up the back stairs and down the dark hall to her room and shut the door tight after her, wedging the chair beneath the knob to be doubly sure. Then she huddled on the bed against the wall in the dark with her feet curled beneath her and the little cat in her lap, her heart pounding and her breath ragged in her ears.

"He'll never dare follow us now, Starlight," she whispered into the kitten's fur. "Most likely we'll never see him again."

Starlight purred his contentment, and licked his rough tongue across her thumb. Cora took comfort in the tiny gesture, and yet at the same time her thoughts raced on.

Had her kitten done the same to the man who'd called him Blackie? Had he mewed happily, and nestled closer in the safe, cozy nest between his chest and the wool of his coat? Would Starlight have been as happy to have stayed with the man, to have shared his life and adventures in the wide world instead of being penned in so tightly with her? Would the man with the blue eyes and dimpled smile have made him happy? And could he have done the same for her as well, and helped her reclaim the freedom she'd thought lost?

"Oh, Starlight," she whispered, heedless of the tears that were wetting the little cat's fur. "What if he was the one, kitten? What if I ran away from him, and he was the one?"

2

Alex stood beside the tall window, his hands clasped tight behind his back, his impatience growing by the moment. Though his mother had worked hard to instill some sense of polite behavior and a modicum of good manners into his resistant soul, nothing she could have taught him in their Massachusetts parlor would have prepared him for the great roaring boredom of a fashionable London drawing room.

And not one glimpse of the girl from the garden. Restlessly he flipped open his watch to check the time. Damnation, where was she? He'd assumed she'd been a guest—why else would she have been inside Lady Waldegrave's private garden, a brown-eyed elf of a girl dressed in a yellow silk gown that had shimmered around her like her own patch of sunshine?—but if she hadn't joined the others by now, she likely wasn't coming at all.

With an exasperated sigh he stuffed the watch back into his pocket. Supper had been bad enough, course after course of French-style kickshaws so overdressed and overwrought that he still wasn't sure what he'd been eating. Then came the stupefying time spent

with the other gentlemen after the ladies had with-
drawn, brandy and pipes and endless inebriated argu-
ments over horses Alex had never heard of, let alone
seen race.

By the time they'd rejoined the ladies here in the
drawing room, the other men were so deeply in their
cups that all they could do was squabble or bray, or
simply fall asleep in the tall-backed chairs before the
fire, snoring shamelessly in the face of some poor,
pained lady.

Not that the women offered much better company.
To Alex they seemed as empty-headed as the men and
as overdone as the supper, so uniformly disguised by
padding and powder and furbelows that he'd had a
difficult time distinguishing one from the other. No
wonder that they'd all swooped down upon his sister
with such cries of delight; Diana was the only female
guest whose beauty was actually *hers*.

The only lady guest, that is, besides the girl in the
garden. She'd been real enough, too, with her pale little face and pointed chin and freckles over the bridge
of her nose that she hadn't bothered to hide with
powder, her dark red hair reminding him of the chest-
nuts back home.

He wished she hadn't run away from him. He
wished she were here now to tell him why she had.

Her speech and bearing had marked her as well
born, a lady, as much as the rustling silk and lace cuffs
she'd worn. There'd been a softness to her speech, too,
that hinted at the country, of those freckles honestly
gotten in the open sunshine. But how did she recon-
cile the honesty of freckles with the unrelenting arti-
fice of society?

Not that his sister was having any difficulty in adjusting to this world of blatant flattery. He looked across the room to where Diana was listening, wide-eyed, to one of the fatuous, foppish men from dinner. She looked lovely, wearing bright blue scarcenet that brought out the color of her eyes and three nodding white plumes in her black hair, but still Alex couldn't help grumbling disconsolately to himself.

God knows this was exactly what his sister had come clear to London to do, but it wasn't easy to watch Diana make a fool of herself. What had happened to all her sound Massachusetts common sense, anyway? From the moment this afternoon she'd been welcomed by Lady Waldegrave and declared to be the most perfect beauty the colonies had ever produced, Diana had been beaming and basking in the attention as if she truly believed every rubbishy word. She'd lapped up the compliments with the same greedy eagerness that Blackie had demonstrated this afternoon with his first saucer of cream.

Blackie. He almost groaned aloud, imagining Diana's reaction when she learned he'd practically given her kitten away, and to another woman, too.

"You frown, Alexander," said Lady Waldegrave, prodding his arm with her furled fan. "Does the quality of my company so displease you?"

"Not at all, ma'am," said Alex quickly, but not fast enough for his hostess.

"You lie, sir," she said, the prodding now more of a jab. "And not particularly well, either. But for your dear mother's sake and your sister, too, I shall forgive you."

"You're too kind, ma'am," he murmured, then realized he'd blundered again, and bowed his apology. "My lady, that is."

"No wonder your mother so despairs of you," she teased, tipping her head to one side to look up at him from beneath her lashes. "Yet I'll forgive you for that misstep, too, though I may not let you forget it. 'Ma'am' indeed!"

She smiled, taking away whatever sting might have been in her words. Alex suspected the countess had been using the same famously beatific smile on men since before he'd been born—in her first year in London she'd been dubbed Lady Angel—and though she was no longer young herself, that smile still had its powers. She was a slight woman with the kind of fine-boned face that had aged well, and she wore her ransom of jewels— the sapphire alone in her necklace was as large as a pigeon's egg—with a properly aristocratic nonchalance.

And as soon as Alex had met her, he'd understood how, long ago, she'd been great friends with his mother: they both were kindhearted and impulsive, both witty, natural coquettes who thrived on centering a room full of adoring friends. But while Anabelle Crosbie had married for love alone, scandalously eloping with a low-bred sea captain from the colonies, Charlotte Vanbrugh had married dutifully, dully, and very well.

Now, nearly thirty years later, Anabelle Fairbourne lived in a cheerfully disorganized house on Massachusetts Bay, surrounded by a husband and children and countless pets who worshiped her even as they tracked sand upon her floors. The widowed, childless Dowager Countess of Waldegrave had three grand residences, two carriages, and a hundred servants, none of which seemed able to make her famous smile less stoic and more genuinely happy.

"I've forgiven you, Alexander, yet still you frown,"

said Lady Waldegrave, sounding genuinely perplexed. "Whatever have we done to vex you so already?"

"Nothing whatsoever," said Alex quickly. He'd be a poor guest to fault his hostess for how she'd chosen to live her life. "If I was frowning, it was because I was missing another of your guests."

"One of my guests is missing?" Now the countess was the one who frowned as she glanced about the drawing room, counting her guests with the proprietary thoroughness of a hen with her chicks. "Why, they do seem to all be present, though Mr. Carlton does seem to be rather sleepy."

To Alex it appeared that Mr. Carlton was rather snoring, though he politely chose not to point this out. "I meant the young lady with the chestnut hair."

"Chestnut hair?" Again Lady Waldegrave surveyed her guests. Diana was the only woman in the room whose hair was not powdered white, and hers was black, not chestnut. "I cannot fathom whom you mean."

"But she was here," insisted Alex. "I met her earlier this afternoon when I left to take Diana's kitten away."

"And a good thing you did, too," declared the countess, dabbing a lace-bordered handkerchief to her nose. "Verminous little beast! Even the memory of a cat in my home is enough to make me weep and wheeze like an old bellows!"

"We never would have brought the kit here, ma'am, if we'd known you'd be so affected," said Alex hurriedly. *That* was certainly true. As soon as Diana had lifted Blackie from his new basket, Lady Waldegrave had begun to sneeze, her eyes turning red and teary as she'd gasped about the pestilence carried by cats. Alex had barely been able to snatch the poor kitten from the hands of a vengeful footman, tucking the trembling little cat into his own coat for protection before he, too, had escaped through the door to the garden.

"You did remove the creature with haste," said the countess, grudgingly mollified. "And I'll grant that you couldn't have known of my affliction."

"No, ma'am," said Alex contritely, preferring to distract her from the recollection of Blackie's unhappy banishment. "It was while I was taking the kitten through your garden that I met with the young lady."

"But not one with chestnut hair," protested Lady Waldegrave quickly, sweeping her fan to encompass the room. "As you see, I've no such lady here tonight."

"Not that I've seen here, no. But she was real enough. Small, a bit of a thing, in a yellow gown like sunshine."

"A yellow gown?" exclaimed Lady Waldegrave, cocking her hands back from the wrists to emphasize how appalled, how *horrified*, she was by his suggestion. "No *lady* would wear yellow, not this season, not if she has any slight wish to follow the fashion, and not if she wishes to be welcome in my home, either!"

But her trilling laugh, like her protest, somehow rang false to Alex's ear. "She *was* there, my lady," he said testily. "And I'd wager you know her name, too."

The countess looked at him sharply, all levity gone in an instant. "You forget yourself, sir, and if you—"

"Oh, Alex, here you are at last!" cried Diana as she slipped her hand into her brother's arm. She was giddy, flushed with excitement and the claret, too, her words sliding over one another. "I wondered if you'd ever come back for me."

He settled his hand over hers, holding her steady.

He didn't like seeing her like this, not on her very first night in London company. He should have stayed here, watching over her, instead of chasing that girl in yellow through the garden. "I came back hours ago, Di. Before we'd even sat for supper. It's you that hasn't noticed."

"Oh, Gemini, and everything's my fault again." She pouted up at him, then giggled. "But then it always is, isn't it?"

"Not precisely always, Di," he said, "but close enough."

She smiled suddenly, brilliantly. "You took Blackie away!" she said, delighted with herself for remembering. "Back home to the *Calliope* and put him to bed!"

"We'll speak of it on the way back to the ship," he promised. They had a great deal to discuss, and the kitten would be the least of it. "Now come, make your farewells."

"But I'm staying here now," protested Diana. "Lady Waldegrave has already given me the most beautiful chamber for my own use as her guest. You can have my things brought over in the morning."

Alex drew in his breath. "That's not what we agreed, Di. As long as I remain here in London, you're to stay with me on board the *Calliope*. You're my sister, and my responsibility."

"Then surely you must see the impropriety of having your sister remain on a *boat*," interrupted the countess. "During your voyage here, doubtless it couldn't be helped, but for her to stay with you now, amongst all those rough sailors, having to be rowed back and forth by some low river barge man, without heed to the arrangement of her hair or dress. What brother could wish such disreputable hardships upon his sister?"

Alex took a deep breath before he spoke, something he wasn't generally in the habit of doing. "I hardly see, my lady, how staying with me would constitute a disreputable hardship to my own sister."

The countess' famous smile appeared again. "Then you simply must trust me, Alexander. If your sister is to meet suitable gentlemen, she must stay here as my guest." She patted his arm, at the same time managing to shift possession of Diana's hand from his to her own.

Not that Diana objected, linking her hand with the older woman's.

"I'm sorry, Alex, but that much *is* true," she said wistfully. "Your *Calliope's* a splendid ship, but what sort of gentleman could I possibly meet moored out in the middle of the Thames?"

He saw how her gaze had drifted away from him and softened, and he turned around to see what—or who— had caught her attention. Across the room, standing beside the fireplace, a young gentleman in a brocaded coat winked back at her from beneath a crested white wig looming like a snowbank over his forehead.

"Lord Oswald was speaking to me of operas, plays, and oratorios," she said as she smiled shyly in the white wig's direction. "He told me which ones were the most droll and pleasing to ladies, and promised to take me to a playhouse whenever I chose. With Lady Waldegrave in attendance, too, of course."

"Damned right," growled Alex. Operas, plays, and oratorios—and overhelpful fops—were only the beginning of the things she'd find here in London that didn't exist back home in New England. "Diana, that winking ass looks like he's tumbled head first into a cask of flour."

Diana glared at him, tossing her head to make the cluster of plumes pinned into the hair quiver with indignation. "He is a gentleman of fashion, Alex, and his manners and his air are impeccable. I do not know why you are being so . . . so churlish."

Alex glowered. Nothing had gone well this entire infernal evening, and he felt completely entitled to his churlishness. "I'd like to see this precious Lord Oswald jump to your defense the next time you get up to mischief at the White Boar."

"Perhaps I wouldn't wish him to," she answered warmly, while Lady Waldegrave, her expression pained, pretended not to hear. "Perhaps I don't wish to visit low places like the White Boar again. Perhaps I wish you'd stop telling me what I should do and say and see, and go back to *Calliope*, where everyone is bound to obey you."

"And perhaps you're getting too damned full of yourself!"

"Hush, Alex, people are staring!" she hissed at him, pointedly lowering her own voice. "Why, to hear you speak I'd believe you wished to keep me trapped forever on the river until I'd no choice but to wed some dreadful old sailor."

"Some old *sailor*?" sputtered Alex. "What the hell is that supposed to mean? Wasn't a *sailor* good enough for Mother?"

"Please, please!" Lady Waldegrave implored, at last fluttering her hands for them to stop. "Your father wasn't any ordinary sailor. He was a captain when your mother met him, with a fine estate of his own.

And sailor or not, he must be a rare gentleman for your mother to have given up so much to wed him."

"Vastly rare," said Diana, giving her plumes an extra, emphatic toss. "If there were more men like Father in Massachusetts, then I wouldn't have come here now."

"*More* men, Diana?" scoffed Alex. "Hell, I thought you only needed one."

But Lady Waldegrave had had enough.

"Captain Fairbourne," she began, her voice surprisingly severe. "Alexander. Doubtless your voyage has been a long, tiring one for you to speak so rudely to your sister. Perhaps you should withdraw for the evening now. I'm sure that in the morning, after a night's sleep, you will see all of this in a far more cheerful light."

But Alex could see it now. He was being dismissed, sent away, packed off, cast adrift; there was no other way to look upon it, and only one way to respond.

"Very well, my lady," he said with a curt bow. He didn't doubt that the countess' intentions were the best, but God help them all the first time Diana chose to empty a glass of that fine claret onto some gallant's snowy wig. "I find I am, ah, weary, and shall say good night. To you, too, Di."

His sister narrowed her eyes with suspicion, every bit as stiff-backed as he was himself. This genteel behavior was going to kill them both.

"Mind you tend to my Blackie," she said, more of a threat than a reminder. "I'm counting on his help."

"Oh, aye," said Alex moodily. "Choose the help of a blasted kitten over mine."

But Lady Waldegrave merely nodded, her beatific smile once again graciously in place. Of course it would be, thought Alex, she'd won, hadn't she?

"In your mother's letters, Alex, she implored me to treat Diana like my own daughter," she said gently. "You have my word that I'll do nothing less."

Alex bowed to the countess again, all the answer he dared venture, kissed Diana on her perfumed cheek, and left, his steps echoing as he marched down the stairway to the great formal hall. He kept his head high as the footman handed him his hat and the porter held the door open, and it wasn't until he'd heard that door shut and latch behind him that he loosed his unhappiness in a bitter, muttered torrent of seagoing oaths.

He'd just been summarily dismissed, treated like some insignificant link-boy. It was bad enough to hear it from a lady who didn't know better, but coming from his own sister—well, hell, that stung, and more than his pride, too. Diana couldn't wait to begin this new life among fashionable London, and she couldn't have made it more clear that he was no longer necessary. She'd be needing him now about as often as she'd need the tarred-over hat she'd worn in foul weather on board the *Calliope*, and feeling thoroughly sorry for himself, he kicked at the tall garden wall and swore again.

She might have thought herself free of him, but he'd be damned if he'd let himself be shed so easily. Diana was still his sister. Their mother might have been perfectly willing to turn her over into Lady Waldegrave's keeping, but their father would raise the devil if he abandoned Diana as she wished, and rightly so, too. No, Alex would be back here tomorrow, as soon as he'd called on Sir Thomas Walton again, to make sure Diana wasn't mistaking Lord Jackass Oswald for a possible husband.

Besides, he'd have to come back here anyway to find her blasted kitten. With a sigh he gazed up toward the top of the wall, remembering the garden—and the girl—that he'd found on the other side. He was positive Lady Waldegrave knew her, and nearly as sure that she was still somewhere close by. He couldn't imagine why the countess would have pretended otherwise, especially insisting on that foolishness about yellow silk.

And why the devil had the girl herself claimed Blackie as her own, anyway? The kitten was no more than a stray from the street, the sort that was born to be drowned by the dozen in London every day, and hardly worth the lie she'd told.

Yet if he were honest, there *was* something special about that seven-toed kitten, just as there'd been something special about the girl who'd stolen him away. It wasn't that she was a great beauty, because she wasn't. She wasn't even really very pretty, when he considered it objectively, and she certainly wasn't the sort of woman he usually fancied.

Yet still he thought of her serious little freckled face before she'd seized the cat, and the way she'd looked up at him from beneath one stray wisp of chestnut hair across her forehead, her eyes fey and tip-tilted at the corners. No wonder he'd called her an elf-girl, and no wonder, too, that he wished she hadn't run away. Standing in the garden with her had been the only entertaining part of this whole wretched evening.

He leaned back, looking past the garden wall to the house beyond. The tall windows of the drawing room remained brilliantly lit, while through the smaller open windows below drifted the bustle and clatter from the kitchen.

He hoped the elf-girl was taking care with Blackie, finding him a saucer of cream for the night.

He wondered if she'd have scorned him if she'd known he was only a shipmaster from the colonies, the way his own sister had.

He considered whether she'd have lingered if he'd worn a white-powdered wig and haw-hawed like a brocaded gentleman jackass.

The light of a single candle suddenly flickered up above on the sill of an open dormer window where the servants' bedchambers must be. He didn't know what had drawn his eye, and was scoffing at his own wayward imagination when he thought he could just make out the silhouette of a little black cat moving inside the window's sill.

Then the candlestick shifted forward, and by its light he could clearly see the pale oval of a woman's face. With one slender hand, she shielded the wobbling flame, and brought the light full upon her face, her chestnut hair tucked haphazardly behind one ear as she drew the kitten against her chest.

Oh, aye, he'd be back tomorrow.

And in spite of everything else that had happened that day, Alex smiled.

3

"Were you already abed and asleep, Cora?" asked Lady Waldegrave, more than a little suspiciously. "I sent for you a quarter hour past."

"No, my lady. That is, forgive me, my lady," said Cora breathlessly, dipping a hurried curtsey as soon as she reached the countess' dressing table. It had seemed only a minute since she'd been summoned; surely she hadn't lingered at her window for an entire quarter hour. "I didn't intend to be so tardy."

"You are a dreamer, Cora, exactly like your father," declared the countess soundly. "You cannot deny it. You have no sense of whether an hour has passed since I summoned you, or an entire day."

Lady Waldegrave sighed dramatically, as if Cora's dreaminess were her own grievous burden to bear. The older woman had already shed her gown, her hoops, and her stays, sitting before the mirror in a loose robe over her shift as her maid took down her hair for the night. Without the whalebone and buckram to give her shape and substance, the countess always seemed smaller, less imposing, which was why she didn't take off her jewels until the moment before she slipped into bed.

But this last hour before bed was also the part of Lady Waldegrave's day that Cora usually liked sharing the most. Her role was a simple one, to listen to the gossip that the countess had heard during the day, to speculate and to smile, and to discuss the plans for tomorrow. This dressing room was made for such confidences, a tiny bijou of a room paneled in aquamarine and gold, with long narrow mirrors to reflect the candlelight from the sconces and chandelier, each winking with a shower of cut crystal teardrops. The armchairs were comfortably overstuffed with feathers and down, the velvet-covered daybed near the window always beckoning with a fur-lined coverlet at the foot and the newest novel from the bookshop.

On the hearth of the marble fireplace, Cora would make a pot of chocolate, rich with cream the way the countess preferred it, relishing the steamy fragrance as much as its taste. She loved the little chocolate cups, delicate French porcelain rimmed with gold and painted with shepherdesses and roses, the china so fine that the heat of the chocolate warmed her fingers as well as her tongue. It all felt cheerful and cozy and safe, and almost—almost—like home.

But tonight there was no sign of either the polished silver chocolate pot or the little tray with the porcelain cups, subtle warnings that the countess wished to speak seriously. As Cora waited, the older woman touched the sapphire centering the necklace around her throat, idly tracing the facets of the stone as she looked in the mirror beyond her own reflected face to Cora's.

"Even now you're not heeding me, are you?" she asked shrewdly. "The moon could drop from the very sky, Cora, and you'd be too lost in your own fancies to remark it."

Forlornly Cora ducked her chin and curtseyed again, as much as admitting her guilt. What the countess said was true. She'd been thinking of Starlight, how she'd finally settled him to sleep curled on her coverlet, and she'd also been thinking of the stranger in the garden. With the man's lopsided grin as a starting point, she'd been remembering how he'd frightened her with his size yet surprised her with his gentleness toward the kitten, his black unpowdered hair and gruff voice and his hands that seemed as large as dinner plates and—oh, she was doing it all over again, letting her mind wander every which way, exactly as Lady Waldegrave described.

But instead of the scolding that Cora had expected, the countess merely waved her maid away and patted the low tabouret before her.

"Come, Cora, sit here," she said indulgently. "Yes, child, you do let your thoughts wander idly, but perhaps, for you, that is not such a wasteful idea. If it helps you forget all your tragedies—well, yes, that is wisest, isn't it?"

"Yes, my lady," murmured Cora as she perched on the edge of the tabouret, struggling to keep her expression properly impassive. She would try to be dutiful, for the countess really was very kind to her. But whenever Lady Waldegrave spoke of forgetting her "tragedies," she could feel her rebellious heart grow so tight and brittle in her chest that she wondered how she'd ever survive.

Why would she want to forget when all she had were memories?

"Indeed." The countess beamed, as if all of Cora's sorrows had been neatly resolved. "I am glad you are so understanding. It will make what I must tell you now more agreeable."

Agreeable: oh, yes, and she could be understanding, too. Cora's fingers tightened beneath the folds of her skirt, preparing herself for the worst.

"There have been changes in my household this day, Cora," continued the countess, "and they shall affect you."

"Change can be a favorable thing, my lady," said Cora warily. "You have told me so yourself. Change keeps us free of tedium."

The countess arched a single shaven brow. "I should hope the young man in the garden this evening wasn't tedious, Cora. If you are determined to risk your safety for the sake of flirtation, then at the very least the gentleman should be amusing."

Cora gulped. How could Lady Waldegrave have possibly known of the man in the garden? "I did not meet the man for a—a flirtation, my lady! I went to the garden for—for a breath of air, and he was there!"

"Well, yes." The countess' expression was slightly pained, and totally disbelieving. "No matter how you came to meet him. What concerns me is that you *did*."

Cora flushed with guilty misery. "I vow it wasn't like that, my lady."

"You didn't tell him your name, did you? You didn't let him coax from you any of the details of your, ah, situation?"

"Of course not, my lady!"

Lady Waldegrave watched her closely. "Have you any notion of who the man is, Cora?"

Cora shook her head. She'd been so careful keeping

her own secrets that she hadn't thought that he'd have a name or identity of his own.

The countess sighed, looking down at her fingers as she twisted her rings in the candlelight. "His name is Alexander Fairbourne, and he is the son of one of my oldest friends. He has brought his sister Diana to me, all the way from the colony of Massachusetts, so that I might help her find a suitable husband."

A sister: Cora tried to imagine a female version of that determinedly masculine face, and failed.

"The girl is quite beautiful and fresh, if somewhat unpolished," continued the countess, "and she is by blood the great-granddaughter of the Duke of Auboncourt. I expect she'll have her first suitable offer within a month."

"Indeed," murmured Cora wistfully. This wasn't unusual; having no daughters of her own, the countess often helped launch the country-bred children of her friends into London's matrimonial waters. Once Cora herself had dreamed of marrying, too, of having a husband who loved her and a home to manage and babies, lots of babies, to spoil and cherish. But not now. What man would want a wife with an outlaw's name, or one whose only dowry was a warrant for her capture?

"Indeed, yes," said the countess, rubbing her ear-lobe as she slipped off one of the heavy sapphire clips. "Here, be useful and help me with the clasp on my necklace. But the brother, Cora, this Alexander Fairbourne—he is altogether different, and not to be encouraged. I saw that at once. I shall have to take considerable care not to let him spoil his sister's chances."

Cora stood behind the countess to unfasten the

necklace, grateful that the older woman could not see her face. "Why would he wish to harm his sister? Surely your friend couldn't have borne one child out of goodness, and another of all that is bad?"

The countess snorted. "The goodness would come from my darling friend, but her husband is said to be a wicked man, little better than a pirate, a low-bred rascal who keeps even lower company."

"A pirate, my lady?" breathed Cora. A pirate could be exactly what she needed, a ruthless, daring man who feared nothing. To stumble over such a man—a *pirate!*—near the garden wall must surely be a sign that her fate was changing.

"Oh, yes, a *pirate*," said the countess. "He practically kidnapped my poor friend, you know, ruined her completely, so she'd have no choice but to wed him and hide her shame in the colonies. You cannot fathom the scandal it caused. Though my friend did not dare say so in her letters to me, I am certain—quite certain— that she has sent her daughter to me so the same will not happen to her. And the first step, you see, shall be to separate her from this dreadful brother."

"But he did not seem so very wicked to me," ventured Cora, remembering how kind the man had been with Starlight. "Perhaps it is simply because he was born in the colonies where life is less genteel."

"The colonies!" The countess shuddered visibly. "Life there is not merely less genteel, my dear, it is savage, hewn from the primeval forest, and so is this man. I have the truth on the best authority that he has—oh, he does such things that I cannot tell an innocent such as you! He is handsome as sin and as dangerous to you as the devil himself, and if you value your life, if not your reputation, you will take care to keep from his path."

"But if he—"

"Cora, child, pray consider the facts," scolded the countess gently. "Alexander Fairbourne has spent his life among pirates and wild savages, learning their cunning ways and habits. He is a sailor and a wanderer by birth and by choice, the precise sort of faithless rascal who abandons the poor women he woos with every new tide. Yes, yes, that's what sailors *do*, Cora, so don't go pretending he'd be any different with you. He hasn't the virtue of a true-born gentleman like your father."

No, thought Cora sadly, he wasn't like her father, not at all. Iain MacGillivray *had* been a gentleman, mild-mannered and loyal. His world had been his library at Creignish House, his best friends the books he'd carefully collected, and if Cora were a dreamer now, then it had been her father who'd showed her how in that cluttered, sun-filled room in the south tower.

She'd loved him dearly, her father, but now she'd also come to realize that the things she'd loved most about him had also been the ones that had led to his ruin. If only he'd been less involved with the long-past worlds of Homer and Virgil and more aware of what was happening beyond Creignish's walls—if only he'd had a share of the boldness that Alexander Fairbourne possessed—then maybe he'd be alive still.

But then that would be something Lady Waldegrave, safe and snug in this house in London, would never understand, nor would she understand why this sort of man was precisely what Cora sought now.

"Could you trust this Captain Fairbourne with your secrets, Cora?" she demanded. "What proof do you have that he wouldn't take them straight to your enemies and sell you like a Judas for gold?"

Silently Cora bowed her head, and settled the sapphire necklace into its fitted kid case. The countess didn't really expect an answer to such a preposterous question, and Cora didn't offer one.

Yet instead of considering her folly, Cora thought about how the stranger's smile had seemed to light the dusk. Her own smile had always been shy, guarded, for her teeth were small and irregular, not at all like the pearls that poets favored. Alexander Fairbourne's teeth had been white and even and faintly predatory, gleaming down at her over the back of the little cat.

And his name: what a splendid great mouthful that was, too, the given name of an ancient conqueror coupled with a family name that sounded like a blessing. Her father would have relished the irony of such a name lavished on such a giant from the colonies, joyfully quoting classic texts that hailed Alexander, the golden Macedonian prince who'd made the world his own.

But this Alexander was a disreputable sea captain from New England, not a prince from Macedonia, and her father wasn't in his book-strewn study but lying cold in some unmarked traitor's grave, and if she let her thoughts wander like this any longer she'd begin to cry, and she would not do that.

She would *not*.

No. Better, infinitely better, to think of all she could achieve with this Alexander to help her. With him beside her, she could be a conqueror, too, Cora the Conqueror to match Alexander the Great, and now instead of weeping she had to gulp to swallow a giddy smile of excitement.

"I shall do my best to help you, Cora, to keep you from temptation," the countess continued, closing the case with a brisk snap before she tucked it inside the strongbox beneath her dressing table. "Beginning tomorrow, Captain Fairbourne will find I am seldom home to him, and you, my dear, won't be troubled by him wandering in my garden."

"No, my lady," murmured Cora, even as she tried to think of how she'd meet this pirate captain again with the garden outlawed.

"And to be doubly safe, Cora," continued the countess, "I must also ask you to keep yourself from his sister, and take care not to venture into my apartments if she is with me. Long ago I swore to your poor father that I'd shelter you, and I shall, but I've no wish to be brought to ruination with you simply because you let yourself be led by some handsome young rogue."

"I am sorry, my lady," said Cora softly. She'd only intended to find her kitten, and dream of a way to free herself from her past. But she'd never wished to send the countess to prison, any more than she wanted to be imprisoned herself. "It shall not happen again."

"It won't because I won't let it." Lady Waldegrave sighed, and took Cora's hand in her own. "Once I've found a husband for Miss Fairbourne, Cora, then you shall be next. I've neglected you that way long enough. A young creature like you shouldn't have to spend the rest of her days trailing me about. I must see you wed."

"I am content, my lady," said Cora, though the tremor in her words said otherwise. "I won't betray your kindness by leaving you."

"Oh, pish," scoffed the countess. "It's common

sense, not betrayal. With your tragedies behind you, it's natural that your eyes wander toward handsome young men like Captain Fairbourne. The ones here in London are out of the question, of course, but come September, we shall journey to Italy. Florence, I think, or Naples. Yes, Naples. Neapolitan gentlemen have always been fond of English ladies."

"Scottish, my lady," protested Cora. "I'm Scottish, not English."

"Oh, Cora, 'twill be all the same to them," said Lady Waldegrave blithely. "I'll find you a charming black-haired *cavalière* of your very own, a younger son perhaps, one with exquisite manners and a fine fortune that will make you forget entirely about that rascally Alexander Fairbourne."

Cora slipped her hand free, and retreated one step back. "No, my lady," she said. "Thank you, but no."

Lady Waldegrave frowned. "You won't do better for yourself, not without my help."

"It's not the . . . the Neapolitan gentlemen, my lady, or your kind offer. It's . . . it's that I've no wish to leave Britain."

"No wish to leave the past behind, you mean," said Lady Waldegrave sharply. "No wish to look forward to a future that could bring you happiness."

Cora lifted her chin, her fingers clasped tightly before her. "No wish to dishonor my clan or my father's memory by forgetting them."

"No wish to give over your own stubborn selfishness is more the truth." Irritably the countess rapped her knuckles on the carved arm of her chair. "This is more of your dreaming, Cora. Your precious clan betrayed you and your father without a care or a thought. They don't deserve a scrap of your loyalty now. It's done, my dear, finished and done nearly two years past, and you'll sooner become the next Queen of Naples than return to Creignish."

"There is nothing wrong with loyalty, my lady," said Cora defensively, daring to say more than she ever had before. She'd been loyal to her father and loyal to her clan, even loyal to the black stray kitten that she'd followed into the garden tonight, and she refused to apologize for it. "Loyalty is most rare and admirable, my lady, especially in women."

She hadn't consciously echoed Alexander Fairbourne's words, but as soon as she'd spoken she remembered his smile again, almost as if he were still here to beam his approval for being so outspoken, real enough to make her smile foolishly herself.

As if his judgment could possibly matter, the careless flattery of a man she'd never see again!

"What rubbish you speak, Cora," said Lady Waldegrave with disgust. "And that simpering grin upon your face is no better than an idiot's. If I were not near perishing from weariness, I should order you switched. Indeed, yes! Now away with you, go, and please take care to show a more civil countenance to me in the morning."

"Yes, my lady," murmured Cora, belatedly contrite as she spread her skirts to curtsey. Though the countess was far too kindhearted to have her beaten, it still wasn't wise of Cora to be so willful, yet at the same time it had felt wonderfully, frighteningly exhilarating. "That is, good night, my lady."

"Good night, Cora." The countess swept away from the dressing table toward her bedchamber, leaving

Cora to bring the candlestick. "And one last word for you, my dear: if you must be loyal, pray choose your loyalties with more care than your father did."

"Yes, my lady." That would be an easy promise to keep, thought Cora sadly, for most of the clansmen her father had followed had died with him. "I shall take care, my lady."

"See that you do." The countess sighed, or perhaps she merely yawned. She settled back against the mounded pillows in her bed, folded her hands over her chest, and closed her eyes, composed for sleep. "And also, Cora, see that you keep Alexander Fairbourne from your dreams tonight."

"Very well, my lady," said Cora softly as she drew the curtains closed around the bed, but she didn't agree. Dreams were all she had, and she wouldn't give them up.

And oh my, how grand those dreams were this night! Curled on her own bed up under the roof with Starlight wheezing contentedly beside her, she tried to find sense in what had happened, to sort what she knew was true from what she'd wished were so, and to separate it all from the bluest eyes she'd ever seen on a man.

Alexander. In Celtic his name would be Alasdair. Her uncle, the laird of their clan, had been called that, too, the one who'd made that final, disastrous decision that had ruined all the MacGillivrays, and she shivered as she considered the dreadful irony.

Her father had maintained that the heathen gods, Zeus and Hera and all the rest, helped the ancients by granting them special signs in everyday things, and he'd always been looking for omens and portents himself, anxiously studying the pattern on the ruddy skin of an apple or peering in the cold ashes of the grate for secret meanings. Indulgently Cora had kept his superstitious ramblings from the vicar, assuming it was only a part of her father's scholarship, but now she wasn't as sure.

Couldn't there be some special significance to Alexander Fairbourne's appearance now? Should she see his given name as some sort of warning, a caution not to follow this other Alexander to the same ruin as the rest of her clan? Or was he going to be more like the Macedonian prince who'd brought such shining glory to his people, here to lighten her lonely, empty days with his smile? What he'd said about her being loyal, about it being most rare and admirable—she'd nearly heard that spoken in her father's voice, the words had been so like his own. Could that have been part of the sign, too?

Or, much more likely, was all of this simple coincidence and no more, born of solitude and grief and imaginings?

She did not know; she did not *know*.

And with a groan of frustration she buried her face in her pillow, trying to do as Lady Waldegrave had said, and put Alexander Fairbourne from her dreams forever.

4

*A*nxiously Cora peeked through the narrow window alongside the kitchen door, hoping to glimpse the milkmaid.

It was still early for Lady Waldegrave's fashionable neighborhood, with the sun only beginning to show itself as a hazy pink glow in the dusty sky over the tops of roofs and trees. From the butler to the lowest maid, the countess' servants knew she never awakened or called for her tea before eleven, and so they, too, kept to their beds well past dawn. To Cora, accustomed to country hours and rising with the cock's crow, this had at first seemed shockingly indulgent, but she'd soon learned to relish the peace of early morning, and of being the only one awake and afoot in the great house.

With Starlight, she was doubly glad. If Cook were awake, she'd grow suspicious, demanding to know why Cora needed milk and scraps left from supper. This way, alone, she wouldn't need to make any explanations.

She reached down to pat Starlight, cozily slung in her pocket like a sailor in his hammock. The pocket was like a large, soft linen bag hanging from the apron strings around her waist, a most comfortable spot for a kitten, and most appropriately decorated, too, with an embroidered pattern of yellow birds. She could feel the vibration of his purring through her thin summer petticoat, and she knew the only thing that could make him happier than the leftover chicken fricassee already in his round little belly would be a visit from the milkmaid.

But the girl was late, and if she didn't appear soon Cora would have to retreat without Starlight's milk before Cook came downstairs. Cautiously Cora unlatched the door and slipped outside, glancing up and down the narrow back lane used by tradespeople and servants. Most days the milkmaid came with the dawn when the air was still cool enough to keep her wares from spoiling. She brought the milk can balanced on her head, walking from the pens of the cow keepers outside of town with a slow, distinctive gait designed to keep the milk from separating or churning into butter curds. In this neighborhood, she wouldn't cry her wares, but instead chalked her order tally each morning on the frame of the door.

Just to be sure, Cora touched her finger to the white chalk mark left from yesterday, then stepped out into the lane to look again, craning her neck to lean past the mulberry bushes.

"Up with the sun, out with the dawn," said the man's voice behind her. "I never expected to find you tumbled from your bed this early, lass."

This time, Cora managed not to gasp, but she still couldn't keep her heart from racing. It was one thing to let Alexander Fairbourne creep into her dreams; it was quite, quite another to find him here on the kitchen step, blocking her only way back inside the house.

He swept off his hat and bowed, then smiled wryly as he rose. "Am I that sorry a sight, then, mistress?"

He wasn't, and Cora was certain he knew it else he would never have dared ask such a question of her. If she'd thought him handsome last evening in the shadows of the garden then he'd lost nothing here in the early daylight. He was as broad-shouldered as she remembered, his features as evenly cut, his dimpled smile as charming, his black hair sleeked back into a neat queue with a silk ribbon, everything as it should be to make him desired in drawing rooms all over London. There wasn't even anything particularly noteworthy about the sword that hung from his waist, for many gentlemen wore them, even if the majority did so for show, not defense.

But here in the morning light, she could see beyond his more obvious attributes, down to undercurrents that would take more than a charming smile to disguise. From what Lady Waldegrave had told her, he must still be in his mid-twenties, yet his face was weathered, browned, far more so than the faces of any gentlemen she knew of that age. The harshness of life at sea had left its mark on his face, and given it this unfamiliar patina of experience.

But something more than wind and sun had made his gaze so keen and sharply knowing, as if he'd already seen more of life than Cora could imagine. With a shiver she remembered how the countess had hinted at dark secrets about him. Cora had assumed these were no more than the usual London excesses, gambling and drinking and keeping company with low women, but now she sensed such activities would be minor peccadilloes for Alexander Fairbourne.

Little better than a pirate, that was what Lady Waldegrave had whispered of him and his father both, a wild man from a wild place, and now, with him blocking her path, Cora was willing to believe every word. For all his charm, he frightened her—not so much because of what he could do to her here on the kitchen step, but of how she might betray herself.

"You shouldn't be surprised to see me again, you know," he said as he straightened, settling his cocked hat back on his head. "I'm not generally in the habit of letting thieves keep what's mine."

Now she did gasp, with indignation. "You stole from me, sir, not the other way around! It is you who should be indebted to me!"

"Then we must agree to differ, mustn't we?" His manner seemed pleasant enough, but still Cora sensed the simmering risk if he were crossed. "Perhaps if you invited me inside, we could discuss our, ah, differences with more civility."

"No!" Cora gulped, nervously sweeping her hands along the front of her apron. "That is, Lady Waldegrave would never permit it."

He cocked a single dark brow, bemused. "No swains for the serving girls?"

"Yes," she said quickly. "That is, Captain Fairbourne, you are not my swain."

His expression grew more intrigued. "So you know who I am, do you?"

She fought to keep her hands still at her sides, and not twist or turn to betray her anxiety. "Lady Waldegrave warned me against you."

"All exaggerations." He smiled, no reassurance at all.

"Then you're not . . . not a pirate?"

The smile expanded into a chuckle. "God in heaven, no! I'm a privateer, and never forget that there's a world of difference between the two. A pirate captures whatever he pleases, but a privateer must think of his king first, and follow all kinds of mannerly rules before he can take a prize and earn his share. Most often there's no real battle at all. I simply chase them down, run out my guns to show I mean what I say, and then they drop their flags in surrender and wait meekly for my prize crew to come aboard and claim them."

She hadn't realized there *was* a difference, and now that he'd explained it, she felt oddly disappointed. She glanced down at the sword at his waist, a plain, rather battered sword that she'd felt sure had seen much use. "Then you have never killed another?"

The smile vanished, and the chuckle with it. "What peculiar questions you ask a man, lass."

She raised her chin. "I have good reasons for asking them."

"Then, aye, I have," he said, his voice heavy. "I've killed by pistol, sword, and knife, but never frivolously, and never without regret for a life lost."

Her eyes widened. "You've done that—killed others, I mean—for the sake of King George?"

"In theory, aye. But mostly I've done it for the sake of keeping myself alive another day."

"Then you do not have a special partiality to the German king that wrongly sits on the English throne?" she asked eagerly. "You'd rather fight for yourself and what you believe is right?"

He looked at her warily. "For a bright June morning, you're talking perilously close to treason, lass."

"Not treason," said Cora quickly, even though she knew he was right. "Truth."

"Very well, then. But this time the truth must come from you. You're not some common serving girl, are you? Not dressed like that." His gaze slid down her body, more than enough to make her cheeks grow hot with embarrassment, and pray that Starlight would stay asleep and hidden in the pocket at her hip. "So is your mistress like the other thrifty ladies of fashion, then, scrimping on wages by gracing her people in her own castoffs?"

Cora nodded eagerly, glad to divert the conversation from treason. "My lady likes to see me looking well, too, for it reflects upon her, and I should never be able to dress so handsomely without her generosity."

"Oh, aye, it's always good to be grateful for charity." He leaned closer, his scrutiny uncomfortably keen. "And charitable your good lady must be, if she'll lavish you with her jewels as well."

Cora's hand flew to her throat, touching the necklace of coral beads that she always wore, day and night. "This belonged to my mother, who died when I was born. My father said she'd always worn it, and now so do I in her memory."

She took a deep breath, almost a gulp. "Not—not that this is any of your affair."

"No," he agreed softly, his brows drawn together as he lowered his chin. "It's not. But still I can say that a scrap of gold's no substitute for your poor mother."

She hadn't expected that from him, and though she knew she should be relieved he'd asked no more questions, instead she caught herself remembering how he'd used that same gruff kindness toward Starlight.

She felt oddly off balance, and worse, she felt that if he said one more word about her mother, she might burst into tears.

"Thank you, sir," she said stiffly. "I do thank you."

He glanced up at her without raising his head, his pale eyes more startling beneath those dark brows. "Yes," he repeated in the same low voice. "Such a loss is hardest for daughters, I think, although I—"

"Milk today, mistress?"

Beside the mulberry bush stood the milkmaid, wide-eyed and expectant, and from her grin obviously enjoying the scene she'd stumbled upon. She was short and stocky, a country girl dressed in a homespun linen bodice and petticoat, her brawny forearms bare below the sleeves of her shift and strong enough to balance the tall can of milk on top of her flat-brimmed hat and kerchief.

"Yes, of course," said Cora, flustered. For the past two mornings, she'd intercepted the milk like this, so at least the girl recognized her as belonging to the household. If, that is, the milkmaid stopped gaping at Alexander Fairbourne long enough to notice her. "You may leave it here, if you please."

"Nay, mistress, I cannot," said the girl emphatically. "I'll not leave my milk can for your cook t'use for ill. Nay, you must give me your jug t'fill, as be proper."

"Very well." Cora looked pointedly at the tall man blocking the kitchen door. "If Captain Fairbourne will let us pass, then I'll fetch the jug."

"Oh, aye, fetch away," he said gallantly, opening the door and holding it wide for them. "Here, lass, let me give a hand with your burden."

The milkmaid tittered with delight, purposefully brushing against him as she came through the door, but Cora only glowered. What she wished to do was to slam the door shut in his face, and leave him there outside on the step until she could call one or two of the footmen to send him on his way. Cook was very strict about who was allowed into her kitchen, and Lady Waldegrave would agree with her. Hadn't she as much as banned Captain Fairbourne from her house last night?

But then Cora would risk having him announce that she'd stolen his cat, a cat she was secretly keeping against Lady Waldegrave's wishes, and since she'd no intention of sacrificing Starlight, her only choice seemed to be to let him follow her and the milkmaid inside. This was, of course, exactly what he'd wanted in the first place, and now she'd have to use all her wits to make him leave. Which, considering how badly she'd negotiated with him so far, was going be a sizable challenge to her beleaguered wits.

Her temper simmered as she watched Captain Fairbourne assisting the other woman, pouring the milk for her into the stoneware jug, clucking and fussing over how heavy the milk can must be for her as if she were the daintiest little creature he'd ever seen instead of the great strapping farm girl that she was.

"I do thank you for your kindness, sir," simpered the girl as she prepared to leave, fitting the lid back onto the can. "I don't much see fine gentlemen like you in th' kitchens."

"Hah," said Captain Fairbourne, and to Cora's disgust he winked. "I'd warrant you don't often see gentlemen like me most places."

The girl giggled as she settled the much lighter can back onto her head, taking care to arch her back and thrust out her breasts. "Aren't you the saucy one, sir, to—"

"Cook will settle your account on Saturday," interrupted Cora, pointedly holding the door open. "We'll be wanting nothing more from you until then. Good day."

"Aye, mistress," said the girl, but the glance she shot past Cora to Captain Fairbourne said volumes more, and none of it flattering to Cora. "Good day, mistress."

Without turning Cora sensed, rather than saw, Captain Fairbourne come stand behind her.

"Sent her on her way brisk enough, didn't you?" he said, his voice sounding much nearer to her shoulder than was proper. "Had her clear off quick, didn't you?"

"You must go, too," she said resolutely.

"She was only following her trade, you know," he continued, as if Cora had never spoken. "You can't fault her for that."

Cora frowned. "I don't fault her, not in the least. But *you* shouldn't have behaved with her as you did, a man of your station taking advantage of a girl of the lower sort like that."

"Of the lower sort?" he repeated with amused incredulity. "And who are you now, lass, to decide whose sort is lower or higher?"

"I'm Miss Cora Margaret—" she began, then broke off abruptly when she realized how close she'd come to telling him her name. She *was* still Cora Margaret Anne MacGillivray of Creignish, regardless of what the English generals and politicians claimed to the contrary, and MacGillivrays had been gentry long enough to know who else wasn't. But that was pride making her speak so, pride and nothing else, and unless she wished that same pride to offer her company in an English prison, she'd better bite it back now.

She took a deep breath, then a second one, her arms folded tightly over her chest. What was it about this man that made her forget all caution?

"I'm Miss Cora Margaret, yes," she finished awkwardly, "and I've seen enough of the world to know my place in it."

"Well, now, Miss Cora Margaret," he said evenly, as if speaking only a matter of indisputable fact. "What I think is a bit simpler than that. I think that the cowherd's daughter made you jealous."

"*Jealous!*" she cried indignantly, and at last twisted around to face him. "How could I ever be jealous of—"

But every thought flew clear from her head as she turned and oh, Lord help her, he was standing every bit as close as she'd feared, looming over her again the same way he had in the garden the night before. Now the morning light streamed in through the open doorway, bright enough to show the faint black gleam on his newly shaved jaw as well as the little flecks of darker blue in his pale eyes.

He rested one hand on the wall to one side of her face, his face coming closer as he leaned toward her. Instinctively she backed away the half-inch that remained to her, her elbows bumping into the rough plaster of the wall, and made herself look anywhere but his face, anywhere happening to be his right hand, resting at his waist and carelessly shoving aside the long skirts of his coat from his hip.

"Jealous of whom, Miss Cora?" he asked, clearly enjoying her discomfiture. "You can tell me, can't you?"

The crisp white linen of his shirt's cuff ruffled over his hand, his fingers browned and nicked white with a score of faded scars as well as the new bruises and cuts she'd seen last night. There were curious little black spots burned into the skin, too, scattered like pepper across the back of his thumb and wrist.

"Of you," she said finally. "The girl was making all manner of forward advances at you."

"And so you *are* jealous, Miss Cora Margaret," he said, his voice low and confidential. "Jealous of a lass of—what was it?—'the lower sort.'"

"You're putting words into my mouth!"

"Not words, or anything else," he said. "Not yet, anyway. But as for the jealousy—ah, Miss Cora, that's your own doing, not mine."

Cora swallowed, wishing she knew how to stop the fearful racing of her heart. She realized now he was teasing her, toying with her indignation as Starlight would a scrap of yarn, but she still didn't know how to reply. Even when she was a child, no one had teased her at Creignish—no one had ever dared such familiarity with her—and she certainly had never been teased by a man like this.

But the worst part of it was knowing that, teasing or not, he was right. She *was* jealous of the milkmaid. She envied the girl her freedom to come and go wherever she pleased in London, even the fact that her rough homespun clothes were her own, and not made over in charity. She could laugh and banter and toss her head at Captain Fairbourne and no one else would notice or care, while Cora must weigh every action against the danger it could bring.

And oh, Lord, how much she hated it!

"You shouldn't make such—such accusations, sir," she said, wincing inwardly at how she sounded, like such a prim, spinsterish scold. "Jealousy is hardly a pretty topic for jesting."

"Not pretty like you, no," he said, and she'd bet her life he was smiling, grinning wickedly to match those wicked, idle words. "Such a pretty, cunning little thief, and perhaps a traitor, too."

Cora gasped. "You're making this worse, sir, not better," she said, her own words tumbling over one another in her confusion. "I am neither a thief nor a traitor."

Nor am I pretty, she added silently, and at the same time she felt Starlight beginning to wake and clumsily stir in her pocket. Why could the little cat shift and stretch with such ease, while she seemed incapable of moving, even to save herself?

She had to end this now, *now*.

"And I say you are, Miss Cora Margaret," he murmured, tracing the line of her jaw with his fingertips and at the same time gently tilting her mouth upward toward his. "All of these, and I warrant a great deal more as well."

Her eyes fluttered shut as her chin rose, the morning sun a bright flash against her closed lids. Instinctively she realized he was going to kiss her, and though a lifetime of training as Creignish's lady expected her to stop him and protest in outrage, she wasn't even trying.

Because deep down, she didn't want to. For once she'd rather be like the milkmaid, who would have let this man steal a kiss and laughed afterward.

Tentatively she pursed her lips, not sure what else to do. She'd seen other people kiss, of course, and she'd read books and poems where it had happened, but not even Ovid had offered enough actual instruction.

But Captain Fairbourne, it seemed, had experience enough for them both.

His mouth covered hers with the same confidence that he'd shown in every other dealing with her, that same boldness that made her think again of rogues and pirates, or at least the part of her head that seemed still capable of thought. Not much of it was, or she wouldn't be letting him do this now.

But kissing was proving another way for him to tease, tempting her to let him claim more of her, and as his lips pressed down upon hers, coaxing them to abandon their pursiness and relax, she gave a little moan of surprise. Her lips parted, and he deepened the kiss in a most amazing fashion. Who would have guessed a man's mouth could be so soft, or capable of giving this kind of sensation? She felt giddy with it, almost lightheaded as her heart raced.

He curled his arm around her waist, deftly easing her backward until she fluttered her hands against his chest more in surprise than protest. He might have taken her flailing hands as an invitation, because he drew her closer to him, the hard length of his body pressing into hers.

But only for an instant, the instant it took for Starlight, in her pocket, to decide he was being crushed and yowl like a miniature banshee.

"What the devil is—*oww!*" Captain Fairbourne released Cora and stumbled back, grabbing at his thigh. "The blasted beast bit me!"

Hastily Cora looked down at her pocket. Starlight's head and one paw were still poking through the opening, his eyes wild and suspiciously bloodthirsty.

"You had him all the time, didn't you?" demanded Captain Fairbourne. "Tempting me, cozening me, distracting me like that to make me forget why I'd come here in the first place!"

"I never tempted you!" Cora covered the cat's head with her hand and scurried across the room, making sure the broad oak kitchen table was between her and Captain Fairbourne. If necessary, too, Cook's knives were within her reach, but she prayed things wouldn't deteriorate that far. "I wouldn't know how to do so even if I wished it!"

"The hell you don't," he growled as in three strides he stood opposite her, his hands on the edge of the table. "You knew damned well what you were doing. Especially when you kiss a man like that."

Cora flushed. From his reaction, she couldn't tell if she'd kissed him badly or well. Yet still he was making her knees weak, her heart thump like a fool's, as he stood there across from her, about as furious as a man could be.

She scooped Starlight from her pocket and cradled him protectively against her chest. "You can't have Starlight."

"Blackie." He glared at her across the table, gingerly rubbing his thigh again. "Blackie, or Starlight, or Beelzebub himself. I came here to take him, sure. But now I'm thinking we might work out a different arrangement."

Starlight squirmed, his nose bobbing as he caught the scent of the fresh milk, and tried to crawl up Cora's shoulder. She didn't want to set him down in case Captain Fairbourne tried to steal him back, but the cat wasn't making it easy for her. "I don't see that there's any question of ownership at all."

He sighed with exasperation. "Hold now, and listen. My sister's powerfully attached to that cat. She sees him as a sort of lucky piece, the way some folk keep a copper coin in their pocket, and she believes this kitten's somehow the key to her finding a husband and being happy and God only knows what else."

"All that from Starlight?" asked Cora, still wrestling with the kitten. Last night, alone in the dark, she'd thought a great deal about omens and portents, but now here in the morning she found it difficult to believe that *he* would believe in such superstitions as well. "That doesn't make any sense."

"My sister seldom does," he said with a resigned shrug. "But she'll make a fine case for it anyway, and tell you about Blackie's seven toes and the seven kittens in his litter, and how that all goes toward making him a cat with special, ah, powers."

Gently Cora touched one of the kitten's many-toed paws as it clung to her shoulder. She'd noticed them, of course, for they were hard to miss, but she hadn't given them any special notice before this. Perhaps she should have. She couldn't doubt that seven was a fortunate number, a magical number. But a matchmaking cat?

Captain Fairbourne sighed. "But since Lady Waldegrave here won't let her keep the cat," he continued, "I'm supposed to be watching over him for her, doing what's best for him and Diana's prospects in the bargain. Oh, go ahead and give the wretched animal a dish of milk before he tears you to pieces, too."

Cora hesitated, wondering if he meant this as another way to get Starlight, then decided to trust him.

Besides, he was right about being torn to pieces; she was certain Starlight was covering her shoulder with dozens of tiny claw marks. She pried him free to set him on the floor at her feet, and ladled milk into a small wooden bowl. Frantically Starlight mewed and begged and butted her skirts, nearly upsetting the bowl in his eagerness when she set it down. Purring happily, he settled down to drink, the rhythmic lapping of his tongue defining his bliss.

"There now, there's my point," declared Captain Fairbourne. "How could I look after a kitten on board the *Calliope*, what with everything else I must consider? You'd do better, hands down."

"I already do," insisted Cora as she bent down to stroke the purring kitten, "because he's already mine."

"I'm not going to battle with you over this," he said firmly, coming around the table to join her. "What I want to know is that you'll keep watch over the cat, that you'll see he gets the proper tending and coddling?"

Somewhere upstairs in the house a door opened and closed, all the reminder that Cora needed.

"You must leave, now," she said hurriedly as she lifted the kitten from the now empty bowl. "You can't be found here, and neither can I. Go, *go!*"

Yet he didn't budge, not sharing her urgency. "Not until you agree."

"Yes, yes, I agree," she said, carefully guiding Starlight back into her pocket, "as long as you agree to tell no one, not even your sister, and especially not Lady Waldegrave, on account of how cats make her sneeze."

"Oh, aye, I figured that," he said. "Otherwise poor

Blackie here'd find himself pitched into the river by some oaf of a footman."

"And—and no more kissing," she blurted. "There must be no more of that."

He considered her for what seemed an endless moment, then slowly smiled. "If that's what you wish, or rather, don't wish. No more kissing. We'll make that part of our agreement, too."

He reached out to pet the kitten's head where it poked from her pocket. The gesture seemed oddly intimate, his hand grazing her forearm just enough to make her jump back, and enough, too, to make him look at her quizzically.

"I must go," she said, ducking her head to avoid his unspoken question, "and so must you. I told you before, Cook can't find us here. Now go, please. Just—just go."

"Very well, Miss Cora Margaret," he said softly, and to her great relief he began walking toward the door. "And I swear if you keep that kitten safe, I'll keep your secret, too."

But Cora didn't answer, and watched him leave in silence. He wasn't the handsome, gallant champion she'd idealized in her dreams last night, and he didn't seem to be the savage cutthroat from the colonies that Lady Waldegrave had described, either. He was, so far, simply a man who'd behaved boldly toward her, no more, no less. She must remember that, especially since fate seemed to have brought him to her for her purpose.

Yet as she watched him walk down the narrow backstreet toward the corner, his coattails swinging with a decided swagger, she couldn't help but feel that her life was changing. The last thing her father had promised her before she'd left was that he'd send some trustworthy man to bring her home to safety. She remembered that as clearly as she remembered the tears in her father's heartsick eyes and how he'd been dressed to rejoin the others, in the once bright red tartan of their clan, now stained and soiled, with her great-grandfather's sword on his hip.

All through the black days that followed, after her father had returned to the battle where later he'd been killed, and as she'd fled for her own life, she'd clung to his promise, holding it tight in her heart. She'd never once doubted that her father would keep his word to her, even from the grave. He always had; he always would. It didn't matter that Lady Waldegrave and others had tried to convince her otherwise. Someday, when the time was right, her father's trustworthy man would come fetch her home to Creignish.

A trustworthy man, a brave, bold man who wasn't afraid to show kindness toward the weak, a man who was as good—or as bad—as any pirate and yet would batter his knuckles defending a lady's good name, a man clever enough to steal a princess from her walled tower and carry her home in triumph, just like the heroes in the old stories her father had loved so well.

She leaned out on the step to catch one last glimpse of him before he turned the corner, and as she did he turned, almost as if he'd sensed she'd be there. He swept his hat from his head with a flourish, and though he was too far away for her to be sure, she thought—she *feared*—he winked. With a little gasp she scuttled back inside the kitchen, bolting the door to be sure.

"Good morning, miss," said Cook, her wide face open with curiosity as she pinned her linen apron in place. "You're below early, aren't you? There's nothing amiss, is there?"

"Oh, no, ma'am," said Cora, keeping her hand in her pocket to stop Starlight from peeking out. "Nothing amiss at all."

Nothing amiss and everything a-kilter, thought Cora giddily, and as she skipped up the stairs two at a time, she had to try very hard not to laugh out loud from outrageous joy.

5

Alex walked quickly through the waking city, his long stride keeping pace with his thoughts. Like most sailors, Alex had always believed in the power of luck, both good and bad, and what greater proof did he need than what had already happened to him this sunny June morning? He'd been drawn back to Lady Waldegrave's house mainly because the hour was still too early to call anywhere else, not because he'd truly expected any of the ladies to be awake and eager for his company. He'd come to idle outside that high brick wall, and perhaps catch another glimpse of the missing kitten, or even the girl with the chestnut hair.

But luck had made that same girl rise with the dawn, too, just as luck had brought her to stand on the steps to her kitchen as precisely as if they'd planned an assignation. Luck had brought the milk-maid to call and given him the excuse to join them in-side the house, just as luck—bad luck this time—had put the wicked kitten into her pocket where it had seen fit to make breakfast from his thigh. Bad luck, aye, but only after the stunningly good luck had made the chestnut-haired girl melt into his arms, nearly begging to be kissed.

He'd thought about that happening, of course—he'd thought a great deal about that girl during the night—but he'd never dreamed he'd be starting the day with her like that. Cora Margaret, she'd said her name was, Cora like the pink corabelles that grew wild in the fields back home. She'd been light as a feather to hold, her body warm and yielding and her mouth hot and sweet, and the unconscious little gasp of pleasure she'd given up to him had at once made him think of taking her, of devising all sorts of interesting ways to make her cry out again. He wanted to know if she'd freckles dusted all over her body, if the hair low on her belly was chestnut red, too, if the rest of her tasted as sweet as her mouth, and all of it to make him hard in an instant in his breeches.

Yet the sharpness of his desire for this Cora surprised him. Granted, he'd just completed a long, chaste voyage, but he usually turned toward buxom, abundant women with creamy skin and golden hair, not slight, pale little women with pointed chins and stray kittens tucked in their pockets. He suspected she was some fallen gentlewoman clinging to her dead mother's dignity and jewelry, well bred enough to make her acceptable as the widowed Lady Waldegrave's servant, but likely too ruined to be a governess, let alone to make a decent marriage.

He'd speculated on who'd done the ruining—some rakish squire in the country county she'd come from, or perhaps a married man here in London. She'd asked such strange questions of him that he wondered if the man had dabbled in politics, too, the way too many idle gentlemen did, giving her notions she didn't quite understand. He remembered how fiercely—and charmingly—she'd defended the little cat; likely, to her sorrow, she'd been as loyal to her faithless lover.

But whoever the man had been who'd abandoned Cora, he'd left her with a wistful longing in her eyes and defiance in her posture. The wistfulness made Alex want to protect her and show her the kindness that a woman deserved, her and the foolish little cat with seven toes and two names, while the defiance was a challenge he'd like to accept.

And, during the next few weeks he was in London, he resolved to do so. He had his sister as a reason for returning to Lady Waldegrave's house and the kitten's welfare as an excuse to go to the kitchen door, and the oath he'd sworn would add to the excitement. But most intriguing of all was Cora herself. Miss Cora Margaret whatever-her-last-name-that-she-wouldn't-dare-tell.

Alex smiled to himself, unaware of the frantic giggling he caused between two passing shopgirls. Good luck, the best of luck, had begun his day. He couldn't deny it. But as much as he believed in luck, he was going to need more than that alone to make a success of the rest of his morning.

He could, for example, use a fresh measure of patience, something that, for him, was generally a subjective virtue. If he needed to wait for a contrary wind to shift in his favor, or the tide to turn before he could sail clear, things that no mortal could control, then he'd patience enough to qualify for sainthood. But when it came to waiting because of another man's whim or carelessness, then he'd turn as short-tempered and restless as a crossed bull, and as determined as one, too.

Which was the reason all the pleasurable thoughts he'd had regarding Cora had evaporated by the time he'd reached Sir Thomas Walton's townhouse off Cavendish Square and begun thumping the brass dolphin knocker, thumping it hard. Though Alex himself had been awake since well before dawn—even on land he continued to follow the ship's watches that divided a sailor's day and night, and through years of habit seldom slept more than four hours at a time—he guessed Sir Thomas kept fashionable London hours, and was still at home, perhaps even still in bed. Alex almost hoped he was, so that he'd have the pleasure of hauling Sir Thomas from his covers.

Oh, Alex had followed the rules in the beginning, not making a social call out of what was more correctly a matter of business and trade. But for the last four endless mornings, he'd been made to wait in the narrow, windowless hall before Sir Thomas' offices, packed into the stuffy space with a dozen other supplicants to wait like a dunning tradesman while Sir Thomas never once showed himself and Alex's temper simmered to a roiling boil.

Now he was done with simmering to no purpose, and he was done with waiting, too. He'd come clear across the Atlantic Ocean to confront Sir Thomas. He'd no intention of being put off another day to do it, and he gave an extra thump to the brass dolphin's tail.

The man who finally opened the door looked finer than most true gentlemen, his crimson livery laced with silver perfectly tailored to his stout body and his tie wig snowy with powder. He had an aristocratic aloofness as well, managing somehow to look down his hooked nose at Alex even though he must have stood half a foot shorter. Pointedly he took note of Alex's plain dark coat with pewter buttons, marks of his unfashionable, unworthy provincialism.

"Tell your master I'm here to see him," said Alex curtly. He'd intended to be as civil as possible—the insistently polite voice of his mother was even now there in his head—but he wasn't going to be scorned by Sir Thomas' butler, either. "Go on, man, and give him my name. Captain Fairbourne, Captain Alexander Fairbourne."

But the butler didn't budge from his post. "Sir Thomas is at his levee," he said with chilly correctness. "He is not receiving at present."

"And I say he is," said Alex firmly, pushing his palm flat on the door to shove it open wide enough for him to enter. "Leastways he'll be receiving *me*."

"No, sir, you cannot do this!" sputtered the indignant butler as Alex swept past him. "I'll fetch the footmen, sir, see if I don't!"

Alex felt a weak tug at his coat sleeve, but it wasn't enough to stop him as he went striding across the marble checkerboard floor of the antechamber. Before him rose a double staircase, while to either side he caught a quick glimpse of other beautifully furnished, but empty, chambers.

Then he heard the faint, plinking notes of a harpsichord in the distance, and purposefully turned toward the tall open door on his right. If Sir Thomas were the kind of gentleman who began his day with a levee, a leisurely sort of open-ended entertainment for friends and flatterers, then he'd most likely have music as an accompaniment, and swiftly Alex moved through the first room toward the music and the muffled murmur of voices.

He hadn't far to go. The second room was a bed-chamber grand enough for a peer, complete with a low railing to separate the huge canopied bed from the rest of the room. That the brocaded coverlet on the bed was tossed back and the sheets rumpled did diminish the bed's stateliness, just as the sloe-eyed young woman in dishabille toying with a tiny white dog offered the most obvious explanation for those same rumpled sheets.

Not that Alex was interrupting any particularly intimate encounter. A man in an oversized Italian wig was playing the harpsichord in the corner, while another musician with a flute stood beside him, leaning sideways to read the music over his shoulder. An architect waited with a bulging portfolio of proposals balanced on his knees while he ogled the young woman with the dog. As a tailor loudly described the latest fashions in waistcoats, his two assistants draped lengths of silk over their arms, turning them this way and that to better catch the morning light.

And in the center of all this fawning activity, in an armchair with a back as high as a throne's, sat Sir Thomas Walton.

It wasn't as if Alex recognized Sir Thomas' face, for in truth they'd never met. But for as long as Alex could recall, his father had spoken fondly of the other man, describing him and their shared exploits as wild young blades with such vividness that Alex had recognized him instantly. He'd changed with time, of course, the same way his silver-haired father was no longer the dashing, reckless privateer of thirty years before, but there was still no mistaking Sir Thomas for anyone else in this room.

He was an imposing man, his features strong if florid from too many rich suppers, and his glittering dark eyes were as sharp as ever, and as ever ready to see through fools who dared present themselves. He sat in his thronelike chair easily, one knee cocked over the other, and the crimson silk banyon he wore settled around his frame like exotic royal robes.

It didn't matter that Sir Thomas hadn't a drop of blue blood in his veins, let alone any royalty, because through cunning and cajoling and exquisite timing, he'd thrived clear to a knighthood. When Alex's father had met him long ago, he'd been Jamaica's youngest and most corruptible royal governor, a thoroughly bribable representative of the crown who welcomed pirates, privateers, and navy officers to the same weeklong parties of drinking, gambling, and whoring that were the talk—and the envy—of the Caribbean.

It was no wonder, really, thought Alex cynically, that in his father's own youthful eagerness to make a fortune, he'd also considered such a rascal his friend; a pity and a shame, aye, but no wonder. He doubted he would have behaved any better himself in the same circumstances. But now, nearly thirty years later, it was up to Alex to repair the damage caused by his father's trust and enthusiasm, and though he'd given the matter endless consideration, he still wasn't sure how the hell he was going to do it.

Belatedly Alex swept his hat from his head and tucked it under his arm as he came to stand directly before Sir Thomas. He took care not to move too quickly and seem overeager, nor too slowly, and risk appearing intimidated. He reminded himself again of who he *was*: a Fairbourne captain, a privateer who'd captured more enemy prizes than any other man in the colonies. He never walked away from a fight, and he'd never backed down from any man who'd wanted one.

But then, the stakes had never been quite this high, either.

"Good day, Sir Thomas," he said, sweeping his hat across his waist as he bowed, yet still managing to keep his gaze level with that of the older man. "Forgive my boldness, sir, but you've left me no other path to approach you. My name, sir, is—"

"Your name, of course, is Alexander Fairbourne," said Sir Thomas, finishing Alex's introduction with obvious relish. "Your father's face betrays you, boy, just as his manners do. Who else but the son of Joshua Fairbourne would dare come crashing into my bedchamber like a brigand?"

"And who else but the esteemed Sir Thomas Walton would dare keep the son of his oldest friend waiting like a lackey in the hall for half a week?" asked Alex curtly. "In London I find that not even a brigand's manners can equal a courtier's for audacity."

"Spoken like your father, too," said Sir Thomas, his dark eyes gleaming with delight. Impatiently he beckoned, the deep lace at his cuff fluttering over his fingers. "Come, come, drop your guard, and let me grant you the proper welcome you deserve. Ah, Crowell, here you are at last, as slow as Martinique molasses."

Alex glanced over his shoulder where the red-faced butler had returned with three stout footmen as reinforcements. Four to one: Alex was flattered.

"He's a dangerous one, sir," puffed Crowell defensively. "Knocked me down and pushed right in."

"Where he could have driven me through a dozen times with a knife," said Sir Thomas blandly, "and fled through the window before you came to my assistance. We shall speak of this further, Crowell."

"But Sir Thomas—"

"Go, Crowell," said Sir Thomas with studied weariness. "Now. And take all these others with you, too. I believe Captain Fairbourne shall amuse me sufficiently for the rest of this morning."

"Very well, Sir Thomas." Crowell bowed, and roughly ushered out the footmen, the disappointed tailor and his assistants, the architect, and the two disgruntled musicians.

Alex said nothing, nor did he claim the chair beside Sir Thomas as his own. He hadn't come here to be amusing, regardless of Sir Thomas' wishes.

"So, Captain Fairbourne," the older man said pleasantly, tamping a fresh wad of tobacco into the bowl of his long-stemmed pipe. "I trust you left your father in good health, and your lady mother, too?"

"They were quite well, thank you, as were my sisters," said Alex. He looked past Sir Thomas to the other person remaining in the room with them, and smiled. "Just as I am pleased to see your own, ah, daughter in such perfect health."

Not that he believed for a moment that the young woman on the bed was Sir Thomas' daughter, but he didn't want her in the room while they spoke, either.

"My daughter?" Mystified, Sir Thomas twisted around to follow Alex's gaze. The sloe-eyed girl with the white dog smiled at them both, blowing a breathy kiss over the top of the animal's fur. "Oh, you mean Antoinette. What father'd wish a daughter like that one, eh? Trot off now, *ma belle cherie,* take yourself away from your betters."

The girl pouted prettily at Alex as she tucked the dog beneath her arm and slid from the bed with a well-calculated display of her legs in plum-colored stockings and fancy garters, the high heels of her backless slippers clacking across the floor as she left the room, leaving behind the cloying scent of her perfume.

Sir Thomas sighed indulgently, lighting his pipe with a reed from the candle. "Clearly Antoinette fancies you, Captain. I'll make a gift of her to you if you wish. She has a great many talents beyond her beauty."

"I don't doubt that she does," murmured Alex. The thought of such a "gift" was enough to make him shudder; not only was he loath to be so intimately connected to Sir Thomas, but he also found the girl's frank availability coarsely unappealing. Instead his thoughts returned to kissing Cora earlier, her slight, straight-laced figure, her warm, startled mouth and freckled nose as different from Antoinette's mercenary voluptuousness as two women could be.

"Antoinette's not to your taste, then?" asked Sir Thomas expansively as he sucked in the first pungent smoke of his pipe, filling his cheeks like a mapmaker's drawing of the west wind. "This town is so filled with hot-tailed little strumpets that 'twill be the work of a moment to find you another you'll like better. Unless it's not the skirts that interest you at all, eh, Captain? Unless you've more an eye for a wayward choirboy from the Abbey?"

"No," said Alex swiftly, and mentally resolved not

to let his thoughts wander again. "Not at all. But I haven't come here for entertainment, Sir Thomas. That I can find for myself. I've come here to ask why you haven't replied to my father's letters, and to take your answer back to him when I return."

Sir Thomas looked up at him through the thin haze of tobacco smoke. "By my 'answer,' I'm assuming you more properly mean my 'money.'"

"Your money, or more rightly my father's. Five thousand pounds, granted as a loan between friends, is not a sum most men would forget."

"Oh, indeed not," agreed Sir Thomas expansively. "Though most gentlemen would not be so vulgar as to remind another of a debt of honor."

"If it were honorable, it would have been paid long ago, and with interest for the trouble."

"And if you were a gentleman," countered Sir Thomas, "you wouldn't be asking. Besides, I'd have judged it a piddling enough sum for a man of your father's situation."

"Perhaps once," said Alex. He'd no intention of sharing all the unhappy details of his father's finances, especially given the lavish circumstances in which Sir Thomas lived. But when the sum in question was considered against how most people existed—how few skilled workers earned a single pound in a month of labor, and how an entire middling family could prosper for a year on twenty-five, while a gentleman could exist quite fashionably on three hundred—it was an unconscionable amount of money for a debt.

"While here in London you might not remark it," he continued, "this war with France and Spain has killed our trade in New England, killed it dead.

There's only a handful of ships that manage to make it through to port each season, leaving goods to rot in our warehouses and sailors' families to go hungry."

"How cursed tragic," drawled Sir Thomas. "But your father has always preferred a more lucrative trade, hasn't he? Carrying straw and chalkware gimcracks for a few pence is well enough, but I recall your father collected the best sort of profits by simply stealing, the way all good privateers do."

"Not now we don't," said Alex, praying for whatever it was going to take to keep his temper. He turned and paced six steps one way, six steps back, feeling as if he'd been caged in the small, smoky room. "This war's run on for five years, and our water's so thick with Frenchmen and Spaniards no decent Englishman can reach deep water."

"And yet *you* did," said Sir Thomas, his smile spreading behind his tobacco cloud. "You're here to plague me, sailed clear from New England, which makes rather a sorry claim for your difficulties."

"Blast and thunder, this is *not* my claim, sorrowful or not," growled Alex. "It doesn't matter whether my father needs this money more than you, or if he's prospering from the war or being ruined by it. What does is that you have owed him five thousand pounds for nearly thirty years, and by God, it is time you—"

"I don't have it."

Incredulous, Alex stopped pacing to stare at the other man. "What the hell did you say?"

Sir Thomas' smile spread pleasantly, as if they were discussing the state of his gardens. "I said I do not have the sum you so crudely demand."

Alex swept his arm through the air, encompassing

the harpsichord, the looking glasses, and the polished marble floors, the French mistress and the Italian musicians and the footmen all in silver-laced livery. "How the devil can you claim such nonsense? Of course you have it. You may not have the amount here, in gold, but surely a note to your banker would—"

"Perhaps an order to 'stand and deliver' will work miracles in certain circles, Captain, but I assure you it will not spin gold from straw with my, ah, banker."

Deliberately Sir Thomas shaped his mouth into an oval, puffing out a vaporous zero of smoke for his own entertainment. "You may prattle on about how the French or the Spanish may be meddling with your thieving out in the colonies—my sugar plantations in the islands have been nothing but a drain to my pocketbook these past three seasons—but things have been no more peaceful here at home in London."

"Your home, sir, not mine."

Sir Thomas smiled indulgently. "Your capital, then. The home of your sovereign, which should, I dare say, concern even the most provincial and benighted soul."

Instantly Alex recalled Cora's unexpected questions about fighting for King George. He'd never once in his life had his loyalty to the crown questioned, even in jest, and he wondered uneasily at the coincidence of it happening twice in one morning.

"Of course we concern ourselves with His Majesty's welfare," he said now. "Living in Massachusetts instead of London doesn't make us any less Englishmen."

Sir Thomas nodded, though Alex couldn't help suspecting the other man didn't agree. "Then you're perfectly aware that not two years ago hordes of Jacobites and Rome-loving Papists tried to rip that throne away from him. Thank God Cumberland and his troops put the rebellion down before it reached London, but those Scottish bastards still caused their share of mischief."

"We heard of the rebellion, aye," said Alex impatiently. "We are not as backward as you believe, sir."

They'd all heard of it in Massachusetts, but by the time the news had reached the colonies, the sense of any real danger to King George and his Protestant England had been drained from the story. Instead the rebellion had sounded like a few hundred ragtag Highlanders stirred together with French Papists under the misguided leadership of an exiled prince, a hopeless mismatch for the superior English troops.

In New England it had all seemed very distant, wasteful, and eminently foolish, though understandable at the same time. They'd only to look north to Canada for proof of the wicked duplicity of French Papists, and as for the Highland Scots, well, everyone knew they weren't much more civilized than the Abenakis or Iroquois in the western forests. Alex could name plenty of captains who wouldn't sign a Highlander on his crew for fear of their violent tempers and general savageness.

Sir Thomas tapped the stem of his pipe against the corner of his mouth. "Five times five thousand, that's the damage they did to my properties in Northumberland. Cattle stolen, crops destroyed, my house looted and burned, and not a penny have I recovered of it."

Alex listened, openly skeptical. Fortune had always showered upon Sir Thomas' shoulders, and he found it hard to comprehend how his affairs could have turned so completely sour in such a short time.

"Surely His Majesty has made reparations to you,

sir," he said. "You have served him too long and faithfully for him to treat you otherwise."

Sir Thomas laughed, a brief, derisive snort. "You're no fool, boy. You don't believe that any more than I do. But there have been promises made that could be of interest to you, a handsome property confiscated from its Jacobite owner, other certain small generosities pending."

"Generosities worth five thousand pounds?"

"You don't relent, do you?" Sir Thomas studied him shrewdly. "Just like your father. But yes, I do believe in time we could both be satisfied."

"How much time?" asked Alex. "I have my ship to attend to. I can't linger here on a whim forever."

The lace on Sir Thomas' cuff fluttered again as he waved his hand. "These matters cannot be rushed, Captain. They need to thrive at their own pace. A courtier's time is not the same as a sailor's."

"We could see if a judge would agree, sir," said Alex, his patience fraying. "I doubt any English court of law would stand against my father in a debt of this size and age."

"What, and let the solicitors grow sleek at our expense?" scoffed Sir Thomas. "I'd sooner take the money and toss it into the river than take it to the Inns of Court to be given over to lawyers and judges. But perhaps you would consider other, ah, arrangements to settle this account? I have heard your sister has come with you to find herself a husband. My introductions could be most useful to her."

"My sister has nothing to do with this," said Alex sharply. "She will have no need of introductions from you."

Sir Thomas' expression turned crafty. "I hear she's a great beauty, your dear sister. She's already being regarded with favor by the best people of fashion, and I've no doubt she'll be quite the belle this season. The whole world knows how your father stole the Duke of Auboncourt's granddaughter for himself. Consider what pleasure he'd take in seeing his daughter become a marchioness or even a duchess in her own right. A word or two in the right ear, and it can happen."

"A word or two worth five thousand pounds?" asked Alex, not bothering to hide the disgust he felt.

Sir Thomas nodded. "Everything in this life has its price, Captain. Surely you understand that. To be the wife of a peer, to share in his power and his estate, to bear his blue-blooded children, must doubtless be—"

"My sister's future is not for sale, sir," said Alex curtly. It was one thing to defend Diana's honor in a tavern, but quite another to be forced into challenging a man like Sir Thomas Walton to a duel. "I'll expect payment to my father in gold."

"How painfully tedious." Yet Sir Thomas' smile returned, putting Alex on guard again. "Then you must, I fear, be willing to wait."

"Six weeks," said Alex firmly. "Six weeks, and I'll sail home with my father's money."

"Six weeks, then, for you and I to see much of each other." His smile widened, and so did the emptiness behind it. "I trust you'll let yourself be my guest. A supper with other friends, say, a bit of gaming or wenching? I should hate to let Joshua's son go unamused."

"If, sir, my schedule permits," said Alex, recognizing his dismissal and almost welcoming it at the same time. Clearly he'd accomplish nothing but further frustration if he remained, and with bitter determination he swallowed back his feelings of failure. "But you may be certain that I'll wish to visit you often to learn the progress of your 'generosities.' "

There came the short bark of a laugh again. "Yes, I rather expect you will. You favor your father admirably, you know. No wonder he's so deuced proud of you."

The older man's glance raked over Alex, measuring him from head to toe. "But when you call on me again, Captain, I'll ask one favor of you. I'll admit that the sword is necessary to a young man's bravado. But could you please kindly show me the small honor due your father's old friend, and leave behind the knives and pistols hidden about your person, eh?"

For an answer, Alex bowed, sweeping his hat over his leg, the same way that he'd bowed when he'd first forced his way into the room. He did in fact have a small pistol tucked in his belt to the back of his waist where it would be well hidden by the skirts of his coat, and in the cuff of his boot he'd slipped his long-bladed sailor's knife. In London, he'd always judged it best to regard all unknown waters as unfriendly ones. It was familiar and comfortable; it was also safest by far.

And he'd be damned before he turned careless now, not even for the sake of five thousand pounds.

Cora was sitting in a chair by the window in her room, her head bent over the Irish-stitch pocketbook she was working, when she heard the raised voices far below in the front hall. It was far too soon for Lady Waldegrave to return with Diana Fairbourne, not with the itinerary her ladyship had planned for the afternoon, and besides, the cross-tempered voices were decidedly male.

She frowned, her needle stilled as she strained to listen while Starlight pounced on the scraps of yarn at her feet. She told herself firmly that it couldn't possibly be Captain Fairbourne again, not twice in the same day, and yet both the timbre and the temper could belong to few others. She tossed her handwork onto the bed, gathered Starlight up in the crook of her arm, and hurried toward the stairs and the voices to investigate.

Yet by the time she'd reached the second landing, the man had gone, slamming the door after himself with such force that she felt the rattle in the arched window here an entire floor above.

But still she wished to know if Captain Fairbourne had been here, and now she rushed through the empty front parlor to the window overlooking the street. Without a thought she sat Starlight on the floor, pushed back the damask curtains, and with both hands threw open the sash, the heavy wooden frame squeaking against the cords in protest. Not that Cora heard, or cared, for there striding across the street was Alexander Fairbourne, her trustworthy man proving his trust.

"Captain Fairbourne! You've come back!" she shouted joyfully, impulsively. "I knew you would, I knew it must be so, and now you have come back!"

He stopped and turned to find where her voice came from, shading his eyes against the noontime sun as he finally discovered her in the open window.

"And ahoy there to you, Miss Cora," he called in return. "I've come back, aye, to see my wretched sister. Which, it seems, I am not permitted to do."

Cora felt a sharp stab of disappointment, buoyed back almost instantly with rationalization. Of course he couldn't *announce* that he'd come here to see her again for all the world to hear—after all, she was the one bellowing from the window like a costermonger's wife—and what better reason could he have for returning than to see his sister?

Nervously she glanced down at the front door, making sure that the butler hadn't heard her and come out to investigate. She certainly didn't wish him reporting back to Lady Waldegrave.

Resolving to be more cautious, she knelt beside the window, resting her chin on her folded arms as Starlight jumped to the sill beside her.

"You can't see your sister because she's not here," she said, lowering her voice. She wasn't about to tell him he'd no longer be welcome in the house whenever he called; she didn't want to risk driving him away, and besides, such a message should come from her ladyship, not her. "She and Lady Waldegrave went out to visit the shops and make calls."

He frowned, considering. "Calls to whom?"

"Oh, Lady Waldegrave's friends, I suppose." He was handsome even when he frowned, she decided, and gazing down at his upturned face like this, without any danger of kissing or other such misbehavior, was exceptionally pleasant. "At least those with eligible sons or nephews. That is why she's here, you know."

His frown deepened. "I trust that jackass Oswald's not on the bill of fare for today."

"Lord Oswald?" she asked, curling her fingers into Starlight's fur. "He's a perfectly nice gentleman with a respectable income, and heir to several titles, too. Your sister could do far worse. Still, I'll grant you he's not very clever, so I could see how you might think him a, um, *jackass*."

It was a vulgar word, not at all appropriate for a lady to say, yet repeating it felt satisfyingly wicked—as had all of her contact with Captain Fairbourne, and she couldn't tell if this made him more trustworthy or less.

"Oh, aye, Miss Cora, be overnice about it," he scoffed. "The man is a jackass, hands down, and I won't have him marrying into my family."

He was teasing her again, she knew it, but it was his using her given name to do it that made her blush. Because she hadn't told him her family name, he'd really no choice but to call her Cora, yet still she liked the sound of it in his rough, gruff voice.

"It's entirely possible that your sister is taking tea with him right now," she said, hoping that from where he stood he couldn't see her blush. "Lord Oswald's mother is Lady Winifred, who is a dear friend to Lady Waldegrave, so it's entirely possible that they're—oh, Starlight, no!"

Vainly she grabbed for the little cat as he wriggled free and jumped from the sill. She cried out as he fell, his paws and tail outstretched as if he thought he could fly, sailing through the air to land squarely on Captain Fairbourne's broad shoulder.

"Hah, there you are, you little devil," said the man as he put his hand over the cat's back to keep him from escaping again. "Always up to some mischief, aren't you?"

"You can't keep him!" cried Cora, leaning far out the window herself. "You can't take him away now!"

He looked up at her over the cat's small black back, beneath the brim of his black hat, his eyes very blue in the sunlight. "I never said I was going to, did I?"

"Then give him back directly!"

"Look here, Cora," he said. "I'm not going to keep shouting up at you. Come down here so we can talk civil."

"There?" She swallowed hard. "In the street?

"Aye, in the street," he said firmly. "You must if you want this infernal cat back. I've had my fill of butlers this morning, and I'll be damned before I'll go back to grovel before the one you keep."

"We're a household of ladies, sir," she explained stiffly, "and Junius is instructed to be most careful about whom he admits to the house."

Most careful: that was how she should be, too, and yet here she was actually considering leaving the house that had been her sanctuary for nearly two years only because he was asking it.

"Step lively, lass, I haven't all morning." He made a great show of first looking down the street, then back in the other direction. "And I see no tigers or lions or other peril lying in wait to gobble you up."

Not tigers or lions, thought Cora, her heart racing and her mouth dry, but enemies that could be every bit as dangerous. Of course she wanted Starlight back, but oh, what she'd have to do to get him.

As if he could read her thoughts, Starlight turned and gazed up at her, blinking in the bright sun from his perch on Captain Fairbourne's shoulder. The little cat shifted, and the man spread his hand over his back.

"Come down, Cora," he called softly, coaxing her. "What harm could there be in a bit of trust?"

The trustworthy man would come . . .

And so, at last, she nodded in acceptance, and closed the window with a thump.

6

Cora was out of breath as she slipped through the front door, her skirts fluttering around her ankles as she hurried down the white steps to join him. After all the rebuffs he'd endured this morning, Alex couldn't help but be flattered by her haste, and by the eager face, pink beneath her freckles, that she now turned up toward him and the small black cat.

"Oh, Starlight, you're so very bad," she said, reaching up toward the cat on his shoulder. Her hands were white, the fingers tapered and unmarked, lady's hands that did no work, and he marveled at how refined her duties for her mistress must be to have hands like that. "Don't you know you could have been killed if you'd fallen so far to the pavement, you foolish, foolish kitten?"

Briefly Alex considered holding the cat out of her reach to prolong this moment of her so guilelessly posed before him. But she so clearly adored the cat that to keep her from it would be cruel, and instead he dipped his shoulder low enough for her to reach it.

"There now, Starlight, come to me," she coaxed as, one by one, she carefully unplucked the cat's tiny claws from the wool of his coat. Though Cora treated the kitten like a naughty child, she didn't speak to him in the high-pitched, sing-song baby talk that Diana had. She seemed too practical for that kind of silliness, or perhaps she'd seen enough suffering in her short life to quash such girlish exuberance. She'd already lost her mother and most likely a lover, unimaginable tragedies to his petted, protected sister, and from how Cora had spoken he wondered if she'd any family of her own left at all. She had a quality of aloneness to her, of being accustomed to keeping her own company more from necessity than from choice. And as disloyal as it was, there was no question in Alex's mind that Cora now cared infinitely more than Diana did for the kitten, no matter how she'd come to claim him for her own.

"I don't know why Starlight jumped like that," she was saying now as she cradled the cat against her chest. "Though I'm vastly glad you saved him, I am sorry that he used your shoulder for a pincushion to do it."

"No harm done," he said gallantly. For his own part, he was happy enough to have sacrificed his shoulder to the kitten's landing; if Blackie, or Starlight, had stayed on the windowsill where he belonged, then Cora, too, would have stayed inside. "I'd venture he has seven lives to match his seven toes, which would make anyone courageous."

Self-consciously she smiled, making him realize how seldom she did. Tiny pinpricks of sunlight filtered through the brim of her straw hat to dapple her face. The hat was broad-brimmed, low-crowned, and without trimming, yet it suited her as much as the pink-flowered muslin of her gown with the white lawn ruffles at the cuffs and the rosy coral beads around her throat, the essence of summer in a woman's dress. She looked fresh and crisp and country-innocent, regardless of her past, and he couldn't help comparing her to Sir Thomas' slatternly mistress.

Not that Cora was *his* mistress, at least not yet. But if she were, decided Alex, then this was how he'd want her to dress.

"Seven lives will last Starlight but seven days if he insists on trying to fly from open windows," she said, fortunately unaware of Alex's thoughts. "But I do thank you for saving him, Captain Fairbourne."

"Alexander, lass," he said softly. "I'm not your captain, nor shall you ever serve on my crew, I think. Better you call me Alexander, or Alex, as my friends do."

Her shy smile faltered with uncertainty. "That seems vastly . . . vastly *familiar*."

"So was the kiss we shared this morning, and yet you managed that."

At once she ducked her head over the kitten's back, hiding her face beneath the broad brim of her hat as she turned away from him, back toward the house. "I must go, sir. I must go now."

Swiftly he circled around her, blocking her path. "Don't leave, Cora, not yet. Walk with me instead. Once around this square, never out of sight of this house. Is that so much to wish for?"

Her uneasiness palpable, she glanced from the steps of Lady Waldegrave's house, across the street to Hanover Square, and back again. This square, like all the fashionable squares being created here in the West End, was not large, an unassuming park the width and breadth of four houses, with a handful of trees bordered by a low whitewashed fence. To walk its circumference, even at a snail's pace, would take no more than half an hour.

"What would be gained by such a walk?" she asked, more to herself than seeking his answer. "To leave this house, to walk as you ask—what purpose would there be?"

"Why, the pleasure to be found in each other's company," he said. What he was finding first, though, was how desperately he wanted her to agree, and he couldn't begin to explain why it suddenly mattered so damned much that she did. "I'd have hoped you'd wish the same."

After a long moment, the broad-brimmed hat nodded, more in troubled resignation than agreement. "Because you wish it, then so must I?"

"That's not exactly it, no," he said, taken aback. Haste to join him was flattering; resignation like this was not. "I've never forced my company on any lady, and I'm not about to do so now."

"But I must trust you," she explained anxiously, as much to herself, it seemed, as to him. "You said so yourself."

"Aye, but not like—"

"You will protect me, Alexander?" she asked, and from the angle of her hat he could tell she was looking at the sword at his waist. He remembered her earlier fascination with his sword, and with the number of unfortunate men it had sent from this life, and if either of them felt uneasy now, it was he. Most likely her interest was the usual one he'd seen in women, a romanticized view of piracy and privateering based on the tales of poets or playwrights who'd never been to sea, let alone to war, yet there was still something odd about her interest, just as there was something odd about her reluctance to leave the house.

But she had called him by his name, her voice quavering a bit when she'd done it, and she'd asked for his protection as well—a request that, like the baby talk, he sensed she rarely made.

"You will watch over me?" she asked again.

"If necessary, aye," he said gruffly, and he meant it. "Though I doubt we'll find much threat here."

"From tigers and lions, no." Gingerly she looped her hand into the crook of his arm, and tipped her head to one side so at last he could see her face. Her cheeks were rosy and her dark elf's eyes danced with such unabashed excitement that he instantly forgot his misgivings. "Now walk and amuse me, the way you have promised. Tell me of your day after leaving me this morning."

"There's nothing much to tell," he hedged as they began, following the wide sidewalk that ran before the houses. "Nothing that would interest you, anyway."

"I am so weary of my own concerns that I'll embrace yours in an instant," she declared, and he thought again of how much she could remind him of a merry little elf. "Tell me whatever—oh, *oh!*"

She gulped and lowered her head to hide her face in her hat like a turtle into his shell as another, older lady and gentleman passed them by. The two were squabbling, so engrossed in their own quarrel that they scarcely managed a civil nod at Cora and Alex as they passed by.

"They're gone," said Alex quietly when the pair had passed. "Were they friends of Lady Waldegrave? Were you afraid they'd recognize you and tell her?"

She shook her head and took a deep breath from inside the hat brim. Her fingers tightly clutched the sleeve of his coat, her skin moist with nervousness.

"Then they're not about to tell her ladyship one blessed thing," he said to the crown of her hat. "Besides, most people are so caught up in their own affairs that they've no time to squander on anyone else's."

"It wasn't that," she whispered miserably. "That . . . that . . . wasn't what I feared."

He kept walking, at a loss. "Do you wish me to take you home? If you're not well, then you shouldn't—"

"No!" she cried unhappily, and now when she looked at him her dark eyes seemed filled near to overflowing with tears of frustration and fear, not excitement. "I'm quite well. Quite! I must be brave, and not be afraid. I can't be a coward. I can *not*."

"You're not a coward, Cora," he said, not sure where this was leading. As far as he could see, there was absolutely nothing to inspire this kind of reaction from her. "I'd never describe you that way."

She shook her head with despair, unconvinced. "Oh, yes, I am a perfect coward, trembling and shaking like this. It's only that—that—oh, pray, simply speak of something else!"

"If you wish." He cleared his throat, and self-consciously patted her hand again. He hated to see women cry, and he didn't want her to do it now. He'd be willing to walk on his hands in the middle of the square if it would keep her from weeping.

But of course now that she'd as much as commanded him to talk, he could think of absolutely nothing to say. The topics that were on his mind—the time-consuming chore of replenishing his ship's stores before the long voyage back across the Atlantic, the patched sail that needed replacing, the worrisome cough of one of his crewmen—weren't the kind that would interest any lady, let alone one as distraught as Cora seemed to be.

In desperate need of inspiration, he scanned the neat little square with its fenced-in lawn beneath the dusty summer sky. That lawn was probably all the greenery that most of the inhabitants of these grand houses saw on any given day, and he thought of how much he himself would hate to live packed so closely to his neighbors, and so far from any forests or open meadows.

And that, he decided, would have to provide conversation enough.

"I don't believe I could ever live in London," he began, feeling as if he were pompously proclaiming his preference from a pulpit. "Oh, I know it's the greatest city in the world, but I'd trade it all for a clear sky and a fresh breeze off the marsh at home."

He could feel her take a deep, steadying breath beside him, a tremor of pure will.

"Is that what your New England is like?" she asked in a tiny voice. "Clear skies and marshes?"

He nodded, encouraged. "There's no other place like it, not in all the world. My home is a place called Appledore, on a long arm of land that curves into the sea called Cape Cod. Compared to this, everything is still new and wild—we Englishmen have only been there for a hundred years or so, you know—and though we've plenty of company, we don't stumble over one another with every step the way you Londoners do."

"But I'm not a Londoner," she said wistfully. "My

home is—was—in a place full of wildness, too, and at night I always listened to the river that ran near our house. The carts, the carriages, the people racketing about are all anyone hears in London, night and day."

Alex nodded. "Then you understand why I can't wait to sail again. Not that the ocean is silent, mind, the way landsmen think—there're the wind and the waves, and the men calling to one another, and the ship's timbers creaking and groaning like an old man—but the sounds have an honesty to them that city noises don't."

He heard her catch her breath and felt her stiffen, and when he glanced up he saw two women with a little boy approaching them.

"Steady as you go, Cora," he said softly. "They mean you no harm."

"I *will* be brave, Alex," she whispered fiercely. "You'll see. I won't be a coward again."

"Look at that lady's kitten, Mama!" cried the little boy excitedly, hopping up and down as he pointed. "Look at where he is on her!"

"This is Starlight," said Cora, bending from the waist so the boy could better see the cat on her shoulder. "He's only a kitten, you see, still a baby cat, so I must keep him with me as if I were his nursemaid to make sure he doesn't come to harm."

"If you didn't, big dogs would eat him," said the boy with horrified fascination. "In one bite."

"Richard!" scolded one of the women as she jerked the startled boy back by his wrist. "What a vastly cruel thing to say!"

"The lad said big dogs would eat him, ma'am," said Alex quickly in the boy's defense, "which is perfectly true. He didn't say he'd eat the kit himself."

"Indeed." Impatiently the woman tugged on his wrist again. "Come, Richard. We can't dawdle here all day."

"Good day, ma'am," said the boy with a jerky small bow. "Good day, sir. And good day, Starlight. Maybe I'll see you tomorrow."

"Aye, lad, perhaps you shall," said Alex heartily. The boy was already being tugged past them, and as he looked back longingly over his shoulder at the black kitten, Alex winked. He remembered well enough what it had been like to be a boy with women keeping him from doing the things that were really interesting.

"You shouldn't have said that, Alex," said Cora, though her smile didn't make it much of a rebuff. "Letting him expect to see Starlight here tomorrow!"

"And why shouldn't he?" asked Alex easily. "If I've anything to say about it, then you'll be back here tomorrow, here with me."

"Oh, yes," she scoffed as she stroked the cat's narrow back, "as if you have any right to say what Starlight and I shall do and when."

"Blackie," he corrected. "Mark the color of his fur."

"Starlight, on account of his lovely little star, and mind you remember it." Her smile warmed, making him doubly glad he'd coaxed her outside. She'd been good with the boy, enough that he'd seen how happy she'd be with children of her own. He wondered if the scoundrel who'd left her had promised her a family; for some women, that would be more alluring than jewels. Cora, he decided, would be one of them.

"Then can I say you weren't a coward?"

"Oh, yes, how marvelously brave of me, not to be frightened of a child!" She tossed back her head so the hat slipped back from her face and let the summer sun wash over her cheeks in a most unladylike fashion. "But then you can't know how much any of this means to me. To be here, standing on the far side of the square I've looked at for so long from my window. It's as if I've seen the same landscape in a painting on the wall, and now somehow I find myself inside it."

"There, then, that's another fault I'd find with London," he declared. "In Appledore the ladies can walk about free as pretty birds to the shops or the market-house or to call on friends, with everything so close that you needn't bother keeping a carriage. Your own legs are perfectly sufficient."

"My legs, perhaps," said Cora doubtfully, "but hardly my shoes."

She paused to pull her skirts back against her legs so the squared-off toes of her slippers peeped out from beneath the hem, and belatedly Alex saw they weren't the best sort of shoes for walking, with high, curving heels and no backs and roses embroidered in silk across the toes. Not for walking, no, but for seduction, for tip-toeing across a bedchamber below the drifting silk of a dressing gown and little else, and with shocking speed he imagined her exactly like that, leaning over *his* bed.

"You would have other shoes," he managed to choke out. "And the breeze from the sea would put the roses on your cheeks, not your toes. That's the reason why the Appledore ladies are so wondrously fair, and without need of powder or paint."

"If you put me onto your beach, all I'd be was wondrously spotted." She flicked her muslin skirts back in place, and grinned at him. "But tell me of your Appledore gentlemen. Are they such righteous paragons as well?"

"Most are, aye." He sighed mightily, bowing his head with feigned sorrow. "Alas, I'm the lowest specimen there is, an unworthy, squat male, the despair of my father and the shame of my mother. Which is why they sent me away here to London."

"You are *not!*" she cried so indignantly that he almost laughed aloud. The best part was seeing the sympathy settle across her face when, for one fleeting moment, she'd been prepared to believe him, and even better, to defend him as well.

"Very well, then. I'm not the most squat," he admitted with another monumental sigh. "I do have two brothers to share the blame. But most all of us Appledore men are of a piece since we all follow the sea."

"You're all privateers?" she asked with surprise, doubtless envisioning some Tortuga of Cape Cod, a buccaneer's paradise among the puritans.

"Not usually, no. Only when wartime makes privateering more profitable than fishing or whaling or carrying plain merchant cargoes." He couldn't help the pride creeping into his voice. "The only thing that's constant is that most Appledore men sail in Fairbourne ships."

Now instead of the fenced green square before him, Alex was seeing the harbor back home, filled with sloops and schooners and ships registered to his family's name, the sky overhead a fair-weather blue and the water sparkling with sunshine. It was a fantasy view, of course, for even before this war, there had never been a time when all the Fairbourne vessels would be in port at once, and besides, the larger ones now sailed from Boston's deeper harbor to the north. But as a symbol for his family, the sunny harbor full of ships made a handsome picture indeed, and one that he cared about fervently.

"That's what has brought my father to such a pass, you see," he continued, still seeing that idyllic scene. "He believes in looking after those who labor for him, and their families as well."

"But that's how it should be, isn't it?" insisted Cora with a conviction that surprised him. "Though you're not all blood kin, from the way you're telling it, your father acts as your town's chief, doesn't he?"

Alex had an unsettling vision of his father as a fearsome Wampanoag chieftain from the time of King Philip's wars, sporting feathers and wampum beads in his hair and a tomahawk and scalps hanging at his waist.

"We're not savages, Cora," he said testily. "Just because we live in Massachusetts doesn't mean that."

"You know perfectly well that's not what I meant," she said impatiently. "About being savages, that is. But your tribe, or your clan, or your town, or your parish, it's all much the same, isn't it? The people in Appledore depend on your father, not just for their livelihood, but for his leadership."

"Even when it brings his own family close to ruin?" He didn't know why it suddenly mattered to Alex that she understand. Perhaps it was because no one else in London did. "Long ago my father made an extravagant loan to a friend in need, a friend who has never seen fit to pay him back. Yet always Father excuses him for his disloyalty, pretending the money means nothing, while he still tries to support half of our town."

Now it was Cora who was patting his arm, offering the comfort of a listening ear. "He sounds like a good man, your father, generous and loyal."

"Father can't do everything, Cora, as much as he wishes to," he said. "Besides, he's not a young man any longer. He must consider his own welfare as well as that of my mother and sisters."

"He doesn't have to," said Cora promptly. "He has you to do that for him."

"Oh, aye, and doesn't he, though," said Alex grimly. "Someone in the family must be practical. Why else am I in London now, praying my sister doesn't run off to Gretna Green with some hare-brained lordling, while I must grovel and threaten and cajole to see that this obscene debt of his is finally settled?"

She smiled up at him sweetly, tiny loose tendrils curling over her forehead from the heat. "So that your father can squander the entire sum on widows and orphans and homeless puppy dogs?"

"Damnation, Cora, I didn't say that!"

"No, you didn't say that," she agreed, "and you never would, nor even dare think it. But it's clear as the sky above that your father trusts you. You make an excellent champion, Alex, which, of course, my father must have recognized, too, or else he never would have—"

"You mean *my* father," interrupted Alex moodily. He didn't see himself as anybody's champion, and he didn't like being called one. "Hell, Father could recognize whatever he wants, but it still doesn't make it true."

Yet she only smiled, sadly, he thought, though he could see no reason for that, either.

"Oh, Captain Fairbourne," she said. "You're not nearly as serious and practical as you pretend, are you? And now you—oh, dear God, please help me to be brave, help me to be brave *now!*"

Swiftly Alex looked ahead. Considering how she'd reacted before, he expected another strolling couple, or more children out with their nursemaids. But instead the two men approaching now were, to his mind, even safer and less threatening. Two soldiers, officers, steady older men decorated for their bravery, were coming along the walk toward them deep in conversation, likely refighting old battles against the French or plotting new ones.

"Do you see them, Alex?" she whispered urgently. "Soldiers, English soldiers!"

"We are in England, sweet," he answered, "and many officers make their homes on Hanover Street, not far from here. Now no more running, mind? You were brave before. Be brave again."

She didn't answer at first, her gaze fixed on the two soldiers ahead of them. She'd slipped the kitten from her shoulder to her arms, holding it tightly like a baby to her chest.

"I can't pass them, Alex," she whispered hoarsely. "What if they see me? What if they know me?"

"Cora, lass," he asked, his own uneasiness growing. "Have you done something that would make them know you?"

"No!" She shook her head rapidly in denial. "I've done nothing wrong, Alex, nothing!"

And yet Cora knew she had. She'd been wrong to come out walking with him, wrong to leave the sanctuary of Lady Waldegrave's house, wrong to trade her caution for the pleasure she found in Alex Fairbourne's company.

But most of all she'd been wrong from the moment she'd been born a MacGillivray, born to a clan renowned for its loyalty and doomed by it at the same time. To Alex these two officers were simply English soldiers, but she recognized their regiments by their uniforms, and knew they were Cumberland's men. They were smiling, chatting pleasantly with each other as they walked around this well-tended square as if Culloden had never happened, as if their hands and souls weren't stained forever with the blood of her clan, her kin.

Her *father*.

"They said the ground ran red with blood and tears," she whispered, her words rushing fast as a river. "They said no mercy was granted the wounded, that the orders were to kill even those who surrendered."

"What in blazes are you talking about, Cora?" asked Alex. "You're making no sense at all."

But she was, perfect sense. The sun glinted off the gold wire wrapped around the hilts of the soldiers' swords, the long leather scabbards slapping gently against their thighs as they walked. What menace did these swords have now, as gaudily benign as a lady's silver chatelaine? Yet they had killed before and would kill again, just like the more humble sword that Alex wore.

He wanted to help her, her trustworthy champion, but she'd be wrong, hideously wrong if she let him. Too much blood had been spilled already in the MacGillivray name. If she ever wished to find peace, if she ever hoped to return home, she'd have to put an end to it now, *now*, while she could.

And the only way she knew how was, one more time, to run.

"I must go," she said, her voice breaking off in a

breathless sob as she backed away, her arms tightening around Starlight. "I must go *now!*"

"Oh, aye, and where would you go?" asked Alex, gently but firmly settling one arm around her shoulder, as much to calm her as to keep her at his side. "If you don't want to be noticed, Cora, then don't go bolting off like a wild rabbit. Don't think of what frightens you, but of what makes you happy."

The soldiers were so close now that she could see the crowns of their Hanover king stamped into the buttons on their uniforms. She was trembling against Alex's side and she couldn't stop. She wanted to do what he said, to be brave, but all she could think of now was her father in his scarlet tartan coat and the white plume nodding in his black hat, how proud he'd been to ride with the rest of the clan, how he had died on that chilly day in early spring while these two men still lived to walk on in the warm summer sunshine.

"Think of the little kit in your arms," Alex was saying. "Look at the white patch on his forehead, how it's like a star, a lucky star for you, Cora."

Mutely she did as she was told, gazing down at Starlight. She touched her fingers to the white patch of fur and he looked back at her, his green eyes slowly blinking, and opened his mouth to mew.

"See now, your luck's changing," continued Alex. "Even that little kit knows it, doesn't he? And now, Cora, so do you."

She stroked Starlight again, and realized, somehow, she'd stopped shaking. "Do I?"

Alex smiled down upon her. "Oh, aye. We've walked right past those two officers, and all they did was touch their hats to you. Not that you noticed, mind."

"I didn't?" Swiftly she turned, saw the backs of the soldiers, and giggled with nervous relief. "I didn't, did I?"

Maybe her luck was changing, just as Alex said, and happily she began to tell him exactly that. But instead, as she turned, she gasped with dismay, and all that joyful relief and good luck seemed to flee as quickly as it had come.

The dark green carriage waiting beside the stone block at the curb was a familiar one, the matched bays waiting patiently while the footman closed the carriage door painted with the understated coat of arms in gold.

Lady Waldegrave had returned home early.

7

"I've been calling and calling for you, Cora," said Lady Waldegrave crossly. "Wherever have you been hiding yourself?"

"I—I was in the garden, my lady," said Cora breathlessly. It was, in a way, true, for the circuitous route she'd taken from Alex's side had in fact passed through the garden and the garden doors to reach her ladyship's bedchamber. She'd barely managed to tuck Starlight away inside her pocket before she'd passed one of the maidservants on the back stairs, and he was making it clear he wasn't happy to be so confined, growling and wriggling against her leg. If her ladyship hadn't been calling for her, she would have taken the kitten upstairs first, but instead she now had to cover him up as best she could with her hat in her hand, and pray he wouldn't yowl at the wrong moment.

"Garden or no garden, Cora, you should have been aware that I needed you." While Mary, one of the housemaids, stood by helplessly wringing her hands in her apron, Lady Waldegrave yanked a mahogany box from a shelf and dumped the contents into a heap of handkerchiefs and lace scarves in the center of her bed. "Here now, look at this jumble! How am I supposed to find anything?"

"What are you seeking, my lady?" asked Cora as she hurried to the side of the bed, still carefully keeping her wide-brimmed hat over Starlight in her pocket.

"That cinnabar box with the cunning little men carved into the side, the ones with the topknots like haystacks," said the older woman as she dug through the handkerchiefs, bright pink circles of vexation visible on each cheek beneath her powder. "Oh, Cora, you know it! The box that Howlin gave me last Twelfth Night! I came all the way home from Lady Julia's house to fetch it, Lady Julia having expressly asked to see it, and here it has quite vanished—quite!"

"It's where it always is, my lady," said Cora, happy to have Lady Waldegrave fuss over anything other than her. She opened the lid of the long chest at the bottom of the bed, reached deep into one corner, and pulled out a small drawstring bag inked with Chinese characters.

"Oh, I knew you'd find it, my darling Cora!" cried Lady Waldegrave, sinking into a pouf of stiff silk skirts as she sat on the chair beside the bed. "Only you know my ways. But oh, how all this has vexed me! Here, Cora, bring it to my hands. Tea, Mary, and take care to make it hot. I find I need a restorative after this distress."

Reluctantly Cora came closer, the box in one outstretched hand while with the other she held her hat close to her hip. Why couldn't Starlight go peacefully to sleep, instead of wriggling and wiggling so fiercely inside her pocket?

"Come, Cora, let me have the box," said Lady Waldegrave, beckoning impatiently. "And see that you take it from that nasty old bag, too. Whoever knows what sort of heathens might have touched it?"

Most likely the same heathens who'd fashioned the box, thought Cora as she struggled to open the bag's drawstrings with one hand.

"God gave you two hands so you needn't be so fumble-fingered," said Lady Waldegrave. "Pray put your hat aside and—and—ah-*choo!*"

Her sneeze exploded at the same instant that Cora had worked the cinnabar box free of its bag, and as she handed it to Lady Waldegrave she added one of the handkerchiefs from the bed as well.

"It must be that wretched bag," said Lady Waldegrave, sneezing again into the handkerchief. Her eyes were already tearing and turning red. "What other explanation could it be? I don't care if Howlin said I must keep the box wrapped in it. Cora, please, toss it in the grate now so it will burn the minute the fire is lit this evening. I won't have it here—here—ah-*choo!*"

She buried her face in the handkerchief while Cora gratefully used the bag's banishment as a chance to retreat across the room to the fireplace, and as far from Lady Waldegrave as she could. *She* knew the explanation for her poor ladyship's distress, of course, the same black, furry explanation still wriggling in her pocket, but she was hardly going to share it. The luck that Alex had promised would come from touching Starlight's star certainly didn't seem to apply to the poor kitten himself.

"Perhaps you should take the air outside, my lady," she suggested, throwing open the nearest window for good measure. "To give the, ah, contaminant a chance to leave the room."

"You are right, dear Cora," said the sniffling countess. "Besides, Lady Julia is expecting me back, and I don't wish to leave Diana unattended for longer than I must."

She rose, dabbing at her nose, and peered through her red-rimmed eyes at Cora. "Are you certain you are well yourself, Cora? Now that I can see you properly beside that window, you appear quite disordered."

"I'm perfectly well, my lady," answered Cora, though she felt her cheeks grow hot with a guilty flush. She *did* feel disordered, though not the way that the countess meant. She had left this house for the first time in nearly two years and she had gone unrecognized past two of Cumberland's soldiers, but most of all she'd walked and talked and laughed with Alex Fairbourne, an experience heady enough to disorder any woman. "Truly."

But the countess wasn't convinced. "Your face is red and feverish, Cora, and I'll not have you ill. Before I leave again, I'll have Cook prepare you a special draft."

"That's very kind of you, my lady, but not necessary, not—"

"Junius was convinced he'd seen you earlier across the square walking with a black-haired gentleman much like Captain Fairbourne."

"My lady!" gasped Cora, too stunned even to venture a defense. She'd thought her greatest worry this morning would be Starlight's discovery; she'd never imagined *this*.

Lady Waldegrave studied her shrewdly over the bunched handkerchief in her hand. "Well, yes, that was my response, too. Dear Cora out walking with a gentleman, bold as an alderman's daughter! Cora risking her pretty neck for the sake of amusing herself with such wrongful company as Captain Fairbourne! Not our Cora, no, no!"

"No, no, my lady," echoed Cora faintly, though she couldn't honestly say if she were agreeing or denying. "No, no."

"And so I told Junius," said Lady Waldegrave briskly, as she wrapped the cinnabar box in another handkerchief. "No, no, and no more bearing such dirty, disgraceful tales to me, either. Now let me return to Lady Julia's house before she fears I've perished at the rough hands of thieves, and calls the constable to search for my body."

"Very well, my lady," said Cora, dipping a curtsey of farewell. "Have a pleasant afternoon, my lady."

"Oh, it will be pleasant enough," said the countess with a final sniffle, "so long as Lady Julia does not feel the urgency to boast once again of her prowess at the faro tables."

But at the doorway she paused, one bejeweled hand on the latch, and turned back.

"And Cora, please be sure that you give poor Junius no further cause for fancifying. I know on occasion he does enjoy a bit more gin than is proper, but I would not wish to have to let him go because of what he has wrongly witnessed. A well-behaved butler is such a comfort to a widow like myself, and so vastly difficult to replace. You do understand, dear Cora, don't you?"

Cora nodded, her mouth too dry to answer. Junius had been with the countess far longer than Cora, clear back to when he'd been plain Ezekiel, before she'd rechristened him to suit the fashion. And Lady Waldegrave hadn't been jesting, either; a good butler was worth his weight in guineas, while Cora . . . Cora was not, and they both knew it.

Starlight shifted again in her pocket, this time twisting around so he could display his irritation by sticking his claws through her petticoat and into her leg, and yet, now, Cora scarcely felt it.

The countess smiled with the well-perfected sweetness that had made her so famous in her youth. "You have always been so wonderfully understanding and accommodating, Cora. I pray those are attributes that you never lose."

But in the depths of her own troubled heart, Cora realized she already had.

Like all captains who loved their ships, Alex ordinarily took an undisguised delight in approaching his darling in an open boat, using the time as a passenger to reflect on her beauty and to fuss and worry over even her tiniest flaws. A warm summer evening like this, when the water was smooth and still, and twilight made the sky and Thames blend together in a soft blue gray, could make the scrutiny even more pleasurable. But regardless of the weather or season, Alex never questioned the time such endless devotion took. He knew well that some day these same details could prove the difference between survival and death to him and his crew.

The *Calliope* had been built first as a merchant sloop for the Caribbean trade, then converted to a privateer as soon as war had been declared. Her rigging had been changed to make her sail faster and closer to the wind to better outrun the enemy, and her sides had been cut for speed and to accommodate the heavy guns she now carried instead of cargo. But because

Alex had been so successful, there were many little luxuries to be found in the captain's cabin, too, from an oversized bunk with pressed linen sheets to a glass-fronted case for his favorite books to the mahogany chest with a voyage's worth of the finest New England rum. Not that there was any mystery to this; in the five years since Alex had taken command, the *Calliope* had become more his home than any house on shore could be.

As the hired boatmen rowed closer, he tried to study the sloop as he always did, looking for ways to improve her, but tonight he found the task more an outright chore than a labor of love, and with a muttered oath of frustration he struck the side of the boat with his fist.

"So we are testy this night, Alex, are we?" asked Johnny Allred, sitting on the bench beside him. "Have the pleasures of London so paled for you already?"

Johnny was the *Calliope's* first mate, and had been since the sloop's launching. But more importantly, Johnny was Alex's oldest and closest friend, and together the two had survived every manner of adventure in their lives, from punishment for filching apples from a neighbor's orchard as boys, through a brief time in a Havana prison for smuggling as young men, to now, where side by side they'd made the *Calliope* one of the most profitable privateers in the colonies. Though Johnny didn't look like any of the Fairbournes—he was short and stocky, fair-haired and ruddy-faced—he'd always held an honorary place in the family from being Alex's friend, and, like any true brother, he'd earned a certain freedom that few first mates could expect from their captains.

Not that Alex was particularly inclined to acknowledging that this evening.

"The pleasures of London are damnably overrated," he growled, "and damnably overpriced, too. I'd as soon see the whole rotten place given over to the devil or the French, whichever wants it more."

"Ah," said Johnny, nodding sagely as he began peeling the orange he'd pulled from his coat pocket. "Then I take that to mean you've passed your day in less than happy circumstances."

Moodily Alex struck his fist against the boat again, this time hard enough to make his hand sting. "You can take it to mean whatever the hell you want."

"It's Diana, then." Johnny tossed the fruit's peel over the side, bright orange bobbing on the gray river water. "She's not behaving the way you want."

"She's behaving like Diana." Alex sighed. Diana and her ridiculous interest in the well-powdered Lord Oswald were only part of what was bothering him, albeit a most important part. But as close a friend as Johnny was, Alex couldn't tell him about his meeting with Sir Thomas because he couldn't share the reason for it. And then, precariously and perplexingly on top of everything else, was Cora, and he didn't begin to know what to make of her, let alone what he could confess.

"That's Diana," said Johnny. "That's the only way she knows."

But Alex shook his head, his shoulders bent low beneath the weight of responsibility. "I should never have brought her here to London. I should have left her behind in Appledore where she'd be a trial to my parents, not to me."

"You liked having her on board during the crossing," reminded Johnny as he broke an orange segment free with his thumb and slipped it into his mouth. "Part of what's vexing you so much now is that you miss her. The entire sloop's gone powerfully quiet with her gone ashore for good. That, and knowing she'll wed whomever she pleases, just like your mother did."

He was right, of course, which only made the gloom settle more completely over Alex. "You should see the miserable excuse for a man she fancies, Johnny. Rigged out in more lace and jewels than any decent male has any right to wear, with a wig as high as the mainmast."

"She'll choose the husband that will suit her, not you," said Johnny firmly. "Besides, Diana can take care of herself better than any woman I know."

That wasn't particularly reassuring, conjuring as it did for Alex memories of his sister's righteous mischief on both sides of the Atlantic. Besides, what did Johnny know about choosing a husband? He'd let himself be chosen by the first girl he'd ever walked out with, one of the miller's sweet-tempered daughters. His home life was so quiet and peaceful that Alex half suspected Johnny came to sea with him simply to avoid perishing from boredom.

But why the devil couldn't Diana have fallen in love with a good, steady man from Barnstable County like Johnny? Peaceful boredom and a shingled cottage full of children would be a good thing for her. Why did she have to come clear to London, where the wider selection of bachelors only increased the chance that she'd make a woeful choice? Here the process seemed infinitely more complicated than at home, more risk-filled on every level.

Which was, really, what was bothering him most tonight.

"I'll grant you that Diana can look after herself better than most women," he began. "Oswald will find that out soon enough. But what about the things she can't settle by dumping a tankard of ale?"

Johnny considered that, sucking thoughtfully on a piece of orange. "London has more than its share of villains and rogues, true enough. But Diana's staying with a titled lady in a grand house on Hanover Square. I'd scarce think there's a safer spot in the city."

"But what if there were something wrong in that house, something not as it should be that might come 'round to harm Diana?"

Johnny's thumbs split the orange. "You're not telling me all, man."

"That's because I don't know it, not by half." Alex sighed, impatient with himself. He didn't like not knowing when he felt he should, but now that he'd begun to tell Johnny, he couldn't very well stop. "It began simply enough. I came across one of Lady Walde-grave's servants in the garden, a fair little lass, and—"

"Hah, so there's the wench in your tale," said Johnny with a sly wink. "I knew you'd have found one by now. I would've been disappointed otherwise. We've been in port nearly a week."

"It's not like that," said Alex defensively. "Least-ways, it began that way, but it's not now. And she's not a wench."

"Then what is she? Another countess?"

"Perhaps so." Alex sighed, again looking across the water toward the *Calliope*.

Because of how the sloop sat at her moorings, the

boatmen were bringing them beneath the prow, close to the figurehead. It had been his mother's idea to repaint the carved wooden figure when the sloop had been fitted out for privateering, and the musical muse had lost her pale gown in favor of one of brilliant golden yellow and her silvery hair had been changed to a more bellicose red.

Now twilight muted the colors, softening them, and when Alex gazed up at the carved woman beneath the bowsprit, to his shock he saw Cora the way she'd looked that night in the garden, her silk gown like gathered sunshine and her tousled hair full of burnished reds as she cradled the black kitten to her breast.

He blinked, blinked hard, and when he looked up again he saw only the wooden Calliope with her perpetual smile for the waves, pan-pipes in her hand instead of a cat. Any other time he would have laughed wryly at the trick the shifting light had played on him, but not now. Now he saw it as another sign that Cora might not be what she seemed, and uneasily he shook his head at such uncharacteristic superstition.

"Either she's a countess," Johnny was saying, "or she's not. A cat may look like a king, sure, but there's no mistaking one for another. Even a dunderhead like you can tell the difference."

"Which is why this girl puzzles me all the more," said Alex, for once letting his friend's good-natured insult go unreturned. "She wears her mistress' castoff clothing and dreads her disapproval, and keeps herself hidden away from company like any obedient servant mindful of her place and wanting to keep it. But she carries herself like a lady—speaks like one, too—and wears coral beads she claims belonged to her mother."

"None of that means she's a countess," said Johnny. "You could say the same of Diana."

Alex shook his head. "And if that were all, I wouldn't be worrying. But there's stranger than that. She speaks daft, Johnny, scraps of nonsense about battles and blood like an addled old soldier instead of a young lass."

Instantly Johnny sobered. "She could have been caught behind the lines of a battle, Alex. She could have come here from north near Quebec or from the settlements to the west, or perhaps one of the islands where there's been so much trouble. You've seen what happens to women."

He didn't have to say more. The wars with first the French, and then the Spanish, in the colonies had been going on as long as they'd both been grown men. While privateering had kept Alex and Johnny away from the worst fighting on land, they'd each seen enough of the aftermath of battles to understand—the desultory remains of towns and villages emptied of their people, blackened fields where once crops had grown, the hollow, ravaged faces of widows and orphans.

"I'd thought of that, aye," said Alex slowly, "and I'd wondered if she might be teasing me by telling worthless tales. But how the devil could the girl have landed in a countess' household on the other side of the world? And why does everyone from that countess to her damned butler want me to believe she doesn't exist, let alone live there?"

"And what does any of this have to do with your sister?" asked Johnny bluntly. "I don't mean to be unkind, Alex, but this city is full of unfortunates. You can't save them all, not even all the pretty ones. You said you feared for Diana, yet I don't see how this poor creature could bring her harm."

"Because I think she's a part of something far worse," said Alex urgently, lowering his voice so the two men at the oars ahead of them wouldn't overhear. "I don't think she's shy or meek by nature, or behaving entirely like a servant. I think she's hiding. This morning I walked with her around the square, and when we passed two officers she nearly fainted away from fear that they'd recognize *her*. But what the devil could a young girl like that have done that officers of the king would know her face?"

Johnny whistled low under his breath. "A hanging offense, I'd warrant, and there under the same roof with Diana."

Alex sighed. "It could all be folly, of course. She might only be some pitiful half-daft niece or cousin, kept safe here instead of the madhouse. I cannot ask the countess, for she's made it clear she won't tell me the truth, and Mother'd have my head if I made a fuss with her friend for nothing. But for Diana's sake, I should know. I *must* know."

"Then ask the girl herself, Alex," said Johnny without hesitation. "Ask her outright. Tell her you'll have her carted off to Bedlam if she tells you falsehoods."

"I'd never threaten Cora, Johnny! She doesn't deserve that!"

"Cora, is it?" Johnny made a low sound of derision in his throat. "Then your questioning will be all the more charming for you both, won't it? But take care, Alex. For Diana's sake and for your own. I've no wish to have to go to your grieving father with the sad news of your passing, brought about by your concern for some half-witted serving girl."

The boat bumped against the tall, dark side of the *Calliope*, and as one of the boatmen used a boat hook to draw them close to the sloop's boarding steps, the other tugged on the front of his knitted cap as he held out his hand for the fee for ferrying the two men.

"Here's fare for us two from shore," said Alex as he pressed the coins into the man's callused palm, "and more to take me back as well."

"Now?" asked Johnny, turning with surprise. "Surely the lass and her trials will keep until morn, and let you have the second watch tonight to consider it."

But Alex shook his head and slid to the center of the bench as Johnny stood. "Better now, and be done with it. And don't go practicing those sad words for my grieving father, mind? I'm not ready to make you the *Calliope's* captain just yet, and especially not for the sake of a woman."

They laughed together, loudly enough for curious crewmen to look down at them from the *Calliope's* rail. But as the boat pulled away from the sloop, Alex knew that, deep down, he wasn't nearly as certain.

Sir Thomas hadn't intended to feel sorry for himself, sitting here alone in his splendid, echoing cavern of a parlor and staring into the fire like some ancient, tedious worthy bent only on the glories of the past.

He wasn't old. Far from it. He hadn't even seen sixty summers yet, a man still in his robust prime. He had power and honor and worldly possessions, a beautiful mistress who was surprisingly faithful to him, and only the mildest twinges of gout when the weather turned damp. He still liked fast horses and young actresses and risking a fortune on a hand of cards, none of which was a pastime for graybeards. His life was rich and full, and God willing, he'd have many more years left to its span.

So why, then, did he sit here alone now, growing drunker and drunker on this fine smuggled claret, letting his self-pity deepen with every sip?

Because this morning when Alexander Fairbourne had burst his way into his life and his breakfast, he'd truly thought he'd found a way to turn back time.

The shock of it had been as sharp and unexpected as a flash of lightning, and gone just as quickly. It wasn't Josh Fairbourne returned in all his splendid rough-hewn youth, but instead Josh's son in his own image, a grown son so full of his father's vitality and bluster that in that moment Sir Thomas had let himself believe that he, too, was once again a young man eager to seize whatever prizes the world might offer.

It had been only a moment, of course, and he'd recovered quickly enough that no one had suspected. But the regret and longing had lingered long after the young man had left, leaving Sir Thomas to wallow in this uncharacteristic melancholy tonight.

His old friend's son was one to make a man proud—clever, bold, impassioned, and loyal—and that, really, was what had cut Sir Thomas the deepest. He had no such son as an heir, nor was he likely to sire one now. He'd wed twice, both brief times to sad, sickly widows who had left him their fortunes unencumbered by any brats. He'd always congratulated himself on his good luck, but today, for the first time, he'd begun to wonder if fate was laughing the loudest. If he'd had an heir to consider, then he might have created a genuine estate instead of a slippery mountain of debt, and he wouldn't be facing such disaster now.

For though he'd shrugged aside the notion of a legal battle, the truth was that this tall, handsome son of his old friend could very likely be his ruin. The debt Alex Fairbourne wished to claim was real enough. Long ago when he'd been a royal governor, he'd condemned a French ship as Joshua's prize that, strictly speaking, should have gone free instead.

In gratitude Joshua had made Sir Thomas—he'd still been plain Thomas Walton then, but no matter— a loan to cover a private embarrassment, and to prevent anyone from correctly regarding this loan as a bribe they'd called it a business loan. There'd been many papers signed and much rum drunk, and considerable celebration for their own cleverness.

But if those papers were still in Fairbourne hands, then any court in the kingdom would take the familiy's side and order Sir Thomas to pay the debt plus interest. He couldn't begin to calculate how much that would be, except that it would be more than he had.

Ruin. Public shame and loss, the humiliation of being a seven days' wonder of gossip; either a corner in the debtors' side at Fleet Prison until his death, or a hasty flight by night across the Channel to France to spend the rest of his days clinging to the shadowy edges of Calais society, dealing faro for his supper. What a shabby end to his life that would make!

No. He'd not sunk so low, not yet, and he took a long swallow of the claret to help collect his thoughts. Though his days of plum governorships were past, he had one last favor owed him, one last reward pending that could save him still.

It was a grand one, too, if only he could be sure of claiming it. In exchange for certain favors and to make up for his own losses during the Jacobite rebellion two years before—property he'd owned in Westmorland had been devastated by the invaders—he'd been promised one of the forfeited estates. Creignish, it was called. Not one of those bleak, drafty Highland castles, but a handsome seat fit for a gentleman, with the lands to support it. Once it was in his name, such an estate was sure to support a mortgage for a pittance like five thousand pounds. It could all be handled by his solicitor, without any scandal or inconvenience.

Except that Creignish wasn't yet his.

Though there was no doubt that the former owner had been the worst sort of Jacobite, dying with his clan at Culloden, he'd also been a special, peculiar friend of the king's father. Sir Thomas had never been able to learn the details—he'd always suspected a woman must have been involved—but for whatever reasons, this particular Scotsman had earned himself a special place in the new king's heart.

Rebellion had changed that. King George had felt the Scot's betrayal sorely, but still he'd sworn to return Creignish to the man's only child, a daughter. Though the search for her continued, most believed her dead with the rest of her clan; the Duke of Cumberland had been thorough in ridding the Highlands of traitors, women and children as well as men. But until proof could be found of her death, Creignish would not be granted to Sir Thomas.

His hand trembled as he poured more claret into the glass. One step at a time, he reminded himself, one step at a time, never looking too far ahead. He'd always done what he'd had to before to survive. Why should now be any different?

He had six weeks before Alexander Fairbourne was determined to sail. Five weeks, then, to accomplish so much. He must find proof to satisfy the king that the MacGillivray girl was dead, and not wait any longer for the dawdlers that had been appointed by His Majesty. He would find proof, or manufacture it. The results would be the same.

He was aware that the girl might in fact still live, hidden away in some wretched cave or hovel on the moors. He would not kill her himself, of course, but neither would he balk at giving the order for it to be done by others. He couldn't risk having her step forth later to make an awkward claim against him. Besides, what was so slight and useless a life worth when measured against his fate at those dismal faro tables in Calais?

He sighed, and held the glass before him. He would not let himself be bested by some whelp from the colonies. He would survive, and he would be the stronger for it.

The fire glimmered red through the claret, red as blood, and at last Sir Thomas smiled.

Ah, yes, he was still a gentleman in his prime, in his prime.

8

*I*t was late, long past nightfall, and long past the time that Cora usually fell asleep. Her room here under the slated roof still held the warmth of the day, but after Starlight had jumped from the sill earlier she didn't dare leave the casement wide open again. It had been dangerous enough to see him go flying from the first floor; two stories higher, and without anyone to catch him, would be a fall he wouldn't survive.

Because of the heat, she wore only her shift, her feet and legs bare and her hair loosely pinned on her head, and yet still the fine linen clung moistly to her back. No doubt the air was cooler outside, and briefly she considered strolling in the garden until she felt sleepier. Lady Waldegrave was out again, off to some affair or another with Diana in tow, and until they returned, the house was quiet and dark, except for the night-light in the hanging blue globe in the front hall.

Cora sighed. What *would* become of her life if she didn't dare to change it? Would she spend the rest of her days here in the countess' beneficent shadow, or was she ready to risk everything to find her way back to Creignish?

She'd believed she'd never forget her home, yet each day that passed here it became harder and harder to remember. Hearing Alex speak so warmly of Appledore and his own family had made her realize that.

It was the little details that were slipping away, blurring with time and absence, and determinedly she tried to focus on recalling them now: the sound of the wind blowing hard off the moors, the mists that would rise from the Inverness River and tangle in the tops of the gnarled old trees near the front of the house, the mixtures of scents in her father's library, the tobacco from his pipe, the earthy smoke from the "honest peat" he insisted on having burned in the fire, the musty, dusty smell of scores of old books, scattered on shelves and chairs and tables and stacked in wobbling towers on the floor.

Yet even that was fading, growing less vivid each day, and with a little wail of frustration she tossed back the wool-stuffed mattress on her bed and pulled out the flat, linen-wrapped secret that she kept hidden there against the rope springs. She tore the linen away and let the wool cloth inside tumble free, a luxurious, oversized square of bright red woven across with emerald green, purple, sapphire blue: her clan's tartan, the shawl, or screen, that all MacGillivray women, rich and poor, had worn to display their Jacobite sympathies.

She wrapped the screen around her shoulders and closed her eyes, the rough wool across her shoulders a poignant reminder of all she'd left behind. She'd smuggled it from Scotland wrapped around her waist beneath her petticoats, and kept it secret ever since for Lady Waldegrave would order it burned in an instant. The Dress Act that Parliament had passed after Culloden prohibited any such dangerous show of clan loyalty, but for now, Cora didn't care. They could pass all the acts they wished, and in her bones and blood and heart she'd still always be Cora Margaret Anne MacGillivray of Creignish.

Tap-thump . . . Tap-thump-thump.

Cora frowned, listening. *That* had not been a noise she'd remembered from home. That was here, now, and with a sigh she cautiously opened her eyes.

Starlight was standing on the windowsill, balanced all rabbity on his hind legs, with his many-toed front paws splayed out flat against the glass. His entire little body was tense, alert with anticipation, with even the fur along his spine bristling stiff with excitement.

"Oh, Starlight, you foolish beast," said Cora, reaching to lift him down. "There's nothing out there for you to hunt, only some foolish moth drawn to the candlelight."

Yet as she set him on the bed, she heard another tap, small but insistent, at the glass. Starlight growled and struggled, eager to return to the sill, but Cora pushed him back and went to the window herself. She peered down in the dark garden, made blacker because of the candle behind her.

Tap!

"Oh—*oh!*" Someone was tossing pebbles from the walkway at her window, and without thinking she indignantly threw open the window and leaned out to confront the thrower.

"You there!" she called. "You stop that this instant or I shall call the watch!"

"Not until you come down to me," said Alex, moving from the shadows onto the path where she could make out his upturned face far below her. "I'm getting powerfully tired of having to hail you like this, Miss Cora."

"Hush!" she hissed with dismay. Lady Waldegrave might be out for the evening, but many of the servants, including that traitor Junius, would be waiting up until the mistress returned home. "Just—just *hush!*"

"Perhaps you didn't hear me proper," he said. "Best I fix that."

To Cora's horror he cupped his hands around his mouth, the way that men did when they wished to amplify their voices from a bellow to a roar.

"Wait!" she called back before he could. "I'll—I'll come."

She didn't trust him not to shout again if she took time to dress, but with the screen around her she was as covered as if she'd been wrapped in a blanket, decent if not fashionable. Hastily she thrust her bare toes into her yellow mules, and wrinkled her nose at her unkempt hair as she caught a glimpse of herself in her looking glass. She prayed the garden would be too dark for him to notice, but then, she'd no intention of lingering with him in the dark garden where Junius might hear them, either.

From the bed, Starlight mewed hopefully, and hopped off the bed to follow.

"Not tonight, lovey," she said firmly, putting him back in the center of the bed. "I've no intention of chasing you through the rose bushes in the dark again."

She chose the front stairs, guessing she'd be less likely to encounter any servants there, and where, too, the candles in the wall sconces would still be lit, making a candlestick of her own unnecessary. To keep from making noise on the marble stairway, she carried her mules in one hand and went barefoot, scurrying down the steps, through the lower parlor and the double doors to the garden.

As she'd guessed, it was much cooler here in the garden, and she drew the screen higher over her shoulders as she stepped outside. Somehow the night seemed darker out here, too, with little light filtering through from the hallway, and belatedly she wished she'd brought a candlestick. The breeze rustled through the leaves above her, and in the distance she could hear the watchman hoarsely calling that all was well at ten of the clock on an evening calm and fair.

Let it stay that way, too, thought Cora, and scanned the empty garden for Alex. He was a large man, not easily mislaid, and though her wicked heart was racing with anticipation, she told herself sternly that she was in no humor for playing hiding games tonight.

"Alex," she called as loudly as she dared. "Alexander Fairbourne. For goodness' sake, sir, please show yourself!"

"And how much more do you wish me to show, sweetheart?" he asked, so near that his voice was little more than a rough whisper. She turned swiftly and there he was, sprawled across the wooden bench, his hat on the seat beside him and his arms spread across the bench's back and his long legs comfortably crossed.

"I'm seeing far too much of you as it is," she said. "Especially since you don't belong here now at all."

"And a good evening to you, too, my dear." He smiled, his teeth white in the half-light. Everything about him seemed reduced to black and white, his dark coat and breeches black against the whitewashed bench, the white linen of his shirt and his unfashionably unpowdered black hair. Black and white and very male, without all the gray layers of drawing room niceties, which in turn made her acutely aware of how, beneath the tartan, she wore only the thinnest layer of white linen over her own body. At least *he* didn't know that, and she tugged the woolen shawl higher over her bare arms.

"Well, yes, and a good evening to you, too, Alex," she said. "But you are always creeping up to surprise me like this, and I don't care for it."

"And you are always bolting away from me like a frightened horse, and I don't care for that, either."

"I—I have my reasons," she said, flustered. He wasn't doing anything beyond sitting there, but the way he was watching her, his gaze warm and lazy and lingering, was making her skin tingle and grow warm in a most unsettling way. "You should go, Alex. You can't stay."

He sighed. "You tell me you've seen too much of me, Cora, while I feel I haven't seen nearly enough of you. Morning, noon, and now the night, a pretty way to mark my day."

A pretty compliment, too, dear enough to make her heart lurch with secret joy. And oh, Lord, had all this really happened in a single day?

"So you're not glad that I'm here, Cora Margaret?" he asked when she didn't answer, his voice low and rough and surprisingly urgent. "Aren't you glad to see me too?"

"Oh, yes," she said at once, honesty getting the better of her intentions, even as she prayed that this wasn't only another of his teasing ways. But she *was* glad he cared enough to come back, and each time he did made her trust him a little further, made her believe in him—and, strangely, herself—a little more.

"Good," he said, and smiled.

The satisfaction in that single word, coupled with the warmth of his smile, nearly undid her. As it was she felt flushed and too warm beneath the wool shawl, and thankful for the dark that would hide it.

"How did you get inside here?" she asked, her voice sounding unnaturally reedy and breathless. "This garden wall is all brick. Did you force the lock on the back gate?"

He shrugged, careless. "I can climb sixty feet to the foretop in less time than it takes to tell. If I'd wished, I could have been through your own window without any trouble at all."

She wasn't sure what a foretop was, but she didn't think she should ask, either, if it might lead to him clambering into her bedchamber.

But it was enough to make her remember Lady Waldegrave's warning, albeit later than she should. "You truly must go, Alex. You can't stay. This afternoon, I—we—were seen together by her ladyship's butler, and she is not happy with me."

"What, servants spying on servants?" Alex clucked his tongue with mock disapproval. "My, my. What sort of household does your lady keep?"

"Alex, be serious!" she pleaded. "Lady Waldegrave keeps a most respectable house—you wouldn't want your sister staying here if she didn't—and if I don't obey her wishes, I . . . I will no longer be welcome here. Is that what you wish? That I be reduced to sleeping in the middle of Hanover Square?"

Instead of answering, he bent forward, resting his arms on his knees and looking down at her feet.

"I do believe, Cora," he said slowly, "that you have the most beautiful pink toes I have ever seen on a woman."

Horrified, she looked down, too. The shawl swaddled her to her knees, and her shift came to the middle of her calves, which left a thoroughly indecent stretch of leg and ankle and toes—*toes!*—on display. Immediately she dropped her mules to the walk, wobbling as she shoved her shameful, guilty feet into them. Gentlemen never noticed a lady's toes, and rarely had the chance to. Why, *why*, had she forgotten her mules until now, and invited such a hideously intimate comment?

"My toes are simply—simply *toes*, Alex," she said, trying at least to sound ladylike, "and there is nothing whatsoever beautiful about them, as any—"

"Cora, sit." He swept his hat from the bench, and patted the seat beside him. He was still leaning forward from viewing her toes, and now, when he looked up at her, she was struck by how ridiculously long and thick the lashes were that shadowed those pale eyes. "Please."

"I will not sit, and I won't have you—"

"I came here to talk to you, Cora, I swear it. Talk, and no more. Your charming little toes distracted me, that's all." He sighed, and shook his head as if to shake away his untoward thoughts as well. "I won't speak of them again. Now sit. Please. Come and sit by me."

She realized that this was as much of an apology as she was likely to receive from him, and that even this much was a rare event. Yet still she hesitated, sensing not danger, but temptation.

"No one inside the house can see this bench," he

coaxed. "It's too close to the wall for that, and the trees take care of the rest."

"Alex, please, I—"

"And if you refuse me and run away again, I'll simply sit here until you come back." He leaned back in the bench, clearly settling in to stay. "Until morning if I must. You've left me with a great many questions, Cora, and I'm not leaving until I have answers."

"Questions?" she echoed faintly. If anyone had questions to ask, it should be her, and not the other way around. "I don't see what right you have to question me about anything."

"My sister is a guest in this house," he said. "If you are hiding from the law or have acted in such a way that you put her in danger or at risk of scandal—"

"I've done nothing that could possibly hurt your sister!"

He smiled again, but this time with more determination than warmth. "Then you won't object to easing my mind on a few matters."

She slowly shook her head. How, really, could she refuse?

Gallantly he held his hand out to her as if inviting her to dance instead of to an inquisition. "Be brave, Cora. All I'm asking is the truth."

"All you're asking is the world, and more."

He shrugged again. "Only if you think of it that way."

"I'm not giving Starlight back to you," she said warily.

"I'm not asking for him. Trust me, Cora. Please."

Again, again, that same word and all it meant. Why must so much of this be tangled together, trust and loyalty and truth and not-quite-falsehoods? With a whimper of frustrated resignation she plopped on the other end of the bench, so far from him that her hip was crushed into the carved armrest; she'd be branded with the imprint of an acanthus leaf, but the distance she'd gained would make it worthwhile.

Until, alas, he slid along the bench to be closer to her, not exactly touching, but near enough that she could sense the shape of that well-muscled thigh every bit as clearly as the acanthus.

"Well, then." He cleared his throat self-consciously, and to her surprise—and relief, too, in a way—she realized he wasn't any happier about this than she. "First things first. Is your name truly Cora?"

"Oh, yes. It was my mother's choice because pink corabelle flowers were her favorites, and though my father thought it rather a silly name, he agreed for her sake."

She gave him a quick, nervous smile. Perhaps if she volunteered more than he asked, then he wouldn't ask about the things that would be so much harder to explain. "He would rather have named me Andromache or Cassandra or even Aphrodite—he was very fond of the old Greeks, you see—but Cora I was, and Cora I am."

"Then why did our old friend Junius tell me that no one named Cora lives here in this house?"

That was an easy one, too. "Because those are her ladyship's orders," she said promptly. "I told you that before, didn't I? A household of ladies in London cannot be too cautious."

"And that is what you are, isn't it?" he asked. "A lady? There's no way in God's green earth that you're

the little lowbred serving wench you want me to believe."

She hesitated, nibbling on her lower lip. He was
watching her too closely for her to try spinning any
more tales. He'd asked her to trust him; maybe this,
then, was the first step.

"No," she admitted. "I'm not. Though I do try to be
useful to her ladyship whenever I can, and I think that
she appreciates that. My father sent me here when . . .
when it was better I not remain at home. Lady Waldegrave has been most generous and kind to keep me
here since then."

Alex frowned. "Yet she has you sleep up under the
eaves like a maid from the scullery, and gives you her
castoffs to wear. That's sure as hell not the way to treat
the daughter of a friend."

"I've never been sure exactly how her ladyship
knew my father," said Cora slowly. She'd often wondered this, and the few times she'd tried to ask Lady
Waldegrave, she'd been told curtly it was only more of
the unnecessary past that she'd do better to forget.
"They do not seem to be people who would have
much in common, and he had never mentioned her to
me before, ever. Yet he sent me to her, and she welcomed me, and she has . . . she's risked a great deal
more for me than you can know."

But Alex seemed to have lost interest in Lady
Waldegrave as he leaned closer to her, his gaze intent
on her. "Tell me about your home, where you're from.
I've rattled on endlessly about my Appledore, but
you've said scarcely a word in return."

"About my home?" She twisted her hands in her
shawl, suddenly shy. For the last two years she'd

been told to forget her past for the sake of her future. Instead she'd locked all her memories so tightly away inside of her that they'd become intensely private, her special retreat and comfort. To be asked to share them now, after so long, felt unsettlingly intimate. It was the same as when he'd called her toes pretty, a part of her not meant to be seen, let alone complimented. If she told him about Creignish, then she'd be revealing far more to him about herself than just her past, and she wasn't sure she was ready for that.

"Aye, aye, your home," he said with an impatient sweep of his hand. "Like it or not, we're all part of the place we were born. Begin wherever you wish. Tell me of the sky, and the land, and the flowers that grow wild. You said there was a river—tell me of that, if it runs fast or slow to the sea, clear with fishes or full of silt and muck."

"The river," she said softly. The river was one of the things she'd missed most. What harm could come from speaking of it now, especially if she didn't say its name or that of Creignish? "The river runs from the loch to the sea, cold and so clear you can see the brown trout dancing beneath the ripples. But it's not easy, our river. Because it must make its way from the mountains, it runs swift and heedless, crashing over the silver rocks that dare stand in its path, blustering with white foam, hiss, hiss, fie, fie on you, laddie!"

She laughed softly, remembering the first nursemaid—Bett, her name had been—who'd told her that.

Unconsciously Cora had slipped back into the old way of talking herself, softening her consonants, warming her vowels, polishing them with the burr that Lady Waldegrave had warned her would be best forgotten with everything else.

"It's never the same, our river," she continued, seeing the familiar landscape in her memory once again. "When the autumn sun sits low in the sky, the river glitters like a thousand diamonds while the leaves on beech trees on the banks shiver and shimmer like gold. That's when you'll see the ospreys, too, hanging high and idle in the sky with their wings scarce moving."

She drew her feet up onto the bench, folding her arms over her bent knees, and brushed her cheek against the wool draped around her. "But it was stormy times I liked the best, when the clouds raced over the glen and everything turned wild, the cairns dark and the sky moody-blue and purple, and the wind wailing mournful as a lost soul outside my window, and the river rushing full of ice and snow from the mountains bound for Inverness and the sea."

"And this, lass," said Alex as he touched the fringed hem of her screen where it lay on the bench between them. "I'll wager this isn't any ordinary shawl, is it?"

"Not to me," she said, and defiantly drew it higher. She'd half forgotten he'd been there with her, but now the memories made her brave and bold, and tired of duplicity. "It's the tartan of my clan, my family's own."

"You're a Scot," he said softly. "One of the Jacobites from the Highlands. Oh, lass, why didn't you tell me?"

"So you could spare your sister the shame of sharing a house with me?" she asked fiercely. She couldn't turn back; what she'd said was said and couldn't be undone, and oh, dear Lord, she hoped she'd judged him right!

"Now will you do as Lady Waldegrave says all Englishmen must, and damn me as a traitor?" she continued, not giving him a chance to say the wrong answer. "Will you summon the magistrate to take me off for the crime of wearing this plaid?"

She was trembling, her first brashness fading into panic that grew with each second he didn't answer. Though he sat on the bench beside her, in the darkness she couldn't read his face enough to know his thoughts, and she felt as vulnerable as if she stood before him naked.

But at least now he knew the worst that could be said of her, and soon, too, she'd know the worst of him.

"Tell me, Cora," he said. "Who was it you lost in the rebellion? A brother, perhaps, or a sweetheart?"

She bowed her head and closed her eyes. "I lost everyone," she said, the bitter finality of her grief making her voice harsh. "*Everyone.* My oldest cousin was killed at Falkirk, his brother mortally wounded. But it was that black-hearted bastard Cumberland who did the worst at Culloden. 'Sweet William,' these Londoners called him, petting him like a great hero for his butchery, but I would call him bloody, stinking William for what he did to my clan!"

Forgetting the man beside her, Cora's hands clenched tight into fists to drum the litany of her losses. "My three uncles, the one that was our clan's chief, my seven cousins, even my poor daft cousin Will who couldn't spell his own name. Two thousand men slaughtered by English muskets in half an hour's time, they say. Two *thousand* men! But that was not enough for Cumberland, not enough by half. My aunts and lady cousins, too, gentlewomen all, were murdered two days later by his orders, driven through with English swords for daring to succor the wounded."

At last Cora's voice broke, torn apart by the weight of the suffering she'd kept so long inside. "Her Ladyship would not tell me, no, to spare me, but I learned of it anyway, from the news sheets the servants forgot to take away, from their gossip in the stairs, from the last letter of my last aunt, before she, too, died of a fever. My poor, dear father, as kind and gentle a man as ever lived, cut to pieces at his prince's side as if his life were worth no more than a dog's instead of the hero he longed to . . . he longed . . . he . . ."

Like a music box that had finally wound down, she was too spent to continue, and as the words deserted her, her emotions welled up in their place, into one final, keening wail of despair and loss as she buried her face in her hands.

"Oh, Cora, here," said Alex gruffly, and without a thought for anything but her, he drew her into his arms. Carefully he stroked her hair as if she were a child, letting her settle against his chest, her knees falling clumsily over his lap.

"There now, Cora," he whispered. "There now, there now."

He prayed that what he said wouldn't matter as much as the feeling that accompanied it, for he'd no notion at all of what to say that would be proper. He was horrified by what she'd told him, appalled that a distant political event that he'd shrugged off had touched her so deeply. In the Boston news sheets at home, the reports of the Jacobite rebellion had been slight, and focused entirely on the splendid defense of the capital and crown by the gallant young Duke of Cumberland against the savage Highlanders. The articles had shared Sir Thomas' attitude: the Jacobites were more a nuisance than a genuine threat, an inconvenience that needed stern controlling, like some virulent garden pest.

There'd been no mention of entire families slaughtered, of gently bred women and the wounded killed after the battles. And as for the savage Highlander, that fearsome wild barbarian equal to the Iroquois or Abenaki in battle and lack of civilization—he'd only to look at the fine-featured girl weeping against his shirt to see again the ignorance of blind prejudice.

He felt like the world's greatest ass for not having figured it out on his own, and for bringing her more pain. All the possibilities that he'd concocted to explain her situation and behavior seemed foolishly inconsequential compared to the truth, and again he silently cursed himself as an unfeeling blockhead. Lady Waldegrave had been right to shelter her. If what Cora said was true—and he'd no reason at all to doubt her—then he'd been selfishly inviting her to court danger by coming outside to walk the square with him.

But all these were things he would consider later, much later, alone in his bunk on board the *Calliope*. With Cora in his arms, her sobs wracking against his chest and her tears wetting his shirt, the only thing that mattered was bringing her some sort of peace, however fragile it might be.

"Cora, sweet," he murmured, still stroking her hair, running his hand along its tangled length down her back. It was soft, springy beneath his fingers, curlier than he'd realized when she'd had it pinned back in a knot. "Cora, I'm sorry, lass. I'm sorry this happened to you."

"But it didn't," she said, pushing herself back from

his chest to meet his gaze. Her eyes were blurry with tears, her nose touchingly red and puffy with them. "That—that's what makes it so hard for me, Alex! I'm the only one left. You say I'm brave, but if I truly were, I would've been there, too, and died with the others!"

"And do you really believe that's what your father would have wanted for you?" countered Alex sharply. "You said he sent you away to London and out of harm's way. Would he have done that if he'd wanted you to die on some godforsaken moor?"

She made a little gulping sound in the back of her throat, letting the shawl slide from her shoulder as she looked down at her hands.

"No, he didn't," she whispered with heartbreaking honesty. "No. Father wished other things for me."

"I'm certain he did, lass," said Alex firmly. "You were his daughter, and he loved you, and he went to a good deal of trouble to see that you were safe."

She nodded, and swallowed hard, flicking her tongue nervously across her lips. Though the tears still clung to the edges of her eyes, she'd stopped weeping, stopped trembling, and he dared to hope the worst had passed.

"Father told me to wait," she said solemnly. "He said that when it was safe to go home, he'd send someone to fetch me."

"If he'd taken such pains with the other plans," said Alex, "why, stands to reason he'd see to that, too."

"He was," she whispered, leaning toward him, "a most wise and thorough gentleman."

And then, to Alex's enormous surprise, Cora kissed him.

It wasn't the kiss itself that was surprising, for that was every bit the sweet, yielding apple of temptation he'd remembered. No, what surprised him was how instantly, acutely aware he became of everything else surrounding that kiss. How pale her skin now gleamed in the moonlight, and how much of it there was to see, from her bare shoulders dusted with freckles to her throat with the coral beads to the tips of those delicious toes that had, miraculously, once again shed the mules and now rested on the bench beside his leg. Because she'd let that shawl slide away, he could comprehend the near-transparency of her thin linen shift, and for the first time appreciate the body inside it without whalebone stays or petticoats. Her breasts were small and high as they pressed against his chest, her nipples taut with anticipation, another surprise, and her bottom and hips were soft and womanly as she shifted across his lap, and across the hard proof of his own arousal, no surprise at all.

And no surprise, either, however shamed he should be of the circumstances, that he kissed her back to make her realize how grateful he was that she'd lived and how she should be, too. With one hand on her hip he steadied her, guiding her instinctive movements into real pleasure for them both, while with the other he tugged the drawstring of her shift so her breasts were free to explore with his fingers and his mouth and his tongue, suckling and teasing until she gasped again, her own hands convulsively clutching his shoulders.

When at last he let her go, her breath was as ragged as his own, her lips swollen from his kissing and her breasts full and tight, and her elfin eyes full of wonder and wantonness, a midsummer nymph from the Highlands beneath the stars and moon.

"I didn't die, Alex," she whispered, her little laugh infectiously husky as she propped herself upon his chest. "You were right. You *are* right. I lived to be here, now, with you, the way Father said I would."

Alex would have wagered his own life that having her sprawled across him in her shift was not precisely what her father would have wanted, but he wasn't about to argue.

"Damned right I'm right, Cora," he growled, reaching for her again. "But why aren't you—"

"Hush," she said, and pressed her fingers over his lips. "No more, no more! You've asked your fill of questions for tonight, Captain. You have your answers, and so, at last, do I."

And before he could stop her, she'd vanished like the wanton sprite he'd swear she'd been.

9

Cora slept so deeply she didn't dream, and when she finally awoke the sun was high in the sky and Starlight was nibbling impatiently at her fingers. With the window still latched, the room was now stifling, and though in the night Cora had kicked off her coverlet, she felt sticky and groggy as she pushed herself upright in the bed.

No dreams, she thought as she sipped water from the pewter mug beside her bed, no dreams, and yet on the edges of wakefulness something still lingered, nagging at her to be remembered.

She yawned, and stretched, and lifted the heavy mass of her hair off her damp shoulders. She should have braided it last night, the way she usually did; it was uncharacteristic of her that she hadn't bothered. She'd have a trial of a time brushing it out now, and with another yawn she reached for her hairbrush and swung her legs over the side of the bed. Blindly her toes crept this way and that across the bare floor, searching for the mules that should be there.

Abruptly her toes stopped as, equally abruptly, she remembered everything that her foggy mind had overlooked. Her screen was draped haphazardly over the back of the chair where she'd tossed it, the neck of her shift still shamelessly unlaced and open. She remembered the bench in the garden, and Alex, and what she'd told him, and what she'd done.

What *he'd* done.

What they'd done *together*.

She'd left her mules in the garden by the bench where she'd kicked them off, and where, if they were found and presented to Junius, she'd be in most serious difficulty with Lady Waldegrave.

But maybe she still had time. If her ladyship had stayed out so late that she was still abed now, if the staff knew it and were all still gossiping over tea in the kitchen, if no one had yet been sent to rake the paths in the garden, then she *might* have a chance to retrieve the incriminating mules.

She dressed as quickly as she could, a plain bodice and a single petticoat without hoops or stays, the minimum required for modesty, and stuffed her tangled, uncombed hair beneath a ruffled cap.

"I'll be back in a moment, I promise," she told the protesting Starlight as she pushed him gently back into her room. "And I'll bring you breakfast, too."

She ran, slipping and sliding along the bare floors in her stocking feet, down the stairs and to the lower parlor. The heavy glass door to the garden squeaked on its hinges as Cora swung it open, and she winced at the sound, guilt magnifying it a thousand times in her ears and making her certain someone else would hear.

But the mules were exactly where she'd left them, kicked off in the grass in front of the bench, just as, mercifully, Alex wasn't, despite his threats to remain.

Ruefully she retrieved the mules, brushing away the dew that glittered on the silk before she slipped them on her feet.

The absolute last thing she needed was to have found Alex here waiting for her this morning, and yet perversely it was also the one thing she'd rather wished had happened.

Lightly she ran her fingers along the curving back of the whitewashed bench, remembering. He'd promised to make her feel alive, and he had. Oh, hadn't he! In one day with Alex Fairbourne, she'd learned more than that old Ovid had ever managed to explain, and she'd done it in plain English, too, without—

"Oh, good morning," said a woman behind her. "I didn't think anyone else was here."

Swiftly Cora turned. She'd never met the young woman standing there in the doorway, but she'd no doubt at all who she was. She was tall and breathtakingly beautiful, with glossy black hair and the kind of flawless, creamy skin that Cora, cursed by her freckles, had always wistfully admired. But what left Cora speechless was the young woman's smile, so unabashedly warm and open and so unsettlingly like her brother's, a most feminine version of a very masculine face.

"My name is Diana, Diana Fairbourne," said the young woman as she came toward Cora. She moved with the easy, natural grace that dancing masters could never hope to reproduce, and was sure to inspire volumes of bad poetry comparing her to her goddess namesake. "I didn't realize her ladyship had other guests as well. That is, you are a guest, aren't you?"

She glanced at Cora's haphazard dress, her doubts so obvious that Cora cringed.

"My name is Cora," she said hastily. "I'm, ah, a friend of Lady Waldegrave's. That is, she and my father were friends."

"That's how it is with me, too," said Diana, again flashing that perfect, uncanny smile. "She and my mother were friends, oh, ages ago. But then I'm vastly surprised we haven't met before this, aren't you?"

Cora tried to smile back, terribly conscious of her own crooked little teeth.

"Her ladyship is, ah, accustomed to her own ways," she said carefully. "She has been alone for so long that she sometimes will forget to think of others' concerns in addition to her own."

"Well, yes, I will suppose there is reason to that," said Diana, dropping onto the bench with the same nonchalance that her brother had done, and in the same spot, too. "If I'd lost my husband as young as she did, I'd be half mad, too. Though more likely I'd have wed again."

"She's not mad, not at all," said Cora quickly in the countess' defense. "She simply prefers to order things to suit herself, and if, or when, she does have us meet, I mean to act surprised so as not to wound her."

"You *are* wonderfully loyal, aren't you?" said Diana, marveling. "And much more noble, too. I shall resolve to follow your lead, and do as you say, for you are as bound to be right as I am wrong. I'm not noble in the least, you see. It's a great failing with me. I'm far too common in my thoughts and sensibilities. Which is why I've been ordered to read *this* and edify my mind."

She held up a small leather-bound book of sermons suitable for ladies, pinching one corner between her thumb and finger to hold it away as if it smelled rank. Cora recognized the book; she'd read it, too, of course, and though it wasn't as scintillating as a French novel, it wasn't horrible, either. Not that she'd dare say so to Diana. Compared to her dash and beauty, Cora already felt as drab and stuffy as that book of old sermons herself. How could Alex find her in the least interesting after growing up with such a brilliant sister?

Diana let the offending book fall to the bench. "I should far rather have preferred to go with her ladyship to play cards, but she wouldn't take me."

"She's already gone out?" asked Cora with surprise.

Diana shrugged with wounded disinterest. "Some friend or t'other sent word to come join a party that had begun last night. She didn't even bother to eat her breakfast before she summoned the carriage, the eager old hen, and left me behind."

"Indeed," murmured Cora, the suitable response to every comment. So that was why she hadn't been summoned this morning to pour Lady Waldegrave's tea; while she'd been snoring away, her ladyship had been racing to the card tables. "You should consider yourself fortunate, Miss Fairbourne. The only guests left will be ones who've lost so heavily that they'll stake most anything in desperation, or those too far in their cups to stagger home."

"But that's when it's most interesting, don't you think?" exclaimed Diana. "That's when you're most likely to win, too, if you can keep your own wits. But that's also why her ladyship forbade me to go. She said that young unmarried ladies should never be tempted into gaming with gentlemen, lest we feel constrained to—oh, how was it she said it?—to 'wager our greatest treasure.' Just like that: Our Greaaaatest Tray-shuu-ure."

Dissolving in peals of laughter, she fell back against the bench, rolling her gaze skyward. "As if I'd be foolish enough to stake my maidenhead upon a hand of cards! I've not come clear to London to be seduced that easily, I can assure you. These fine titled gentlemen are going to have to be vastly more clever than that to have a chance at *my* Greatest Treasure!"

"Indeed," stammered Cora again, her face flaming with embarrassment. She'd had few friends her own age as a girl, but she could never recall any lady in her clan, young or old, speaking so freely and about such things. She didn't envy poor Lady Waldegrave, charged with keeping this wild colonial from mischief here in London until she found a husband.

"But we shall make our own amusement, won't we, Cora?" said Diana, twisting eagerly to face her. "I'd already half decided to go call upon my wicked brother, and meeting you here has made up my mind. I shall take you with me. Lady Waldegrave has taken her carriage, but we can go to the river in a hackney."

"Your brother?" gasped Cora. "But he will be on board his ship, won't he? You mean to go there, to the docks, among the sailors?"

"Well, yes," said Diana, unperturbed. "I have spent my entire life around sailors—my family is thick with them, absolutely thick—and I can tell you they are not nearly as fearsome as people claim. Alex is captain and master of the sloop *Calliope*. She'll be easy enough to find. I remember perfectly where she's moored. We'll hire a boat at the quay to take us out to the sloop. We'll flush that rascal of a brother out of hiding, won't we? Do you know he has not called on me once since he left me here, not once?"

"But he has," protested Cora, her head spinning at such an elaborate plan. "He came twice yesterday while you were out."

"He *did?*" Diana scowled, fuming. "Then why in blazes didn't that fussy old butler tell me?"

"Miss Fairbourne, I'm not sure that this is such a good idea. If her ladyship learns—"

"Oh, please, call me Diana. We are much too close in age and circumstance for formality. And her ladyship won't find out, not if we go now and are back before her." Diana hopped to her feet, ready to leave instantly, until she glanced again at Cora's dress. "Well, we shall leave as soon as you shift your clothes a bit. But you will find Alex most amusing. All my friends do."

And Cora already did, but she wasn't about to tell *that* to Diana, either. "I'm not sure this is wise at all, Diana, and—"

"We'll simply have to coerce Junius into silence," said Diana with a conspirator's grin, "so he won't spill everything to Lady Waldegrave. What useful private wickedness do you know of him?"

"About Junius?" asked Cora uneasily. "I don't know anything private about him."

"Of course you do," insisted Diana. "In a household such as this, there are usually precious few secrets. You must have heard something, from the maidservants or the footmen."

Cora considered. She'd overheard Cook once confiding to the butcher. "I don't know if this is strictly true or not, but I did once hear that he kept a terrier trained for rat baiting in the stable, and that he'd invite other butlers to come watch and make wagers."

"Perfection!" cried Diana gleefully, clapping her hands together. "Exactly the thing to make him lose his place! I'll speak to Junius, and we'll have a hackney in no time. Hurry, Cora, hurry!"

But Cora didn't hurry. In fact, she failed to move at all beyond twisting her fingers nervously in her necklace.

"You said you wished to be more noble, Diana," she said hesitantly. "I'm quite sure that blackmailing Junius this way is not noble."

Diana sighed. "Is Junius a special friend of yours?"

"Junius?" Cora shuddered, remembering how he'd spied upon her and Alex and reported to the countess, and the more she considered it, the less deserving he seemed of any nobility whatsoever. "I should hardly say so."

Diana nodded. "And if I am trying to be more noble, Cora, then you should be trying to improve yourself as well. What would you wish most as betterment?"

"I?" Cora thought only a moment. "I should wish to be more brave, I think."

"Very well, then." Diana rested her palms on Cora's shoulders, and earnestly searched her face. "Do you truly believe you shall grow any braver at all hiding here in this house? Wouldn't it be much more brave of you to come with me, and dare to see a bit of London on our own?"

Alex had told her again and again to be brave. What better way to prove it to them both than to go visit him on board his sloop?

"Be brave, Cora," urged Diana, "and come with me."

And before the tall case clock in the hall struck the hour again, she had.

Alex's day did not begin well. In his exhausted mind, the day never really began at all, since the day before it seemed never to have ended. When he'd left the countess' garden, he'd walked restlessly through the night streets for at least another hour, trying to make sense of what had happened between him and Cora. He'd gone to her with his head full of questions, and she'd given him more answers than he'd expected, as well as a heady taste of the passion she'd bottled up in that neat little body of hers.

But in some ways what Cora had told him had only added to her mystery. To be the single survivor of her clan was beyond his comprehension—Alex's own family was so much a part of who and what he was, both good and bad, that he couldn't fathom life without them—and the circumstances of their deaths made her grief all the more understandable. It also explained her skittishness and very real fears for her own safety, as well as her peculiar position in the countess' house.

But he still didn't know her family's name, or where exactly in Scotland she'd called home. Though he suspected she was gentry, he didn't know how high in the aristocracy her father had been. At least three Scottish dukes had been executed for treason, and for all Alex knew, Cora could have been one of their daughters. The final battle at Culloden had been over two years ago now, and the ordinary Englishman's hostility toward the Jacobites seemed to have faded and turned back toward that more time-honored enemy, the French. Unless Cora's father had been particularly notorious, then most likely by now she'd be no more than one more sad, sorry, anonymous victim of war. The world, alas, was filled with them.

At least that was what Alex told himself. It made sense until he remembered Sir Thomas' tirade against the Highlanders, how he'd blamed them for all his current misfortunes and looked vindictively toward their confiscated lands to make good his own reverses. If a man as well connected at court as Sir Thomas still carried so much hatred and suspicion against the Jacobites, then perhaps Cora's fears were well founded.

And that was what kept Alex walking.

When he'd first met Cora in the garden, hunting for her lost kitten, he'd welcomed her as a diversion, a saucy little lass to amuse him while he was in London. It was a familiar enough arrangement for him; as a mariner, he was seldom in one port long enough for anything more lasting.

But it hadn't taken long for Cora to change that. She wasn't like any of those other women in other ports, and he'd felt that way before he'd known her circumstances, too. While she wasn't conventionally pretty, she had charmed him with her bright, tip-tilted eyes and chestnut hair and her small, round body. She was clever and brave and loyal to her lost family, quick-witted and resourceful, and trying as hard as any woman could to stay that way in the face of terrible disaster.

Yet somehow all that trying made her more vulnerable, more fragile, and to Alex, oddly more appealing. He wanted to see her luck change. He wanted to see her survive and flourish, and he didn't want to sail away and leave her behind until she did.

He told himself his life was complicated enough at present. He didn't have time to spare watching out for anyone else. He was always faulting his father for doing exactly that, and he wasn't about to fall into the same bottomless pit himself.

But this wasn't just any hapless soul. This was Cora, and he smiled to himself as he walked, remembering how her face had glowed when she'd told him about the river running through her father's land, or how she'd chuckled, deep and husky with delight, as her wondrously plump bottom had settled across his lap last night.

He smiled, then cursed himself for being a besotted fool, and began the whole despairing argument with himself all over again.

By the time he'd finally had himself rowed back to the *Calliope*, his temper was as black as it could be. Until, that is, Johnny had glumly greeted him on deck. One of the crew had been taken up by the watch for brawling in a rumshop, and unwilling to lose even one Appledore man to His Majesty's navy, Alex had at once gone back to shore to buy back the man's freedom before he disappeared. The horizon was already brightening with daybreak before he returned to the sloop with the shamefaced seaman, both of them smelling ripely of the time spent in the gaol, of old rum and stale vomit.

But Alex's trials still weren't done. As soon as he'd retreated to his cabin, a messenger from the customs house had arrived, bearing a score of complicated bills and queries about the cargo that needed his immediate attention.

By the time it was all resolved and the messenger gone, the sun was rising high through the hazy sky and Alex's head was aching with exhaustion. With a curt order not to be disturbed for anything short of the Apocalypse, he retreated at last to the sanctuary of his cabin. He didn't pause to eat or shave or wash, taking the time only to strip away his boots and all clothes save his breeches before he sank into the welcoming oblivion of his own bunk, and sleep, sleep, with one final, fleeting image of Cora smiling impishly as she bent over to kiss him one more time. . . .

"I know perfectly well he's on board, Johnny, so don't try telling me otherwise unless he has some wretched low woman there in the cabin with him."

Slowly Alex opened one eye, then the other. How the devil could he have gone to sleep with Cora's smile and awakened to his sister's voice? His sister was in Lady Waldegrave's keeping now, not his, and somewhere causing mischief on land and far from here. Doubtless he was imagining things, and with a grumbling yawn he bunched the pillow up in his arms and closed his eyes again.

"Oh, Johnny, please," his sister was saying from the deck overhead, wheedling in that molasses-sweet voice that inevitably got her her way with men. "Won't you be a lamb and fetch my brother here? Or must I skip past you and find him myself?"

Now the unfocused image floating before him was of his first mate covered with unlikely fleece, meekly saying "baaa" while Diana tapped him with her shepherdess' crook. He wanted to laugh aloud, Johnny looked so foolish that way, and he would have, too, if at that exact moment the door to his cabin hadn't burst open with a very real Diana on the other side.

"Oh, my, my, brother," she said with arch disapproval, her hands at her waist to mimic their mother. "There may be no doxies hiding in here with you, but fah, it surely does stink like a brothel!"

She ostentatiously fanned the companionway door back and forth as Alex sat upright on the bunk to glare at her. He'd let his habits return to being more comfortable and bachelorlike since she'd gone to stay with the countess, and he didn't like having Diana surprise him like this, unshaven, undressed, unwashed, and sleeping in the middle of the day.

"I won't ask how *you* know about such things," he retorted, bunching the pillow into his hands, "my dear sweet *sister.*"

At the last word he hurled the pillow across the cabin at Diana's gleeful face. With a lifetime of dodging such offerings from her brother, she instinctively ducked. But the person in the companionway behind her had had no such experience, and the pillow that flew over Diana's head thumped against the edge of the door exactly even with Cora's startled face.

"Jesus," he groaned, and lunged off the bunk and across the cabin to snatch the offending pillow from the deck. This was a nightmare worse than any he could have dreamed, and with the pillow in his hand he finally dared to meet Cora's gaze.

She'd been startled, yes, but she hadn't shrieked or screamed the way most females would, and she hadn't scuttled away, either. She'd stood her ground, and though her cheeks had pinked becomingly beneath her freckles, she'd kept her expression pleasantly even and ladylike. She was dressed in the same flat straw hat and flower-covered muslin that made her look like an engaging and fresh little blossom herself. It also made him acutely aware of how unengaging he must look himself, half naked and with his hair untied and sticking up every which way like a wild man's, and self-consciously he rubbed his hand across his stubbly cheek and jaw.

"You might apologize, you know," suggested Diana, reappearing beside Cora. "Grovel for our forgiveness a bit before I introduce you properly to this lady."

Introduce her. Damnation, so Cora hadn't told his sister they'd already met. Considering all that had happened between them, it was probably just as well that she hadn't, but it sure as hell was going to make this little visit of Diana's a challenge for them both.

"I—ah, um," he began inauspiciously, and at last remembered to toss away the pillow clutched in his hand. He was usually good at groveling to ladies, but the combination of having Diana there as a witness with Cora's own twitching little half-smile was making this damned difficult. "I, um, ask your pardon for my, ah—oh, blast, Diana, you were the ones who forced your way into my cabin!"

"And a powerfully uncivil place it is for ladies, too." Unperturbed, Diana pushed the door open the rest of the way and sauntered past Alex into the cabin, her lace fichu trailing from her shoulders. "No matter. Cora, I would like to present to you my brother, Captain Fairbourne. Alex, I'd like to present Miss—why, Cora, I don't believe I recall your family name."

"Cora is sufficient," said Cora, still lingering in the

doorway. "That is, if we are all to be friends, then given names should be enough. Captain Fairbourne—Alex—I am honored, sir."

She spoke in perfectly clipped London English, without even a hint of the Highland burr that had colored her speech last night, and because Alex knew how much it must represent to her, he missed it in her voice now.

"And I am honored, Miss Cora," he said formally, reaching for her hand as he bowed, "to meet so charming a lady."

Her fingers were warm, and surprisingly damp, and he wondered if, inside, she were nervous. God knows she should be, coming here like this. It wasn't that he didn't wish to see her—he did, immeasurably—but now that he knew more of her past, he couldn't help feeling oddly responsible for her again. He wanted her safe; he wanted her happy. But for someone who'd spent the past two years in hiding, he couldn't imagine a more dramatic way to burst back into view than to choose Diana for a companion.

As he straightened, he glanced up to meet her eyes, and realized that she'd been staring quite pointedly at his bare chest, and he smiled. Though he might wish to be more genteelly dressed for receiving ladies, he wasn't ashamed of his body, and neither, apparently, was Cora. When she realized she'd been caught, she blushed, and hastily looked down, but not before she let her gaze be trapped for an instant by his. Wicked, wicked, he thought, and savored the moment between them, keeping hold of her hand a good deal longer than he should for a lady he'd just met.

Not, fortunately, that Diana seemed to notice. "Alex, where's Blackie?" she asked, bending to peek beneath his desk. "I came here specifically to see him. Puss, puss, where are you hiding?"

He heard the tiny gasp from Cora, and he wondered if she really believed he'd betray her now.

"He's not here, Di," he said quickly. "He's, ah, gone ashore with Solomon. Being a land-bred cat, I thought he'd like to run about a bit."

Solomon was the ship's cook, known to be fond of dogs and cats, and it was entirely plausible that he'd take a kitten for a stroll. Alex would just have to tell him.

"I suppose you're right," said Diana, disappointed. "But I'm sure I'd be doing much better at finding my true love if he were here to guide me as he's supposed to."

"The hunt isn't prospering?" asked Alex, striving to keep the hope from his voice. "What of Lord Oswald?"

Diana sighed. "Lord Oswald prides himself on his fighting cocks, and as a great favor he showed me the special silver spurs he'd had made for them. I had to tell him that cockfighting was cruel and barbaric and disgusting, and that any man who enjoyed such a hideous pastime would never suit me. Oh, Alex, I'd had such hopes for him!"

Alex smiled. Likely she'd told Lord Oswald a good deal more than that: farewell forever, Lord Oswald. "There'll be other gentlemen, Diana. London is a large place."

"I suppose so." She sighed again. "Otherwise I might as well have stayed in Appledore and married the first cod fisherman who'd have me. But I do wish Blackie were here to grant me a bit of luck. You are finding ways to amuse yourself, I trust?"

He didn't dare look back at Cora. "Tolerably, aye."

"At least that makes one of us." Absently she glanced at her reflection in Alex's looking glass, plucking a curl back into place. "You know, I do believe I left my tortoise combs, the ones with the silver chasing, in my little cabin here. I can't find them anywhere among my things in my trunk. Cora, you don't mind staying here with Alex while I run down and look before we leave?"

She didn't wait for an answer, but swept from the cabin in search of the tortoise combs.

And, to the great uneasiness of them both, left Cora alone with Alex.

10

"They must be monstrously fine combs," ventured Cora at last, "to be worth such an effort."

"Aye, and only one pair out of the hundred my sister must own," said Alex, finally turning to face Cora. She was standing in an angled beam of sunlight slanting in from the stern windows to make her hair glow bright around her face, and he caught himself thinking how remarkable that she'd be as appealing in the day as she was by moonlight.

Appealing and oddly right standing there, though he couldn't fathom why. Women didn't belong on privateering ships. He'd had trouble even accepting Diana on the voyage here. How could this copper-haired elf-girl possibly look at home among his disordered male belongings, his charts and pistols, his leather-covered spyglass and battered old mug?

Not that he'd let himself be distracted by such things. He'd more questions to ask of her first, or maybe it was again. Damnation, she *was* distracting him.

She smiled uncertainly, tipping her head to one side. "Thank you for not telling her I have Starlight."

"You're welcome," he said, and took a deep breath.

He would *not* be distracted. "Cora, why in blazes are you here? Why aren't you back at the countess' house where you'll be safe?"

Her smile blossomed into a grin, forgetting to be self-conscious of her teeth. "I'm doing exactly as you said, Alex. I'm being brave. I'm not thinking about dying any longer. I'm *living*. And I can't tell you what a wonderful time I've had today with your sister."

"Oh, aye, Diana, the perfect model of decorous behavior," he said grimly. "Have you told her your history as well?"

"No, no," said Cora emphatically. "I've never even told much to Lady Waldegrave. Only you, Alex."

But Alex simply shook his head with exasperation, unconvinced. "Cora, what were you thinking? Two young women, unattended, and near the docks, too! What would've happened if you'd been recognized, eh? What then?"

Her smile seemed somehow to soften. "So you do care what becomes of me, Alex?"

"Of course I care!" he exclaimed, flinging his arms outward with impatience. "I'm the one who incited you to this foolishness of being brave, so I better damned well be the one to take responsibility for it as well. No more wandering about the town, mind? Especially not with my feather-headed sister. You stay with the countess where I'll know you won't come to harm."

"You do care," she said, marveling, her voice dropping to almost a whisper of wonder. She pushed her hat back from her face, letting it hang by the ribbons down her back, and stepped closer to him, eagerly searching his face as if seeing him for the first time. "I was so afraid that all you wished was a—a flirtation."

Having Cora gaze at him like this, her lips parted and moistly inviting and her eyes half closed and almost dreamy, was making him forget everything but kissing her again, and again, and filling his hands with her breasts, and perhaps even easing her toward his bunk for a good deal more.

Which would, of course, lead to nothing but out-and-out disaster. If he felt any sort of bond with her, it shouldn't be sealed with her on her back. How could he bluster about protecting her one minute, then want to tumble her like some slatternly tavern wench the next?

"You're a brawny, bonnie man, Alasdair," she murmured, the burr thick in her voice now as she let her gaze slide down his bare chest again. "How could I have known you were so well made beneath your clothes?"

Well made, oh, yes, and hard as a bar of iron inside the last bit of clothing he wore. Whoever dreamed disaster could appear in such an enticing package? He was so close to giving in he could taste it, near enough that he could smell it along with the musky, womanly scent of her skin and flesh on a warm summer's day.

So close, and so damnably wrong.

With a groan he turned, snatched another shirt from the peg on the bulkhead, and yanked it over his head, letting the tails hang untucked in front to hide his obvious arousal. Alasdair, hah. He was Alexander Fairbourne and no one else, and the sooner he started thinking with his head instead of his cock, the better for them both. Furiously he began raking his fingers through his hair, pulling it back so he could tie it with a scrap of leather from his pocket. At least he could look the part of a sane, civilized man, even if he couldn't act it.

"Come along now, Cora," he said heartily as he pulled on his boots. "Best we get on deck before Diana hunts us down."

She didn't answer at first, standing in the slanting sunbeam where he'd left her. Carefully she set her hat back on her head, looping the ribbons beneath her chin in a neat bow before she glanced at him sideways, from beneath her lashes.

As glances went, it could have meant anything or nothing. Eyes like hers could convey a great many things without a word being spoken.

Anything or nothing: could she have interpreted his caution as rejection, that he'd found fault with her? She wasn't a practiced coquette, but rather a young, sheltered girl still discovering what pleased her as well as the power she'd have in pleasing others. Her enthusiasm for that first discovery was one of the things he'd found so intriguing—and exciting—about her, and he'd hate to think he'd inadvertently dampened it in any way.

Swiftly he grabbed up his coat, shrugging his arms into the sleeves as he hurried to follow her into the companionway.

Anything or nothing. But what if she'd seen his holding back in an entirely different light? What if she thought he'd been too cowardly to claim what she'd clearly been offering?

She hadn't gone far, only a few steps ahead. Her head was bent forward as she gathered her skirts and looked down to watch her foot on the companionway steps to the deck, the nape of her neck a creamy pale triangle above the linen kerchief, made whiter in contrast to the line of coral beads.

"Cora," he said, his voice rough with longing. She

turned toward him, a single graceful movement of expectation that he ended for her, slipping his hand around her waist to pull her from the step and against his chest.

Hungrily his mouth found hers, nothing sweet or gentle as he kissed her this time, kissed her hard and fast, enough to tip her hat back from her head and to make her catch at his shoulders to keep from losing her balance entirely. That Alex did for her, pressing her back against the bulkhead as he deepened the kiss. Now his body was striving to learn hers, the soft curves and valleys of her hips and thighs and breasts and the stiff, unnatural angles of her stays and hoops, and all of it fiercely exciting because it all belonged to Cora.

From the deck above he could hear the voices of two of his crewmen laughing, calling to each other, and he knew at any moment one of them or even his sister could come down these same steps and discover him and Cora. Yet he relished the risk, daring to be caught with her, the same way he'd dared capture in the *Calliope* a hundred times before.

And so, to his surprise, did she, almost vibrating with it beneath him, her breath quick and shallow as she kissed him back. Was this, then, part of the reason she'd dared come with Diana, the thrill of risking everything to danger? It wasn't his sister's style of blundering now and apologizing for the consequences later. This was more a matter of seizing a challenge and bettering it, a kind of dare against one's self. He'd never passed up such a challenge, even as a boy, and it was the single reason he'd done so well at privateering.

But by nature women didn't like taking risks. Was

this what she'd meant about being brave? Or was it simply that she'd nothing left to lose?

"You are . . . you are *wicked,* Alex," she whispered when he finally let her go. Her eyes were dark with excitement, her cheeks flushed and her lips red. She wobbled on her feet, groping behind her for the railing to steady herself, and swiped her tongue around her lower lip as if to taste his kiss again before she smiled. "But you know I'd never doubt you, don't you?"

Then she laughed, deep in her throat, and bunched her skirts in one hand and raced up the steps, her hat bouncing by its ribbons against her back. He grabbed at her ankle, but she was faster, her red-heeled shoes already clicking across the deck by the time he bounded after her. She was standing at the taffrail when he reached her, holding fast to the polished wood as she looked out over the water.

"It's beautiful like this, isn't it?" she said breathlessly. "All the ships and boats with their pretty sails and banners in the sun, and even the dirty old Thames sparkling like diamonds!"

He tried to see the river with her eyes. To him the Legal Quays, squeezed in here between London Bridge and the Tower, made for one of the worst anchorages in the world, overcrowded and costly, with unpredictable currents and more floating rubbish and dead dogs than he'd seen anywhere in the world. Even the quays and wharves were overburdened, with cargoes piled so high for want of enough porters that many of the goods spoiled before the tariffs had been set.

Yet still there was an undeniable grandeur to a city of this size, spreading golden along the river banks, seemingly without end. Towers and church spires punctuated the summer sky, centered by Wren's great dome on St. Paul's. Many of the ships had hung their sails to dry in the sunshine, the canvas bleached as white as the few clouds in the sky, and the striped pennants of different shipping houses flew below the red and blue overlapping crosses of Britain.

But what remained most beautiful to Alex was Cora herself, with her bright hair coming unpinned in the breeze and her skirts fluttering around her legs, and he'd give a great deal to kiss her again. But already the other men on the deck were far too interested in watching them, and what he'd dare to do below decks with the risk of discovery he wouldn't try now, for her sake, with that audience a certainty. There was nothing like a ship's crew for gossip, and nothing like gossip to undermine a captain's authority. Instead Alex contented himself with placing her hat back on her head, letting his fingertips trail down the back of her neck where he wished his lips could follow.

"Don't let yourself burn, lass," he said, ever the captain solicitous for a passenger's welfare. "The sun bouncing from the water is an entirely different fish, especially for one so fair."

"Meaning one who already has more than her share of spots and freckles." Absently she looked past him to the gray and white gulls bobbing over the water. "I've been on a big boat like this only once, when I sailed from Inverness to London."

"You came by sea?" he asked with surprise. From her telling, he'd imagined her escaping by horseback, dashing through woodlands and across moors, accompanied by fierce Highland warriors as guards.

She nodded, her smile fading as her thoughts

slipped into the past. "It was Father's idea. He thought I'd be safer, that no one would expect a Jacobite to be clever enough to flee like that, and he was right. He sent me with Mr. Abraham, the kind old man who brought Father books from Vienna and Paris, and if anyone asked, I was to say I was his granddaughter. We were nearly three weeks on that boat, and not once did I set foot from my quarters. It was so cold, and the seas were rough, and I—oh, there were other reasons as well."

It was a pitiful enough scene to imagine, poor Cora huddled in a tiny cabin aboard a north sea coaster in the icy storms of early spring, nursing seasickness and grief and loneliness with only an elderly book dealer for company. There wouldn't be much Alex could teach her about bravery after that.

"You'd find it different on the *Calliope*," he said, wanting to cheer her. "You can ask Diana. This sloop fair sails over the waves instead of through them, and my sister had nary a day of seasickness the entire voyage."

"I imagine she didn't," she said, and though she smiled, it was a sad smile, not at all what Alex had hoped. "How long before you must sail home?"

"The beginning of July, God willing," he said, and hoped that God would be willing Sir Thomas' money into his pocket before then, too. "Five weeks or so. Even that is a gamble, for I want to make the crossing before the fall storms begin in earnest. Hurricanes, we call them, and evil things they are to ships, too."

"Five weeks, you say." Restlessly she ran her hands back and forth along the polished wooden rail. "That's what I wish, too."

"To sail to Appledore?" Indulgently he let himself

imagine her there with him, showing her all that made him proud about the town, walking with her barefoot along the sandbars to gather shells, sweeping her into the middle of the often raucous family suppers around his mother's long mahogany dining table.

"Oh, no," she said quickly, squashing his sentimental daydreams, "though I'm certain it's a lovely place. No, I meant that I want to go to my own home."

Her home. He let that sit awkwardly between them, unsure of how to respond without wounding her. It was all fine and good to remember fondly the place where one had been born, but with her there was a very reasonable certainty that her home had been destroyed. And even if by a miracle the building itself had remained untouched, what kind of homecoming could she expect if all her family were dead?

He thought of the grand welcome that always greeted the *Calliope's* return to Appledore, with his parents and assorted siblings, aunts, uncles, cousins, and friends gathered on the wharf to wave and cheer, the bells in the two meetinghouse towers ringing, the small fishing and pleasure boats sailing alongside them as escorts into the harbor, the whole spectacle like a joyful, sweeping embrace that enveloped every happy, homebound sailor onboard.

And then he looked again at Cora, small and alone beside the rail, leaning her pointed little chin on her hands as she stared steadfastly out across the river. He knew it wasn't the Thames she was seeing, but rather her river, there in the past that was gone forever. Unrealistic though her determination might be, even foolhardy, to Alex, who understood how powerful an attachment to home could be, it was simply heart-breaking.

"Yes," she said firmly, as if hearing his unspoken doubts. "I mean to go home as well. But you knew that already, didn't you, Alex?"

She smiled at him over her shoulder, so warm and open an appeal that he couldn't help but smile back, and think again of how tangled together their lives seemed to be becoming.

"Aye, Cora," he said softly. "I suppose I did."

"Oh, Cora, there you are!" called Diana cheerfully as she clambered up the companionway to the deck, waving the newly retrieved tortoise combs in her hand like tiny signal flags. "We must be off directly anyway, or Gemini, the trouble we'll catch if we don't!"

The *Calliope's* boat was already being lowered to the water to carry them back to shore while Johnny Allred was testing the bo'sun's chair that would allow Cora and Diana, one by one, to be swung from the deck to the boat without compromising their modesty in a revealing flutter of petticoats. Johnny would go with them—it was his turn to go ashore, anyway—and make sure they returned safely to Lady Waldegrave's house.

Lightly Alex rested his hand at the back of Cora's waist, guiding her across the deck to where the others stood. All he could feel now was the stiff whalebone of her stays, the lacing zigzagging up her spine, while he remembered instead how soft and yielding she'd been in his lap last night, all her lovely, sweet-smelling flesh beneath the thin linen shift.

He wished he could go with them in the boat. No, better yet, he wished Cora would stay with him here in his cabin. It was impossible, of course, but he wished it still, and for a moment he spread his fingers possessively around the curve of her waist.

Waiting at the sloop's side, Diana waved her hand impatiently for them to join her.

"Oh, Cora, I should have warned you about how tedious my brother can be," she said. "If you let him begin talking about his darling *Calliope,* then he'll bore you to tears in no time. This sloop is his only true love, you know. He'll never have another. He's quite broken the hearts of all my friends that way."

Alex snorted derisively. "That's because my *Calliope's* a sight more faithful than any of your friends."

"You don't know that," retorted Diana, smoothing her fichu over her shoulders. "It's hardly the fault of my friends that you make them so, well, so *distracted.* But I will say, dear Cora, you do seem to be at ease with my ill-mannered old brother."

With considerable interest her gaze slid downward, noting that possessive hand of Alex's resting at Cora's waist. Diana had always been attuned to such nuances, a dubious gift, in Alex's opinion, that she'd inherited from their mother.

"I know it's not possible, of course," she went on mischievously, her blue eyes shining with the delicious possibilities, "but I'd almost believe that you two had already been long acquainted."

"But we have," said Cora blithely. "I do believe we've known each other, oh, simply forever."

Diana laughed as if Cora had said something tremendously witty and clever, but Alex knew she wasn't jesting, not about this. She believed it without any doubts at all.

The unsettling part was that Alex was beginning to believe it, too.

Most days when Sir Thomas came to Will's Coffee-house, he'd claim as his indisputable right one of the best seats, one of the few chairs as opposed to a seat on the trestle benches, and one beside the windows overlooking the street. With a cup of steaming coffee before him and his favorite long-stemmed pipe in his hand, he'd scan the latest papers and broadsheets through a tobacco haze while keeping his ears open for the scandal that was being whispered rather than printed. In his long curled wig and beautifully embroidered waistcoats, he liked to be the first that others saw when they entered, to prove he still had his place of importance in politics and at court.

But when Sir Thomas had left the drizzle in the street and climbed the narrow stairs to Will's today, he'd waved off the boy who'd tried to usher him to his usual chair. Instead he'd made his way alone to the murky depths of the coffeehouse where the daylight rarely reached and the smoke seldom cleared, especially on a damp, rainy morning like this. Today his waistcoat was plain and his wig tied back in a simple queue, for this morning he sought neither audience nor attention. The man he was meeting would be company enough.

Impatiently Sir Thomas shook the last raindrops from his coat, scanning the faces of the men huddled around these more anonymous tables. From the description he'd been given, the man should have been easy to spot. Blast the rascal if he dared be late! He should know not to keep his betters waiting, particularly those willing to pay his outrageous fees. Sir

Thomas gave his walking stick one last irritable jab at the floor and turned on his heel to leave.

"Sir Thomas, ain't it?"

"Deadmarsh?" Sir Thomas looked in the direction of the man's voice, squinting to make his eyes focus into the shadows beside the cold fireplace where the man had chosen to sit.

"No names, milord, no names, if'n you please." The man coughed and slid along the bench to make room for Sir Thomas to join him. "The less we know about each other, the better."

Reluctantly Sir Thomas joined him. Deadmarsh—that was all the name he knew, and apparently all he'd learn—had the leathery look of an old soldier accustomed to bad food and sleeping on the ground, his clothes worn and patched, the buttons and lace on his once jaunty uniform coat long ago snipped and sold for food or drink. His face was seamed and puckered by the same old sword wound, the same one that had taken his eye. Now he wore a soiled red kerchief slanting over his face to mask the empty socket, and when he spoke he twisted his head oddly to give the remaining eye a better angle for seeing.

"You've information?" asked Sir Thomas, thanking Providence that he'd chosen to meet this man here among the crowd at Will's rather than some other less inhabited spot. "As you know, time is of the greatest importance in this matter."

"I've had my success, milord," said Deadmarsh, smiling to show teeth broken and yellowed. "Ye will be happy, milord."

"You've found the chit?" demanded Sir Thomas,

excitement making him inch forward. "Blast it all, man, I must see her now if you have!"

"Ye can see her, aye, but ye can't have her," said Deadmarsh with maddening patience. "But I have her trail now."

Glancing about first to see if they were noticed, Deadmarsh drew a small, grimy bundle from his pocket. Slowly he unwrapped the strip of cloth until a thin folder of soiled leather slipped into his hand. He dug his thumbnail along the edge, seeking an opening, and as he did Sir Thomas could now see the faded glints of stamped gold leaf that once had made an elegant border. At last Deadmarsh found the hidden fastening, and with a grunt of satisfaction he popped the folder open and held it out for Sir Thomas to see.

It was the kind of case that wealthy travelers often had made to carry a favorite picture of a loved one with them on their journeys. The once-fine tooled morocco leather was now stained with blotches of rusty brown, but the colors of the small oval portrait, painted on ivory, were still clear and bright.

A young girl of perhaps twelve or thirteen years, still child enough to wear her chestnut hair curling untied down her back. Her plain white gown was sashed with red tartan across one shoulder, and around her throat was a strand of coral beads. Her features seemed too sharp to Sir Thomas to be considered pretty, though he'd be generous and fault the painter for that.

"This is the girl, then?" asked Sir Thomas. Regardless of her lack of beauty, her face was one he'd remember, and if he saw it again he told himself he'd be sure to recognize it. "You're sure?"

"I don't make such mistakes, milord," said Dead-marsh almost primly. "That be the girl."

Sir Thomas nodded. "She'd be older now, of course. More of a woman than a child. And she wouldn't be wearing that scrap of plaid to give herself away."

"But she do wear the beads, they say. Leastways she always did," said Deadmarsh. "They'd be enough to mark her."

Sir Thomas stroked his fingers over his mouth, hiding his growing excitement. This was exactly what he needed to win his case, the kind of proof that would convince even the king. When that puppy Alexander Fairbourne came to his door again—which he seemed to have fallen into the vile habit of doing most every morning—he'd be able to greet him more warmly, without that unpleasant mixture of anxiety and dread. Surely at last his luck must be changing!

"This picture is all well and good, Deadmarsh," he said, "but it's only a beginning. You must go to Scotland where the girl last was seen. I'll need her found within three weeks."

Deadmarsh's single brow arched with surprise. "I heard 'twasn't the girl ye cared for, but the proof of her death."

"Yes, yes, of course," said Sir Thomas impatiently. The rascal was reputed to be experienced and as trust-worthy as could be expected; why, then, must he spell out all the unsavory details? "But whether the girl is already dead, or dies, ah, at some time in the near fu-ture, doesn't concern me. All I must know is that she is beyond troubling me."

Deadmarsh nodded, smoothing the red scarf over his face. "Ye shall have yer proof, milord. This picture, an' the beads, an' maybe a curl o' that ruddy hair. That should be plenty, aye?"

"Plenty, yes." Again Sir Thomas glanced at the girl on the ivory; in a way he wished he hadn't put a face to this last obstruction in his path. But it was her insignificant life or his own ruin, and when he considered it like that, the choice was easy enough to make. "You are certain this is the girl?"

"Oh, aye." Deadmarsh's face twisted into a smile more like a smirk. "This be taken right from her Jacobite father's own fingers on the moor at Culloden afore his body be even chill. Look, and mark the letters in gold on the back: his sign. This belong to him jus' as she was his daughter."

"I'm sure it did," said Sir Thomas hastily. Now he realized to his great discomfort that the stains on the leather case were the blood of a dying man whose final wish had been to see his daughter's face—distasteful, disturbing details that he'd rather not have known.

Abruptly he rose, wanting nothing more to do with this man or the bloodstained portrait of the girl. "You will send word to me when you have done, ah, what you must, and we'll meet again then. But three weeks from this day and no more, else you'll not have a farthing."

"Aye, milord." Deadmarsh touched his fingers to his forehead, then tucked the portrait back into his coat. "Ye won't be disappointed, nay. Ye shall have yer proof."

11

Cora sat alone in the corner of Lady Waldegrave's print room, concentrating on making the tiniest possible snips around the plumed tail of an ostrich. It wasn't a real ostrich, of course, but a fanciful version, black ink on cream paper, as interpreted by an Italian engraver who, from the inaccurately hooked beak to the spreading phoenixlike wings, had probably no more seen the actual bird than had Cora. Neither of them cared. The artist had sold his ostrich in great lucrative quantities to English gentlemen and ladies touring the continent, while Cora had been happy simply to find an image that was sufficiently long, exotic, and lushly curved to balance the palm tree and monkey that she'd already cut out earlier.

"How do you judge it, Starlight?" she asked as she held the ostrich, now cut free of his background, in her outstretched hand to consider. "He certainly is a silly sort of bird, I'll grant you that."

But the kitten was too involved with diving and pouncing upon the curling scraps of paper at Cora's feet to be able to reply, and with a sigh Cora carefully lay the ostrich on her worktable alongside the monkey and his palm tree. She was restless and she was lonely, and on this too quiet morning with only the rain tapping against the windows to disturb her, no ostrich, no matter how perfectly cut, was going to make her happy.

Oh, there'd been a time not long ago when she'd loved working in here. Like most ladies of fashion, Lady Waldegrave had craved a print room for taking tea and generally impressing her friends. She'd spent a fortune at Mr. Bushell's shop, buying French and Italian prints by the armful, but when it had actually come down to the work of choosing which prints would look best on which wall of the room, of cutting and trimming and arranging the borders and swags and columns to frame the prints, and then the final tedium of pasting them in place to the walls—that had all been far beyond the countess' interest. She'd gladly given the entire project over to Cora, who'd found peace and pleasure in the painstaking work.

But that had been before Alex Fairbourne had come into her life. She smiled ruefully, and scooped Starlight into her lap.

"What's become of me, kitten?" she asked, tickling his nose with a sliver of paper. "Once you were the world to me, and now see how fickle I've become! I thought he was the one, Starlight, I truly did, and yet four days have passed without a single line or whisper from him. I know he promised me nothing, nor did I promise him, but I did think he was special, Starlight. I *did.*"

This time the kitten chirruped in sympathy, rubbing his muzzle against her thumb and looking so foolish as he lay on his back with his paws in the air that she had to smile. Perhaps she wouldn't have felt so sorry for herself if she'd had Alex's sister to talk to, but on the same afternoon that they'd visited the *Calliope,* Lady Waldegrave had introduced Diana to a young marquess who'd claimed every last waking minute of her day, and likely a good deal of the sleeping ones, too.

"Maybe you did find a splendid husband for Diana after all, Starlight," she said softly, stroking the downy black fur on his round little belly. "I'm not as particular, you know. All I really want is to go home."

She kissed the white star on his forehead, and resolutely turned back to her scissors and prints. The ostrich and the palm tree both would need something to set them off: matching archways, perhaps, or a border of curving vines. She reached across Starlight for the pile of printed borders, and as she did the kitten curled over in her lap, peeking over the edge of the table. To Starlight, one scrap of paper looked as tasty as another, and before Cora realized what he'd done, a small paw had dragged the ostrich over the edge. Snatching the hapless bird in his teeth, Starlight then bounded off Cora's lap and across the floor, the ostrich flapping ungallantly from his mouth.

"No, Starlight, no!" shrieked Cora, dropping her scissors to grab him. In all the prints the countess had bought there was only one ostrich, and she'd notice if it didn't appear somewhere on her walls. "Come back with that, you little thief!"

But Starlight was already through the door and racing down the hall, his claws clicking on the black and white stone floor and his tail puffed with the new thrill of freedom.

Cora followed, bunching her skirts to run better.

She should never have brought Starlight downstairs with her to the print room for company, and she hated to think what would happen if one of the servants found him before she did.

"Starlight!" she called, her own heels skidding on the slippery floor of the hall as she ducked beneath the staircase. "Starlight, where—*oh!*"

She stopped instantly, yet it still didn't feel fast enough. She didn't have to call Starlight any longer because she'd found him. He was curled up, proud as a little lord with a half-chewed bit of ostrich paper dangling from his mouth, blissfully content in the arms of Alex Fairbourne. She understood that bliss; she'd felt it herself.

Alex was standing there in the hallway where he'd just arrived, his black cocked hat still glistening with raindrops. Unlike the last time she'd seen him, his jaw glistened sleek and clean from the razor, his black hair was combed back in a perfectly tied black silk ribbon, his clothes were brushed and pressed for calling. Not that she cared; she'd welcome him in tatters if it came to that. He smiled, and she felt her whole world lurch with joy.

"Good day, Miss Cora," he said, and gave her a shallow bow with the cat.

"Good day, Captain," she managed to squeak out. Her curtsey ended on the down sweep, with her bending to gather up the tattered remnants of the now headless ostrich.

Carefully Alex lifted Starlight, cradling him in one hand. "I thank you for once again finding my sister's cat."

"The cat must leave directly, miss," intoned Junius with baleful righteousness. "Her ladyship's orders."

Cora blinked and looked up at the butler. Had she really been so blinded by Alex's appearance that she'd overlooked Junius looming there as grim as death?

First Starlight, and now Alex. The minute Lady Waldegrave returned, Junius would be whispering at her side, eager to tell all. He'd worry and tear Cora's reputation with the same fierce pleasure that Starlight had shown with the paper ostrich, and with about the same results.

But as her despair deepened, she suddenly remembered what Diana had done with Junius. Though she'd never have been daring enough to devise such a plan on her own, she certainly was desperate enough to borrow it.

"Her ladyship's orders are quite clear, miss," said Junius again, and with relish. "She has never permitted cats in the house."

She smiled at the butler, the same way she'd seen Diana do it. "Oh, my, Junius, then I must have been mistaken," she said disingenuously. "I'd rather thought her ladyship had said no *rats* in the *carriage* house. Wasn't that it?"

Junius stared at her, his eyes bulging and his florid face going purple-red about his tight-wrapped neckcloth. For one endless moment, Cora feared she'd somehow said the wrong thing, and that instead of silencing Junius, she'd only managed to confound herself more.

But then, without a word, the butler bowed curtly, and took a step backward, and she realized, at least for now, that she'd won.

"Captain Fairbourne, sir," she said, striving to emulate Lady Waldegrave's own hauteur as she swept her hand through the air. "Would you care to come view her ladyship's print room?"

"Rats and cats?" asked Alex as he followed her down the hall. "What the devil was that all about?"

"Something I learned from Diana." Cora gave her shoulders a little shrug, as if, like Diana, she behaved questionably like that all the time. "We'll have no more trouble from Junius now."

"Be careful what you learn from Diana, lass," cautioned Alex, "and be careful, too, who you make into your enemy."

"Junius already was an enemy," said Cora defensively, "and resented my place here. I didn't do anything to change that."

"All I'm saying is to mind yourself, Cora," said Alex. "And how is my wily sister faring herself?"

"Most well indeed," said Cora, relieved to move to another topic. "Starlight is doing exactly as she bid. She has a grand new admirer, a marquess."

"A marquess," repeated Alex, clearly unimpressed. "How blessed grand. And does my sister admire this marquess as much as he does her?"

"Oh, yes! For one thing, he collects Roman intaglios, not fighting cocks, which made him immediately superior to Lord Oswald. And her ladyship says he is perfection in fortune, title, and figure."

Alex snorted. "He better damned well have a fortune considering how much Diana likes to spend it."

"He must, or Lady Waldegrave wouldn't have encouraged him. Now this, Alex, is the print room."

She waited just inside the doorway for him to join her, her hand still holding the headless ostrich.

Though the walls were only half covered, she was still proud of her handiwork. But to her disappointment, all Alex did was give the walls a most cursory glance, with Starlight perched on his shoulder like an insolent parrot.

"Very fine, Cora," he said, without even a hint of genuine interest as he hooked his hat on the back of Cora's chair. "You may tell the countess I said so."

"It *is* very fine," she protested indignantly, and took the kitten from his shoulder. "Very fine indeed, and I should like you to say more than that, considering how many of my hours have gone into cutting and composing!"

She swept past him to the opposite wall, raising her hands to smooth her fingertips across a large print she'd pasted up this morning. It was one of the countess' favorites, an improbable domestic scene engraved after a French painting. A plump kitchen maid was refusing the attentions of a fashionable gentleman. Yet though the maid's face was modestly averted, her hands raised to stop her seducer, the artist had placed plenty of signs that the gentleman would eventually succeed: the broken eggs on the table, the overturned pitcher with a cat lapping up the spilled milk, the unraveling knot in the apron strings around the maid's waist.

While Cora had been trimming the print, she hadn't given much thought to its moral message, but now, she suddenly found to her shame she could think of little else beyond kissing Alex, and touching him, and all those other lovely, wicked things she didn't yet comprehend that were represented by broken egg shells and spilled milk.

"I need to border this with flowers, I think," she

said, rattling on to hide her thoughts as she held the tattered ostrich up to the wall. The last two times she'd been with Alex she'd behaved most wantonly, without any of the kitchen maid's protestations, and the worst part was realizing she wouldn't protest now, either. "I was going to use this ostrich, until Starlight stole it and ripped it quite apart, and now I'm not certain what—"

"I missed you, Cora," he said softly, so close she felt his breath on the back of her neck and smelled the scent of the soap he'd used for shaving and the raindrops scattered over his coat. "God knows I've wanted to come to you these last days, and if I'd—"

"Hush," she said breathlessly. "Don't say more. The first three words were enough. Any more will spoil it."

"You don't give orders to a captain, Cora," he said, his voice dropping to a raspy growl that made her shiver. "Not a minute has passed that I haven't thought of you. You've bewitched me, lass, plain and simple, until I don't know fore from aft, east from west."

She still stood with her hands raised against the wall, and now he settled his palms around her waist, his thumbs meeting over her spine. When she'd dressed she hadn't bothered with hoops beneath her petticoats, but she had laced on her stays, and now he muttered an oath in frustration as his hands discovered it, too.

"Why in blazes must you ladies rig yourselves out like this, eh?" he said, sliding his hands higher along her sides, pressing against the long strips of whalebone. "I liked you better the way you were that night, soft and warm, the way God intended women to be. The way my Cora *is*."

She caught her breath as he kissed her on the side

of her throat, there on the pulse beneath her ear, where the heat of his lips sent tremors racing straight to her heart. His hands slid higher, beneath her outstretched arms, higher, until he reached the top of her stays and the stiffened edge of her bodice to where her breasts were raised fashionably high.

He teased his lips against her throat, nipping at her, almost as if he were tasting her, and at the same time eased his hands into the front of her bodice to free her breasts. She gasped, pleasure spiking through her as he settled his fingers over her nipples, rubbing his palms across the lush flesh of her breasts. Gently he guided her bottom and hips back against his, and against that mysterious hard place in his breeches. Even as she arched deeper into Alex's embrace, the warning of the broken eggs and spilled milk remained framed between her outstretched hands and before her gaze.

"Sweet Cora," whispered Alex hoarsely. "*My* Cora. Ah, lass, can you tell how much I want you?"

She could guess if she could settle her befuddled wits to think again; but what she knew was how much *she* wanted him, even without understanding all that that meant. Instinctively she pressed back against him for support, her knees so weak that he easily nudged them apart with his own until she felt herself riding the hard muscles of his thigh with only her petticoats between them.

And now, when through the haze of desire she saw the demure kitchen maid and the broken eggs, her only response was to close her eyes and give herself to Alex. If she was his Cora, then he must be her Alex. How could it be otherwise, when he could make her feel like this?

"Alex," she whimpered. "Oh, Alex, please!"

"Damn," he said through gritted teeth. "Blast and double damn to high holy hell, and God give me strength."

Breathing hard, he abruptly stopped moving, stopped his hands from caressing. Instead, with a groan, he simply held her, his arms loose around her waist, letting her head slip back against his shoulder.

"Oh, Cora, sweet, I'm sorry," he said. "I'm sorry. But thank Jesus you stopped me in time."

She slid free and turned toward him, resting her balled hands on his chest. Her heart was thumping as if she'd run a race uphill, and her whole body felt heavy and inexplicably on edge.

"I didn't stop you, Alex," she cried, confused and searching his face for a clue to his meaning. "I'm not stopping you now!"

"If you've any sense at all, Cora, you sure as hell better stop me," he said, his voice rising with an anger she didn't understand. "Where in blazes do you suppose this sort of game ends?"

She didn't want him believing she was ignorant, not like this. "We were—were giving pleasure to each other," she said, her voice wobbling with uncertainty. "Because we—we like each other's company."

"Pleasure, hell," he said with grim fury. "In another half minute, you would have been on your back on that table with your petticoats over your head and your legs over my shoulders and my cock buried up to the hilt, giving me more *pleasure* than any man in this life deserves. But that wasn't what you wanted, was it? Was it?"

"No," she whispered, shocked as much by the crudity of his language as the scene he'd described. "No."

"No," he repeated, and closed his eyes for a moment as he composed himself. "No, Cora, you wouldn't, not like that. And I'd be the lowest bastard on earth if I didn't agree."

Gently he reached out to tug her bodice back over her bare breasts, and clumsily she finished the task, turning away from him to smooth her shift back into her stays and tuck her kerchief into her bodice.

She hadn't been ashamed of what they'd done when they'd been doing it, but now, as the giddy heat passed from her body and cold reason came in its place, she felt every ounce of the guilt and sin that the kitchen maid's print warned against. Before, she'd thought of herself as a trifle wanton, a word which sounded exciting and daring and somehow brave. Now she felt merely tawdry as well as wretchedly innocent, and she could see nothing brave or daring in either one.

"I swear I came here to talk to you, Cora, and that was all," he said, standing beside her worktable with his back to her and his hands clasped tightly behind his waist. She couldn't tell if he meant to give her privacy, or if he needed to look away to compose himself as well.

"I wanted to know you were safe," he continued, "and that you hadn't gotten yourself into any more scrapes or mishaps with Diana. I swear that's all I wished, and yet you make me forget reason, Cora. I forget everything reasonable with you, and become no better than the village bull in rut, and I'm sorry for it. If you do not wish to ever forgive me, I'll understand. Damnation, I'll *understand*."

She was glad one of them would because she still

didn't. One moment he'd been kissing her throat in the most delicious manner, and the next he was saying she'd tempted him into wanting to do the most shameful things.

But she still liked him—oh, yes—and still trusted him. That hadn't changed, and when she saw how his shoulders were so bowed that the even the silk ribbon in his hair seemed to droop, she knew he felt the same regrets and shame she had about their actions. Wistfully she hoped at least he'd felt some of the joy, too.

Because what had happened wasn't entirely his fault, or blame, or guilt, or whatever he chose to call it. Half was hers. She'd been there, too, in case he hadn't noticed. Claiming it all for himself might be a noble, gentlemanly gesture to make, but it wasn't true, and she wasn't going to let him do it.

That decision was easy. The hard part was figuring out how exactly to tell him. There she was at a complete loss, and the only sounds now between them were the random *splats* as the last raindrops trickled from the trees to the garden paths outside.

Oblivious to all of this, Starlight wove his way among the paper scraps, sliding on his belly to squeeze beneath the rungs on the chair. He paused for an instant, as still as could be with his tail outstretched, then wiggled his bottom, lunged forward, and pounced on Alex's polished shoe buckle, biting it as savagely as he could.

"Shove off, you rascally beast," said Alex when he noticed him, but instead of kicking him off he bent and lifted the cat back to his shoulder. This was Starlight's favorite spot in the world to be, and to make sure Cora knew it, he blinked at her, and yawned, too, for good measure.

The sight of Starlight misbehaving made her recall how all of this had begun, and slowly she uncurled her left hand. Pressed into the damp creases of her ink-smeared fingers and palm was a damp, tattered scrap of smudged paper, all that remained of the unfortunate ostrich.

"Look," she said softly. "You and Starlight have quite ruined my ostrich."

"Your what?" asked Alex, scowling down into her hand. "Oh, aye, the ostrich. It looks ruined enough, sure. Where did it come from?"

"From Africa, I suppose," said Cora. Tentatively she let her other hand creep into the crook of his elbow. To her great relief, he let it stay. "Isn't that where ostriches live? Then by way of Italy. Though being a bird, at one time it must have come from an egg."

Alex sighed impatiently, but his face was relaxing, too, the harsh lines on either side of his mouth softening.

"A paper egg, I'll warrant," he said. "But where in blazes does one purchase a paper ostrich in London?"

"At Mr. Bushell's shop," she answered promptly. "In St. Paul's churchyard."

"Then come along," he said, plucking his hat from the chair while Starlight peered down with interest from his shoulder. "And bring what's left of your bird if you expect Mr. Bushell to identify it."

He took her hand in his, frowning down at the pulpy, inky mess. "I should like to say something clever about a bird in hand, but I can't put it quite right."

She looked up at him from beneath her lashes. "I think you already have."

"Then you forgive me?" he asked, running his thumb lightly along the heel of her hand. "For the ostrich, I mean?"

She narrowed her eyes. "You're forgiven, Alex. For everything. But you must forgive me for my part, too."

"Damnation, Cora, a lady shouldn't have to—"

"Then I'm not a lady," she said evenly, "if that makes it any easier for you to swallow. You didn't make me do anything I didn't wish."

He sighed, and she knew he'd surrendered. "You're a holy trial to me, Cora, that's what you are. Now, go, fetch your hat. Seems I owe you an ostrich, and I mean to pay my debt now."

They sat across from each other in the hired hackney, mostly because the cab was too narrow for them to sit side by side, but also so that Cora could face forward, and see everything she wanted from either window. Starlight slept peacefully curled on the seat beside her, for neither of them had wanted to leave him behind with Junius.

Alex smiled again as he watched her crane her neck and gasp in wonder at some new marvel of the city. What a waste for her to have been hidden away for two years in the countess' house when all of London was waiting for her to discover! Her reactions now were so wonderfully guileless and genuine that it was almost as if he were guiding a child through the city for the first time, and as a result he was enjoying himself enormously, too. For once he was thankful for the snail's pace of London's congested streets and lanes, of having to creep along among the sea of carriages and wagons, chairs and handcarts and horses and pedestrians, because it gave Cora more time for looking at the city, and for him in turn to look at her.

With delight she surveyed the sprawling market of farmers' stalls at Covent Garden, never having realized that this was the source for most of the food served at the countess' table. She laughed at the lurching, overcrowded coach from Greenwich, resplendent with a dozen roaring, drunken midshipmen clinging to the top, and she stared wide-eyed at the troop of trained monkeys dancing on a street corner in matching satin jackets while their master played the fiddle. She critically studied the dress and hair of the ladies of fashion, whether squeezing their oversized hoops and petticoats through the doorways of shops or parading in carriages glittering with gilt striping and coats of arms painted ostentatiously on the doors. With awe she stared up at the spires of churches and the towers of public buildings, and at huge houses built of Purbeck and Portland stone in the latest Italian style, a hundred times more imposing than the countess'.

But not everything pleased Cora. She was horrified by the number of beggars and ragged children to be found in nearly every street, by the number of pinched and ravaged faces that showed disease and madness, too much to drink and too little to eat.

"Englishmen say we Highlanders live like base creatures, scarce worthy of being called Christian men and women," she said, her face troubled. "But not even our poorest crofters suffer like this."

"Then they wrong you, sweet," said Alex softly. He knew how she was feeling; on his first boyhood voyage with his father to London, he'd been so outraged, so sickened by the yawning difference between rich and poor, unknown in Appledore or even Boston, that he'd vowed he wouldn't return. He had, of course, like every other traveler, just as he still felt the same revulsion. The only difference was that, as a man of the world, he'd learned to hide it.

But Cora had not, and he saw how her mouth twisted with horrified sympathy as they passed a girl younger than herself, her garishly painted face still unable to hide the desperation in her eyes as, with her near-naked baby tied to her back, she vainly tried to tempt the sailors staggering from a corner rumshop.

"Father would have found her a place at Creignish," said Cora, her unhappy gaze following the girl. "Stranger or friend, we never turned anyone away. Everyone was given food and a blanket and shelter as long as they wished it. No woman would have been forced to do . . . do that."

"Nor would she suffer in Appledore, either," said Alex. "Creignish, now, is that the name of your town?"

"Not my town," she said absently, "for we live in the glen, but our house is called Creignish, after—"

She broke off when she realized what she was saying, her eyes suddenly sharp with accusation.

"That wasn't meant as a trick, Cora, I swear," he said gently, "and I wouldn't ask now if I hadn't a reason."

"I would have told you outright if you'd asked," she said reproachfully. "Don't you know that?"

He sighed and looked down, fiddling with one of the buttons on the sleeve of his coat to avoid meeting her eye.

"In these last days I've learned my business here in

London will likely conclude sooner than I'd thought," he began, wishing he didn't sound so damned pompous, "and let me sail earlier for home."

"Oh," she said, a single, wounded syllable, and from the corner of his eye he could see her lift the sleeping kitten into her arms for comfort. "Sooner, you say. On account of the hurricanes?"

He nodded without looking up from his sleeve. Blast, he'd been trying to help, not hurt her! "Like any captain, I have to put the safety of my crew and ship first. That doesn't leave us much time. If I'm to help you, Cora, I'll need to know more about you. Hell, I don't even know your family's name."

"My clan," she said, her voice icily formal. "The MacGillivray. You may call it a family, but to us it's our clan. I am Cora Margaret Anne MacGillivray, and my father was the Honorable Iain MacGillivray, younger brother of our laird, my uncle, the Earl of Aviemore. His name was Alasdair, too. Like you."

He kept his relief to himself. Because Sir Thomas was being so much more obliging than he'd expected, Alex had been able to spend these last days discreetly asking about the Jacobite rebellion and how the government regarded the Highlanders now, learning whatever he could to help Cora. His worst fear had been that she would turn out to be the daughter of one of the three Jacobite peers brought to London for trial and execution—Lords Kilmarnock, Cromarty, and Balmerino—and he was relieved to learn she belonged to a less infamous clan instead. Granted, it didn't make the MacGillivrays any less dead, but the lack of notoriety still could make Cora's own future less of a challenge.

"So Creignish was the house on the river," he asked, "your father's house?"

"And mine," she said defensively. "Which is why I wish to return to it."

He sighed wearily, wishing she wouldn't fight him so. The heroes in ballads might come sweeping in with swords and pistols to save the lady in distress, but this week he'd served Cora best by asking a great many tedious questions of a great many dry and tedious men.

He still didn't have any guarantees that the home she loved so dearly wasn't already in ruins. And even if it still stood, Alex hadn't yet been able to find out much about the Scottish inheritance laws. Unless they differed dramatically from the English ones, then her father's house—this Creignish, wherever it was—would go to the next male heir instead of Cora. Considering how far the executors would have had to go to find a living male MacGillivray, the chances were that anyone residing there now would hardly welcome Cora's return.

He forced himself to look away from the button on his sleeve and at her instead. Though her chin was high, her nose proudly in the air as befitted the last of her clan, she was also clutching Starlight so tightly against her chest that Alex couldn't believe the kitten wasn't protesting.

"I'm guessing Creignish lies somewhere not far from the sea, Cora," he continued carefully, "since that's how you escaped. But you can make this all far simpler if you tell me exactly in what county it stood."

She looked at him sharply over the back of the kitten. "You don't believe my house still stands, do you?" she asked, her rising voice managing to sound both defiant and plaintive at the same time. "You're just like

Lady Waldegrave. You think Cumberland burned it like everything else. You think that I've no home left to go to, that I should forget everything about the past, that I'm a sad and sorry burden for wishing it were so."

"Cora, please," said Alex, reaching across for her hand. "I only want to help, sweetheart."

But she shook him off, and though he was sure he saw tears shining in her eyes, through pure will alone she did not shed them, nor did she let her voice break.

"I would know it if Creignish were gone, Alex," she said. "I would *know,* just as I knew when Father died. I'd know in my heart, here, without you or Lady Waldegrave or anyone else having to tell me."

Before Alex could answer, the hackney lurched to a stop and the driver thumped on the roof to let them know they'd reached their destination. Before the man could open the door, Cora unlatched it herself, and clambered ungracefully out onto the curb. There she waited for Alex with Starlight held high on her shoulder, stubbornly studying the prints displayed in the shop window to avoid looking at him.

Yet as soon as Alex had paid the driver and joined her, she reached for his hand at her side, linking her slender fingers into his as tightly as a drowning man would grasp a lifeline tossed his way.

"I would *know,* Alex, and nothing you can say will convince me otherwise," she whispered fiercely beside him. "Just as I know I'm right about you."

12

"*G*ood day, sir," said Cora, hoping Mr. Bushell wouldn't see how anxious such a simple request could make her. "I—that is, we—wish to purchase an ostrich."

"To replace the one that was eaten," explained Alex, sounding so reasonable and unarguably captainlike that she smiled with relief. No one would question anything she said as long as he was there beside her, and no one would believe nearly three years had passed since she'd last stepped up to a shopkeeper's counter like this one.

"Yes, eaten," she echoed now. "Devoured. As soon as I'd cut the poor ostrich from the paper, my kitten seized it from the table and ran away."

Mr. Bushell regarded Starlight with open hostility, doubtless picturing the kitten savaging his entire stock. "If you wish, miss, I shall ask one of my boys to watch your animal outside where he'll be more content."

"Oh, the kit won't be any trouble," said Alex confidently. "All he wants to do is sleep right now after so much devouring. Go on, sweetheart. Show the man what's left of the bird."

Cora began to reach into her pocket, but Mr. Bushell hastily put up his hand to stop her. He was a small, tidy man, dressed in the same black and white of his prints, and accustomed to anticipating the wishes of his lady customers.

"That won't be necessary, miss," he said with a neat bow. "Not at all. We've only the one print with the ostrich, the Antonio Parisi. A most handsome and excellent choice, miss, very popular with ladies of taste like yourself. Allow me to fetch one for you, if you please."

Shyly Cora nodded, and as the man bustled away to find her ostrich, she relaxed enough to look around her. Lady Waldegrave had complained that while this shop was the most popular in London, she'd found Mr. Bushell's own personal taste lacking in refinement.

Now Cora understood why. Taste had less to do with Mr. Bushell's choice of stock than a firm knowledge of what would sell, and to customers that ranged from titled ladies composing their print rooms to tavern keepers looking for an entertaining picture to pin to the wall over the bar. While most of the prints were stored in large, flat portfolios, those most in demand were displayed in the window and in neatly hierarchical rows along one wall.

On the top row, as in society, were the portraits of stern-faced clerics and divines. Next came a row of heroes, modern generals such as the Duke of Marlborough beside ancient ones like Hannibal and Caesar. Below that were copies after famous paintings— Guido, Tintoretto, Raphael, Rubens—as well as fanciful scenic views peopled by nymphs and satyrs, French courtiers, or commedia dell'arte figures.

Finally, on the lowest and most accessible two levels, came the prints that had offended Lady Waldegrave's sensibilities: vulgar scatological satires of current politics, lascivious portraits of popular actresses and royal mistresses lolling half-dressed on day beds, and titillating vignettes of bawdy encounters. No wonder the clerics on the top row glowered downward with such righteous fury!

As soon as the content of this last row registered, Cora's conscience ordered her to look away with maidenly haste. Yet one picture on the lowest row seized her attention and refused to let it go: a grinning soldier, his long musket pointing suggestively toward the sky, was pulling a sly milkmaid back against his chest. His hands buried deep into her bodice and his unbuttoned breeches hung around his knees, her legs were splayed and her bottom pressed up eagerly against him with her petticoats tumbled every which way, the entire scene dreadfully like the one Cora and Alex had enacted in the print room this very morning. Cora flushed with embarrassment, even as her body grew hot and languid at the memories that viewing the print was churning within her.

"See something you like, pet?" teased Alex, and to Cora's horror she realized he'd followed her gaze and was looking at exactly the same print of the soldier and milkmaid. "Another edifying picture you'd like to add to the countess' print room wall?"

"No!" she exclaimed, turning away so fast she nearly crashed into Mr. Bushell.

"Here is your ostrich, miss," he said, laying it upon the counter to untie another portfolio for display. "Perhaps I can interest you in some of our newer offerings as well. These are views of some of the finest houses in Britain, belonging to the highest families in the realm. They are in the most perfect taste, miss, and provide an excellent balance to a collection of grand vistas taken on foreign soil."

Gratefully Cora bent to admire the prints as he turned them one by one. There was nothing suggestive about blandly grand vistas and fine houses, and she forced herself to concentrate on them and to forget the solider and his milkmaid.

"Pray, will you excuse me for a moment, miss?" asked Mr. Bushell as an overdressed woman beckoned furiously to him for assistance from across the shop. "Might I leave you to amuse yourself?"

"We'll do well enough on our own," said Alex, and the shopkeeper retreated. Alex bent close to Cora, resting his hand lightly on the back of her waist as she turned the prints in the portfolio.

"I do believe I liked those others on the wall better," he said idly. "They held more . . . *excitement*, didn't you think?"

"Hush," she scolded, her cheeks flushing again. "Just you *hush*, Alexander Fairbourne! Simply because I agreed to take half the blame for our—our lapse this morning doesn't mean I wish to speak of it here now."

"We weren't speaking of it, Cora." He chuckled and leaned closer, smoothing a loose tendril back around her ear. "We were *looking*. Faith, can you imagine a print room lined only with pictures of that sort?"

She could, and what was worse, she could imagine being inside such a room with him, and oh, lord, the mischief they'd find together. Instead of chastising him the way she should, she giggled, every bit as wicked as he was himself.

"Stop, Alex," she ordered, even though she was unable to stop her own laughter as she turned the next sheet. "Stop now, before Mr. Bushell returns and we're—oh, Alex, *oh!*"

She stopped then with a cry that made Alex stop, too, bending over her with instant concern. Yet how could she explain, how could she tell him?

"What has happened, Cora?" he demanded gently. "Are you unwell, Cora? Cora?"

She nodded, holding her hand out over the print before her. "This picture, Alex," she whispered, her gaze held fast to the image. "This . . . it's Creignish."

He whistled low, as speechless a response as she'd had herself.

And why not? The artist had drawn it exactly as she remembered it herself, and excitedly she began explaining the picture to Alex.

"This square tower here is the oldest part of the house, more of a watchtower, really," she said, her words rushing over one another in her haste to explain, to make him *see*. "But this other tower was built by Father, and there's nothing inside but his library and all his books, with the tall windows to let in light in every weather. And these windows here, overlooking the river—those are my rooms, Alex, except that I would never have them latched on such a bonnie summer's day."

" 'The Highland Estate of a Scottish Gentleman,' " said Alex, reading the elegantly penned description along the lower edge, " 'as Described from the North.' Nary a word about it being Creignish, though."

"But it *is!*" cried Cora frantically. "Look, here, I can tell you which chambers lie behind every one of these casements, and how the mists will rise from the river here to make the stones wet, and—"

"Hush now, sweetheart, hush," soothed Alex. "I wasn't doubting you, only reading the legend, that's all."

"It's only because Father's dead," she said, fighting her panic. "If he were still alive, then it would say his name as master of Creignish, instead of a 'Scottish Gentleman.'"

"Is there a difficulty, miss?" asked Mr. Bushell hurriedly, drawn back by her outburst. "Pray, if there is anything I can remedy—"

"Not a thing," said Alex easily. He slid the print of Creignish across the counter. "But I believe we'll take this one, too, for the lady, along with the ostrich. No, let's take two of the ostrich, in case the kit grows hungry again."

The shopkeeper bowed, with one last suspicious glance at Starlight. "Excellent choices, sir. Let me wrap these for you, sir, I'll return in a moment with your reckoning."

Cora stared at Alex, overwhelmed. From the night she'd left home, she'd been urged to forget her past. Yet Alex wanted her to remember it, so much so that he was buying this print of Creignish. For that she'd forgive him his earlier doubts, and she'd forgive him teasing her about the bawdy print, too. How could she not when he'd do such a wondrous thing for her?

But oh, what would she do when he was gone?

"Forgive me for being bold, sir," interrupted a slight young man with dark, lively eyes and a turned-up nose. "But does the lady have an interest in things Scottish?"

Instantly Alex's face hardened, and he moved to shield Cora from the young man and from his question. "The lady's interests are of no concern to you."

He spoke in a tone that, to Cora, offered no encouragement and less invitation. But the young man persisted, tugging off his red woolen cap as he inched around Alex to better speak directly to Cora.

"But the lady's interests could very well become my concern, sir," he said, smiling winningly at Cora, "and my concerns her interest as well."

"Ah, so you have met our Mr. Curlew?" said Mr. Bushell, returning with the wrapped prints and reckoning. "Mr. Curlew is our resident genius, you know, with his chamber above stairs to facilitate the timeliness of topical subjects. He is the author of so many of our most popular prints."

" 'The Lady Challenges the Wit, or A Candlelight Conversation between True Rivals,' that's mine," said Curlew with considerable pride. " 'The Most Secret Pact between the Devil and the Duchess of R.' That was mine, too."

Uneasily Cora thought of the soldier and the milkmaid, hoping that wasn't one he'd claim as well. "You are an artist, then?"

The young man bowed grandly with an actor's flourish over his ink-stained leather apron. "Jacob Curlew, your servant in all things, miss. I am not like other gallants, miss, for I desire neither your person nor your virtue but merely your phiz, your face, to preserve for all time."

Mr. Bushell clapped his hands and beamed with delight. "Ah, miss, how many ladies would weep with joy to hear such a request! To have Mr. Curlew conceive an admiration for your face! You must honor his request, miss, you must not deny his talent!"

"She can deny anything she damned well pleases,"

scoffed Alex, taking Cora by the arm to lead her from the shop. "Ladies don't have their faces posted in shop windows for all the world to ogle. Come along, sweetheart."

"Not as herself, sir, oh, no," agreed Curlew quickly. "Not with her own name beneath. I'd never ask that of a lady. Only the actresses wish it, seeing as it helps them in their trade to be known. When I portray a lady, it's as a muse or goddess or other some such."

Reluctantly Cora shook her head. As flattering as the artist's interest was, having her picture in this shop would be far too dangerous.

"Oh, pray consider, miss!" cried Curlew. "Olympus has been overdone of late, and the public thirsts for variety. Instead I'd draw you as Caledonia. I thought it the moment I spied you, miss, and it fair shouted out to me. There's my Caledonia, I thought at once. Brave, beautiful Caledonia, even in defeat!"

"That would sell wonderfully well," agreed Mr. Bushell eagerly, "especially with a bit of sentimental poesy printed beneath. There's such an interest, such a sympathy that way lately. Tastes will change as swift as politics. Once I could sell scores of Cumberland as the brave and valiant prince, and now that he's fallen from favor with the people, I cannot keep a one in the shop for fear of criticism. Oh, yes, a new Caledonia would do well indeed."

"Then you can sell your wretched Cala-nothing without this lady's help," said Alex firmly. "High time we were on our way, lass."

"A sketch, then, miss?" pleaded Curlew. "For myself alone? A half an hour sitting, that is all?"

Cora hesitated. Even though the drawing would

never become a published print, she liked the idea of personifying Caledonia. Let the London ladies be Venus or Hera; she'd be the symbol of her own Highlands. "Very well," she said slowly, "and only if you promise it will go no further."

"You have my word!" cried Curlew, twisting his knitted cap in his hands in eager anticipation. "I promise to be swift in my work, to capture your essence in as little time as possible, miss, ah, oh, I do not believe I caught your name?"

"Because she didn't tell it," said Alex sharply. "Lass, are you sure of this?"

"Yes," she said shyly. "I know it seems vain, but I would rather like to do it, Alex. And it's only a half an hour."

How could he refuse her, the least vain woman in the world? At least she had sense enough not to tell the little weasel of an artist her name, thought Alex glumly as he followed them up the narrow stairs at the back of the shop, up to the Curlew's chamber—a chamber that Alex half-suspected was used for more nefarious purposes.

But though there was an unmade cot and a trunk of clothing in one corner, the room was definitely first and foremost a studio. Light streamed in over the neighboring rooftops through the uncurtained windows, and battered plaster casts of famous statues stood as grubby, ghostly sentinels. Fresh-pulled prints, creamy white and midnight black, hung to dry like laundry, while the dark stains that mottled the floorboards told of countless inky mishaps.

Clearly Curlew was the artist as he'd claimed, and grudgingly Alex conceded that to him.

He wasn't inclined to concede much else. Because

Alex himself had always been a man of deeds rather than thoughts, he wasn't comfortable around others who instead sat about and depended on their wits for their livelihood—artists and musicians, teachers and writers and lawyers—and he never quite knew what to say that wouldn't make him sound like a thick-headed dolt.

He watched Curlew help Cora to a shallow platform that served as a kind of stage, and listened to them earnestly discuss how she should stand and hold her head, referring to other artists and paintings that he'd never heard of. Before this, he'd believed that he and Cora were much alike, companionably so. But seeing her now with Curlew made him wonder if he really knew her at all. Would she have snapped at him before if he'd known more about pictures, like Curlew, or if he'd known that Caledonia was some dead old Roman's way of saying Scotland?

He thought of the print of the house that Cora said was Creignish. From the way that she had spoken about her home, he'd been imagining a good-sized gentleman's house in Massachusetts, something similar to his own family's on the hill overlooking Appledore. But this Creignish had turned out to be larger and grander than any house he could name in Boston, let alone humble Appledore.

Hell, he thought gloomily, the entire town of Appledore could fit into the front hall of Creignish, with whistling room to spare for the wind. She'd never acted the fine lady to him, and she'd never complained about wearing hand-me-downs or sleeping up under the eaves among the servants, yet now it seemed she'd been born to a station far above his own. The more he thought of him and Cora, the less it now seemed that they had in common. He could worry all he wished about appearing a dolt: the most doltish thing he'd ever done was to fancy a bond existed between him and Cora MacGillivray, and that she fancied him as much as he did her.

And, perversely, the more he realized he'd never have her, the more dear she became in his eyes.

"You wish me to turn my head this way, toward the window?" she was asking, fussing with an old coverlet that was serving as a cape around her shoulders. "I've only sat for an artist once, you know, years and years ago, when I was scarce more than a child, and I wish to do it properly now. Oh, Starlight, hush. If you don't behave, I shall have to put you down."

Obviously something about the coverlet cape didn't smell quite right to Starlight, and for the first time since he'd eaten the ostrich he was wide awake, sniffing suspiciously and growling at the coverlet as he clawed his way higher along Cora's shoulder.

"You're a wicked cat boy, that's what you are," Cora scolded, and with an impatient sigh she lifted him free and held him out, claws and legs outstretched, toward Alex. "Here, Alex, you mind him. He always calms with you, especially after he's been naughty with me."

Dutifully Alex reached for the little cat. So much for being a dashing ballad hero; here was the final indignity, his pistols and sword idle and useless while he played nursemaid to his lady's kitten. At least he and Starlight could commiserate about becoming wretched inconveniences before the glory of Art.

But Curlew was disappointed. "Oh, but I did like that pose! The cat was to represent an orphaned babe in arms, you know. He presented a most poignant element to the composition."

"If you are quite set upon it," said Cora reluctantly. "Perhaps if you offer him a saucer of milk, he will be more agreeable."

Milk was ordered, and miraculously produced, and swiftly lapped up while Curlew prepared his paper.

"You're not finding this too tedious, Alex?" asked Cora anxiously. She stood on the edge of the platform in her stocking feet—apparently Curlew's vision of Caledonia excluded shoes—with her hair curling loose over the makeshift coverlet cape, altogether too charming, in Alex's eyes, to represent a vanquished country. "You're not too terribly bored?"

"Not at all," lied Alex, striving to be understanding and noble. "As long as you feel this is, ah, right for you to do."

"Only a half an hour," she promised, leaning forward to kiss him, so quickly he barely realized she'd done it, but more than enough to reassure him. She wouldn't have offered that to just any old dolt, he thought wryly, but he couldn't deny that the kiss did improve his mood.

But what the hell was he supposed to do next? Pack Cora off into a coach for the Highlands, and wave a cheerful farewell as she rode off to a country that, while no longer filled with violence, certainly could offer its share of uncertainty for a penniless, homeless young woman?

He reminded himself how she wasn't really his responsibility, not the way that, say, Diana was. She wasn't family, and she wasn't from Appledore, and besides, hadn't he sworn he wouldn't be like his father and let himself get so woefully entangled in other people's affairs?

But he'd only done as much as he had for Cora because she'd been so obviously in need of a friend. That wasn't the same as being entangled, was it? He also liked her. Aye, that was the tricky part, wasn't it? He liked her, liked her so well that he was having a very hard time thinking about clearing London for home and leaving her behind. In the beginning, all he'd set out to do was to amuse himself and make her happy. So why, then, didn't he now feel happier himself?

He was thinking about this together with that sudden, sweet kiss she'd given him as he watched her fussing with the kitten. Eventually the furry babe in arms, now docile with a belly full of milk, was loosely swaddled in a length of cloth to hide his tail and claws. Only his small whiskered face—a thoroughly humiliated face, thought Alex—was permitted to peer out from his impromptu hood while Cora cradled him against her shoulder.

Yet still Curlew wasn't satisfied. "Your expression, miss. You're stiff and unfeeling as a marble statue, without betraying any emotions at all. Cannot you compose your features into a more tragic cast? Something a hair more wretched?"

"I'm not an actress, you know," said Cora plaintively, to which Alex offered a silent, heartfelt *amen*. "How can I feel wretched when I'm standing up here like a porcelain vase on a stand?"

Curlew sighed, and turned to appeal to Alex. "Perhaps if you spoke to her, sir?" he pleaded. "Distracted her, sir, and lifted her mind from the labor of posing?"

"I can try." Alex came to stand where Cora, with

her head dramatically twisted over one shoulder to display her profile, would be able to see him. She smiled hopefully, and Curlew squawked.

"No, no, no smiles," he ordered. "You are conquered, you are grieving! Sir, speak to her only of serious, somber matters, if you please."

"Serious and somber, aye." Alex cleared his throat, realizing how damned near impossible it was to converse on command, especially with an audience. "You tell me, Cora. What should I say to you that's sufficiently serious?"

"You don't have to say anything, Alex," she answered. "It's what you did, buying that print for me downstairs. *That* was serious enough."

"How could I have done otherwise, eh?" he asked gruffly. "Who else should have had it but you?"

Who else, indeed? Though Cora wasn't smiling as she'd been ordered, her expression had softened as she looked at him, so unmistakably full of affection for him—for *him*—that he couldn't help but grin in return. Alex wasn't sure if this was what Curlew had wanted, but it sure as hell pleased him.

"The house lies to the southeast of Inverness, two days' journey when the weather is fair and the paths are dry," she said softly, so Curlew couldn't hear. "On the largest bend in the Findhorn River. That was what you asked me earlier, wasn't it?"

"That should make it easy enough to find," he answered softly, "especially a house like that."

She smiled sadly, and nodded. "Everyone from Edinburgh north knows Creignish, and the tale behind it. It wasn't always so grand, you know. Father had first loved a beautiful girl he'd met on a visit to Bath, the only daughter of an impoverished viscount. But because she was from the lowlands and he was a Jacobite Scot, neither family would approve the match."

Though Alex had been the one ordered to speak, he was now the one listening to her spin a story that had obviously been polished by retelling. In his family, the past was seldom mentioned and the intangible future considered far more interesting, but for Cora the past had become a treasured legend because, in many ways, it was all she had left. Her voice now carried the gentle lilt of her homeland while her face seemed to glow as if lit by a candle from within, her eyes misty as she looked back to far happier times.

"Brokenhearted, Father wed instead the lady his brother suggested," she continued, "a plain-faced, plainspoken heiress from Glasgow who was no more happy with the marriage than he. They'd nothing in common, you see, and they began to improve Creignish because it was the one thing they could agree upon. Soon the house became their shared passion, the passion that joined them, finally, in love. He forgot the first lady from the lowlands. She forgot her gay life in Glasgow. Their home was built with love, and love filled their home, the home they'd made together."

"Yet the poor lady died giving birth to their daughter," said Alex softly.

"Aye," said Cora, more with regret now than sadness. "But her husband never ceased building and refurbishing, a testimony to his wife and their love that would survive beyond them."

"Splendid!" cried Curlew, jumping up from his stool to dance a quick jig of joy. "We are done, miss, we are done, and such a marvel you have given me!

No actress, hah. You, miss, rival the best of Drury Lane. Such pathos! Such a poignant air! Ah, if you would only let me share it with the world!"

He turned the paper for Alex and Cora to see, and Alex whistled low. Curlew had captured Cora, the sweet, sorrowing wistfulness that wasn't like anyone else, and immediately Alex could imagine the drawing framed in his cabin. "How much will you take for it, Curlew?"

Curlew smiled expansively. "I can make you a copy, sir, ready the day after tomorrow. And because of the pleasure I've found doing it, I shall charge you the barest pittance."

Alex doubted that, but he wanted the picture too badly to argue before Cora. "In two days, then, and mind no one else sees it. Now time we were on our way, pet, and quickly."

Yet though the driver of the next hackney drove faster and with more adeptness through the crowded streets, to Alex the ride still had an odd, otherworldly quality to it. This time he and Cora gave up the entire facing seat to Starlight, and chose to ride side by side, her head resting on his shoulder and her fingers linked loosely into his. How could it be that in the course of one day this same woman could be capable of driving him nearly mad with lust, and then bringing him close to unmanly tears with tales of her lost family? Now they spoke little, but the silence between them was peaceful, so much so that several times Alex suspected Cora had fallen asleep.

But she wasn't sleeping, not entirely. She was thinking, too.

"I never would have done that a fortnight ago," she said drowsily. "You've helped make me brave, you know, and that has made me feel free to dare to do, oh, such things!"

"You were already brave, lass," he said. "I didn't have anything to do with that."

"Oh, yes, you did, Alex," she said with complete conviction. "You *did*. Now that you've come, I'm an entirely different Cora than the one cowering up beneath Lady Waldegrave's roof."

She sighed contentedly, burrowing her cheek into his shoulder, but Alex himself was anything but content. He'd never have a better opening to tell her the cold truth, that he'd met her entirely by accident, not design, that he wasn't her hero, and that he'd neither time nor intention to go traipsing across Scotland with her to a house that had ceased to be her home.

He should have told her all of this, and been truly as brave and honorable as she believed he was. Yet instead he sat silent like the greatest coward in the world, and watched the little kitten yawn and stretch his paws against the wrapped print of the Highland estate of a Scottish gentleman.

And the lost paradise of one slight, beautiful, impossibly brave Scottish lady.

13

Cora stood in her room in her nightrail, her face washed and her hair braided for the night, the sheets of her bed turned back and waiting, and Starlight giving himself one final bath on the coverlet. The rest of the house was quiet and dark, and once again she'd be the last one to bed.

In a few minutes she would sleep, too, but now she'd one last thing to do, one last obligation to perform. She'd put it off all afternoon and evening, letting it nag at and fester in her conscience, and now, at last, she knew she couldn't wait any longer.

What if she'd been wrong? What if she'd imagined it all or let her imagination concoct a vision of what she'd wished to see rather than what actually was there?

With the forbidden tartan screen around her shoulders for courage, she gulped a deep breath and tore away the rough paper covering the print Alex had bought this afternoon.

Her gulp became a sigh of longing and joy as she carefully propped the print on the table beside her bed. It was Creignish in all the detail she'd remembered and some that she'd traitorously forgotten. She bent closer, hungrily studying it as if the house were a long-lost friend, and in a way it was.

"Oh, Starlight," she whispered to the kitten on the bed. "Do you think Alex knew? In all the prints in Mr. Bushell's shop, how would I have discovered this one without his help?"

In return the kitten mewed, all the opinion he could offer, and Cora gathered him up from the bed into her arms, holding him again as she'd held him while she'd posed this afternoon.

"I think he did know, my handsome kit," she whispered into the fur on the top of his head as she gazed at the print. "He pretended he didn't, of course, because he is so good and modest. First he gave me Creignish like this, paper and ink, and next he will take me to the real one."

"Cora?"

She turned quickly with Starlight in her arms, not certain she'd heard her name whispered. No one else was awake, and certainly no one would come up here to her room at this hour.

"Cora?" came the whisper again, and then, to her horror, the door began to inch open. It was too late to wonder why she'd neglected to latch the door, but if she'd any of her wits about her, she should have hidden the kitten under the bed and shoved the shawl beneath the sheets, or at the very least tossed the wrapping back over the print to hide it. But instead she stood frozen in place like a deer in the lantern's light, watching the door open wider and wider.

"Cora?" came the whisper again, and now, finally, the whisper was attached to Diana's wary face peeking through the opening. "Is this your room? I wasn't sure, you know. What a cunning little rookery you have! Might I come in?"

Because she was Alex's sister, Cora wouldn't turn her away. But the difference between what Alex knew of her and what Diana did was a vast one indeed. Cora liked Diana as much as her limited experience with friends would allow her, but she hardly knew her well enough to trust her with the number of guilty secrets now on display by the light of a single candlestick.

But to Diana, there was only one that mattered.

"You have Blackie!" she cried, rushing toward Cora with her hands out to take the cat. "Oh, Cora, you have my darling little kit!"

But Cora shrank back, shielding the kitten with both hands. "He's not yours, Diana. You . . . you must be mistaken. I know Alex believed he was yours, too, but he's mine, and has been since I found him in the garden. And he's a secret, Diana, a secret you must swear to keep, for if Lady Waldegrave learns he's here, she'll have him taken away and tossed into the street!"

Diana frowned, letting her arms drop to her sides. She, too, was dressed for bed, with her nightrail covered by a loose yellow silk dressing gown patterned with blue roses that fluttered gracefully around her as she moved.

"But I recognize him, Cora," she insisted. "His little face with the white star, his paws with all those toes—he's my Blackie, no mistake. The old woman near the tavern had a basket with the whole litter, and he was the one I picked. Or rather, he picked me."

"Then let him choose again," said Cora. Quickly, before she changed her mind, she walked to the center of the room and set the kitten gently on the floor. He looked up at her, perplexed, but she hardened her heart and walked back to Diana's side.

"There," she said, tucking her hands inside her tartan. "We'll neither of us call or beckon. We'll just stand here, and let him come to whichever one he pleases."

But as she stood there, watching him look first at her and then to Diana, she wasn't nearly as convinced as she'd sounded. If she'd been a cat herself, she'd probably have gone to Diana simply based on appearance. With her thick black hair, still crimped from the evening, her clear skin and blue eyes, Diana looked as lush and welcoming as the first rose of summer, while Cora . . . Cora could picture herself well enough, her reddish hair braided tightly back from her freckled face, the rough wool tartan pulled snug over her shoulders, every bit as severe as the rough-hewn land she'd come from.

Remember who has fed you, Starlight, she urged silently, *and petted you, and given you a much nicer name than Blackie, and taken you to play in the garden!*

And remember Starlight did. He rose to his paws, blinked, and trotted directly to Cora, ducking beneath the hem of her night rail to butt his head against her bare ankle.

"You must have called him in some way," grumbled Diana. "There had to be some reason he went to you so quickly."

Cora scarcely managed to keep her triumph—and her relief—to herself. "Then we shall do it again," she said, returning Starlight to the center of the room, "and this time, so you're quite sure I'm not influencing him, I'll stand farther away, over here."

Diana nodded in agreement, but the results were the same, and Starlight again headed straight to Cora.

"Wicked little beast." Diana sighed with resignation, and dropped onto Cora's bed in a soft rustle of silk, tucking her feet up beneath her. "I'll grant he's yours, but I cannot fathom how it came to pass. Unless, of course, my wretched brother meddled somehow."

Cora flushed, thinking how that was exactly what Alex had done.

"Would you like to hold him?" she asked, holding the kitten out to Diana as a way of changing the subject. "You do recall how much he likes to be petted."

"Oh, yes, and what male doesn't?" said Diana wryly as she took the cat into her lap, letting him settle and stomp a nest against her leg without a care for what those tiny claws were doing to the yellow silk of her dressing gown. "What a sweet, wicked little beast you are, Black—no, what was it you called him, Cora?"

"Starlight," she said, beaming like any proud mama. "On account of the white star on his forehead."

"Starlight, then." Diana scratched him behind his ears. "Very well, Master Starlight. I must thank you for your efforts on my behalf, for you've given me a quite perfect gentleman in my Lord Roxby, just like the old woman said you would."

"Lord Roxby?" asked Cora, duly noting the implicit familiarity. "Is that the marquess? The one who collects the Roman intaglios?"

"The Marquess of Roxby, Earl of Ashburnham, Baron Knowles." Diana smiled proudly over the cat's head. "He truly is quite perfect, Cora. I couldn't improve upon him if I'd invented him myself. I would never have met anyone like him in the colonies. He's handsome and charming and he's not old at all, only twenty-eight, even though he's already come into his title. And he's perfectly mannered, Cora, a true, true gentleman. Why, he respects me so much he hasn't once dared to try to kiss me, even though he's had several opportunities!"

Again Cora was thankful that the single candle wouldn't show her blush. Whenever she and Alex found opportunities alone, they'd made instant and exciting use of them. But she'd never regarded this as a lack of respect, any more than she could imagine Alex stammering over asking for much of anything.

"I do believe he's the one for me, Cora," said Diana softly. "I cannot count how many men I've considered and had consider me—I am, after all, nearly twenty-one, which is so monstrously old you must swear never to tell a soul—and yet Lord Roxby is the only one who's ever made me feel like this. He's the one, Cora, I'm sure of it."

Cora smiled, though her thoughts and heart were racing with confusion. How strange to hear Diana use that phrase, for that was how she'd always thought of Alex, as "the one," the man who'd come to rescue her, lead her, help her find her way back home. She'd never considered it in the way that Diana evidently did, as the single man in the world destined to be her husband. In the depths of her grief after she'd left Scotland, she'd put aside any notion of marrying, despite Lady Waldegrave's matchmaking offers, and she certainly hadn't looked at Alex as a potential husband, any more than he would have contemplated her as his wife.

Yet what if that *had* been what her father had intended? That the man she must wait for would not only deserve her trust, but earn her love as well? Father had spoken often of seeing her happily wed, of her finding a man she'd love as much as he'd loved her mother. He'd wanted to see Creignish filled with grandchildren, and though he'd never forced the matter, he'd been quietly disappointed that she'd never attracted any interest from the young men in their clan.

She'd never dared to have such bold dreams before, and she couldn't afford to do it now. Hadn't Alex told her this very day he was leaving for his own home even sooner than he'd planned? He'd never once mentioned love to her, and she hadn't expected it. And there certainly had been no hint of the kind of lasting, wedded love that her father had wanted for her.

"Aren't you happy for me?" asked Diana wistfully. "Lady Waldegrave treats it all like a grand game, and Alex is too protective to ever approve of any gentleman I like. You're the only friend in London I have to share this with, Cora."

"Oh, Diana, of course I'm happy for you!" cried Cora, genuinely sorry she'd become so preoccupied with her own thoughts that she'd forgotten Diana's news. "Though he's the fortunate one, you know, to win a prize like you."

Diana smiled with surprising shyness. "That is what he says, too."

"And he's right," declared Cora, sitting beside her on the bed. "But where shall you live if—*if,* if, if—you wed him? Will he go back to Appledore with you?"

"To Appledore?" Diana laughed, but to Cora's ears there was a hollow ring to it. "If I wed Lord Roxby, I doubt I'll ever go back to Massachusetts. He'd have no wish to go, I know that, and my place would be to stay with him. It would be the same with any man, Cora, and I'm quite resigned. The woman must always be the one who accommodates herself to the gentleman's wishes."

Cora thought of how fondly Alex spoke of Appledore, and how close the Fairbournes seemed to be, and she couldn't imagine Diana feeling any less strongly about their home.

"But what of your parents?" she asked, thinking of how she'd willingly cross the ocean a dozen times if she could see her own parents again.

"My mother will understand," said Diana softly, "for she left her own past behind when she fell in love with my father. She's never once been back to Ireland in nearly thirty years. She says to find happiness a woman must follow her love, and she's proof enough that I should believe her."

While at first it struck Cora as strange that Alex had never mentioned his mother was Irish, the more she considered it, the less strange it seemed. His mother had been so completely absorbed into his father's world that to Alex her previous life had virtually ceased to exist, and certainly to matter.

But though Diana seemed willing to follow her mother's example, Cora wasn't. To forget the legacy of her clan and her parents, to abandon Creignish forever for the sake of a single man, even a man as fine as Alex—could any love be worth making such a sacrifice?

"But what about you, Cora?" asked Diana, deliberately lightening her tone to be more playful as she stroked the purring kitten. "If you are Starlight's mistress, then what lover has he found for you?"

"For me?" Cora laughed self-consciously, praying that Diana hadn't been reading her thoughts. "And where, pray, would my poor little kit begin to look?

I'm not beautiful like you, Diana. I've never had a score of adoring gentlemen gathered in a flock around me, nor, truly, would I know what to do with them if I did."

"You don't need a flock," said Diana coyly. "Only one. And I'd rather thought my brother seemed interested. Alex is worth every last one of your mythical 'flock' combined. If there'd been another like him in Appledore, I would have gathered him up for my own long ago!"

"Now you do sound like the countess, seeing ripe bachelors hanging like apples from the trees," said Cora defensively. "And I rather think your brother isn't the kind agreeable to being 'gathered up,' nor do I see myself as a gatherer."

"Oh, Cora, I *saw* how my brother looked at you on the *Calliope,* and I—what's that?"

Instantly Cora held a finger over her lips to warn Diana to be silent, and both of them froze, wide-eyed, listening.

"Miss?" came the muffled whisper again from the other side of the door. "Miss, do you be awake?"

Cora hurried across the room and cracked the door to peek into the hallway.

"Hurry, miss, you must come," whispered the maidservant, her mobcap pulled low over her sleepy eyes. "It's her ladyship, miss, callin' and callin' for you something dreadful."

"Tell her I'll be there directly, Mary," said Cora, and swiftly closed the door again before she could see Diana. She tore the shawl from her shoulders, folded it, and lifted the corner of the mattress to tuck the tartan back into hiding.

"I must go to her now, Diana," she explained hurriedly, "though if you wish to stay here with the kit you may. There's no telling when I'll be back."

"Oh, at last you are here!" cried the countess plaintively from the bed as soon as Cora stepped into the room. With her painted cheeks wiped clean and her jewels and wig put away for the night, Lady Waldegrave looked older, sadder, her shadow-ringed eyes haunted by old regrets and new fears. She sat propped up by a feather-filled mountain of pillows and bolsters, the sheets tossed about and the curtains of the bed haphazardly thrown open, all sure signs to Cora that the countess was having trouble falling asleep.

"I came as soon as Mary called me, my lady," she said, reaching out to smooth the coverlet back over the older woman's knees. "Would you like me to read to you to help you sleep?"

"No, no, that's not why I wanted you, Cora," said the countess querulously, making nervous little pleats in the edge of the bedsheet with her fingers. "Though I do wish I'd had you here earlier when I put away my things for the night. Mary is so clumsy and slow and common, not like you at all. But I've come home so late with Diana that I've tried not to rouse you. I've tried to make do, Cora, I've tried, truly."

"But why, my lady?" murmured Cora, tucking another pillow behind the countess' head. "You know I'll always come if you need me."

"You've looked so unlike yourself lately, Cora, that I thought it best to let you sleep." The older woman sighed restlessly, and shook her head, the laced ruffles on her bed cap trembling. "You haven't been well. I could see that. Flushed, feverish, forgetful—if I hadn't been so occupied with Diana, I should have taken you to be bled to settle your humors. And if I had—taken care with you, that is—then perhaps I wouldn't have had that dream."

Cora paused uneasily. She didn't like dreams, and for a good reason, too. Despite her father's learning, he had been as superstitious as any pagan, and a great believer in the messages and warnings that came to him while he slept. He'd claimed it was a dream predicting his own death at Culloden that had brought him back to Creignish that last time, only long enough to say farewell. "The dream, my lady?"

"Yes, yes!" cried the countess anxiously, clutching at Cora's hand to draw her closer. "It was as clear as life itself. I had been careless with you, and somehow you'd been carried back to Creignish."

"In a dream, that's where I *would* be," said Cora gently. She went to the cupboard to find the powder that the apothecary had given to the countess to help her sleep, and measured and stirred a small amount into the glass of water beside her bed. "I often imagine myself there, too."

Lady Waldegrave nodded eagerly as she took the glass, sipping at the water. "Then that's doubtless why I saw you there, too, walking beside the river. In the beginning, everything was peaceful and golden green, the exact way your dear father described it. But then suddenly you were in a kind of sailboat on a river, and the sky turned black with clouds and the wind began to blow and blow."

"It was only a dream, my lady," said Cora, trying to calm her even as her own uneasiness built. Lady Waldegrave had never mentioned Creignish before except to tell Cora not to speak of it. So why, then, was she dreaming of it now, and in such a nightmarish way?

"But it seemed so vastly real, Cora!" cried the countess. "I kept running along the shore, trying to call you back, but you couldn't hear me on account of the wind. And then the sail shifted, and I saw you weren't alone, but with that dreadful pirate brother of Diana's, and you were weeping because he was taking you away into the black clouds and the storm and—"

"Hush, my lady, you're awake now," said Cora as firmly as she could. She'd found it unsettling enough that the countess had dreamed of Creignish, but now to have added Alex carrying her off in a sailboat was infinitely more disturbing. Why were they all at Creignish, anyway? Was the little sailboat supposed to be the *Calliope?* But Alex would never make her weep, let alone appear in the middle of a storm to carry her off to—off to where?

"It was only a dream, my lady," she said, pushing away her own fears. She'd be wrong to place too much stock in her ladyship's ramblings, especially now, when the sleeping powders were likely already taking effect. "I'm here with you now, and I'm perfectly safe. You see? How could I be holding your hand otherwise?"

"But it was so real, Cora," protested the countess in a quavering whisper. "I was so sure I was going to lose you like that, even after I'd promised your dear father to keep you safe. But I'll make it up to him, and to you, Cora. In the autumn we'll go to Italy, to Rome, to Florence, and I'll show you all the places your father liked best. Naples! How Iain did love Naples, and the grotto there!"

In her urgency to speak, she was clutching at Cora's hand so tightly that her bony fingers were leaving red marks. "I'll show Naples to you, too, Cora," she whispered fiercely, "and I'll keep you safe from that pirate who made you cry. He'll never hurt you, I promise."

"But Alex never has made me cry, my lady," protested Cora without thinking, "nor is he a pirate."

"Alex!" The countess' eyes grew round with distress beneath the ruffled cap, and her upper lip quivered. "*Alex?* You would call a man like that by his Christian name? You would dare show such familiarity with a rogue determined to kidnap you!"

"My lady, he has never—"

"In my dream he had pistols in his belt and a sword in his hand, while with his other he held you tight about the waist!" There were tears in the countess' eyes, tears of sorrow and fear from what she'd seen in the dream. "He had taken you away by force, Cora, else why would you weep? From your home, from me, away to your ruin beneath a black sky of shame! What other explanation can there be?"

With a start Cora remembered these same weapons scattered so carelessly around the captain's cabin on board the *Calliope*. But they would be part of a privateer's trade, not necessarily any indication of his personality, or any special portent of the future in Lady Waldegrave's dream.

Yet hadn't her father dreamed of guns and swords before his death, and claimed to see his own end with the same clarity that the countess now had seen Cora's? What of the boat on the river, and her tears, and the black sky of shame? What had she and Alex done to deserve that, even in a dream?

Or what would they do?

"Oh, my lady," she said, guilt and confusion rushing her words. "Please, it was only a dream! I never meant to bring you—"

"Please, Cora, please, *please*," gasped the countess, and with a deep sigh she sank heavily back against the pillows, her eyelids fluttering shut.

"My lady!" Swiftly Cora leaned close, chaffing the countess' hands. She'd never seen the powder work this fast, but then she'd never seen Lady Waldegrave so agitated over a dream, either. "My lady, tell me, please! Are you unwell? Do you wish me to send Junius for Dr. Wiley?"

With another sigh, this one almost a groan, the countess' eyes flickered open.

"I will save you, Cora," she breathed faintly. "Don't be afraid. He . . . he won't hurt you. Now let . . . me sleep."

And with no other choice, Cora did.

But she sat by the bed and held the countess' hand long after her fingers had relaxed and her breathing had turned slow and regular. She sat until the tapers in the candlestands had guttered out, and the first light of dawn had begun to brighten the sky outside the heavy curtains of her ladyship's bedchamber. From the garden she heard the first cheerful chirps of the London sparrows, and the early carts rumbling sleepily through the streets to begin their deliveries. The new dawn brightened into full day, the sunlight a glowing strip that outlined the drawn curtains.

Yet still Cora sat beside the sleeping countess, with only her fears and her conscience for company. Though her back ached with weariness, she kept it straight and fought back the sleep that tried to claim her, and all for the simple reason that if she didn't sleep, she wouldn't dream.

And dear Lord, she'd enough of dreams to last the rest of her life.

"Within a fortnight, then, Sir Thomas," said Alex, waving aside the maidservant hovering with the silver teapot. "I'd not expected your affairs to settle themselves so quickly."

"Nor I, Alex." Sir Thomas smiled pleasantly, setting his own empty saucer down beside the cup for the girl to clear away. "But I've every assurance that it's so. I expect the last piece of evidence being gathered to arrive any day now, and then my, ah, contacts in the government assure me the final documents will be signed at once. Occasionally, good fortune does smile down upon us, even where government ministers are concerned."

He chuckled drolly, pleased with himself and good fortune, and Alex couldn't help smiling back. The man was the worst kind of crooked old rogue, but in these last weeks, over tea or chocolate in the morning, he'd actually grown almost fond of him. He still didn't trust him, of course—he wasn't as great a fool as that—but he did appreciate the way the man could charm the apples from a tree while conniving to steal the very bark from its trunk, and beaming benignly the entire time.

"If there's anything I can do to help with the paper gathering, Sir Thomas," he said, "you know I'm at your complete service."

Sir Thomas leaned forward, lowering his voice confidentially though the two of them sat alone in his great echoing sitting room. "It's actually not a paper being gathered, Alex, but an individual who has proved most slippery and cunning to find."

"Then you must let me help!" offered Alex again, eager for the challenge. With his head—and heart, if he were honest—so uncertain over what was happening with Cora, the idea of a simple, achievable task like this seemed endlessly appealing. "I've chased ships across hundreds of miles of empty ocean. Finding some poor braggart here in Britain couldn't be harder than that."

But Sir Thomas only shook his head. "Ah, I know, I know, the thrill of the hunt," he said with a sigh. "I'd be after the creature myself if I were your age. But I've heard from my people that the hunting is done, and it's only a matter of bearing evidence now, the sort of dry, dull work left to the legal monkeys."

Alex's smile turned polite as he pushed back his chair to leave. According to his father, Sir Thomas had always been more inclined to direct others than do much for himself, and regardless of his age, the only thing he'd be likely to chase would be petticoats. Still, Alex was thankful that Sir Thomas had done whatever ordering needed doing so he could sail with the debt paid and the money in the *Calliope's* strongbox.

"Here, Alex, I've something for you before you go." Sir Thomas held out a folded, sealed note. "You've devoted so much of your sojourn here in London to me and my affairs that you've scarce had time to amuse yourself. Give this letter to the greeter at King's Theatre in Haymarket tonight and you shall have my box as your own. I've put your name in the appointment book for tonight, for David Garrick and Hannah Pritchard in *The Suspicious Husband*. Garrick's become vastly popular—though I must say I still crown old Quin as king of players—and Mrs. Pritchard is a cunning little morsel herself. Go on, I mean for you to enjoy yourself! Free your sister from Witch Waldegrave's clutches, and take her with you."

He was right about taking Diana. Alex had hardly spent five minutes alone with her since she'd traded his care for that of the countess, and now the days he'd have left in London were dwindling to a precious few. Leaving Diana behind as she wished was going to leave an enormous hole in their Appledore family, and his pleasure in returning home would be forever tempered by her absence.

And Diana would love to see a play. The theater had been one of the things she'd anticipated most about London, and even Alex had heard of David Garrick's new, more natural manner of acting. Walking down the street outside Sir Thomas' house, he was happily imagining his sister's enthusiasm and delight when he bumped into a ragged old soldier.

"Beg pardon, gov'nor," the man muttered, stumbling unsteadily away from Alex, while tugging on the front of his hat in a show of deference that also managed to hide his face. "Meant no harm, gov'nor."

"None caused, sir, nor taken," said Alex, reaching out to take the man's arm to steady him. He couldn't fault the man for backing away—battle scars like the one that had obviously claimed his eye beneath that soiled red kerchief were sights that made most civilians recoil with horrified disgust, even as they enjoyed the freedom such soldiers had won for them. Surreptitiously he slipped a coin into the man's pocket, and patted him gently on the shoulder. "You take care of yourself now, sir. This city's full of rascals and thieves."

The man muttered something Alex didn't catch, and reeled off down the street, his shoulders hunched and his head down. Alex sadly watched him go. Whoever he was, or had been, he'd no place now in an elegant neighborhood like Cavendish Square, and if he wasn't careful he'd be taken up as a nuisance by a constable from the parish.

But the one-eyed old soldier was as careful about avoiding parish constables as he was crafty about appearing as a pitiable beggar, and he knew exactly what he was doing in Cavendish Square.

"Deadmarsh!" exclaimed Sir Thomas as soon as he saw the man waiting for him in the hallway, with a footman hovering suspiciously to make sure he didn't steal anything. "What the devil are you doing here? I thought I'd made it clear that you were never to come to my—"

"The girl's alive, milord," interrupted Deadmarsh, "and she's here in London."

"Blast it, man, hold your tongue!" Sir Thomas dismissed the disappointed footman with a curt wave of his hand, and lowered his own voice before he spoke again. "You must be mistaken, Deadmarsh. You were sent to Scotland to prove the chit was dead, not tell me she's here in London."

" 'Tis no tale, milord." Grimly Deadmarsh pulled a creamy white paper from his coat, unfolding the thick folds before he held it out to Sir Thomas. "There she is, milord; no mistake. I spied it first on Monday in an Edinburgh tavern, but it come from London. Drawn from life last week in St. Paul's court, though the artist swears he never learned her name."

Stunned, Sir Thomas could only stare at the print in his hands. The drawing was crude, the sort of cheap, mawkish illustration that would find a place over rumshop bars and in boardinghouse parlors, but the subject was one that would find an immense market: a young woman gotten up to represent the grieving, conquered Caledonia, standing in a barren landscape replete with fresh graves and tattered flags, and holding her now-orphaned baby in her arms.

But all Sir Thomas saw now was the young woman's face, her unusually upturned eyes and small chin, her thick, curling hair, and the distinctive beads around her throat.

"Look'ee, milord," said Deadmarsh, shoving the bloodstained portrait of the young girl beside the print. "Just you look, and tell me it's not the same face."

His fingers trembling, Sir Thomas folded the print. He didn't need to look again. The proof was clear enough.

Truly fate was mocking him, playing with his future in such a cruelly barbarous way that if this had happened to anyone else, he would have laughed aloud at the poor bastard's misfortune.

But it wasn't happening to anyone else. It was happening to *him*. He thrust the print back into Deadmarsh's hands.

"Find her," he said. "Then make her disappear. Completely, forever. I don't want to be troubled by her like this again. Find her now, and do it."

14

"*H*ere you are, Cora!" With a gleeful flourish Diana closed the door to the print room and leaned back against it, as if daring anyone else to try to follow her. "I knew you had to be somewhere in the house! But dear Lord, how do you do such tedious small work as this? I'm hopeless at handwork, hopeless and clumsy."

"Diana, you shouldn't be here," said Cora uneasily, the sharp-bladed scissors still in her hand, the table covered with scraps of paper. "You forget we're not supposed to be acquainted."

"Oh, pooh, we *are*," said Diana blithely, "and I've never stopped doing anything simply because I wasn't *supposed* to. Besides, Lady Waldegrave is having all sorts of evil words with the poor man come to dress her wigs, and I doubt she'll have any to spare for us this morning. Which you knew, too, Cora, else you wouldn't have dared bring this little darling with you."

She bent down to scoop Starlight from the floor, displaying scandalously fashionable yellow stockings below a red petticoat, and swung the cat up into her arms. "Besides and more besides, I have a great surprise for you from my brother."

"From Alex?" asked Cora excitedly, smoothing back her hair as she rose to her feet. "He's here?"

Shrewdly Diana narrowed her eyes. "And you pretend you don't care for him! Alas, the great coward didn't come himself, but sent a boy from the ship with a message."

"Oh." Disconsolately Cora dropped back into her seat, not even bothering to defend herself. "So what manner of surprise is there for me in that?"

"This manner, my dear." Diana pulled a folded paper from her pocket, waving it rapidly before her face like a fan. "Through doubtless devious means, Alex has obtained two places in a private box at the King's Theatre for tonight's offering of *The Suspicious Husband,* and he has most dutifully asked me to join him."

"Oh, my," said Cora wistfully. "That's the new play with Mr. Garrick. Even Lady Waldegrave said he was so handsome and amusing that she nearly swooned with delight. You'll enjoy yourself mightily."

"Not *myself,* you ninny," corrected Diana. "You're not heeding me at all. I am already engaged for this evening with Lord Roxby. But I cannot very well send Alex to watch Mr. Garrick by himself, can I? He would be vile and ill tempered if I did. Thus when he comes to fetch me this evening, you shall be waiting in my place."

"The theater," breathed Cora uncertainly. "Oh, Diana, I do not believe I should."

A simple walk around the square, a visit to the *Calliope*—after two years in hiding, these had been great adventures for her. But to go to the theater, to sit in a box and watch the most popular actor in the wittiest play, and to do it all in Alex's company, was almost beyond imagining. Perhaps Diana had never stopped doing anything simply because she wasn't supposed to, but for Cora there still seemed to be a bit too much at stake to be so blindly impulsive.

Not that Diana would ever understand. "Of course you can go," she said, unperturbed. "I'll insist."

"But surely Lady Waldegrave—"

"Lady Waldegrave will be with Lord Roxby and me, making certain that neither of us compromises the other," said Diana. "We shall leave before Alex arrives, and as long as you are back before us, she'll never be the wiser."

Yet still Cora hesitated. How could she tell who'd be there in a crowded theater?

"Alex will watch over you," said Diana kindly, almost as if she could read Cora's worries. "I know. He makes the best watchdog in the world, and likely the largest, too. And you do know that if I make you a loan of my brother, I'll give you a gown to match as well."

"A gown?" asked Cora in astonishment. From what she'd seen, Diana's wardrobe was as beautiful as she was herself, and a far cry from Lady Waldegrave's castoffs. "One of your own? Oh, Diana, I couldn't."

"You can," she answered, "and you will."

"But why are you doing this for me?" protested Cora. "Why are you doing any of this?"

"Because it amuses me," answered Diana promptly. "Because I like you. Because after all the years that my brother has claimed that he cares only for that silly sloop, at last he's tumbled into love."

"But not with me," said Cora quickly. Love wasn't the reason Alex had come into her life; she'd already resigned herself to that. "Not me."

"Oh, and who else would it be, Mistress Ninny?"

Diana frowned as Starlight gnawed on her knuckle. "Come, come, let's go pillage my trunks and cupboards. I've one patterned silk in particular that I've never worn, but I think it will suit *you* wondrously."

And it did.

Cora knew it the moment she stepped before the looking glass in Diana's room, or maybe even before that, when she'd first felt the silk sliding over her skin. This was the kind of magical gown that little girls always dream about, and women rarely find: a gown so perfect for her in every way that Cora felt perfect, too.

This was not the sort of gown she ever would have ordered for herself, not even when she'd been the indulged daughter of Creignish. It was far too fashionable, too daringly stylish and modishly French in its lavish details, and French, too, in the seductive way it displayed Cora's body. The fabric was cream-colored moiré silk faille that rustled like a whispered secret around her body. Dozens of swirling, exotic flowers—rose pink, golden yellow, sapphire blue, emerald green—had been hand painted across the silk, with the same flowers in tiny silk replicas to festoon the lace *engageantes* on the sleeves and give Cora's every gesture significance. The neckline was deep and square above a stiffened stomacher that pressed Cora's breasts into such a high, voluptuous display that only the ruffle of lace on her shift protected her modesty.

The hoops she wore—also borrowed from Diana—spread the silk skirts outward and exaggerated the sway of her hips when she walked, while the long, pointed bodice and the split in the front of the overskirt, all enhanced with rows of eyelash fringe, seemed to draw the eye suggestively to that tantalizing, peculiarly distracting place between her legs—a place that, before Cora had met Alex, she'd never given much thought to at all.

"Oh, you'll turn Alex into a blithering idiot dressed like this," said Diana with approval as she smoothed the silk of one sleeve over Cora's arm. "The hem is too long for you, though. Your shoes should show, and the clocks on your stockings over your ankles."

" 'Tis fine this way," said Cora hastily, feeling that quite enough of her showed already. "I may not be as tall as you, but I'm not as . . . not as . . ."

"Bold?" suggested Diana. "Wanton? Brazen?"

"I didn't say that!"

"You didn't have to, Cora," she said with a low laugh that managed to be bold, wanton, brazen, and thoroughly pleased with herself all at once. "But here, here's something else about this gown. Look, see how it's lined with this dark rose silk, even though the outside is ivory? That's terribly, terribly wicked, you know."

Cora turned back one of the edges of the slit overskirt so the pink lining showed. "Why is that wicked?"

Diana twisted her mouth and tried to look worldly wise before, at last, she sighed and merely shrugged. "I don't know," she admitted. "But it was sufficient to horrify my mother so that if there'd been time before we sailed, she would have had the lining ripped out and replaced. She said the pink inside the white would give gentlemen unseemly notions they shouldn't have. She made me promise never to let any of them see it, either, on that specific account. But she didn't make *you* promise, so Alex can look at it all you want."

"But when?" asked Cora, still mystified at the idea

that gentlemen could be incited by the lining of a gown.

Diana smiled archly. "I'm told that when the lights are dowsed and the play has begun, the private boxes at the King's Theatre are most private indeed. But I shall leave that to you and Alex to discover for yourselves. Faith, how I wish I could see his face when he sees you!"

"Of course my sister is here," said Alex impatiently. "She's expecting me."

Somehow Junius managed to make his expression both professionally impassive, as befitted the butler in his ladyship's house, and self-satisfied as well. "Miss Fairbourne is not here at present, sir. She left an hour past with her ladyship, in the company of the Marquess of Roxby."

"Well, hell." Alex stared down at his shoes and at the new pair of cut steel buckles he'd bought special for this occasion to impress Diana. Not that she was going to see them now, and not that she'd be impressed with a pair of twenty-shilling shoe buckles, either, when she had some double-blasted marquess dancing on her whim.

He knew that dancing noblemen were the reason his sister had come to London. He knew he should be happy for her sake that she seemed to be having such a success.

"Alex?"

He glanced up, surprised, and instantly forgot his sister.

Cora was standing at the top of the stairs, one foot tentatively forward. He'd never seen her dressed like this. She looked older, more worldly and womanly, less like the sprite who'd first surprised him in the garden and more like the fashionable lady she'd been born to be.

And also far, far more seductive. Unlike Cora's usual clothes, this gown instantly made him remember how warm her skin was to touch, how soft her breasts had felt in his hands, and how the last time they'd been alone in this same house, he'd come unforgivably close to tipping her back onto the table and driving himself hard into her and stealing for them both every bit of the pleasure that that neat little body of hers promised.

Then she smiled shyly, and he remembered all the other things that he'd come to find so special about her: her merry, chuckling laughter and her unselfconscious charm and the freckles scattered over her skin like nutmeg over custard, the way the one moment she could be defiantly loyal to her doomed clan and yet the next shed tears of delight as she cradled that foolish little black kitten with more tenderness than most women showed their babies.

And then, being male, he marveled once again at how splendidly displayed her breasts were by this gown, and how he'd have to kill any other man—slaughter him outright—who dared look at her.

"Diana asked me to go with you in her stead," she said, hovering there on the top of the step. "To the play, that is. If you do not object."

What kind of idiot did she honestly believe him to be? "If you wish to come, aye," he began, "since Diana can't."

Blast, but that was awkwardly put! He wasn't prepared to see her. He'd only been expecting an uncomplicated evening with his sister, not the confused whirl of attraction and desire that he always found in Cora's company.

"I'd be honored to have your company," he tried again. "They, ah, they say this fellow Garrick is clever as they come."

"Oh, he is." Happily she skipped down the stairs, her bosom quivering deliciously with every step.

Alex heard a strangled sound from Junius behind him, Alex's own reaction precisely.

"That's a, ah, handsome sort of gown," he managed to choke out.

"You like it?" she asked anxiously, brushing her hand over the skirt—as if anyone was going to notice *that.* "I want you to be proud of me. You don't think it's too elegant for a playhouse?"

He cleared his throat again. "Perhaps if you have some sort of kerchief or shawl."

"Oh, I forgot." She tugged a filmy triangle of linen from her arms over her shoulders and breasts: better than nothing, but not much. "Your sister dressed me. This is her gown, you know."

He should have seen Diana's hand in this. He had a hazy recollection of this gown appearing at home from Mademoiselle Lacroix's shop and causing some sort of uproar between Diana and his mother. Now he understood why.

She looped her hand through the crook of his arm, and he couldn't avoid looking down at her bosom again. He'd remembered her as being slighter than this, not overabundant but most pleasing, yet something about the way this gown was constructed was certainly changing his mind.

"You know, Cora," he said with gloomy certainty, "I shall have to throttle at least one leering jackass on your behalf tonight. I'll have no choice."

She grinned impishly and patted his arm. "That's exactly what Diana said you'd tell me."

He grumbled wordlessly even as he enjoyed the touch of her fingers on his arm, anticipating an entire world of trouble ahead for them both this evening. He'd have no choice in any of this, no blasted choice at all.

Yet when she smiled up at him, her face radiating happiness and excitement as he helped her into the hackney, he caught himself thinking less about trials of defending her honor and more of the rewards of being her champion.

And realized that, where Cora MacGillivray was concerned, he'd already made his own choice long ago. The only decision left was how to tell her.

"Cora," said Alex, the hired carriage's window framing a square of light over his shoulders. "We must talk, you and I."

"I'd rather thought, Alex, that that was what we *had* been doing." Cora tried to laugh, to dismiss the horrible solemnity she'd heard in his words.

But there was talk and there was Talk, and she understood the difference. When she'd been chattering on about Diana and her marquess, that had been talk. But the seriousness she suddenly found in Alex's face meant Talk: words fraught with meaning and heavy with portents, the kind of words that seldom, if ever, seemed to bring good news with them.

And clearly this time would be no exception. The summer evening was hot and still, unusual for June, the London dust hanging in the air with a heaviness that begged for the release of a thunderstorm. Even if her hoops would have permitted it, this wasn't the evening for cozily sharing a seat in a hackney. Alex sat across from her, one hand planted decisively on each knee as if he were willing the heat away, as miserably ill at ease as she was herself. The sweat plastered his dark hair to his forehead beneath the brim of his hat and to his neck in tiny damp curls, while beneath his coat the white linen of his shirt clung in dark patches to his chest and his neckcloth hung in moistly strangling folds around his throat.

"We were talking, aye," he admitted. "But Cora, it's about other things I wish to speak now. About you and me. About my *Calliope's* sailing. About your Creignish."

She should have known this was coming. She didn't know whether to be excited or frightened that everything would finally be settled. She clasped her hands tightly in her lap, partly to keep them occupied and partly to keep her sweaty palms a secret from Alex.

"I've been expecting this, Alex," she admitted in an eager half-whisper. "From the beginning. On that last night, Father had promised me that a man would come to take me home. And it's time now, isn't it? It's *time.*"

"Cora, I never met your father," he said, an unexpected, almost defensive edge to his voice. "I'm certain he was a rare and kind gentleman, and his loss a grievous one. But I never did have the honor of meeting him, let alone promising him anything in regards to you."

"And how could you tell me anything else?" she said at once. "My father died in disgrace. Unless you wished to be branded as a traitor, too, you must pretend you didn't know him."

"I'm not pretending, Cora," he said firmly. "I never met your father, and I've never been to Scotland, let alone to Creignish."

"But you could have met Father somewhere else," she said, her voice rising with urgency. She wished she hadn't let Diana lace her stays so tightly; she felt as if the whalebone and the heat and the awfulness of this moment were all crushing in on her at once. "He traveled many places, the same as you. Yes! He could have met you most anywhere!"

But Alex shook his head, refusing to accept her desperate conviction, and the close air in the little hackney was as charged as the thunderclouds gathering overhead.

"Cora, sweetheart," he began again, leaning forward to reach for her hand. "Cora, please. If we're to have any future ahead of us we have to be honest with each other. I can understand that after all you've suffered, you would have, ah, looked for ways to comfort yourself, to ease the pain of your loss by—"

"Alex, this isn't some *story!*" she cried, jerking her fingers away from him. "My father and my uncles and my cousins were all killed in one day, one single day. My home is all I have left to me. What *story* could I possibly have created to account for that?"

"I'm not some blasted hero, Cora! I'm an ordinary man from Massachusetts, and the sooner I—"

"*No!*" She closed her eyes, protecting herself against the kindness she didn't want, the understanding she couldn't accept. He'd given her back a dream she'd desperately wanted, and she wasn't going to let him take it away from her, not now when she could almost smell the wild heather on their glen. "You're the one who'll take me home, and nothing you can say now will change my mind!"

His mouth was a tense, tight line, with little beads of aggravated sweat collecting on his upper lip. "It's not a matter of changing my mind, Cora. It's more than—oh, hell, now what?"

The hackney lurched to a halt, accompanied by a volley of curses from the driver. Alex leaned from the window to see the reason, then swore himself.

"There's carriages and hackneys from here clear to the damned playhouse," said Alex. "If we wait our turn, we'll miss the music for certain."

"Then perhaps I should step down and walk," said Cora, grabbing the handle to the door. "Better that than sitting here and waiting for a blasted *hero* to rescue me!"

"Damnation, Cora, stop it," he said as he tried to wrestle the door shut. "Cora, be reasonable!"

But the hackney's horse took one irritated step sideways, enough to help Cora pitch herself out the door and into the street. It was hardly the most graceful of exits, but she did manage it without tearing her gown or falling face first, and with the extra impetus of emotion to carry her, she plunged recklessly into the crowd.

"Cora!" Alex shouted in that captain's roar of his, loud enough to be heard over a gale. "Cora, come back here!"

She didn't, of course. She wasn't about to answer to an order bellowed in the street like that, and swiftly she turned the corner.

"Miss MacGillivray!" called a quavering voice as unlike Alex's roar as possible. "Bless th' saints, I dinna believe 'twas you!"

Stunned, she stopped sharply, and looked for who'd called to her in an accent she hadn't heard for years.

"Miss MacGillivray, miss, here, here!" The frail old man was standing in the alley between two buildings, keeping himself out of the path of the rushing theater goers. His shoulders were bent and twisted with age, his hat pulled low over the red scarf that covered a blind eye, and the hand he held out to her shook with palsy.

"Bless ye for stopping, Miss MacGillivray, a bonnie, brave lady like ye!" he said, coughing weakly against the sleeve of his shabby blue coat. "I knew your poor father, lass, and saw him at th' last, there on th' bloody moor of Culloden!"

"You did, sir?" she asked excitedly. "You followed the prince, too?"

"Aye, Miss Cora, I did." He coughed again, squinting up at the sky with his single eye as he lurched unsteadily backward, and beckoned for her to join him. "Och, but my eye canna bear th' light, miss! Come here wit' me, where 'tis gentler on these ancient eyes."

Eager to hear more of her father, Cora followed the old man into the alley. But as soon as she'd joined him in the shadows, away from the others, he suddenly stood upright and his palsy vanished, and in one horrifyingly fast motion he'd locked his arm around her neck and was dragging her backward through the alley into a dank, rubbish-filled yard. Frantically she kicked her heels and clawed, but the pressure of his arm against her throat was making her gasp to breathe, let alone scream for help.

"Cora?" called Alex from the street, a thousand miles away. "Blast it, Cora, where are you?"

Desperately she kicked again, this time striking a

half dozen rotting barrel staves stacked against the wall with their rusted hoop, scattering everything with a noisy clatter.

"Cora?" Alex's voice echoed in the alley's narrow walls. "Cora, lass, is that you?"

The old man swore, and to Cora's surprise, released her. Gasping for air, she pitched forward, catching herself against the wall. But then she was choking again as he hooked his fingers into the back of her necklace and jerked it hard across her windpipe. The old gold clasp gave way against the force, and then as suddenly as he'd appeared, the man had vanished, the sound of his running footsteps disappearing behind her.

"Cora!" Alex pulled her around, holding her upright as her own knees buckled. "Cora, sweetheart, what happened?"

She gasped again, still struggling for air. She touched her hands to her throat, and tears welled up in her eyes as she realized her coral beads were gone. "He—the old man—he stole my necklace."

"Your mother's beads?" Alex's face hardened; he knew what the necklace meant to her. "I'll get them back for you. Which way did the bastard—"

"No!" she croaked. "Don't go, Alex. Please—please stay with me instead."

Reluctantly he looked back to her. "Did he hurt you, lass?"

"Not much," she said, rubbing at the raw patches the brick wall had scraped into her palms as the tears slid down her cheeks. "I'll be well—well enough. Oh, Alex, he said he knew Father!"

"Did he?" Alex's frown deepened as he handed her his handkerchief. "Cora, we should find a constable.

This has gone too far. If the man knew your father's name, then he wasn't an ordinary thief."

"I won't talk to a constable about Father. It—it wouldn't be right." She dabbed the handkerchief at her eyes. "And maybe I heard the man wrong. Maybe I . . . I heard what I wished to instead, just as I saw only a shabby old beggar pretending to be half-blind, instead of a thief. I was the fool, ripe for the picking. All he wanted was my . . . my necklace."

Again she touched her throat, now so painfully bare, and fresh tears rose to her eyes as she remembered how terrified she'd been. "Besides, they weren't diamonds or rubies. What constable in London would bother with a Scottish lady's old coral beads? They're gone now, and I . . . I must accept that."

But she couldn't, not yet, and when he pulled her into his arms she went gladly, burying the sorrow of her loss against his chest. Here, then, was the closeness she'd craved in the hackney; but oh, what a price she'd paid for it!

"I should never have let you run off like that," he said over the top of her hair. "What the hell was I thinking, anyway?"

She sighed, wishing he wouldn't blame himself. "It wasn't your fault, Alex. I was the one who jumped from the hackney. It wasn't as if you pushed me out into the street."

But he shook his head, his first fear for her safety shifting into anger. "But what if I hadn't found you in time, eh? What if I'd hadn't heard that racket you made or if I'd turned down a different street?"

She pushed away from him far enough to see his face. "But you didn't, Alex. And you couldn't have."

She tried to smile. "You have to take me back to Creignish first, remember?"

"Damnation, Cora, that's enough," he said roughly. "I'm done with being your savior, handpicked somehow by your father from beyond the grave. What do I have to say to make you understand? God knows I'm only a man, not some bloodless saint. Why can't you accept it, too?"

"But I do, Alex!" she cried breathlessly, the feeling welling up from inside her chest. He'd said before he'd wanted the truth, and suddenly that was what she was telling him, whether either of them wished to hear it or not. "I never wanted a saint. All I wanted was a man, one man, and the only one I ever wanted was you!"

Before he could answer she flung her arms around his shoulders and pulled his face down to kiss him, to prove that what she'd said hadn't been words alone. Not that she'd planned it: she hadn't even known it herself until she'd spoken.

For one ghastly instant she felt him begin to withdraw as he warred with himself. Her pride, her past and her future, her heart: didn't he realize she'd nothing left to offer? When he lifted his hands from her shoulders, she pulled him closer, kissing him with a shameless, fervent urgency until she heard him make a deep, growling noise in his throat, a masculine sound of surrender and desire.

Then he was kissing her back with the hunger of a famished man, his hands settling at her waist and curving her body to meet his. His hat toppled back from his head and they didn't stop; her hoops bowed and creaked, the silk of her skirts snagging against the bricks behind her, and she gave them no thought.

"You're mine, Cora," he said against her throat, his voice rough with desire. "You're mine, Cora Margaret, understand?"

She smiled, her joy boundless, and enough to make her legs weak beneath her. "I always said you were the one, Alex," she whispered. "You just didn't listen when I told you."

He grunted, and with an effort eased back away from her, at least as far as he could in the narrow alley. "Nor did you, sweetheart."

She wrinkled her nose as she reached up to smooth a lock of his hair back from his forehead. "Oh, yes, I did. I've heard every single word you've ever said to me."

"Aye, but how much did you heed, eh?" he asked. From his expression she guessed he didn't share the same joy she'd felt. He didn't even look happy. "Cora, about Creignish—"

"Not now," she said skittishly, laying her fingertips across his lips to silence him. She found she needed to touch him again and again, in small, intimate ways that would reassure her. "We can talk later, after the play."

Lightly he kissed her fingers where they touched his lips, then bent to retrieve his hat, frowning as he brushed the dust from the crown with his sleeve. "Better I should take you home to Lady Waldegrave's instead. You've had your share of excitement already."

"But the play, Alex," she said. "Isn't that why we came? To see Mr. Garrick? To amuse ourselves?"

He sighed, and tapped the hat back onto his head. "Mr. Garrick or no Mr. Garrick, we are going to speak of Creignish later, Cora, and a few other things as well. Nothing's been settled yet."

"Nothing?" she asked wistfully, twisting the ends of her kerchief around her fingers. She'd thought he'd meant what he'd said about her belonging to him. She'd certainly meant what she'd said to him. "Nothing at all?"

Alex paused, and silently cursed himself for making her look like she was ready to weep again. Damnation, he'd deserve it if she did. Why hadn't he been able to control himself when she'd kissed him like that? Kissing was all well and good—very good, really, where Cora was concerned—but kissing her then, when she'd still felt so helpless and frightened after the attack, had been about the wrongest thing he'd ever done.

But why the hell couldn't she see that he couldn't be honest with her until she was honest with him? He wanted to tell her how he felt, plain and simple and direct, but he couldn't do that until she'd quit believing her dead father had somehow ordered him to take her back to her ghost-filled Scotland. It was heathenish nonsense, that, and gave him chills just to consider it.

He wanted her safe, he wanted her happy, and most of all, he wanted her with him. He didn't expect her to deny her past—he'd never demand that—but he did want her to be reasonable about the future, leastways if she wished to share that future with him.

But their immediate future had her gazing up at him with her mouth pinched and her elfish eyes more sad and mournful than any elf had a right to be, and him feeling like he'd just put his big foot down square in the middle of his mother's flower garden.

He swept his hat from his head as gallantly as he could in the alley, and bent to kiss her, sweetly this time, more as a pledge and a promise than in passion.

"Everything about you matters to me, sweetheart,"

he said gruffly, holding his face level with hers. "It's only the details that must be sorted out. Now come, we can't keep Mr. Garrick waiting."

She smiled then as he took her hand, so tremulous that he worried all over again that she'd begin crying. How could a woman who had survived as much as Cora had turn weepy over something *he* said?

But as they walked to the theater, she seemed to regain her composure as well as her earlier excitement, her eyes again bright with anticipation instead of tears. Yet even as she commented on another woman's hat or the oversized nosegay in a gentleman's hand, there was still a wariness to her as they moved through the crowd, and she was careful to keep her hand tight around his.

But Alex, too, couldn't shake the feeling that others were looking at Cora with more than the passing admiration for her gown or face. And it wasn't just men, either. Women and girls, too, old and young, well dressed and poor, stopped to gaze at Cora, some unabashedly open-mouthed with awe.

Cora noticed it, too. "I don't believe I'm ready to be a lady of fashion," she said with a nervous little laugh. "How does your sister bear it, having people stare at her?"

"Oh, Diana thrives upon it," he answered, trying not to share his concerns as he guided her inside the open doors of the playhouse. "You know that's why she came to London. She'd exhausted the supply of people to ogle her in the colonies."

With Sir Thomas' signed note as their passkey, they were quickly ushered to his box. Once again Alex thought of Sir Thomas' claims to poverty, for his box was one of the very best, on the first tier and near the stage. The standard seats had been replaced with more comfortable armchairs, the cushions covered with silk plush, and a private servant at once appeared to offer them food or drink. There were curtains, too, to screen the box holders from the gazes of the other theater goers, especially if the play served to be less interesting than what was happening in the box.

"Oh, how splendid!" exclaimed Cora with delight as she took her seat near the front of the box. Fluttering her fan, she leaned forward to admire the crowd that was still milling about beneath them or making their way to other boxes. Candlelight sparkled off silk-satins and jewels, both real and paste, and lighthearted laughter and conversation rose with anticipation as the orchestra began tuning their instruments for the overture. "Oh, Alex, have you ever seen a more beautiful sight?"

None more beautiful than Cora, he thought, sitting there in profile with her cheeks still flushed and her hair a bit disordered from their kiss in the alley, her eyes reflecting the dozens of candles. In that same weak moment when he'd kissed her, he'd also told her she was his, and with her here beside him, he found how desparately he hoped it was true.

But as he leaned forward to tell her again, a movement from the seats below caught his eye, a sudden flash of waving white. A tall, older gentleman, distinguished in a clergyman's somber coat and fluffed gray wig, was holding his hand over his heart as he waved his handkerchief in their direction.

"Do you know that man, Cora?" asked Alex, slipping his arm around her shoulders. Sometimes it didn't hurt to be possessive. "That one, there. The minister."

"I've never seen him before in my life," she whispered uneasily. "Who is he?"

"I haven't a notion, sweetheart." Alex watched as others noticed the man's gestures, following his gaze to look up toward Sir Thomas' box themselves. Some of the upturned faces were easily bored, uninterested, and soon looked away, but here and there Alex saw the same excited recognition he'd noticed in the crowd in the street, with people pointing up at their box.

"I don't like this, Cora," he said slowly. "Why the devil are they peering up here, anyway?"

But the answer came soon enough.

"Hail, hail, fair Caledonia!" called the minister, his voice ringing out with the clarity of his pulpit training. "Hail to thee, brave, grieving Caledonia!"

Cora gasped, her cheeks losing all their color beneath her freckles. "Mr. Curlew promised the picture was for himself! Alex, he *promised!*"

"*Damn* that bastard!" he swore furiously. "Come, Cora, we—"

But as he glanced past her down into the sea of fascinated, upturned faces, one stood out, though the man most likely would have wished otherwise; he no more belonged in this well-dressed crowd than he had on Cavendish Square.

The grimy red scarf was still pulled across his face, the same ragged uniform coat still hanging from his shoulders, but the unfocused, shuffling demeanor of a worn-out drunkard had vanished, replaced with the predatory edginess of a longtime mercenary. Even from this distance Alex could recognize it, just as he recognized the bulge of a pistol beneath the man's coat. The Jacobites and their rebellion might be long done, but somewhere a bounty or reward must still be offered for traitors—and their daughters.

A shabby old beggar pretending to be half-blind. . . . Damnation, how had he let himself be fooled like this?

The old soldier was staring up at Cora with his single eye, and a slight smile of unmistakable triumph flickered across his face.

And that was more than enough for Alex.

"We're leaving, Cora," he said sharply as he grabbed Cora's arm and pulled her back with him out of the box. "No questions, no argument. We're leaving now."

15

Cora huddled low in the corner of the hackney, pulling her shawl tightly across her chest as if the sheer linen had the power to protect her.

"But I still don't understand, Alex," she said unhappily. "You've said yourself that I'm no longer at risk for being my father's daughter. No one in London knows it, anyway. Why would anyone wish to harm me now?"

"I can't say, sweetheart," said Alex, keeping his voice low so the driver couldn't possibly overhear. "You were in danger, and that was all that mattered to me."

Though they sat together, her hand clasped tightly to his, he looked past her and out the window, watchful as a hawk even as the carriage rolled through the deepening summer dusk. She was seeing a different side of him tonight, hard-edged and supremely capable, and to her wistful regret she realized this was probably the Captain Fairbourne that he showed the rest of the world.

She sighed forlornly. None of this made any sense to her, but she wasn't sure she wanted it to, either. "You're not telling me everything, are you?"

"I'm telling you what I saw," he again explained patiently. "The man below us had a gun, and he was watching you."

"So were a great many other people!" she cried, but without much conviction. Pistols had no place in a playhouse. How could she argue with that? " 'Tis all the fault of that wretched, lying artist."

"I know, and he'll answer to me tomorrow." Alex sighed heavily. "Cora, the man who stole your necklace. Do you remember what he looked like, what he wore?"

"Of course." She shivered as the thief's face came rising up again in her imagination. "Though he was pretending to be an old beggar man, I think he was younger, and stronger, too. Much stronger. His coat was blue, with the buttons cut away, and he wore a dirty red scarf to hide one eye."

"You are sure?"

She nodded. "But why, Alex? Why does it matter so much now?"

He shifted uneasily in the seat, not answering at first. "Because I'm thinking that man was the same one I saw with the gun in the playhouse, Cora," he said finally. "And if he is, then he knows who you are, and he has a reason for following you. And I don't like it at all."

She looked down into her lap. She tried to tell herself she should be grateful for his caution, thankful for his experience, but instead all she felt was the fear settling around her again like a worn and familiar old gown that she couldn't quite make herself throw away. Thanks to Alex, she'd thought she'd finally been done with hiding and secrecy and pretending she was someone she wasn't. She'd convinced herself that bravery was enough to make her free, and that the world was ready to welcome her back.

But ten minutes in the playhouse had shown her how wrong she'd been, ten minutes and a threadbare thief with a gun. She bowed her head, fighting the old terrors that now had a new face.

And yet Alex had been the one who'd made the difference tonight. She didn't want to consider what could have happened without him. Over and over he'd denied that he was her savior, her rescuer. But what more proof did she need than how he'd looked after her tonight?

"Perhaps I'm wrong, Cora," he said, relaxing enough to brush his fingertip over her cheek. "I hope I am. But long ago I learned to trust my instincts about things like this, and because of it I'm still alive. And so, thank God, are you. Ah, here's Lady Waldegrave's house."

He climbed down first, paying the driver and scanning the square for more strangers with hidden pistols before he hurried her up the front steps.

"Fetch your mistress at once," ordered Alex sharply as he pushed their way past Junius into the hall. "Tell her I must speak to her directly."

"Her ladyship is not at home, sir," said Junius, almost scolding. "If you'd care to leave a message, I shall deliver it when she returns."

Alex swore, then turned back to Cora. "I must go back to the *Calliope* now, lass. But I'll return as soon as I can. An hour, no more."

She remembered the pistols and swords that she'd seen in his cabin and knew they were the reason he needed to return to the ship. Once she'd found his weapons exciting proof that he was as familiar with danger as his reputation suggested. Now they only reminded her of her father's farewell, how the scabbard with his battered sword had bumped clumsily against her side when she'd hugged him for the last time.

And oh, please God, she didn't want to have to do that again with Alex, any more than she wanted him to leave her now.

"You don't have to go," she said, fear making her abandon all pride as she clutched at his sleeve. "Stay here with me, Alex, please!"

"I told you, Cora, I won't be gone long," he said more gently. He held both her hands in his, his gaze focused so entirely on her that she couldn't look away even if she'd wished it. She'd never seen him so earnest, nor so intense. "You stay in this house, and you don't leave, not even to take Starlight to the garden, mind?"

"But Alex—"

"You've been safe enough here for the last two years, sweetheart," he said firmly. "You'll be safe for another hour. Even Junius knows that, else by God, he'll have to answer to me. Isn't that so, Junius?"

Junius nodded stiffly, not quite a bow, but not a denial, either. "I always follow her ladyship's orders, especially those regarding Miss MacGillivray."

Alex smiled. "There now, lass, what did I tell you? You wait for me here. As soon as I'm back, Lady Waldegrave and I will decide what we'll do next with you."

"*Do?*" asked Cora, stunned, her panic growing. "You'll decide what you'll *do* with me?"

"Only good things, sweetheart, I promise you." He winked, trying to lighten the mood. "Be brave, Cora. Don't fail me now. Be brave the way I know you can be. No, the way you *are.*"

Only good things, he'd said, and suddenly Cora gasped as she understood the obvious meaning behind his words. Before Junius, he'd be oblique, so the butler wouldn't tell her ladyship first, but Cora understood.

Creignish.

That had to be it, didn't it? Of course, of course, of *course*, and she nearly clapped her hands with excitement and joy. He was going to take her home to Creignish, and they'd begin their journey tonight. That must be why he was going back to the *Calliope*, to gather clothes and whatever he'd need. She'd have to pack her own little trunk, too, and contrive some way to carry Starlight, depending on how they'd travel: coach, or horseback, or perhaps by water, the way she'd come to London with Mr. Abraham. Perhaps Alex even intended to sail the *Calliope* himself, and she could scarcely contain her delight.

It was all exactly as poor Father had wished. There'd be no more English soldiers, no more hiding, no more guns. She'd be home, and she'd be there with Alex. She smiled shyly, wanting to give him some sign that she'd understood.

"That's my lass," he said gruffly, and before she could answer he'd slipped his arm around her waist and was kissing her. Swiftly, surely, his mouth moved across hers, another promise and farewell, and then he was gone without looking back, his broad shoulders slipping through the door before Junius bolted it shut. Almost dazed, she stared at the closed door as she touched her fingertips to her lips.

"Her ladyship requests you come directly, miss," Junius was saying. "She is waiting in her sitting room."

Cora frowned. "Lady Waldegrave isn't here," she murmured. "She's with Diana and Lord Roxby."

Junius bowed, his well-polished heels together and smugness glinting in his eyes. "Her ladyship returned earlier than expected. She called for you immediately, miss, and was distraught to learn you were not available. *Most* distraught."

Cora shook her head, her confusion turning to suspicion. "You told Captain Fairbourne she wasn't here."

"I always follow her ladyship's orders," repeated Junius primly, "especially those regarding you, miss. Will you come with me, miss?"

It was true enough that the countess had standing orders never to be at home to Captain Fairbourne, but considering the circumstances, Cora thought Junius might have relented, and it all seemed more than a bit peculiar.

"Why should I go with you, Junius?" she asked warily. "Why should I trust you at all?"

"That is your decision, miss," said the butler, keeping his expression impassive while his voice dripped with reproach. "But if I might venture to speak, I would say that her ladyship does deserve such trust from you."

Cora sighed, guilt sweeping over her. Junius was right. The countess did deserve her loyalty, and besides, if she was going to leave tonight with Alex, then who knew when she'd see Lady Waldegrave again?

But as Cora followed Junius up the stairs, she dreaded the conversation before her. Over and over she'd disobeyed the countess' wishes, and though Cora thought she'd the best of reasons for doing so, she doubted her ladyship would agree. Junius had said she was "most distraught," but Cora was certain being distraught was only the beginning.

Without thinking she touched the bruised, empty place on her throat where her necklace had once been, wincing. True ladies like the countess would never have to contend with street thieves, for true ladies never scampered off unattended into alleys.

Ruefully she glanced down at the gown she'd borrowed from Diana. Any of the magic those hand-painted flowers had held earlier was certainly gone now, and she prayed that the countess wouldn't recognize the gown as Diana's. If she hadn't kept her ladyship waiting so long, she would have gone to her own room first to change, but then again she was already in such deep trouble on account of Alex that knowing Diana and borrowing her clothes likely couldn't make it much worse.

"You will show Captain Fairbourne upstairs when he returns, won't you, Junius?" she said as she hung back before the door to the countess' sitting room. "It's most important that you do."

But Junius was already announcing her to Lady Waldegrave, and Cora had no choice but to follow him into the room with a sweeping curtsey.

"My lady," she said as she rose, daring to meet the older woman's gaze. "You, ah, wished to speak to me?"

"Indeed I do, my dear Cora," she said with surprising mildness. "Sit here, do, and have a dish of chocolate whilst we talk."

The countess swept a gracious hand toward the chair beside her. She was still dressed for her evening with Diana, her throat and wrists glittering with jewels and two nodding black plumes tucked into her powdered wig. But what Cora noticed first was how she didn't seem angry at all, her expression instead mild, even cheerful, her famous smile beaming as she filled the second cup. Uneasily Cora took the chocolate and sipped at it as she perched on the edge of the offered chair.

"It would seem we hardly have time at all to converse these days, my dear," said the countess, "what with Diana being such a belle about the town. But you've found other ways to entertain yourself, haven't you, Cora?"

Nervously Cora gulped the rest of the chocolate to keep from answering, then set the empty dish down with a clatter.

Not, though, that the countess seemed to expect a reply. Her smile strained as she glanced at Cora's gown. "You are looking well this evening, my dear. I could have found a peer for a husband for you, too, dressed to show yourself to such advantage. What a shame you've chosen to squander yourself on that Fairbourne man!"

"But I haven't *squandered* myself!" cried Cora defensively. "Alex is a good man, just like Father was!"

"I shall not hear such nonsense!" The countess set her cup down on the table with a rattle of porcelain. "Your father was worth ten of Fairbourne—no, a hundred! He was a true gentleman, Cora, and he would no more deign to *speak* to a creature like that pirate, let alone give his daughter into such a man's keeping!"

"But Alex isn't like that, my lady," protested Cora. "From the beginning, he has cared for me in the best way."

"Oh, I'll show you the *best*," said the countess with withering sharpness. She reached across the table for a sheet of thick cream paper, holding it near the candle to read the printed words.

> *Mourn, hapless Caledonia, mourn*
> *Thy banished peace, thy laurels torn!*
> *Thy sons, for valor long renowned,*
> *Lie slaughtered on their native ground;*
> *Thy hospitable roofs no more*
> *Invite the stranger to the door;*
> *In smoky ruins sunk they lie,*
> *The monuments of cruelty.*

"Of cruelty, Cora, of *cruelty!*" continued the countess, her voice now scathing with bitterness. "The real cruelty is what you have dared do to me and my kindness, to cast it all away for the sake of a worthless man who will do *this* to your good name!"

"Let me see that, my lady, please!" cried Cora desperately as she tried to grab the paper. "Please, I must see the print!"

But the countess held it high in her hand. "So you do know what it is, don't you? You have sold your face like the lowest harlot, common on every street corner, and for what? For what?"

She tossed the print scornfully to the floor, and Cora dropped to her knees to retrieve it. Mourn hapless Caledonia, indeed, she thought as she held the paper up to the light, and spare a bit for poor Cora, too: for Jacob Curlew had risen far beyond his meager talents to create his masterpiece. There above the verse, composed by one Tobias Smollet, Caledonia walked on her sorrowful journey across the ravaged Highlands, with her orphaned, starving baby.

That much Cora had expected. But Caledonia's face was so completely her own that she gasped, a portrait so true, so eloquent, that it was worthy of Sir Joshua Reynolds himself.

"But no one knows who I am, not by name," she whispered, still on her knees. "They'll see me as Caledonia of the Highlands, not Cora MacGillivray of Creignish."

"Anyone who knew your dear father—and there are many who mourn him still, Cora—will see his face in yours in that drawing, and know the truth. And I cannot think of a surer way for you to have broken his heart than with this."

The truth, the truth: the more Cora stared at the print, the more her face did in fact seem to dissolve into her father's. But then the rest of the room seemed to be dissolving as well, blurring into shadows that crept in closer and closer from the edges of her vision. She tried to stand and couldn't, her whole body suddenly as heavy and unresponsive as sand, and instead of rising upward she found it much easier to sink forward, her silk skirts billowing around her as she curled on her side on the floor, the print slipping from her fingers.

The chocolate, she thought with the last murky bit of her consciousness. *Her ladyship must have put the draft she used for sleeping into her chocolate.*

"Poor sleepy Cora," crooned her ladyship, crouching down to tenderly stroke Cora's forehead, the last thing she saw before her eyelids, too, became too heavy to keep open. "I am so sorry to do this to you, my dear child, but it truly is for your own good. For my darling Iain, I always do whatever I must. And now, you see, I have."

* * *

"I know there's no love lost between us, my lady," said Alex as soon as Junius ushered him into the countess' sitting room. "So I'll not waste time. I've come for Cora."

"Oh, you *have*, sir," said Lady Waldegrave. She was sitting in a high-backed armchair with tall candlesticks on the table beside her, carefully placed to flatter her the best. He had the uneasy feeling that all had been as precisely arranged as anything he would have seen tonight on the playhouse stage, and with as little grasp of truth or reality as well.

"Yes, ma'am, I have," he answered firmly. "Now shall you call her, or will I have to go find her myself?"

"Such impertinence, sir," she said archly over the top of the languidly waving fan. "Surely your mother has taught you how barbarously ill mannered it is to make demands of a lady of rank."

"Aye, she has," he answered evenly. He would have to work hard to rein in his temper, for losing it now would accomplish nothing. "But she also taught me not to be swayed by the influences of others, and to do what I believed was right."

The countess snapped the fan closed. "Did you believe, sir, that it was right to insinuate yourself with an innocent like Miss MacGillivray? Was it right, sir, to encourage her to disobey those who loved her best, to lead her into dangerous situations that could only result in her ruin?"

"Was it right to make her a prisoner in your house?" demanded Alex, remembering Cora's lonely face as she'd gazed from the window up under the roof. "Was it right to keep her as another servant?"

"I kept her safe, sir," she answered fiercely, "and I kept her from such tawdry displays as this."

She snatched a paper from the table beside her and thrust it toward Alex. He didn't have to take it from her to know it was the print of Caledonia.

"But it is of no consequence now, sir," she continued. "You have done your damage to Miss Mac-Gillivray, and you'll do no more. I have sent her away until you have sailed, and placed her safe and well beyond your wicked reach."

Alex hesitated, desperately trying to decide if the woman was telling the truth. "She was here not an hour ago."

"And now she is gone." The countess' eyes gleamed. "You can search this house if you doubt me, sir, and you'll find nothing. I've done what's best for her, and for her happiness, and that, sir, does not include you."

"And who the devil gave you the right to decide that for her?" he demanded furiously, his resolutions to control his temper unraveling as his anger grew at what she'd done. "You're not kin, nor even a friend, to choose her fate like that!"

She raised her head, drawing on a lifetime of practiced dignity. "Her own father gave her into my keeping. Iain MacGillivray was a rare gentleman of great wisdom and grace, and when he knew he would die, he entrusted me with his greatest treasure."

Alex snorted with disgust at such pretentious talk. "Then he'd surely feel like the greatest damned fool in the world to see what a sorry mess you've made of Cora's life!"

"He would not!" she declared, thumping her furled fan on the arm of the chair for emphasis. "He would see that I have done my best for her at all times, and far, far more than any rascal like you could offer."

"Oh, aye, what could I possibly have to offer Cora?" asked Alex, so angry now that each word came out with the fire that would have sent his crew scurrying to obey. "Only a home where she'd be free to come and go as she pleased, and a family eager to pet and cosset her. Only an end to the lies and secrecy, and to the fear that makes her jump at her own shadow. Oh, and me. Did I mention that? I mean to make Cora my wife, too, if she'll have me."

The countess gasped with shock, pushing herself up to her feet. "And why should she marry you?" she said, for the first time losing rein of her tight-laced self-control. "What titles, what station can you give her?"

"Mrs. Captain Fairbourne has always been title enough for my mother," he said. "I doubt Cora would want for more, especially in Appledore."

"In *Appledore*," scoffed the countess contemptuously. "How could she be content in some little place in the colonies like that after London?"

"Because I love her," he declared. He'd decided in the carriage from the playhouse that he'd ask Cora to marry him; that had been easy and noble. But the part about loving her—he hadn't even been able to admit that to himself, let alone say it to Cora. Yet now that the words were out, they sounded fine. They sounded *right*. "Damnation, because I *love* her."

"But that is not enough!" cried the countess, her voice turning shrill. "That was what they told *me*, and they were right! I am the proof, sir, because I became a countess, a lady of property and fashion received by His Majesty himself! That is what lasts, sir, not your *love!*"

"And I say you are wrong, my lady," answered Alex heatedly. There was more being said here than he'd first realized, but he was too caught up in his own emotions to sort them out. "My mother gave up all these things you covet to wed my father. She doesn't miss them, not for a moment, because of the love they share instead."

But the countess shook her head in vehement denial. "Iain was a wise man, sir, the wisest man I have ever known, and even he believed what they told us, because it was the truth. Love will not last, sir, love *will not* last!"

"Lady Waldegrave!" Diana appeared at Alex's side, glancing sharply at him before she dipped a hurried curtsey to the countess. "Are you unwell, my lady? I heard you from my chamber and I came at once."

"She has sent Cora away to be clear of me," said Alex bitterly. "I was going to ask Cora to marry me, Di."

"You *were?*" Diana gasped, her eyes round with gleeful surprise. "Oh, Alex, that is the most perfect news! I knew you should, of course, but I wasn't sure you'd actually do it!"

"I haven't," he said grimly. "I couldn't. When I returned here, Cora was gone."

"But I did what was right," protested the countess piteously as she sank back down into the chair, her head bowed. "All I wished was to ensure Cora's happiness. She should have been my daughter, you know. She would have been a beauty if she'd been mine. If love had been enough, she would have been."

The English lady Cora's father had first loved— now Alex remembered her from Cora's story of her parents while she'd posed for Jacob Curlew. So Iain MacGillivray had trusted his daughter to Charlotte Waldegrave, the woman he'd dutifully left behind at his family's insistence. No wonder the countess' feelings toward love were so confused!

"But you can still make it right for Cora, my lady," urged Diana, kneeling beside the older woman's chair. "If you tell Alex where you sent Cora, then he can follow and bring her back."

"It's too late," moaned the older woman, shaking her head. "They'll be outside the city by now."

"Were your men armed, my lady?" asked Alex urgently. "Tonight Cora ran afoul of a man I believe was a bounty hunter who recognized her. He nearly carried her off then, and I can't swear he won't try again."

The countess' shoulders sagged, scattering powder from her hair as she buried her face in her jeweled hands.

"I sent her with two footmen in a hired carriage to Waldegrave Hall." She sobbed once, a broken cry from a long-broken heart. "And oh, may God and Iain forgive me for what I have done!"

The bed lurched with a life of its own, and no matter how Cora tried to twist and turn, she couldn't find a quiet spot to sleep. It had to be Starlight bouncing his way across the mattress, ready to play regardless of the hour, and with an unhappy groan she reached out to shove him away. Why couldn't he understand that her head ached abominably and that she needed to rest?

"Be still, you wicked little beast," she grumbled sleepily. "I've no wish to play with you now."

"Oh, so it's a beast that I be now, is it?" said a man's voice. "You wouldn't be here a-tall if you hadn't been playin' with someone."

There shouldn't be a man in her bedchamber, especially not one who spoke like that to her, and with a great effort Cora forced her heavy-lidded eyes to open and help her make sense of what was happening.

But seeing did not mean believing, let alone making sense. Instead of her familiar little bedchamber, she was in a closed-in rocking box hazy with pipe smoke and stinking of drink: a carriage, then, and one she didn't recognize. Through the windows she could see the night sky, and the occasional black outlines of trees to show that they'd left the city. Over the rhythmic, muffled clop of the horses' hooves on the dirt road she could hear the same distant thunder that had rolled across London, oh, so much earlier when she'd been on her way to see Mr. Garrick with Alex.

Alex?

She pushed herself upright, everything before her spinning as if she still were half in dreams, and blinked. She'd slept awkwardly flopped over onto the seat, and her face was sticky from having pressed against the worn leather, every muscle in her body ached in protest, and her hair was unpinned and clinging moistly to her neck and shoulders.

And most definitely no Alex. By the light of the single small coach lantern, she could see her only companion in the carriage, a young man in the unadorned livery that Lady Waldegrave gave to her servants in the country for every day. He was also a young man being entirely too familiar with her in his speech and in his manner, sprawled as he was across the opposite seat with a clay pipe in his teeth and an insolent expression on his face as he let his gaze wander over her rumpled silk gown.

"Who are you, pray?" she asked, striving to make

her voice carry the countess' authority. "And why aren't you riding outside on the top where you belong?"

The young man smirked and preened. "I'm Toby, miss, thank'ee for askin'. I come down to town with some parcels for her ladyship, an' come back up to the Hall wit' you, an' I be ridin' inside, here, to make sure you keep yourself safe, an' on account of David an' the doxie he's got ridin' on top with him. On top o' *her*, is what he wants to be ridin', but he takes what he gets first."

As if on cue, Cora heard from overhead a woman's shrill laugh made giddy with drink. So there was the doxie; but where was Alex, and worse, where was she, and how had she come to be here?

"We're taking you to th' Hall, miss," volunteered Toby, more kindly. "Waldegrave Hall. Her ladyship, she wanted you gone from town an' away from that rake. We just changed horses at that last inn while you was sleepin'—that be when David found the doxie—an' we should be at the Hall by daybreak."

Waldegrave Hall. Vainly Cora tried to recall where that was—how far from London, how far from Alex. But why would her ladyship take the trouble to banish her to the country? And how had she come to be here now, with a queasy stomach and an aching head and a buck-toothed footman leering at her?

"If'n you want to sleep more, you can," said Toby as he leaned forward to offer her a drink from the bottle of gin in his hand, "but if'n you want to play instead, Toby here's your man. Aye, I am, miss."

"I need to get down," said Cora urgently, holding one hand over her stomach and the other close to her mouth. "I feel ill. Stop the carriage. I need to get down *now.*"

Toby swore, then leaned his head from the window to bawl at the driver to stop.

"It's looks fit to storm something fierce," he said as the carriage lumbered to a halt. "You're not expectin' me to come out there wit' you while you puke, are you?"

Cora shook her head as she fumbled with the latch on the door, struggling not to trip as her skirts billowed around her legs. They'd stopped in the middle of an overgrown woodland too scrubby to be called a forest, but full of black shifting shadows with the moon hidden by clouds. The wind had gathered, gusting wild enough to make the horses whinny and shift uneasily in their traces, and the leaves on the trees overhead blow bottoms up and silvery.

"Clear off, my *lady,*" said the frowsy woman who'd been riding on top with David as she pushed past Cora to climb inside the carriage. "I'll not have my clothes rained upon while you retch."

But Cora didn't care. After the stuffy carriage, the wind whipping against her face felt good, sweeping away the last sleepy cobwebs from her thoughts and settling her stomach as well. Now she could remember drinking the chocolate with her ladyship, and realizing too late that there'd been sleeping draft mixed in as well, and her ladyship whispering that everything was for the best.

But it wasn't for the best, not when Cora could also remember how Alex had promised to come back. What had he thought when he'd returned to find her gone? What tale had Lady Waldegrave told him as an explanation?

Holding her blowing hair back from her face, she looked back at the carriage. The driver was busy controlling the restive horses, and the two footmen and the woman, silhouetted in the lantern's light, were equally busy consuming the gin. No one was bothering with her.

And so, with her skirts bunched high in her hands, she plunged into the scrubby bushes and ran. She ran heedless of the shadows, heedless of the first flash of lightning, heedless of how her kerchief fell away and her stays dug into her sides and her high-heeled shoes hobbled her steps, heedless of the branches that snagged and grabbed at her clothes.

Behind her, back on the road, she heard loud voices—quarreling, angry male voices—yet she didn't stop. She heard the dry crack of pistol shots, and a woman scream, and the terrified squeal of horses as the carriage rumbled into motion, and still she ran, faster, faster. The lightning flashed again, the thunder now rumbling close on its heels, and she did not stop.

Until the man's arm hooked around her waist and yanked her back against his chest, his other hand pressed tight over her mouth to silence her instinctive scream.

Terrified, she thought of how helpless she'd been in the alley, and how, this time, there'd be no Alex to rescue her.

"Don't move," rasped the man into her ear, "or by God, you die."

16

Don't move, he'd ordered, or you die; and yet Cora couldn't help but twist in his arms to face him.

"Alex!" she gasped, and tears of relief welled up in her eyes as she flung her arms around his waist, her heart pounding from running and from fear. Though she could barely make out his face in the shadows, she'd still recognized his voice, his touch, even his scent. "Oh, Alex, how did you ever find me?"

"Hush, Cora, hush!" he whispered urgently. "I meant what I said! We're not alone here!"

"I know," she whispered, her voice quavering with relief. "Oh, Alex, Lady Waldegrave was sending me away with two horrid footmen, and—"

"I don't mean them, Cora," said Alex. "There are others, too. Highwaymen, I'd wager. We can't stay here. We have to leave now."

"Highwaymen!" Her hand brushed against something hard tucked into the belt at his waist, and without looking she knew it was a pistol.

"Oh, Alex, they have guns, too," she said anxiously. "At least I heard—"

"I heard it," he said. "Now untie your hoops."

She stared at him. "My hoops? Why ever would I—"

"Do it now, Cora, else I'll do it for you," he ordered. "Handsomely now, hurry!"

Modestly she turned her back to him before she pulled up her skirts, fumbling in the dark with the double-tied ribbon that held the cane hoops at her waist, over her shift and beneath her petticoats. Behind her she heard Alex swear with impatience, and before she'd realized what he was doing, he'd flipped up her skirts from the back. She gasped as she felt a tug in the ribbon, then the hoops were dropping free over her hips and to the ground. Swiftly she turned around, just in time to see him tuck a long-bladed knife back into its sheath under his coat. Dear Lord, who was following them that he'd needed to bring so many weapons?

He grabbed her hand and pulled her forward through the bushes to where, to her surprise, he'd tethered a large dark gelding. The horse seemed equally surprised, shying back away as they came closer.

"Hey now, lad, be nice to the lady," murmured Alex as he untied the reins. " 'Tis good you're such a big fellow since you're going to have to carry two of us."

"But how did he come here, Alex?" asked Cora breathlessly. "How did *you*?"

"On his back, of course," he said, bending down to link his hands to make a step for her foot. "Fortunately that carriage of yours was slow as January molasses, else I never would have caught up with you in time. And I can't tell you how happy I was to spy you leave on your own, as neat and tidy as if you'd known I was waiting."

"I told them I was going to be sick," she confessed. "I did think I was."

"Well, no matter," he said. "Here now, up you go."

In one easy move he'd lifted her up onto the horse's back, then climbed up behind her, shifting her forward. The horse whinnied in protest, and shied away again from the pale swath of her trailing skirts.

"Damnation, I should have cut off your petticoats, too," muttered Alex as he wrestled to control the skittish horse. "Can't you haul them in somehow, Cora?"

Clumsily she leaned forward to gather the hand-painted silk into a bunch, trying not to think of how her legs were now uncovered clear above her garters.

"Now hang on, lass," said Alex, "and we'll see if we can make London by dawn."

They soon left the tangle of trees and bushes and came out on the London road, to the south of where Cora had run from the carriage.

"We came this way before," said Cora slowly. "I recognize that tree, and the—oh, dear God, Alex, *look!*"

The shadowy shape of the man's body lying beside the road was unmistakable, even on so dark a night. He lay on his back, his legs outstretched and his arms flung over his head like a broken jumping jack. Lightning flashed, shining bright as a beacon to illuminate the startled expression frozen in his open eyes, and the crimson swath that had once been his white shirt.

"That's one of the footmen from the carriage—his name's Toby," said Cora, staring at the body with horror. "What has happened to him? Why is he here?"

"Someone killed him, Cora," said Alex grimly. "Those shots we heard earlier—one of those must have found him. Likely he fell from the carriage then, or the others tossed him out."

Once her father had been like this, spread on the cold ground while his life's blood had spilled from his body, his arms and legs too still and his eyes unseeing.

"Oh, Alex, we must stop!" she cried, not so much for the footman as for her father, her uncles, her cousins, all those that she'd loved who'd died like this. "We must try to help him!"

"He's past our help, lass."

"But we must do something," she whimpered, twisting around to look back at the black shape by the side of the road. "We can't leave him like that."

"The best you can do for that poor bastard is to pray for his soul," said Alex, "and ours, too, if we linger."

He pulled the horse's head to the right and urged him up the side of the road and into an open field, newly plowed for sowing and soft beneath the horse's hooves. Here in the open, the wind blew harder, and with it now came the first drops of rain—large, cold drops that landed heavily on Cora's bare face and arms. The drops quickly became a downpour, and as the horse bent his head and labored across the now muddy field, Cora turned more into Alex's arms and chest, bowing her head to shield herself from the wind and rain. She was shivering now, as much from grief and the realization of what she'd escaped as from the wet cold.

"Here we are," shouted Alex over the rain. "This should do for us tonight."

Cora lifted her head and saw a large, rambling building looming before them, the walls of starkly patterned timber and plaster with brick in a style old-fashioned a century ago. But her hopes for a sanctuary plummeted when she saw how every window was dark, every chimney empty of smoke, the family clearly still in town or away at another house. If there was a housekeeper or caretaker, then she or he was squirreled away in some other, distant corner of the great house.

"We'll have to keep going, Alex," she shouted back. "No one's home."

"No one but us," he answered, "which is exactly how I like it tonight."

He guided the horse around a brick wall, surrounded by a stand of ancient, gnarled yews, to stand beneath a decorative porch at the far end of the house. Here they'd be sheltered not only from the rain but also from sight of anyone happening across the field.

Alex swung down from the horse, then helped Cora to the ground before he went to the nearest window. These were old-fashioned as well, not modern sashes but antique casements pieced together from dozens of diamond-shaped pieces of glass. With the same knife he'd used to cut the ribbon on her hoops, Alex pried at leaded strips that held the glass together, until several of the diamonds popped out and he could slip his hand into the opening to unhook the latch. He pulled himself up onto the sill and slipped inside, leaving Cora anxiously holding the horse's reins.

"Alex?" she called nervously when he didn't reappear at once. She didn't like being left alone in this strange place, and she kept thinking of the empty eyes and blood-soaked shirt of poor Toby, and worse, whoever had left him there for dead. She was shaking again, and she couldn't stop. "Alex, are you there?"

"Here, sweetheart." He dropped back to the ground

beside her, dusting his hands on the back of his coat. "It's not the tidiest of accommodations, but it will do handsomely for us tonight."

He tethered and unsaddled the horse inside the wall and near an ornamental urn that had conveniently filled with rain water, and slung the saddlebag over his shoulder and, more carefully, the rucksack over his arm before he helped Cora climb inside the window.

"It's—it's very dark, Alex," she said, hugging herself while she heard him fussing with something in the bags. She wanted to be brave, the way he was always telling her she was, but she kept thinking of what could be lurking in the blackness of this unknown room. "Alex?"

"I'm here, sweetheart." With a little flash, he lit a scrap of tinder with a spark from his flint, and then in turn lit the mouse-nibbled tapers in the candlestand on the floor beside him. But also on the floor were Alex's two pistols, and before he did anything else, he deftly began emptying the rain-wet powder to reload them.

"I'll only be a moment," he explained. "It's far better to be prepared than not. One time I was careless and didn't bother to check my powder, and the pistol misfired into my hand."

He held up his hand to show the faint black peppering that she'd noticed soon after they'd met. "I'm lucky I've five fingers left for counting. And now I always take care to check my own powder."

"Do you think you'll need those tonight?" she asked, watching how expertly he handled the guns. She hated seeing the size of the lead balls, as large as her thumbnail, and thinking how pitifully defenseless human flesh and bone was in return. "In here, I mean?"

"I'd wager not," he said evenly. "But I'd rather be ready than otherwise."

But she'd wish *all* of this otherwise, if she could help it, and she turned swiftly away so he couldn't see her tears. Pistols and dry gunpowder might make him feel safer, but what she wished for most was for him to hold her tight, and kiss her until she forgot the dead young footman, and the one-eyed man in the alley, and oh, everything else that was making her feel like a hopeless, weeping coward.

He must have lit more candles behind her because the shadowy chamber brightened further. This wasn't a large room, most likely a bedchamber for guests, though from how all the furniture and the looking glass were shrouded in ghostly linen covers, and from the musty smell of dust and mice, there'd been no guests here for years.

More ghosts and shrouds and signs of death to match the ones that were already filling her thoughts, that seemed to follow her wherever she went.

"Cora?" he asked softly. "Cora, love. What's wrong?"

She cupped her hands together over her mouth to smother her emotions, and shook her head. He'd never called her *love* before, and to hear it first now, in these circumstances, was nearly unbearable.

"You know who killed Toby, don't you?" she asked without turning.

He sighed. "I'm not sure, sweetheart."

"But you can guess. You *have* guessed."

"Cora, there's no point—"

"Will you at least tell me if the man who killed Toby is the same one who is . . . is seeking me? The man with the red scarf?"

She could hear his hesitation; he'd stopped cleaning the pistols, and the only sound left was the rain outside.

"Yes," he said at last. "I won't lie to you. I didn't before, and I won't now. It could have been a highwayman who killed that footman, a random whim of fate, but I don't believe it was so."

Death, and more death, and she rubbed her arms to banish the chill. Jacob Curlew's drawing of her walking among the graves had been more accurate than he'd realized. All she prayed now was that she didn't bring the same dreadful fortune to Alex.

"Oh, no, you don't," muttered Alex crossly. "Where the devil do you think you're bound, eh?"

Cora frowned, for that made no sense. She wasn't bound anywhere else tonight, and Alex should know that.

She heard an odd scuffling noise that had nothing to do with his pistols, then another oath from Alex, and finally the equally cross little meow that explained it all.

"Starlight!" she cried as she turned and saw the little cat standing beside Alex.

Clearly not a happy cat, Starlight lashed his tail indignantly as he eyed one of the lead balls rolling gently on the floor before him. At Cora's voice he looked up, startled, and meowed querulously, relieved to have someone more understanding to complain to.

"Oh, Starlight, you wicked little beast," she said as she scooped him from the floor and cradled him in the crook of her arm. "How did you come to be here, anyway?"

"It was Diana's idea," confessed Alex, sitting back on his heels as he pulled off his wet coat and waistcoat; he'd already shed his wet shoes and stockings.

"She thought he'd be a comfort to you. She's the one who found him the basket for traveling, here, tucked inside the rucksack. I was afraid he'd suffer, but you can see for yourself how unaffected the little rogue is."

Cora looked down at the wicker box with the lid now unfastened, and remembered the care that Alex had taken with the rucksack. "He's been with you all along?"

"Except when he wasn't charming the innkeeper's wife," said Alex as he finished with the gunpowder and flints, "begging beef broth and chicken scraps in the kitchen—far better than the bread and cheese we'll have—while I dickered for a fresh horse. I tell you, Cora, that creature eats more than most men."

"That's because he's only a kitten and still growing. Hey, la, where are you going now?"

Starlight pushed from her arms and jumped to the floor, eager to capture the lead ball before Alex tucked it away.

"Very well," said Alex, holding the ball poised between his thumb and forefinger, "if you really wish it that badly, then yours it is. Go on now, chase your prize!"

He rolled the lead ball across the floor like a marble, grinning as he watched the little cat go racing after it, skittering over the floorboards and around chair legs. After spending so much time in the basket, Starlight was ready to play, and he batted the ball back and forth with a satisfying clatter, bouncing it against the wall to chase again and again, his tail puffed like a black pinecone with excitement.

And for the first time that evening, Cora laughed, clapping her hands with delight as she watched.

Starlight might not have enjoyed his journey today, but she was mightily glad to have him here tonight.

"There now," said Alex, coming to stand behind her, "the world isn't always such a grim old place, is it?"

"I don't think Starlight's world ever is," she said wistfully. "But wouldn't ours be much improved if all pistols and musket balls were used as toys instead of for killing?"

"My poor Cora," said Alex softly. "This wasn't exactly what I'd hoped for you this night."

"Nor I." She smiled sadly. "But I'll grant you it's greatly improved over what it was earlier, even if you feel you must have those pistols."

"I'm only being careful, sweetheart," said Alex. "It would take a miracle for anyone to track us to here. We're likely safer in this house tonight than anywhere in London."

"When I was little," she said, "being safe meant lying snug in my own little bed with the curtains drawn and the shutters open so I could see the moon and the stars over the glen, and the door to my bedchamber left ajar so I could hear Father and his friends talking over their whiskey downstairs. It didn't matter if I could make out their words; it was the low rumble of their voices that made everything seem right and peaceful."

She shivered and ran her hands over her forearms again, hugging herself. "But that was when being safe had nothing to do with pistols or tracks or breaking into an empty house to keep from the rain."

"And to find a bed worthy of a queen," said Alex, with a flourish whipping the linen dustcover from the great bed. Beneath it were a coverlet and bolsters of patterned cut velvet edged with tarnished gold fringe, as out of fashion as the bulbous turnings on the four corner posts and the heavy cornice, carved with scowling cherubs. Next he flung back the coverlet, and beneath it the bed had been left made up, the linen sheets still bearing the creases of a long-ago iron and smelling faintly of wild lavender.

"I'm not sure I should sleep there," said Cora, striving to match his banter.

"No?" he asked, his expression so full of question that she realized, too late, that he'd read something altogether different into her refusal. She'd meant sleep, and sleep alone, while he'd been thinking quite otherwise.

"No," she said, blushing furiously. "You English don't do well by Scottish queens. You brought poor Queen Mary to London only to cut off her head."

"That wouldn't have happened had she been with me." He smiled crookedly. "If I'd been her champion, she would have kept her head."

"How reassuring," she murmured, but as he came to stand before her, her heart was racing. The rain had stopped, the thunder done, and the cooler air that came in through the broken window seemed charged with possibilities.

"I'll be comfortable enough sleeping in one of the chairs," he said, reaching out to take her hands. "You and Starlight can have the bed to yourselves. You're precious cold, Cora. Your clothes are soaked."

"So are yours," she said. The candlelight flickered across his face, wavering in the breeze like her emotions.

"But I'm a sailor," he said, his voice low and gravelly, the way it had been that night in the garden. "I'm as accustomed as a codfish to being wet."

"Not in wet silk like I am." With regret she looked down at the ruined gown, the creamy silk torn and stained with grass and mud. "Your sister will never share anything with me again."

He followed her gaze and frowned. "Silk or sackcloth, you're still too cold. What's the point of saving your life if you squander it by taking a mortal chill instead?"

She met his gaze, raising her eyes without lifting her chin. He was Alex, and she'd trust him wherever he led her, whether it was to Creignish or that queenly, old-fashioned bed. Without looking away, she deliberately began unpinning the front of her bodice, one slow, careful pin at a time.

"Diana told me that your mother had judged this gown most improper," she said, lowering her voice to a husky whisper as her fingers moved from one pin to the next. "She said your mother nearly sent it back to the mantua-maker for being too scandalous. 'Twas the lining, she said, calculated to put gentlemen into a ferocious state. But Diana and I were both too much the simpletons to know exactly why. Perhaps you could tell me, Alex?"

Alex felt as if he'd been hard for her from the moment she'd come bouncing down the stairs at Lady Waldegrave's house, her nearly naked breasts raised up for him like some sort of tempting, pagan offering. He'd instantly remembered how her breasts felt in his hands and how her nipples had tightened in his mouth, how she'd moaned with startled delight when he'd tugged at them with his lips, and he'd remembered it again each time that evening he'd looked at her in that gown.

Oh, aye, that gown was calculated to put gentlemen, and ordinary men, too, into ferocious states; his mother was no fool about teasing men into attention. But how could either of them know that the gown's powers would only increase, that the more ruined it became by rain and mud, the more it made him think of the ruination of its wearer, too?

Without the contrivance of hoops, the silk skirts slipped and slithered over Cora's hips and bottom as she walked, displaying curves that were never intended to be displayed. The little tears and rips caused by thorns and branches revealed unexpected patches of her skin like jagged private peepholes he longed to rip larger, while the pale silk itself, soaked by the rain, had become so translucent on her paleness that it was almost as if the bright flowers had been painted directly onto her bare skin.

His state was ferocious, all right, and that gown—with Cora's delicious self inside—was entirely to blame. How much torment could one wretched garment make him suffer?

He learned the moment Cora began to take it off.

He'd rescued her with the most honorable intentions. First of all he'd meant to save her life, which he had, thank God, accomplished. But he'd also meant to tell her he loved her, and ask her to marry him, which he hadn't begun to do. He told himself he must not look down, that to ogle her now when she was so vulnerable would be far, far worse than kissing her in the alley after she'd been attacked and robbed. Jesus, hadn't he already sunk low enough?

"Diana vowed it was the color that was wicked," Cora was saying as she clicked the last hook open and eased the bodice open with both hands. "Though for the life of me, Alex, I cannot fathom why. How can pink be wicked?"

And with a groan of despair and resignation, he looked.

And looked. Through the sheer lawn of her shift, her blue satin stays raised her breasts full and high, and her nipples were clearly visible, already pebbled with excitement, and eager for his caress. That was enough to bring a cockstand to a dead man; but then there was the question of the gown's real wickedness.

Ivory silk nearly the color of her skin, split to reveal silk that was a deep pink, nearly red, glistening, and so blasted, blatantly suggestive he choked.

"So why is it wicked, Alex?" she innocently asked again. "And I can tell you think so, too, from the expression on your face."

"Because, sweetheart, it reminds a man of your— of a woman's—oh, hell, Cora, I cannot think of a polite name to call it!"

"Then show me," she whispered desperately, reaching up to kiss him. "Make me forget about death and . . . and everything else. Make me think only of you, and of me, of us together."

As her lips found his, at last he understood. Damnation, here he'd been holding back, trying to be noble, when nobility was the last thing she desired. She didn't want to feel protected. Protection was the other side of feeling weak and vulnerable, and she didn't want that, either. She needed to feel strong, with life surging through her, so she could banish forever the ghosts that seemed so determined to haunt her. She needed to feel *alive*.

And he knew exactly how to do it.

He kissed her hard, hungrily, giving in to all the desire and passion he'd been keeping so tightly in check. She parted her lips at once for him, welcoming him into her mouth with a kiss that could have scorched. He circled his arm around her waist, pulling her closer, but though he could feel her breasts press against his chest, he also felt the unyielding whalebone of her stays, keeping her away from him.

"This must go," he ordered, shoving his hands inside the open front of her gown, inside all that lubricious dark pink silk, and pushing it back off her shoulders, down her arms. "I want to feel *you*, Cora."

Her eyes were dark with excitement, her lips parted and begging for another kiss as she shrugged her way free of the bodice. She began to untie the ribbon that held her petticoats, but impatiently he hooked his fingers inside the ribbon and snapped it in two. She gasped as the silk sank with a *shush* into a heap around her feet, then grinned as she stepped free of it with a little hop.

"What will Diana say?" she whispered with gleeful guilt as she reached out to tug his shirt free from his breeches. "When she sees that broken ribbon, she'll—"

"Who the hell cares what Diana thinks?" he growled, pulling his shirt over his head and tossing it aside. "It's you I'm thinking of now, Cora, not my sister."

"And it's you I'm thinking of, too, Captain Fairbourne," she said, her voice husky as she gazed at his bare chest with unabashed interest. "Thinking and looking."

"Take down your hair," he ordered hoarsely, watching her as closely as she was him. "Make it loose."

"It's hardly up at all," she protested, but still obeyed, reaching up to find and pull out the last pins and shake the gleaming russet curls free over her shoulders. "I can't guess how untidy it must be after the rain."

"I like it that way," he said. "If you wished to please me, you'd never wear it up again."

She smiled, and he watched how her breasts trembled over the top of her stays as she held her arms up, how the candlelight made filigree shadows on her skin through the lace that trimmed her shift. The sheer fabric came only to her knees, and below her stays he could clearly see the dark shadow of curling hair at the top of her thighs.

Carefully he slipped his thumbs beneath the drawstring's casing along the neckline of her shift, slipping it down to leave her shoulders bare, then sliding forward to pull the sheer fabric off her breasts entirely, leaving the drawstring's little bow dangling uselessly beneath and the lace now no more than a frill. He'd always delighted in slowly undressing a woman in pretty underclothes, teasing them both in the process, but he'd never found as much pleasure in the game as he was here now with Cora.

"I suppose you like this, too?" she asked, tossing her hair back over her shoulders, as if she needed to draw his attention. She learned quickly, his elf-girl. "Though I must say, Alex, I feel rather foolish."

"Liar," he said before he kissed her again until she chuckled into his mouth. "Whatever you're feeling, sweetheart, it's not foolish."

"Queenly, then?"

"More likely wanton, I'd say."

"Then I'd say likely more wanton," she said, teasing

and coy, and he smiled, remembering a time when she'd no idea how to banter like this.

"Turn about, your wanton majesty," he said, and steered her so her back was facing him so he could begin to unlace her stays. She bunched her hair up in both hands to help, and he paused to press his lips to the nape of her neck, inhaling her scent. He loved the way the freckles dusted her shoulders, like nutmeg grated on vanilla custard; no wonder he thought of her as delicious. Slowly he tugged the cord through the eyelets, letting her feel how her body was gradually released from the cage of whalebone, losing the fashionable silhouette and regaining her own curves.

When he reached the last eyelet, the stays slipped forward on her arms, and she dropped her hair to let them slide off. Before she could turn, he settled his hands on her breasts, relishing the way her nipples responded to his rough palms as she gasped with pleasure. Possessively he slid his hands down the length of her body, lingering over the full curves of her hips and bottom as he pulled her back against him with a groan.

Too much, he thought, his restraint shredding at the feel of so much sweet female flesh pressing against him, and as she yipped with surprise he scooped her up in his arms as easily as she did Starlight. In three steps he'd reached the bed, setting her a little back from the side with her feet stretched out before her like a doll on a shelf.

"Now, Your Majesty," he said, kneeling before her. "You may keep your head, but not your shoes."

"But what of my stockings, my garters?" she asked

breathlessly as she watched him unbuckle each shoe and toss it aside. "Will you have those, too, Captain?"

"Nay," he said, sliding his hand across her ankle, along her calf to her knee. "Yellow silk stockings show far better on you."

He heard her little gulp. "And the garters, Captain?"

He pushed his hand higher along her leg, above her knee to where she tied her stockings.

"You can keep those, too, Your Majesty," he whispered, leaning closer to kiss her throat and beneath her ear as he found the soft, warm skin of her thigh, tracing tiny, teasing circles with his fingertips. "I'll claim them another time."

"I—I thank you, Captain," she said, closing her eyes as she restlessly ran her hands across his back.

"Don't thank me, Cora," he murmured as he pushed her gently back onto the bed. "Just feel."

And how, thought Cora, could she possibly do anything else? She felt as if every inch of her skin were alive with sensation, her body yearning for the promise of rare pleasure that Alex held before her. The candles he'd lit earlier were beginning to gutter out, one by one, deepening the shadows in the room, and to Cora the darkness only intensified her other senses. But in a way all this was frightening, too, because with Alex her body was behaving in some new and very unfamiliar ways.

When he lay atop her, pressing her deep into the soft featherbed, she welcomed his weight, languorously arching and wriggling beneath him so that he groaned again. There was a part of him inside his breeches that was long and thick and hard, a part of him that she'd remembered feeling that morning in the print room, and the more she pressed against it now, the more he pressed back in a way that was infinitely more exciting than anything she'd read about in Ovid.

His mouth was hot and demanding, his tongue exploring every corner of her mouth in a way that made her body move beneath him even more. He trailed wet kisses down her jaw and the little hollow of her throat and to her breast, drawing her nipple into his mouth and tugging at it with his lips and tongue until she was gasping, her fingers tangled in the black silk of his hair.

He'd shoved her shift up over her legs and she didn't protest, pushed it to her waist, and she welcomed how he'd freed her to feel more of her skin against his. Then the shift was gone altogether, flung aside, and though she now wore nothing beyond her stockings and garters, she shamelessly didn't care.

And all because of Alex.

Eagerly she explored the broad, sweat-sleeked planes of his muscular back, marveling at the differences between her body and his, sliding her hands to follow the way his waist tapered and the shallow valley of his spine. She'd wanted to do this since the morning she'd seen him in his cabin, to touch and learn his body. The coarse black hair of his chest was like another caress as he moved heavily over her, and when she pressed her face to his chest, breathing his scent, she could hear his heart racing as fast as her own.

She felt his hand move across her belly, then slide lower, through the short curls she had there. His fingers slipped lower still, teasing a small nubbin of sensation that she'd never dreamed existed. Gently he caressed her, and she whimpered as the joy built, then exploded, leaving her limp and dazed and gasping to catch her breath.

"Another minute, Cora," he promised inexplicably as he slid from the bed, breathing hard. "Only another minute."

"Alex?" she asked breathlessly in the dark, the loss of only that moment seeming like an eternity, and then he was back, smoothing and kneading the insides of her thighs as he eased them apart to make room for himself.

"I'm here, sweetheart," he said as the bed's rope springs creaked beneath his weight. "Do you truly believe I'd leave you now?"

She smiled in the dark, reaching out to touch him, and realized he'd shed his breeches just as she'd lost her shift. Now she wished the candles were still lit so she could see and admire whatever male mysteries he'd been hiding there.

But before she could consider this he was touching her again in her special woman's place, parting her swollen lips to stroke that hot little nubbin once more. Mindlessly she called his name as she clung to him, desperate for him not to stop. He truly was her captain, taking her to places she'd never dreamed of visiting, and her pirate, too, dark and strong and ruthlessly sure as he claimed her for his own.

She was shaking with need as he shifted to settle his body lower between her spread thighs, and she scarcely realized at first that he'd replaced his clever fingers with something else, something substantially larger. She wriggled impatiently and then she felt him pushing against her, pushing into her and stretching her and *filling* her and oh, dear Lord, she feared she'd be split in two and she couldn't breathe and it *hurt*.

He stopped moving to look down at her, his face hidden in the dark but his concern still palpable.

"Oh, Cora," he rasped. "Damnation, I've hurt you."

She shook her head even though he couldn't see it, but when he touched a fingertip to her cheek and found it wet with tears, he knew the truth.

"My own brave Cora," he said. "I'm sorry. But it will get better, I promise."

She *would* trust him, even if she couldn't see how he'd be right. She shifted a fraction, trying to ease his weight, and he swore, struggling not to move in return. Yet strangely, as he'd promised, moving lessened the ache of invasion, and tentatively she rocked her hips upward. That felt better, much better, and she realized now Alex was moving with her, too, teaching her the rhythm.

"Here," he said, guiding her legs over his hips. "Like this. Oh, aye, lass, that's it."

Now she was embracing him with her legs as well as her arms, and though it seemed to draw him deeper inside her, she was beginning to feel the first fluttering of the same pleasure he'd brought her before when he'd teased her with his fingers. But this was better, stronger, more intense, the tension coiling tighter in her body. He angled himself a fraction higher across her body, dragging himself over that most sensitive part of her, and with his next strokes she cried out, frantic for more as her body arched against his, higher and higher and higher until, when she was sure she could bear no more, her release came and she wept and shuddered with joy and so did he, driving two more times into her body before, with a roar, he spent his seed.

"You're mine, Alex," whispered Cora later as they

lay drowsily together, their bodies still intimately twined. "You're mine, just as I am yours."

Alex smiled in the dark, his heart filled to overflowing as he gently smoothed the damp curls of her hair back from her face. "That's because I love you, Cora," he whispered. "I love you, mind?"

But she didn't mind because she was already asleep, her body soft and relaxed and her breathing regular, and tenderly he pulled her closer.

Aye, he loved his Cora, he thought happily as he, too, drifted off to sleep. He'd be sure to tell her again in the morning when she was awake enough to appreciate it. He loved her, and there weren't any finer words in all of England.

17

As Cora woke, it seemed like the most usual of mornings, with Starlight standing on her chest to butt her nose with his muzzle, purring as loudly as he could for extra emphasis. Reluctantly she opened her eyes, squinting at the sunlight, then smiled at the little cat's face so close to hers.

"Wicked beast," she muttered sleepily, and yawned. "Isn't there any chicken left in your dish from last night?"

To answer he butted against her nose again, and with another yawn she pushed herself higher on the pillow, then frowned. This wasn't her bedchamber, and this wasn't her bed, and suddenly a very male arm flopped over onto her stomach, sending Starlight flying from her chest with an indignant yowl.

"Hush, hush, you'll wake Alex!" scolded Cora in a hurried whisper as, in a heady rush, she remembered exactly where she was, and how and why she'd come to be there.

There included Alex, lying in the bed beside her. He was sprawled peacefully on his stomach, one arm pillowing his head and the other thrown over her, and some time in the night he'd kicked off every scrap of sheets and coverlet.

And oh, what a glorious sight he made, his long muscular body so completely at ease, his black hair tossed over his shoulders and his face relaxed, the harsh lines softened and his lips slightly parted in the center of the dark bristle of new whiskers. She guessed that, in warmer seas, he must parade about his sloop as the most scandalously half-dressed of captains, for above the waist and below his knees he was well browned by the sun, while in between his skin was nearly as pale as her own—almost, she thought with amusement, as if he wore invisible breeches all the time.

But Starlight decided such admiration was taking far too much time from his breakfast, and with a slight wiggle of his rear end, he leaped from Cora squarely onto Alex's bare back.

With a roar Alex was instantly awake, rolling off the bed to grab a pistol from the floor, turning and aiming it back at the bed. But Starlight, who had fled at the first roar, now cowered beneath the bed.

Not that Cora could fault him, either. "Put down that pistol at once!" she cried indignantly, pulling the sheet up higher as if that would offer some sort of protection against an irate naked man with a gun. "What sort of good morning is this?"

"Damnation, Cora, I could ask you the same thing!" Sheepishly he uncocked and lowered the gun, shaking his rumpled hair back from his still-sleepy face. He didn't bother to cover himself, though, making Cora blush yet again even as she studied him in the morning sunlight with considerable interest. "I was asleep. How was I to know it was only that hell-cat of yours? Where the devil is he now, anyway? Trying to flay me alive like that—he's lucky I don't skin him in return."

Gingerly he reached behind to pat at his back, assessing the damage, then turned to show Cora. "Look now, there must be blood running in rivers from his blasted claws."

"He's barely scratched you at all," said Cora softly. She hadn't known he'd put the pistols within reach of the bed; she wished she still didn't, even if such caution had been necessary. Being reminded of danger and death that way somehow took away from the joy she'd felt with him last night. "You'll be fine."

But clearly he wasn't listening, instead staring intently at one of the small, dark paintings on the wall. He set the pistol carefully on one of the chairs and leaned closer to the painting, whistling low with amazement.

"What is it, Alex?" asked Cora. She slid from the bed, and found her shift on the floor, shrugging it over her head before she joined him. She might have been wantonly abandoned last night, but in the bright light of morning she felt considerably more modest.

"Don't these beat anything in Bushell's shop?" he asked, laughing as he moved aside for her to see. "I'd wager this wasn't a chamber for stowing the visiting dowager aunts."

Cora looked, and gasped. Though the painting in the gilded frame had darkened beneath old varnish, the subject was still clear enough: a well-muscled Roman warrior, his helmet and shield discarded on the grass beside him to show he'd just returned from the wars, was being welcomed, or congratulated, or perhaps merely entertained by a beautiful long-legged woman dressed in the merest wisp of fabric around her waist. With her head tossed back in ecstasy, she straddled the warrior with her bottom conveniently tipped up to display the warrior and his oversized member claiming a bit of ecstasy for himself, too.

"Oh, Alex!" murmured Cora, shocked, her face hot with embarrassment. "What an exceptionally rude painting! Whyever would anyone have such a picture in their house?"

"Because he liked it, I'd say," said Alex, chuckling at her response as he stood beside her. "Because it made his lady friends act just the way you're acting now. Every last painting in the room's like this one. Quite a collection."

"That's not very well mannered, having pictures for shaming ladies!"

"But you're not truly shamed, are you, Cora?" he asked, teasing, as he slid his hands beneath her shift to rest upon her hips, his fingers splayed as he began caressing her. "You're saying you are because that's what a lady like you is supposed to say, but inside you're not shamed at all. You're pretending you're that Roman lady there, and thinking how powerfully happy she seems, and wondering if I could make you feel happy like that, too."

"I am not," she denied weakly, though in truth he'd read her thoughts exactly. She *was* imagining what the Roman lady was feeling, and that imagining was making her heart quicken and her palms grow damp and that now familiar warm, heavy feeling grow low in her belly. Having Alex, as thoroughly undressed as the Roman warrior, running his hands over her body, molding and kneading and pressing against her breasts and bottom, was only making the imagining even more vivid. She almost felt as if she *was* the woman in the painting.

"Please, Alex," she gasped. "Please!"

"Oh, aye, please," he whispered roughly, his caresses growing more demanding. Her knees seemed to weaken and she leaned back against him for support, feeling how hard his arousal had grown. " 'Please, Alex, please take me like that.' That's what you're thinking, isn't it? That's sure as hell what I'm thinking, lass. Once we leave here, who knows when we'll have this chance again?"

Gently his fingers slid between her thighs, stroking her so she shuddered and closed her eyes, but still the painting remained seared into her consciousness to tempt her. Perhaps Alex could speak of the future, of what would happen to them next, but all she could focus on now was the heat he was stirring in her body.

"I—I am not sure I could do that," she said, her breath coming in such short little bursts that she almost couldn't speak. "That is, I'm not sure my—my limbs will be so—so accommodating."

"I'm willing to wager they can, Cora," coaxed Alex, leading her back to the bed. "We're not about to be outdone by a fusty old painting, are we?"

Soon she'd lost her shift once again and her worries with it, and to their shared satisfaction she demonstrated that her limbs could be as effortlessly accommodating as her imagination already was. She was brave, his Cora, in this as in everything else, and her daring only made him love her more.

Last night he'd considered himself the tutor because of his greater experience, most of which had been expensively purchased in various Caribbean houses that catered to shipmasters. But now, with her rocking atop him, her hair tumbling down and her eyes dreamy with passion and wonder as she rode him, he realized how much in turn she was teaching him. There were at least a hundred different words for what they were doing now, but for the first time for him *lovemaking* was the only one that seemed right.

She smiled and leaned forward to kiss him, guiding him deeper into her willing body. With a groan he kissed her back, holding her tightly by the hips as he brought them both to the final pleasure.

She collapsed on his chest, panting and spent, with her legs sprawled out on either side of his. Sunlight streamed through the diamond-patterned windows to dapple the sheets, and the only sounds were their own ragged breathing and the insistent buzz of a dragonfly outside the glass.

"I love you, Cora," he whispered hoarsely. "I love you."

She raised herself up on her arms to gaze at him, her eyes swimming and her smile wobbly. "I love you, too, Alex. I think I always have."

"I suspect I've felt the same for you as well, though I've been too much the dunderhead to admit it." He brushed the tangled curls back from her forehead. "There now, sweetheart, it's nothing to weep over, is it?"

She shook her head, one tear spilling out anyway. "I'm happy, that is all," she sniffed. "I never thought you'd ever say such a thing to me."

"I never thought I'd say it to anyone," he confessed.

She giggled, the vibration traveling down to where they still lay joined. "You can say it again, you know. I'm scarcely weary of hearing it."

"Well enough. I love you, Cora Margaret MacGillivray. I love you, and I want to marry you, if you'll have me. Marry me, Cora. Marry me, and you'll never be done hearing how much I love you."

But instead of the joyful acceptance he'd expected, her smiled wobbled into infinite sadness.

"I love you, too, Alex," she said softly, and now that first solitary tear was being joined by others, "and I always will. But I cannot marry you."

"Don't be foolish," he said quickly, fear making him impatient. "Why the devil can't you? I love you, Cora, and you love me. I've always thought that was reason enough for most women and men."

She shook her head and pushed herself away from him, leaving his chest feeling chilly and empty. "But we're different, Alex. You must know that."

"Well, hell, forgive me if I don't."

"Alex, no."

"I won't hear that, Cora," he said swiftly, and he meant it: he wouldn't hear her refusal because he couldn't accept it. "I swear I'll make you happier than any woman alive. We'll wed as soon as we return to London, and you and Diana can go to whatever shops you please. You've done without for too long. Once you're Mrs. Captain Fairbourne, I'll want you to buy whatever you please, mind? Then, when we go back to Appledore, why, you can have your choice of houses, and—"

"You have it all planned, don't you?" she said with more than a little bitterness. "You've always faulted your father for wanting to arrange everyone's life for them. I don't see that you're doing anything that's one whit different with me. Perhaps I don't wish to go to Appledore or try to spend you into debtor's prison or be called Mrs. Captain Anything. I love you, Alex, but I don't wish to *become* you."

"But damnation, you'd be safe in Appledore, Cora," he argued, hauling himself upright in the bed. He didn't like being compared to his father. He wasn't the same as the old man, not at all. "This is for your own good."

"Is it now?" She scrambled off the bed and found her shift, pulling it over her head and tying the drawstring at the neck with quick, jerky motions. "I wanted you to take me back to Creignish, not to haul me back to London and then across the ocean to some godforsaken little town in a colony I can't even say, let alone spell."

"It's called Massachusetts, and it's a hell of a lot easier to spell or say than some of those Scottish names of yours!"

"That is not the point," she said, combing the worst knots from her hair with her fingers before she began braiding it, subduing the curls he loved so much into a single tight plait. "The point, Alex, is that my father—"

"How many times must I tell you, Cora," he roared with frustration, "that I never met your father, and that he never asked me to do one blessed thing on your behalf!"

Up went her chin in defense. "I'm not one of your sailors, Alex. My hearing is perfectly fine without your raising your voice to me."

"Then why the devil aren't you *listening* to what I say?"

She didn't deign to answer, her expression mutinous, and flipped the finished braid back over her shoulder. "Did you think to bring any more practical clothes for me? Or are those only for Mrs. Captain?"

"Diana packed *you* some things in the saddlebag."

Furiously he flung back the sheets and swung his legs over the side of the bed as he reached for his breeches. If she were going to dress, then he damned well would, too, and so much for any more frolicking in bed.

"Would you leave Appledore and the sea for my sake?" she asked abruptly. "Do you love me enough to live at Creignish with me?"

"I can't do that, Cora!" he said, aghast. "The Fairbournes have always been mariners. The sea is part of me as much as my own blood!"

"And so Creignish is to me!"

He shook his head. "But to give up my trade, my livelihood—how the devil could I support you? What kind of useless husband would I be to you then?"

"Then you can't expect me to give up Creignish," she said. "I told you, Alex, we're not the same as other folk."

"Cora, what do you think will happen *if* you finally do get back to this infernal Creignish of yours?" he demanded. "That every last brick and flower pot will be the same as when your father lived? That the moon will still be shining on you as you sleep each night in your little nursery bed?"

"Of course Creignish won't be the same," she said, lacing up the front of a plain wool bodice. "Without Father to tend to things, how could it? I'm not a fool, Alex, and I—*oh!*"

She'd reached into the bag, hunting for a petticoat, and instead she'd found the tartan shawl, the one she'd been wearing that night in the garden. He'd told Diana to be sure to pack it, hoping it would have the same pleasant memories for Cora that it did for him. But when he saw the emotion in her face as she sank to her knees and wrapped it over her shoulders, he realized too late that while the shawl did bring back memories for her, too, they weren't ones that included him.

"Creignish is my home, Alex," she said, her anger fading to melancholy as she sat on the floor, with Starlight finally reappearing from under the bed to climb into her lap. "It's the one thing that I have left, the one thing that kept me through losing everything else, and I'm not going to abandon it now."

"Not for me?" he asked urgently. "Not for love? Think of what we share, sweetheart, think of how well we just loved each other. We're good together, Cora, damned good. You don't want to let that go."

Her eyes troubled, she looked away from him and down to the black kitten in her lap, and he realized, perhaps, he still had a chance of convincing her.

"You're a young woman, Cora," he continued. "You could live another forty years or more. Do you want to live it alone at Creignish, with only that sorry moon for company at night? Think of it, sweetheart. The rest of your life without the kind of love I'm offering? Without the children we'd have?"

She looked up at him sharply, and blushed, hugging the kitten as tightly as she would a real baby.

"Aye, that's right, lass," he said. "Children don't come from under the cabbage leaves. Considering how well we, ah, pleased each other, I wouldn't be surprised if you're already sprouting a tiny babe in your belly. Our child, Cora."

She made an odd snuffling sound in her throat that he couldn't decide was a good sign or not. Perhaps with everything else that had happened to her yesterday, Cora hadn't quite made the connection between lovemaking and babymaking, or at least had chosen to ignore the possibility. God knows she wouldn't be the first virgin who hadn't. But unlike most of the others, Cora did have him eager to marry her and give their child a name, if only she'd be reasonable enough to agree.

Damnation, why wouldn't she say yes?

She rose awkwardly to her feet, still clinging to the cat in her arms. "I must remember who you are, Alex," she said with a certain desperation in her voice. "You may be from Massachusetts, but you're still an Englishman, while I'm a woman from a Jacobite clan in the Highlands."

"That has never mattered to you before, Cora," he said roughly. "Don't lower yourself by saying it does now."

"That's because there's never been so much at stake, has there?" She tried to smile, and bowed her head instead. "I love you, Alex. Don't ever doubt that. But my duty to my father, to my clan—"

"Who are dead, Cora," he said bluntly, "and the dead don't care. You know that as well as I. It's over, lass, the rebellion and that foolhardy prince and your life with your father at Creignish. It's over and done forever."

She winced visibly. "Not all of it is, Alex."

"My poor lass," he said, reaching out his hand to her. "Keep all the memories you wish, Cora. But if you believe you owe them your happiness, you'll become another Lady Waldegrave, living your life for duty's sake instead of with the man you love."

But to his surprise, she didn't take his hand. "What do you know of Lady Waldegrave?" she asked, with mingled suspicion and dread. "What could you know that I do not?"

He sighed, dropping his offered hand. He hadn't intended to open this particular hornet's nest, but there wasn't any way out of it now.

"She loved your father, Cora," he said. "She still does. Nay, look at me. That sad old woman with too many jewels was the English girl your father once loved, the match their families ordered broken. It's no tale, sweetheart. You can ask her yourself as soon as we go back to London."

But Cora didn't need to. She felt as if everything she'd known these last two years of her life were breaking apart into fragments and reforming in a different pattern, clicking together to form a new, unsettling, unavoidable whole.

Now she understood how the countess could treat her as fondly as a favorite daughter one moment, lavishing her with confidences and promises of journeys to Italy, then demean her like an unworthy rival the next, treating her as little more than an unpaid servant. It made sense now, perfect, horrid sense.

Not that her father's role was any less complicated. He'd always painted Cora's mother as the great love of his life, when clearly he'd maintained his relationship with Lady Waldegrave long after they'd both wed others. Cora's mother had died at her birth, but Lord Waldegrave had lived until three short years ago, and Cora shrank from the new unsavory truth of Father's frequent "book buying" trips to London. Yet clearly Father had cared for the countess, and relied upon her as a friend as well as a lover. Why else would he have sent Cora to her, making her the one person in England whom he trusted the most?

Both of them had tried to turn their backs on love,

and obey their families instead. Both had married well, their obedience handsomely rewarded in the greedy eyes of the world. The countess had gained jewels, gowns, servants, and houses along with her titled husband; Cora's father had taken his wife's fortune to build Creignish into the fanciful villa of his dreams. But what price had they paid with their hearts and souls?

And what lesson, now, had they left for Cora?

So much had happened in this last day and night, so much for her to digest and decipher and sort out for herself! Her head was spinning, and her heart with it, and she hadn't felt as helpless as this since the night she'd fled Creignish.

Creignish, her Creignish. Desperately she reached for the memory of that perfect place where she'd been born, wanting to hold it like a magic talisman against the rest of her wildly imperfect world.

"Cora," said Alex, his voice rough with emotion. "Cora, love, please. I'm asking you again. Marry me and be my wife."

He stood before her in his bare feet and breeches and an untucked shirt dappled with yesterday's mud, his jaw shadowed with black stubble and his black hair tossed impatiently back from his face. He looked every inch the pirate he was supposed to be, yet all she saw was the uncertainty that she'd put into his blue eyes, the doubt and the desperation that she'd cast into the harsh lines of his face. But she loved him, loved him more than she would ever love any other man. That would never change. He had offered her his heart and his hand, and promised to love her better, finer, longer than any woman in creation, and she wanted desperately to believe every word.

And yet because of Creignish, because to say yes to Alex would mean saying no to Creignish, because of Father and her clan and who she *was,* she could not make herself accept.

"No, Alex," she whispered. "Thank you, but no."

She looked down at the kitten in her arms, the white star on his forehead blurring before her eyes.

"I—I cannot stay in here," she said abruptly, turning away to wrench at the latch on the broken window. She couldn't bear to remain in this room where they'd shared such joy, not for a single moment longer. "I must go outside, now. The—the kitten needs the air."

"Oh, aye, do that," muttered Alex bleakly. "You love the wretched creature more than me anyway."

He reached over her shoulder to unfasten the latch for her, his arm grazing her skin just lightly enough to create a wayward ripple of desire. She didn't look up at his face—she didn't dare—but pushed her way through the window to hop down to the grass, the horse turning to whinny at her. Her feet were bare, the grass cool and wet with last night's rain still clinging to the blades. The early morning sky was clear and blue, the sun hanging low in the trees, and doves on the roof cooed mournfully to one another.

"I'll see to the horse," he said as he followed her out the window, trying hard to sound as if nothing had changed between them, and failing miserably. "We should clear off soon anyway to make London in good time. Don't stray far, mind?"

But Cora didn't answer or turn around, afraid that if she did and saw the pain she'd caused him, she'd change her mind for all the wrong reasons. Instead she walked away from the horse, closer to the wall, and crouched down to place Starlight in the grass. Gingerly the little cat spread his many toes, confounded by the strangeness of tall, wet grass on his city feet.

"Feels odd, my wee kit, doesn't it?" asked Cora softly, stroking the cat's back to reassure him and herself as well. "After two years in the city, it feels powerfully odd to me, too, and I a country-born lass."

Tentatively Starlight nibbled on a blade of grass that was jabbing his nose. A half dozen paces before him, a pale yellow butterfly meandered over the grass, lazily searching for a flower to sip. This was the first butterfly Starlight had ever seen—in Lady Waldegrave's walled garden there'd been nothing as amazing to resemble or rival it—and with a low growl of excitement he bounded after it, across the lawn and beneath a prickly hedge of holly and through the arched opening in the wall behind it.

"Oh, Starlight, not today of all days," cried Cora softly, and bunching her skirts in her hands she raced after him, not through the holly hedge, but around the wall. The last thing she needed this morning was for Starlight to run away, for from what he'd said about her loving the cat more than him, she wasn't at all sure Alex would be willing to wait until Starlight allowed himself to be found.

"Starlight!" she called in an urgent whisper, and stopped to catch her breath, her hands on her hips. She knew the kitten had come this way, but now he seemed to have vanished—meaning, of course, he was hiding beneath some bush, blinking at her and purring at this wonderful new game. "Starlight, come! Oh, please, you wretched kit, this isn't funny!"

"Cora?" shouted Alex from the other side of the

wall, and she could hear the worry in his voice despite his sea captain's roar. "Where are you, lass?"

"I'm fine, Alex," she called back. "I'll be there in a moment when I'm finished."

She heard him grumble, but she knew he wouldn't argue or come looking for her as long as he thought she'd gone to the other side of the wall for privacy's sake—there'd been no chamber pots in the room last night—and once again she called the cat.

"Starlight, please!" she implored softly, bending low to peer into the holly. "Please, else you'll be left behind!"

She heard a rustling of leaves, enough to make her look and see a branch shake suspiciously, down where the wall turned a corner and followed the rambling shape of the house.

"Starlight!" she called as she hurried to the end of the wall and the shaking branch. "You wicked kitten, so help me, after this I'll—"

But what she'd do was never said, the rest of her threat left unspoken and driven completely from her thoughts by mute and unthinking terror.

For just beyond the corner of the wall, standing slightly crouched and poised with a long-bladed knife clutched in his hand, was the one-eyed man in the blue coat from the alley. She gasped, wanting to run, to scream for Alex, to get away, but fear held her as still as if she'd been made of stone.

"Ye thought ye got free, didn't ye?" he said, his mouth twisting into a mockery of a smile, broken teeth and rotting gums, his single eye glinting with satisfaction. "Ye thought ye'd ne'er see me again. I saw *ye*, aye, through the window, there wit' yer legs spread all shameless as a whore to take that big buck o' yours.

Ye thought ye were done wit' me, I know. But Deadmarsh be like a terrier, worryin' at ye 'til he breaks yer back."

He grabbed her wrist, his fingers sinking into her skin, twisted it roughly behind her back, and smothered her cry of pain with his other dirty hand across her mouth.

"Ye have sung yer last, Miss MacGillivray," he said as she arched back to try to lessen the wrenching agony of her twisting elbow. "Ye shall be in hell wit' the rest o' yer heathen Jacobites soon enough, an' me all th' richer for sendin' ye there."

She was fighting him now, gasping as she struggled to escape the pain that ripped like wildfire from her wrist to her elbow clear to her shoulder and the fear that went with it. But oh, he was strong for so old a man, she should have remembered that, his grasp like a vise that tightened only to hurt her more. In the corner of her consciousness came a sudden bright flash of morning light, and almost too late she realized it was reflecting off the blade of his knife, slanting close, too close, to her face, and *she did not want to die like this.*

With a last effort she jerked away from the knife and the man and screamed Alex's name once. Then she ran, cradling her wounded arm before her with her other hand, whimpering as each step jarred the torn and throbbing muscles. Still she did not stop, running as fast as she could, running, she knew, for her life.

But the grass was slippery beneath her bare feet and her arm with the helpless fingers could not hold her skirts clear of her legs, and when she reached a place where the ground rose her heel hooked in the hem of her petticoat and she fell, tumbling forward and crying out as she struck her arm on the ground, a shriek of pain and fear.

"Enough o' this," ordered the man harshly, breathing hard from having chased her as he hauled her upright onto her knees. "I've killed ye once afore this, I won't be doin' it again."

With one hand grabbing hold of her hair, he yanked her head back to bare her throat. She felt the blade, cool, sleek, pressed against her throat, and the tears wet on her cheeks, and her heart thumping for maybe the last time, the last time she could think of how much she would miss Alex.

I loved you, Alex, never doubt that I did. . . .

The sound above her was muffled, a wet thump, followed by a mangled cry torn from the man's mouth. The knife slipped from Cora's throat and then she was slipping, too, thrown forward to the wet grass, falling hard, and yet there was more that was wet, and warm, splattering over her skin as she lay in the grass and trembled and wept and heard the frantic *whirrr* of the doves' wings as they flew over her.

And, slowly, she realized she was alive.

"Cora!" Alex was beside her, the scent of acrid gunsmoke still clinging to his shirt and the pistol in his hand. "Lass, look at me! God in heaven, if I hurt you, too—"

She shook her head, and tried to smile through her tears. "I—I love you, Alex," she quavered. "I was so—so afraid I would never say that to you again."

"And I love you, too, sweetheart, ah, so much." He raised her to sit upright, and she cried out as unwittingly he held her arm. He frowned with concern. "I did hurt you. Where, Cora?"

"You didn't do anything, Alex," she said, struggling to explain when she didn't understand it herself. Though her arm made her shy from an embrace, she leaned her cheek against his shoulder, letting him rest his hand lightly on her back to comfort her that way. "It was that—that dreadful man with the red scarf again, the same one who—who robbed me. He twisted my arm, and he was going to . . . was going to—"

"I know, love," interrupted Alex, wanting to spare her. "But thank God he didn't, and he won't hurt you ever again. I'll find someone to tend to your arm as soon as we reach an inn."

With great care he felt along the length of her arm, making sure the bone wasn't broken. Then, his expression grim, he began to wipe his handkerchief over her face and chest. Confused, she looked at the handkerchief, and gasped when she saw the blood.

"It's his, not yours," said Alex quietly. "I'm sorry, Cora, but there was no other way to do it."

Now she noticed the legs of the man stretched out on the grass, the rest of him carefully blocked by Alex. She'd realized from what Alex had said that the man was dead, and from the pistol she'd known that Alex had shot him.

But it wasn't until she saw how terribly still the man's legs were, the worn soles of his shoes turned up toward the blue morning sky and the toes turned in toward one another, that she began to comprehend the finality of what had just happened, and, more importantly, what hadn't. She'd been so much affected by death these last two years, but until now it had never come so close to her.

She leaned forward to see around Alex, wincing at the pain that even that slight motion caused her arm.

"Don't look, Cora," he ordered quickly, but she'd already seen too much. The man lay facedown in the grass, mercifully hiding where the pistol's ball had torn into his face, but the thin hair on the back of his head was red with blood and brains, an image that would remain with her a long, long time.

If Alex hadn't come when he had. . . .

If he hadn't made such a difficult shot so perfectly. . . .

If the one-eyed man hadn't taken those last few seconds to curse her and her clan before he'd slit her throat. . . .

"Did you hear him?" she asked, her voice still unsteady. "Or me? What made you come for me?"

Alex frowned, turned, and stretched out across the grass to, once again, retrieve Starlight from where he'd strayed.

"Here's your reason," he said, dropping the kitten into her lap. "I could hear you calling him, but the little rogue had come prancing up to me, fine as a lord. I brought him around to find you, and then saw the rest."

"He's not a rogue, Alex," she murmured, gathering the kitten awkwardly with her uninjured arm. She was overjoyed that Starlight was safe; she'd decide later, when her arm didn't hurt and her head was clear, whether the kitten deserved the blame for making her wander, or the credit for bringing Alex to her rescue. For some reason she suddenly remembered what Diana had told her long ago about the kitten leading her to her true love. Having accomplished that, perhaps now Starlight's responsibilities included keeping her alive for Alex.

But when she looked up for Alex now, he was

kneeling beside the dead man's body, searching rapidly through his pockets, sifting through the usual rubbish and scraps of paper and small coins.

"He said he . . . he'd watched us, Alex," she said softly. "This morning, through the window. He called me a . . . a very bad name because of it."

"Then he only got what he deserved, the sneaking bastard," he said firmly, "and whatever he said about you was wrong."

She nodded, hugging her arm, wanting to believe he was right. Though she didn't regret what she'd done with Alex, she wasn't starry-eyed enough to think that the rest of the world wouldn't call her that same ugly name again given the chance.

"I'll only be a moment more, sweetheart," he was saying, "and then we'll be gone. I wanted to see if he'd anything on his person to tell who he was. Maybe he'll even still have your mother's beads, though likely they're long gone for—oh, sweet Jesus, Cora, it's a picture of you."

Swiftly he handed her the small folder he'd unwrapped, letting the grimy cloth drop to the grass. As soon as she saw the leather case, she sobbed once, a final cry of grief. She didn't need to open the case any more than she needed to ask what had caused the ugly, rust-colored stains on the white leather. The portrait inside would be of her, painted at a time when her world was still innocent, and the bloodstains would be her father's, the last he shed in this life.

"Father carried this with him whenever he left home," she said, her voice hollow as she bowed her head. "He claimed it brought him good luck. Nothing in this life would have made him part with it."

"Nothing in this life did," said Alex rising to his feet. For a long moment he seemed lost in his own thoughts, looking silently down at the dead man lying at his feet. "But now that the picture's come back to you, sweetheart, perhaps your luck will change, too."

He turned, his long shadow stretching across the grass, and held his hand out to help her to her feet.

"Come, lass. Time we were done with this place and on our way."

She rose clumsily, tucking the portrait into her pocket, the better to cradle her wrenched arm.

"To London?" she asked, hoping he meant to spare at least a day and night for her to mend, and to stay at the inn he'd mentioned before.

He smiled wearily, and bent to kiss her on the forehead.

"Nay, Cora," he said. "To Creignish."

18

*I*dly Sir Thomas Walton tapped his walking stick against the glass of the carriage window, matching the rhythm of the horses' hooves, and wondered for the thousandth—no, at least the millionth—time on this journey why the devil anyone would wish to live so damnably far from London.

He'd always thought the pleasures of travel were so greatly overrated as to be out-and-out lies. To him the point of travel was the destination, not the process, and though he'd brought as much to amuse himself as his carriage would hold—books, pipes, wines, and a spyglass, a folio of puzzles and a hamper filled with sweetmeats, preserves, and nuts—he'd still felt bored to exhausted distraction before they'd crossed York-shire, and by the time the horses were laboring over the Cheviot Hills into the lowlands of Scotland proper, he almost wished he'd brought Antoinette along just to hear her prattling complaints as a diversion.

Only one thing kept Sir Thomas in the carriage and on this journey, and that was the sweet satisfaction of knowing that fate was, in this last month, treating him so phenomenally well that to complain of anything could only bring disaster. All his worries, all his troubles, seemed to have dissipated like the mist in the morn, and now when he thought of the worn baize table coverings for cards in Calais, he could chuckle benignly at his own pessimism.

Deadmarsh had worked miracles exactly as he'd promised. Though the MacGillivray chit had reappeared briefly in London—seeing her face on that ludicrous print had been nearly enough to give Sir Thomas apoplexy—Deadmarsh had put a swift, deadly end to that folly. To stage a robbery of the carriage in which she'd been a passenger was a clever move, but to make sure that everyone else in the carriage was shot dead and so beyond testifying was brilliant. The discovery of the wrecked carriage at the bottom of the hill where it had crashed and burned from an unfortunate combination of a travel lantern with an open bottle of rum: London had spoken of nothing else for days.

And when the distraught Lady Waldegrave had come forth to identify Cora MacGillivray by the blackened remains of her coral necklace, Sir Thomas had been forced to remain in his house for the afternoon, his gleeful celebration so inappropriate. The MacGillivray heiress was undeniably dead, and her estate granted instead to Sir Thomas. His influence and patience had been well rewarded; for once the courts of law moved swiftly in his favor. All he must do was visit the lands once, take possession to please the law, and then he was free to sell or mortgage it however he wished.

Sir Thomas chortled again, unable to help himself. As close to perfection as Deadmarsh's work had been, the one-eyed old soldier had managed to get himself killed as well, and before Sir Thomas had had to pay him, too. The gamekeeper at a large country house north of London had claimed the honor, saying he'd mistaken the highwayman for a poacher, but had shot him anyway. Regardless of the details, Deadmarsh *was* dead, as dead as Cora MacGillivray, and as dead as the threat of that bleak little room in Calais.

Even Alexander Fairbourne seemed to have vanished, his near-daily morning calls coming abruptly to an end. Perhaps he'd thought better of his father's suit; perhaps he'd grown impatient and sailed back home empty-handed. But regardless of the reason, Sir Thomas now dared hope he'd not only won the prize, but would be able to keep it, too, and that chortle expanded into a full-fledged laugh.

Ah, yes, thought Sir Thomas as he pinched a few expensive flakes from his snuffbox, occasionally fate and good luck smiled even upon old rascals like him, and with a happy sigh he settled back against the down-filled squabs and pulled the soft wool rug higher over his knees, determined to enjoy the last, luckiest part of his journey to his new holdings at Creignish.

"Are you sure you want to push on to the next inn tonight, Cora?" asked Alex. "McKay here says there's a smaller tavern only a mile or so to the east."

"Or perhaps we could sleep beneath the stars like Adam and Eve," she answered, "frolicking stark naked in the garden, at least until the constable comes to take us up."

McKay, the old man in a leather jerkin and high boots that they'd hired to serve as their guide, stared in open-mouthed fascination at such a suggestion from a lady, but Cora only grinned playfully, as if she hadn't been riding since dawn that morning, as if being stark naked would not perhaps be an improvement over being coated with the gray dust of the road.

"No paradise here, Cora," said Alex, wishing the guide wouldn't be quite so open in his eavesdropping. But all the guides they'd found since crossing into the Highlands had been like that, rough-hewn, forward old men as wiry and shaggy as the small horses they all rode now. "Though I wouldn't doubt there's a serpent or two out there to lead you into mischief."

"Ye canna trust th' weather, lady," said McKay emphatically, tugging on his grizzled red beard. "Ye canna trust it nae to turn on ye."

"Well, no, of course not," she answered cheerfully. "I didn't mean it exactly so. Sleeping among the rocks and gorse isn't the most comfortable place to be. But I do think we should continue, paradise or not. It cannot be more than an hour to the inn, can it?"

"We'll push on, then." Alex sighed, wiping his sleeve across his face as he urged his tired horse on. "If you weren't a female, Cora, I'd sign you on as my bo'sun in an instant. I've never known anyone could drive a man as hard as you're driving me."

She laughed, a merry, pealing sound that could have made him let her drive him all night as well as all day. For nearly three weeks now, since her arm had healed, she'd been like this, her mood growing more and more cheerful, almost giddy, as their travel conditions had deteriorated.

She never complained about how long or uncomfortable the day's ride was, though he was sure in the beginning she'd been as stiff and sore as he'd been himself. He preferred to travel by wind and water, not on an unpredictable animal's back, and for the last two years Cora's only exercise had been running up and down the countess' staircases. Yet twenty miles a day was the goal they'd set, and twenty miles a day was what they'd kept to.

She didn't fuss about dressing simply to avoid notice, the way Diana would have, and she'd accepted the new freckles that had appeared across her nose and cheeks from the sun. She didn't snap at their garrulous guides, or hang back from the wildness of the steep, narrow passes pretending to be roads. The summer heat of the southern counties had faded as they'd come north, yet instead of shivering on the days when they'd been shrouded in damp mists or sudden rain showers, she'd reveled in it, turning her face up to the clouds as if they were old friends.

And in a way, really, they were, and all part of Cora's homecoming. Each step drew her closer to Creignish, and each day she seemed to throw off another layer of the grief and gloom that had burdened her so in London. He remembered how Lady Waldegrave had cruelly dismissed Cora as no beauty; if the countess could see Cora now, she'd take back those words in an instant.

He smiled, watching Cora settle the little cat more comfortably in the sling she'd fashioned for him across her chest for riding on horseback. The kitten wasn't really a kitten any longer, more of a cat and too large to travel in her pocket and more of a challenge for Cora, too, thought Alex as he watched her fussing with the animal. Lord, how she loved that cat; he could only imagine how much affection and attention she'd lavish on a child, and how blissfully happy she'd be doing it.

It was easy for him to share Cora's happiness, loving her like he did. But while she might focus on Creignish as an end in itself, single-minded and determined, he could not. He was taking her home because he loved her. That was simple enough, and true, too. He'd willingly put this journey before his own voyage home, and he'd sent word to Diana and to Johnny Allred to sail the *Calliope* home without him if he didn't return by the end of July. How could he do any less for his Cora? At night she slept curled in his arms, and by day not a quarter hour passed that she didn't find some way to tell or show him how much she loved him.

He was gambling, bringing her back to the Highlands like this, hoping against hope that the love and life he was offering could succeed against the golden dreams of the past. The gamble was that she'd have to see the difference for herself. He didn't want her to feel he'd somehow forced her decision. He wanted her to come with him freely, without any regrets. He'd always considered himself a man who liked taking risks, but this one was the greatest he'd ever chanced: did he love her enough to be able to leave her behind at Creignish if that was what she decided would make her happier? He did not know; he did not know. For despite all their tender words and love-play, she'd pledged nothing lasting and neither had he.

And nothing was exactly what Alex feared, in the end, he'd be left with.

Even Cora was silent with fatigue when they finally reached the inn, a humble square building with flaking whitewash and a thatched roof. While McKay saw to the horses, Alex led Cora inside, ducking his head beneath the low beam over the door to enter directly into the public room. Though the fire in the hearth was cheery enough, the room was gloomy, the walls and ceiling grimy and dark with peat smoke, and there were too many empty chairs and benches, with only one table in the corner occupied by two men drinking whiskey and tossing dice.

"Good day, sir, mistress," said the keep's wife, wiping her hands on her apron as she hurried forward to greet them. " 'Tis glad I am to see such weary faces, knowing we've fine food and drink to ease your cares."

"What my wife and I would like most would be a room," said Alex, falling back into the same easy, troubling pretense of husband and wife that he and Cora had used since the beginning of their journey. He'd told himself it was safer, more convenient and economical for them to share a room like that, but his conscience had not always been easy when they'd made love in a different bed each night. "Water for washing, a good fire, and supper brought up as soon as you can."

The woman's mouth constricted into a tight, anxious knot. "We have but the one chamber, sir, to th' back. I can fetch ye water from the well, sure, but I canna make a fire for there's no fireplace, and I canna bring ye supper for there's naught room in the chamber for any but th' bed."

"That will be fine," said Cora quickly, answering before Alex could. She recognized the signs of poverty hiding behind frugality, and though she knew Alex wanted the best for her sake, she didn't want the woman's humble hospitality shamed. "I'll wash, and we'll dine out here, by this fire."

"You didn't have to be so damned agreeable," said

Alex as she washed her face in the bedchamber and Starlight investigated it for interesting scents and bits of dust. It was as small as the woman had warned, with the bedstead touching three walls, a single chair, a washstand, and a rushlight pegged to the wall. The beams in the ceiling were as low as the doorframe had been, and Alex was forced to hunch his shoulders or risk striking his head. "Likely we'd have done better out there under the stars like your Adam and Eve."

"It will be fine, Alex," she said gently, too tired to quarrel. She pulled her tartan shawl from their bag, needing its comfort and warmth tonight, before she wrapped her arms around Alex's waist and rested her head against his chest. "Besides, my handsome Adam, you can make paradise out of whatever place you choose to lay your head."

"Oh, aye, my own Eve, as long as I lay the rest of me alongside you," he said, and kissed her, a heady promise of more lovemaking to come. "Though I surely wish this particular paradise had more headroom to it."

But as she sat in the tall-backed bench beside the fire, she found herself so tired she'd little interest in the food before her, even though the skirlie was just as she'd always liked it, with more onions than oatmeal and plenty of wild thyme.

"Are you unwell, sweetheart?" asked Alex with concern, nothing wrong with his appetite. More men had wandered into the inn as evening had stretched into night, and their conversation and laughter served to keep their own conversation more private. "You should be eating. You look pale."

"I'm tired," she said, surreptitiously slipping more of her food to Starlight waiting on the bench beside her. "A night's sleep is all I be wantin', an' then I'll be mended fine."

He looked at her curiously. "You're talking more and more like the people here," he said. "Can you hear it in yourself?"

She shook her head. "I suppose I canna—can *not*—help it. Everyone who worked at Creignish spoke that way, with bits of Gaelic tossed in, too, but Father always insisted I speak 'proper' English with him. Otherwise, he said, I'd be treated like a crofter's daughter instead of a lady."

"I'll treat you exactly the same," said Alex with a wink, "especially since I've no notion of what a crofter is, let alone how I should treat his daughter."

"A crofter is a farmer, so you can decide what his daughter should be." She smiled. "But that's probably why I'm so tired tonight, too. For so long I've wanted to return home, and at last I'm nearly there. I can see it in the color of the sky, and smell it in that peat burning in the hearth, and feel it in the wind on my cheek, and taste it, here, on this plate, and . . . and it's almost too much for me to bear, Alex, as if I'm afraid I'm going to wake and be back in my little room in Lady Waldegrave's house."

"It's no dream, lass," said Alex, reaching across the table to cover her hand with his. "And because it means so much to you, I'm glad I brought you here."

"So am I," she said softly, pulling the tartan shawl higher over her shoulders. "Because having you here to share it with me makes everything so much better. Oh, Alex, I can't wait to show you—"

"Captain Fairbourne, sir," interrupted the innkeeper gruffly. "I must ask ye to put your wife's screen aside and from sight."

"Aye," said another man, coming to stand behind the keep with his arms folded across his chest. "We don't be wantin' that kind o' Jacobite trash in our village."

At once Alex was on his feet. "I trust I misheard you, sir," he said sharply. "Else I must believe you have insulted me and my wife, sir, and I don't intend to let it pass without an apology."

"Don't be getting all feisty now, Captain," said the innkeeper hastily, his palms held up for calm. "Guthrie here meant ye no insult. Most likely yer dear lady doesn't be knowin' the mischief she's caused. But wearin' the plaid of a clan like that, well now, that be unwise, even for a lady."

Alex's anger gathered like storm clouds. "Are you telling my wife what she can wear?"

"Aye, we are," declared Guthrie belligerently, pushing past the innkeeper. Behind him others added their voices, some thumping their tankards on the table in agreement. "And so says th' king's own law."

"Guthrie says th' truth, sir," said the innkeeper apologetically, edging his way back between the two men. Beside the hearth Cora could see the innkeeper's wife, wringing her hands in her apron and doubtless already foreseeing a brawl and damage to her crockery. "Th' law says no one's to wear tartan, or face prison or transportation. I canna permit it in my house, sir, not even on yer lady wife."

If Alex had seemed tall before beneath the low beams, to Cora he now seemed to fill the room. It was easy to imagine him like this on his own quarterdeck, facing down an enemy ship.

"Permit it, hell," he thundered. "I've never heard such out-and-out—"

"Please, Alex, don't," pleaded Cora urgently, slipping her hand around his arm to hold him back. She didn't want him to fight for her, but she could feel the tension rippling through the room, and all of it seemed centered in Alex. "They're right about the Dress Act. I thought things would be different here, so close to home and away from London, but I was wrong. *I* was wrong, Alex, not them."

But before he could answer, Guthrie had again pushed around the innkeeper, this time to stand before her, not Alex.

"MacGillivray," he said scornfully, his gaze raking over the plaid of her clan. "What a low lot o' sneaking, traitorous bastards they were!"

Alex's fist caught Guthrie square on the chin and lifted him clear from his feet. To Cora it seemed Guthrie hung there, a look of outraged surprise on his round face, before he crumpled heavily to the floor. He groaned, holding his jaw as he flopped from side to side like a beached fish.

"Does anyone else have something to say?" demanded Alex. "Any other words for my wife's clan?"

No one else in the room moved, and the only sound besides Guthrie's groaning was the hiss and pop of the fire. It was, decided Cora as she stared down at Guthrie, a thoroughly horrible moment.

But not for Alex.

"Very well, sweetheart," he said, smiling, not in the least winded as he returned to the table. "Shall we finish eating?"

"I am done," she answered swiftly, reaching for

Starlight. She had not wanted this to happen, and one look around the room at all those faces watching them, Scottish faces, faces that could have come from her own childhood, made her cheeks burn with misery and shame. "Alex, please come outside with me to—to take the air."

She marched outside, stiff-backed, with the cat in her arms and the offending tartan fluttering from her shoulders. The evening air was chilly, the sky clear and full of stars.

"Whatever were you *doing?*" she cried as soon as Alex joined her. "Have you given leave to all your wits?"

"I was defending you, Cora," answered Alex, surprised by her reaction. She couldn't see his expression in the dark, but she could hear how perplexed he was by his voice. "I had to do that."

"But to strike him like that, as if he were no more than a sack of flour!" For emphasis she shoved him, her hand on his chest. "And then to challenge everyone else in the room as well!"

"Cora, men like that don't listen to genteel persuasion," he explained impatiently. "Sometimes you have to hit them to make them listen. You heard what he said. I couldn't let that pass, Cora, not about you."

"But it wasn't about me! The Guthries have always hated the MacGillivrays, and always will. When he said that, he meant my clan, not *me.*"

"Sure as hell sounded as if he meant you," he said defensively. "Besides, you're always telling me how much your clan means to you. If that's so, then when a cowardly little weasel like that one insults your clan, then he's insulting you, too, and me, because you're mine. At least you are for now."

"You're making this far too complicated, Alex!"

"Am I?" he asked. "It already seems pretty damned complicated without any help from me."

"It's not complicated, not truly." She was shaking, hugging Starlight so tightly he mewed in protest, and she wished Alex hadn't reminded her about how uncertain their future together was. "Or rather, it is, but it's always been that way. Oh, Alex, I wanted so much to believe that things had changed! I thought after two years, after all the English have done to hurt us, we'd be ready to stop harming each other. I thought that perhaps things would be different."

"It's not 'things' that you want to change, Cora," he said. "It's people, and two years is nothing to families who have hated one another for 'always.' "

She sighed with frustration, turning away from him to gaze out at the glen before her. "Then I suppose I am wrong once again, just as I was about wearing this tartan."

"Not wrong, Cora," he said gently. "Not really. The world would be a much happier place if you *were* right instead."

She gave a single desultory sigh. "I know *I* would be happier."

"Then come here, Cora, and hand me that damned fool cat." Carefully he swung Starlight up onto his shoulder, pausing to let the little cat settle. Then he took the shawl from Cora and wrapped it around her, somehow managing to pull her back against his chest and into his arms at the same time.

"There," he said with conviction. "I'm happier already. Now since you're all snared up into what changes and what doesn't, I'll show you something that never does, not in a million years."

"Alex, please, I—"

"Hush," he ordered, "and mind me for once. Look up there, now, up at the sky. How many of those same stars did you see from your window when you were a tiny lass, eh? Every last one of them, I'll warrant, because they're every one of them the same now as they were then, back as far as the day God hung them there."

She sighed again, but she looked, too, her gaze following to where he was pointing. It might take a swift knock to the chin to get the attention of a man, but Alex also seemed to know how to get her attention as well, his voice low with the exact amount of roughness to make it masculine and interesting. And secure: she'd never felt as secure and safe as she did when he held her like this, those great strong arms of his looped around her to keep away the rest of the world.

"Look up at those stars, love," he continued. "Same stars I have to guide me at sea, same stars over my family's house in Appledore, same as over you snug in your home at Creignish."

Snug in your home at Creignish. For the first time the words jarred her ear. She'd always thought of Creignish as her haven, but that was before she'd known how it felt to stand like this, with her head against Alex's chest so she could feel the thrumming of his words as well as hear them.

"I love you, Alex," she said quickly, needing him to hear it again. "I do love you!"

She knew he smiled over her head. "Look at those

stars, sweetheart, and remember we stood here like this. Starlight will help you, seeing as he's got one of them right there on his forehead."

"But Starlight's supposed to find me my true love," she protested, "not make me look up into the sky!"

Alex chuckled. "That was Diana's favorite story, too, and I'd say Starlight did his best for her. When I saw her last at Lady Waldegrave's, she told me she'd almost landed a marquess for a husband."

"But Alex—"

"The stars, lass," he said firmly. "Mind the stars; they'll be there long after Starlight has grown into a fat old beast with a white muzzle. Wherever you are, you look up at the stars, and know those same stars are shining down on me, too, wherever I happen to be."

Her chest seemed to tighten as she realized what he was saying, how he was anticipating the time they'd part. Abruptly she remembered something that Diana had once told her, of how Diana's mother had said that to find happiness a woman must follow her love. Then, she'd dismissed it as a foolish sentiment; now, she wasn't nearly as sure.

"I love you," she said again, fiercely, desperately, as if those three words could somehow stop him from going away. "I love you, Alex Fairbourne!"

"And I love you, too, Cora MacGillivray." He kissed the top of her head, his arms tightening around her waist. "McKay says if the fair weather holds, we'll make Creignish in three days."

"Yes," she said unhappily. She'd already recognized enough of the landscape today to have figured that out for herself. "And you'll have brought me home to Creignish, Alex. Just like Father said you would."

"Aye," he said softly. "I'll have brought you home. Though I do wish that old father of yours had explained what would happen after that."

And so did she, thought Cora bleakly.

So did she.

19

On the third day, the sun disappeared but the rain held off, leaving patches of silvery mist to drift across the glen like wayward spirits. Though the pale green of the deer grass was dotted with lavender wildflowers, there was little else about the landscape to remind Alex of summer. The mountains—beinns, Cora and McKay called them—that loomed on either side of the glen were grim and bare, their tops lost in the mists, and the stream, or burn, that they followed was icy cold as it skittered and danced over its shallow, flinty bed. More huge rocks lay scattered through the grass as if tossed there by some long-ago giant, and the few trees and bushes were low and stunted by the wind.

Yet still he could understand how Cora could love this landscape. The wildness and the emptiness of it, the endlessly varying colors of silver, gray, and purple reminded him enough of the Massachusetts coast that he felt a twinge of homesickness.

"This doesn't look right," said Cora as they rode slowly, lessening the risks of their horses stumbling over the rocks and rough ground. "I'm sure there once was a barn there, near that cairn, and a cottage beside it."

"There was, lady," said McKay, twisting around in his saddle to answer her, "before th' English came."

He spat emphatically, and swore far worse and more violently than Cora had ever heard from Alex.

"That's enough," said Alex sharply, cutting him off. "Mind the lady's ears."

But McKay wasn't done. "If th' lady asks, then happy I be t' give her th' answer. Th' prince's men fled this way, lady, them that still lived after th' butchery o' Culloden, and Cumberland, may his black soul rot forever in hell, Cumberland came this way after them, slaughterin' an' burnin' everythin' before."

At once Alex looked to Cora, her face so pale and pinched that he reached across to steady her.

"I'm fine, Alex," she said, her voice more even than he'd expected. "My father was killed fighting with our clan at Culloden, McKay."

"White ribands in his bonnet?" asked McKay, watching her closely. "Or black?"

"He wore the white cockade for the prince," she said sadly. "No one else could have made him go to war."

The guide nodded, a wave of sympathy and understanding passing between them that excluded Alex. "Then ye know, lady."

"Aye," she said, two years of grief in the single word. "I do."

But as they made their way north through the glen, Alex's uneasiness grew. The barn that had been burned was only the first landmark that was missing. Though neither Cora nor McKay remarked aloud upon them, Alex could recognize the signs well enough: a collapsed stone wall that had been part of a house, an overgrown square indentation that was once a kitchen garden.

Though two years had softened the physical scars of war, perhaps the greatest blight on the landscape was what wasn't there: people. The small inn where they'd stayed last night had been run by a single, elderly woman, with them being her only customers for the week, and since beginning their ride this morning, they'd seen no one else at all. No men tending the unsowed fields, no women washing clothes in the burn, no children playing hide-and-seek upon the cairn: only a whole valley full of ghosts, with a few shaggy sheep to watch them pass, and none of it a good omen for what they'd find at Creignish.

It was late afternoon when the burn they'd been following merged with a river, not wide, but deep enough for a small boat, and deep enough, too, to be home to the salmon visible through the rippling water. They said farewell to McKay here, too, for Cora knew the rest of the way.

"This is my river, Alex," said Cora as they paused for the horses to drink, letting Starlight dabble in the water, too. She wasn't pale any longer, the first shock over, but the anxious flush that now stained her cheeks wasn't, to Alex, an improvement. "My river. The one that runs outside my bedchamber window. We're almost there."

"Cora, lass." Alex looked down at the reins in his fingers. God knows he'd had long enough to decide what to tell her, but he still didn't have the faintest notion how to begin. "Cora, about Creignish. About what we might find there."

"I know what we'll find," she said quickly, so

quickly he knew she was trying to convince herself as well as him. "It's my home. It's only a mystery for you, Alex, and you can't know how I hope you'll love it the way I do."

He sighed uneasily, and forced himself to meet her gaze. She was slipping away from him—he could feel it—and he was losing her to a rival of mortar and stone and memories.

"That's not what I meant, sweetheart," he began again, raking his fingers back through his hair. "Recall what we spoke of two nights ago, about how some things never change while others always do. This war, or rebellion, or whatever other damned thing you choose to call it—I don't have to be a Scotsman to see how it's changed this land, and not for the better."

She shrugged, as if she could shrug away the truth. "You don't have to tell me, Alex. I've eyes of my own, haven't I?"

"What I'm saying is we don't have to go on, Cora. I won't think the worse of you if you don't."

"But I must," she insisted. "I have no choice. I'm the last of my family, at least that I know. Creignish is my home, where I belong. I have to go back to Creignish, the way Father wished, the way that my clan—"

"Damnation, Cora, do you think I care a tinker's damn about any of that?" he said roughly. "All I want you to know is that I'll still want to marry you, no matter what happens at Creignish. I love you, mind? I love *you*."

Before she could answer he pulled her into his arms and kissed her hungrily, desperate to make her know how much she meant to him, how much he didn't want to lose her. She belonged with him, among the living, and not buried here in this bleak, empty valley.

"Fie on ye, Cora Margaret, I see ye!" shrieked the woman's voice. "I see ye, an' there'll be no hidin' from me!"

At once Cora pulled free from Alex's embrace, her eyes wild as she tried to see from where the voice had come.

"Bett!" she called back excitedly. "Bett, I've come home! Where are you, Bett?"

"Home, is it!" The woman laughed, shrill and mad, from the other side of the river. She was gaunt with hunger, her clothes worn and patched, her eyes hollowed by suffering as she danced through the grass, swinging her apron back and forth like a flag. "Hiss, hiss, fie, fie on ye, Cora Margaret!"

"I see you, Bett!" called Cora, but the eagerness in her voice had lessened as she saw the woman, and she sought Alex's hand at her side while Starlight cowered at her feet, his tail stiff with fear. "Bett was my old nursemaid, Alex, the woman who tended me as a babe."

Bett cackled back, flicking her apron up and down. "It's Creignish ye be comin' home t', is it, Cora Margaret? Come back t' mock us that have none? Burned out, we be, with naught left for comfort, while ye come back t' Creignish!"

Cora's fingers tightened in Alex's, though somehow she managed to keep her voice even. "Then come with me, Bett, back to Creignish, and I'll see you'll want no more."

"Creignish, ha," scoffed Bett angrily. "What would I be wantin' there? Ye canna pretend t' be one o' us. Ye nivver were. So why should I come with ye, Cora Mar-

garet, comin' back *home* with yer bonnie laddie, kissin'
an' lovin', while th' bones o' my poor Jamie lie cold an'
lonely beneath th' heath? Fie, fie on ye, Cora Margaret,
an' t' hell with yer *home!*"

She ducked down to pick up a rock and hurled it
toward Cora and Alex before she bolted off across the
glen.

"Mad old witch," said Alex grimly, slipping his arm
around Cora's shoulders. "I'm sorry that happened,
Cora, but you must pay her no heed. She's lost her
wits, and doesn't know what she says."

"But she does," said Cora, obviously shaken, staring
after Bett's disappearing figure. "I didn't know about
Jamie. He was her husband, her only sweetheart since
they'd been children. No wonder she's lost her wits if
she lost him first."

"Aye, but she didn't have to go hurling rocks at
you," said Alex. "And that nonsense about you coming
home—"

"It wasn't nonsense," said Cora slowly. "She was
speaking the truth. Alex, there isn't one cottage left
along our glen. *Not one.*"

"You can't blame yourself for this, Cora," he said,
appalled she'd even think that way. "You've lost a great
deal yourself."

She shook her head, unconvinced. She'd slipped
the miniature portrait from her pocket, her fingers
tracing over and over the bloodstained leather. "I keep
thinking and talking about Creignish, but Bett lost her
husband and her home, and she's lived through things
I can't imagine, while I—I hid safe in Lady Waldegrave's house. I should have been *here*, Alex, here with
the others."

Alex frowned, turning her horse for her to mount. "Don't let yourself start thinking that way, Cora. That's not the fate your father wished for you, and anyway, it's not what happened. If you start believing you missed something by not suffering enough, why, then, you're just acting as mad as she is. Come now, climb up."

But she didn't, instead standing still with the bloodstained miniature clasped tight in her hands like a prayer book. "But if I'd stayed, there might have been something I could have done to help, for Bett and the others."

"And if you'd stayed, you could be dead as well," he said, more curtly than he'd intended. Knowing they were so close to Creignish and not knowing what would happen when they arrived was making him moody and short-tempered. "Armies and generals don't heed the whims of young ladies, Cora, and that bastard Cumberland doesn't sound as if he'd have stopped if God himself had asked him."

She looked back down at the miniature, at the mottled patches of rusty red. "Once Bett loved me," she said softly. "She called me her wee bonnie bairn, her own sweet lass."

"I'm sorry, Cora," he said, the only thing he could think to say and that damnably inadequate, too. He held out his hand to her, and she came to him, her arms around his waist and her head against his shoulder. "I'm sorry for everything."

"Oh, Alex, as if any of it were your fault." She looked up at him, and though she tried to smile, her eyes stayed dark and sad. "But now it's time to go to Creignish, isn't it? It's time for me to go home."

They rode the last mile in silence, following the

twists and turns of the river. The sky grew darker, or maybe it was simply that the mists drew together to make a heavier blanket against the sun, and the wind swept down through the valley, nipping sharp and chill at their backs for all that it was summer.

"Because we've come along the river," said Cora, "we'll come in through the back gate. You'll recognize the house from there; it's the prospect in the print you bought me at Bushell's shop."

But Alex wasn't so sure. The print had showed a prospering, well-kept manor surrounded by lush gardens and greenery—"The Highland Estate of a Scottish Gentleman"—on a balmy summer afternoon. The path he and Cora were taking now was neither well kept nor lush, and when they reached the stone wall, the pillars capped with two round stone finials, the gate itself was gone, leaving an awkward gap like a missing tooth. Silentley Cora reached out to brush her fingers over the broken iron hinge, guiding her horse first through the entrance without looking back at Alex.

But there wasn't any way she could pretend to overlook the condition of the once formal garden they rode through next. The edgings of the paths had been kicked to pieces, the white crushed shells scattered into the beds. Most of the boxwood and the rose-bushes had been snapped off or pulled up by the roots—for firewood, Alex guessed, a constant need for any army—and though a few sorry perennials showed their faces, the flowerbeds had gone to ugly, ungainly weeds. There was no sign of her father's garden follies or the summerhouse in the shape of a tiny Doric temple that he'd remembered from the print; all of those must have been broken up for firewood, too, and the benches with them. What had been the kitchen garden was also gone, but when Alex remembered Bett's gaunt face, he doubted even the most common cabbages had survived through last summer.

Her expression painfully blank, Cora slid down from her horse, freeing Starlight to roam, and bent to touch the shattered remains of a marble *putto,* his fat-cheeked cherub's face still laughing up at the sky from the mud where he now lay.

"Father brought him from Rome, you know, on his first tour as a young man," she said. "As a statue, he was only a copy and not worth much, but I always liked him anyway."

"I'm sorry, sweetheart," he said again as he dismounted to join her, and again he felt the uselessness of such words. "I'm sorry."

"So am I." Cora rose, dusting the dirt from her fingertips. From this part of the garden she could only make out the chimneys and the very tops of the roof of the house. At least it still stood; she must be grateful for that much. But still she was putting off going there, stalling like a coward as long as she could. After the ride through the glen, she had thought she'd be prepared for what she'd find, but after seeing the garden—only the garden!—so wantonly destroyed, she wasn't sure she could ever face what had happened to the house.

She felt Alex's hand take hers, his fingers warm and strong while her own felt as cold and bloodless as ice. "I'll tell you again, lass," he said. "You don't have to do this."

"But I do," she said, thinking of all the other people in the glen who'd suffered so much worse than a broken marble cherub. "I *must.*"

"Then be brave, Cora," he said, his voice a rough, urgent whisper beside her ear. "You can do this. Be brave, and I'll be there with you."

She nodded, and steeled herself, and walked to the crest of the last hill, to the prospect that her father had labored so hard to perfect.

Now her father would have wept.

The house still stood, yes, the walls straight and square, the sandstone façade still a warm, rosy red even on this bleak day. But the shutters had been pulled off every window and at least half the glass panes in the casements were jaggedly broken. The soft red sandstone was peppered with gunshot holes, while large chunks of the carved pediments and overdoors had simply been blown away for amusement by the soliders, with all the cast-metal hinges and latches pried off to be melted down for new musket balls. Weeds had sprouted in new cracks in the steps, and through the jagged, blackened remains of a long-cold fire in the courtyard.

Cora pressed her hands over her mouth, beyond tears. How could the house that had always represented so much love and happiness to her now look so frighteningly barren?

"Cora, love," began Alex beside her, but she shook him away. She must be brave; Father would wish it. She hurried down the hill toward the door, almost running, not daring to stop until she'd done what she must.

"Cora, be sure," said Alex beside her. In his hand he held one of his pistols, cocked and ready, and she nearly smiled at the sight.

"I'm sure," she said quietly. "I'm home."

She shoved open the door, and with a deep breath

stepped inside, and into a nightmare version of her childhood.

Everything of value that could be carried off had vanished, gone with the looters; what remained had been broken or defiled. The black and white marble tiles in hallway had been pulled up, exposing the rough wooden floor beneath, the balustrade broken off to ugly stumps, the blue glass lantern gone, the two goddesses, Athena and Aphrodite, that had stood on the landing, decapitated and toppled like the cherub in the garden.

But she would be brave; she would see it all. In the dining chamber the paintings of her ancestors had been slashed, the painted canvases hanging in long ribbons from the cockeyed frames. The wall cloth and paper had been peeled back and the plaster knocked out in chunks, down to the house's wooden frame. Frightened pigeons swooped down over her in the back parlor, where the brittle, glittering shards of broken looking glasses littered the floor. In the drawing room, feathers still drifted like snow into the corners where the plump cushions of the chairs and settee had been cut open and scattered, and tattered curtains drifted raggedly through the broken windows.

Swiftly she moved up the stairs to the chambers that had held the most personal treasures, treasures that now were lost forever: paintings and statues, tapestries and looking glasses, carpets and curios, a lifetime of her father's careful collecting, all gone, and him with it, the grief as sharp as if she'd lost him a second time.

"You've seen enough, Cora," said Alex, trying to steer her back downstairs. "You don't have to go further."

"Not yet," she gasped. "The library in the tower. I must see the library."

She raced down the corridor to the one place that had been more Father's than any other. Somehow he'd still be here, among his books, ready to look over his spectacles and smile and welcome her with a kiss and all the love that had filled her girlhood.

The door was closed, the jamb stuck, resisting, until Alex forced it open with his shoulder.

"Father!" cried Cora as she pushed past Alex into the room. "Father, I'm home!"

But only the wind rushed to meet her, the wind that entered through the yawning openings that once had held glass. Not a window remained, and through the broken glass two years' worth of snow and rain and wind had done their destructive work. The books, Father's books, his wisdom and his amusement and his companions, lay scattered and tumbled and torn across the floor, the spines broken and the countless words on their pages smudged and illegible.

And at last she knew he was gone.

"Oh, Father," she sobbed, standing in the middle of the room as the wind ruffled the ruined pages around her feet. "Oh, Father, why did you leave me alone?"

"But he didn't, Cora," said Alex with a fierce urgency, gathering her into his arms, holding her tight, stroking her hair. "Your father's still where he's always been, lass, in your heart, in your memory. The whole English army can't take him from there, Cora. They may have ruined your father's house, but they can't touch his love. They can't, mind?"

"But they *have*," she cried through her tears. "Why else would it hurt so much now?"

"Because you're really missing him for the first time, that's all," said Alex, his voice so warm and deep and male, like Father's, that fresh tears burned in her eyes. "You'll see, sweetheart. He'll always be there with you. Things can always be lost, Cora. It's people and love that last."

"Then why would he have wanted me to come home again?"

Alex considered this only a moment. "Maybe he thought you needed to come home one more time so you could leave again," he said. "Leaving because you wished it, not because you had to."

She'd never doubted how much her father had loved her, loved her enough to send her away that she might live while he died. Father had understood what Alex was saying. Creignish, and all the lost paintings and books and furniture, none of that really mattered at all any longer. Except in her dreams, the Creignish of her childhood was gone. What remained, what was most important and most lasting, was love.

And oh, how much she loved Alex!

"I—I love you," she said through her tears. "I love you, Alex, and I swear that will last!"

He smiled down at her, his mouth charmingly lopsided. "I love you, too, lass," he said, "enough that I'm willing to risk asking you again. Will you marry me, Cora Margaret MacGillivray, and be my wife?"

And this time she didn't hesitate, thinking how perfect he was and how right this seemed for him to ask her here in Father's library.

"Oh, yes, Alex," she cried, her eyes now filling with tears of joy. "I'll be your wife if you'll be my husband, for now and forever and always!"

"Aye, that sounds like enough, doesn't it?" He laughed, and swung her off her feet so she laughed, too. "But who else have you told before me, I wonder?"

"How could I have told anyone?" she asked breathlessly. "How could I, when I've only learned myself?"

"Someone knows," he said, going to look from the window. "There's a carriage at the front door."

"A carriage?" She went to join him, looking down at the elegant small carriage drawn up before the front door, the footmen lolling idly as they waited for their passenger. She hadn't heard anyone knock. Perhaps it was simply a visitor interested in wandering the grounds; well-bred strangers would often come when she was a child, drawn by Creignish's reputation as a landmark.

"Here now, don't get too close," cautioned Alex, protectively pulling her back from the open window. Here in the tower they were perhaps fifty feet above the river; without the glass, he was wise to be careful. "Will you come with me, Mrs. Captain Fairbourne, to see who's calling?"

She smiled shyly at the title, and shook her head. "I'd rather have another few minutes here, if you don't mind."

She knew once they left the house today, she would not return. Though she wished to remember this room as it had been when Father still lived, she still thought she'd look for some small memento, a book that wasn't too badly damaged, to take with her.

"Very well," he said, kissing her again. "Keep from mischief, and I'll be back for you soon."

She sighed as he left, crouching down to sort through the tattered, stained books. She'd seen so many things today that would have broken her father's heart, but she felt sure this would have been the worst. In many ways, she almost wished the English had burned the house with the others outright, instead of treating it and the contents with such willful disrespect.

She picked up a small book half hidden beneath another, one whose pages weren't too badly fanned and the print still legible.

"Ah, forgive me, miss, for disturbing you," said a man's unfamiliar voice. "I did not believe anyone else was within."

Startled, Cora rose swiftly to her feet, and the man in the doorway gasped. He was older, her father's age, and she wondered if perhaps they'd been friends. From his dress, he was a gentleman, and a wealthy gentleman at that, with golden fur lining his velvet coat, and silver buckles on his shoes, and from his speech, he was an Englishman, a London Englishman at that.

"Good day, sir," she said with a modest curtsey. "My name is Cora MacGillivray, sir, and I lived in this house in happier—oh, sir, are you ill?"

"I am fine, miss, perfectly fine," said the man, though the shock on his face said otherwise. He held a small coach lantern in his hand, a useful thing so late in the afternoon of this gray day. "It was the, ah, surprise of learning who you were, that is all. But now that I see your face more clearly—yes, yes, you are who you claim, no doubt."

He stepped over the books to enter the room, holding the lantern higher and coming closer to study her face, and uneasily Cora backed away. For all that this man must be a gentleman, there was something about him that she didn't trust. Surely Alex should return soon, especially since the visitor he'd gone to meet was here with her.

"Did you know my father, sir?" she asked. "Is that why you are here?"

"No, I hadn't the honor, Miss MacGillivray," said the man, glancing around the room as if appraising it. "I came for a rather different reason. I am, you see, the owner of this house."

"But that is not possible, sir!" exclaimed Cora indignantly. "This house is mine until my death."

"Exactly," murmured the man, smiling. "You see, Miss MacGillivray, you've already died once. Oh, it was most tragic—highwaymen robbed your carriage by night, shooting everyone save the horses before they set the carriage on fire. Your friend Lady Waldegrave was forced to identify you by the beads found around your neck, somewhat blackened, to be sure, but still recognizable. Quite a distressing experience for the countess."

"Oh, her poor ladyship!" cried Cora softly. "I must return to London as soon as I can so she can see I'm still alive!"

"But that would be most inconvenient for me, Miss MacGillivray," said the man, carefully setting the lantern down on a bare place on the floor. "I've gone through a great deal of difficult arrangements to secure this house, and I've no desire to see them account for nothing. Though it is not in the condition I'd wished—I must say, Miss MacGillivray, you've hardly done your best to maintain the property—it still seems to have a value sufficient for my needs."

Suddenly Alex appeared in the doorway. "I couldn't find anyone, Cora," he began, "not in the—Sir Thomas!"

With relief Cora hurried to join him. But before she could reach Alex, Walton grabbed her by the waist and shoved her face-first over the sill of the open window, holding her there with her hands pinned behind her back. She struggled briefly, then froze as she realized how unbalanced she was, and how very far from the river and the rocks below. The wind stole her cap, and she watched the scrap of white linen carried down, down until it seemed no more than a speck on the sharp rocks beneath her. When she'd been little, she wouldn't even stand beside these windows, she'd been so scared of falling, and now to be held out like this brought back all the old fears a thousandfold.

"My dear Alexander, good day," said Sir Thomas over his shoulder, smiling though he was breathing hard from the effort of holding Cora. "Though I cannot explain your arrival, it is indeed most fortuitous."

"Let her go," ordered Alex sharply. "By God, let her go now!"

"I've every intention of letting her go, Alex," said Sir Thomas, "once I've your word that you'll swear her death was an accident."

"Damnation, I meant to save her, not let her fall!" Alex stared in horror, afraid to do anything that might break the tenuous balance that Sir Thomas had on Cora's body.

Sir Thomas frowned. "You won't say that when I tell you who the chit is, Alex. You recall how I was to receive a certain property, confiscated from a Jacobite owner, a property that would oblige my debt to your father. When I received—"

"Creignish is the property?" demanded Alex, stunned. "Cora is the difficult owner?"

"Not for much longer," said Sir Thomas with satisfaction. "Swear you'll tell the constable you saw her jump, and you'll have your money in a week."

"The devil take your money," said Alex, biting off each word with his frustration. "Do you think I'd take it at the cost of her life?"

"Bah, what is her life worth to you? To anyone?" scoffed Sir Thomas. "She's nothing but a traitor's daughter, a plain, fatherless hussy that the world won't miss."

Alex's eyes narrowed with anger and hatred, and despite his intentions he took a step forward, his hands knotted in fists. He'd never felt so damned helpless in his life. He hated seeing Cora like this, trapped there beneath Sir Thomas with her eyes squeezed tight with terror, her chestnut curls blowing back in the wind off the glen, the wavering light of the candle in the lantern making her seem to him at once achingly beautiful and hideously vulnerable.

"Cora is priceless to me," he said sharply, "and she's going to be my wife."

"Your wife?" repeated Sir Thomas incredulously. "What will your father say to that, eh? His oldest boy bringing a Jacobite drab like this into his family?"

"He'll like it just fine," growled Alex, "because I love her."

"Love," repeated the older man with bitter scorn. "I cannot see Josh Fairbourne swayed by *love.*"

"You would, every time he looks at my mother," said Alex. "Not that you'd understand that, you murdering old bastard. I *love* her, mind?"

He saw how Cora opened her eyes at that, his own dear, brave lass, how she turned just the fraction she needed to catch his eye, to let him know she loved him back. It couldn't end like this, not before they'd truly begun. He wanted a whole lifetime with her and then some, children, lots of children, in a big sunny house on Massachusetts Bay, as far as he could take her from this bleak and ruined place. All that he tried to tell his Cora with just a single shared look; and somehow, from how she looked back at him, he thought he had.

Then suddenly her gaze was shifting to his right, to the doorway, surprise flickering through her eyes.

"Starlight!" she called softly.

Alex looked back, just in time to see the little black cat in the doorway. His tail was straight in the air, his back arched and the fur upright, his mouth open to hiss, as confident as any jungle panther that he owned the world.

Determined to reach Cora, the cat bounded deftly across the piles of tattered books, racing from one to the next as if they were floes of ice in the river.

"Where'd that damned cat come from?" demanded Sir Thomas uneasily. "A black cat like that's no good luck to anyone. Come any closer, you hell-cat, and I'll toss you out the window, too."

As if he understood, Starlight paused with his ears flattened back, flicking his tail with displeasure. Then, with feline precision, he leaped onto a book that was haphazardly tossed on a pile of others. He tipped his weight enough to make the book begin to slide beneath him, from the top of the pile, faster now, fast enough that when it finally struck Sir Thomas' lantern on the floor, the lantern toppled over onto its side and the lit candle inside jarred free, spilling a trail of hot wax over the spread pages of another book. Instantly the dry, brittle pages ignited, a hot puddle of fire so bright and fast it seemed to explode, jumping swiftly from one book to the next.

"Clumsy brute!" shouted Sir Thomas, pulling Cora with him as he lunged toward the lantern and the fire. But as soon as Cora realized she was clear of the window, she plunged wildly to try to free herself of his grasp, twisting desperately to reach Alex.

"Stop wriggling, you foolish bitch!" said Sir Thomas. "Stop it, I say, at once!"

But as he shielded his face against the growing flames his heel skidded on another book and his feet flew out from under him. Alex raced forward and grabbed Cora, pulling her free just as Sir Thomas fell backward.

And fell. The fragile lead tracery that remained in the paneless window behind him gave way instantly beneath the weight of his fall. He flailed his arms, almost as if he were trying to fly, and then he was gone over the sill, his last cry echoing against the wall as he dropped, clear to the rocky riverbed below, and the cry ended as abruptly as his life.

Swiftly Cora hugged Alex, relief and joy and love all mingled together into one instant. There wasn't time for more.

"Quick, Cora, this way," said Alex, yanking her toward the door as the fire spread from the books to the dry old floorboards and beams, the wind through the open windows fanning the flames higher and hotter.

"Not without Starlight!" protested Cora, squinting into the smoke and flames for the little cat. "Starlight, here, here!"

"Cora, love, we can't let ourselves get trapped in here," said Alex, raising his voice over the fire's crackle and roar. "We must go now."

"Oh, please, Starlight, no games!" pleaded Cora, coughing from the smoke. "Come *now!*"

And come he did, racing through the flames straight into her arms, overjoyed to be rescued.

"Now, Cora, now!" shouted Alex, and with his hand linked with hers they ran from the room and down the stairs and past the twin headless goddesses. Already the wind was carrying burning scraps of paper through the rest of the house, igniting fresh flames wherever they landed—on the curtains, the wall cloths, the bare floorboards and beams. Still Alex and Cora ran, from the burning house and back toward the gardens.

"Wait!" cried Cora when they'd reached the first hill, pulling on Alex's hand to make him stop. "Please, for me!"

Gasping for breath, she forced herself to turn for one last look here on the hill where the prospect of Creignish had been most celebrated. By now the flames filled every window, the heat roaring into the night and shattering the last windows with dry little pops. The entire house glowed like a giant lantern on the hillside, a sight surely visible for miles away.

Cora held Starlight tight in her arms, her eyes dry but her heart aching with loss. It was done, it was over, and though she knew it was for the best—for much better, really, because of Alex—Creignish burned with a fierce finality she'd never dreamed she'd see, and that she knew she'd never forget.

"Goodbye," she said softly, dropping to her knees on the scattered white stones. "Goodbye, and farewell."

EPILOGUE

Cora sat alone on the bench in Lady Waldegrave's back drawing room, her bouquet of white and yellow roses beside her and her stockinged feet tucked up under her skirts where no one could see how she'd kicked off her high-heeled shoes. She could still hear the voices and laughter of the guests gathered in the front parlor, an unlikely crowd of sailors from the colonies and lords and ladies from London society that had been blended joyfully together by an excellent, and excellently potent, wedding punch of Junius' secret concoction. Cora smiled to herself, remembering the wickedness of some of the toasts that had been raised to her and Alex; she'd have to go back soon before she was missed, but she'd needed this time alone, a moment to reflect on the happy whirl her life had become.

Three months ago she'd been squirreled away in her attic room. Now she was Mrs. Captain Alexander Fairbourne, swept into her new station with all the pomp and display (and even a bishop's blessing) that an ecstatic Lady Waldegrave could muster on short notice, and bound tomorrow for a new home in Massachusetts. In that same time Cora had been declared dead, and then declared alive, and the undisputed heiress of a great deal of land in the Highlands. Though Creignish itself was gone, she'd found a man with new ideas for farming and boundless energy who'd leased the land from her, and had promised work and fair pay for all in the clans who wished it, regardless of their politics.

Alex, too, had seen the courts smile on him. Because of the circumstances of Sir Thomas Walton's death, Joshua Fairbourne had been the first creditor recognized by the dead man's estate, and when Alex returned home he'd be able to give his father the full amount Sir Thomas had owed him, plus the thirty years' interest the judge had awarded. It would, all in all, make for a most joyful homecoming to Appledore for Alex, and a most auspicious welcome for Cora.

"Here you are, sweetheart," said Alex, his smile full of love as he came to join her, and quickly she gathered her roses to make room for him on the bench. "Tell me you're merely hiding from the happy horde, and not having second thoughts."

"Oh, no, Alex, I'd never—" she began, then realized he was teasing, and contented herself with swatting him with her bouquet.

Not mortally wounded, he laughed, and slipped his arm around her waist. She liked the feel of that arm, one of the countless small ways her new husband had of making her feel cherished and loved. Her *husband*: the very notion still amazed her, especially when that husband was the astoundingly handsome man beside her.

"I have been thinking, yes," she admitted, "which was impossible to do in there with so many bawdy toasts flying about."

"All meant with the best possible wishes," declared Alex, then his voice dropped lower. "You were thinking of Creignish, weren't you?"

She nodded. "How could I not? But only good things, Alex, and no regrets. Not even Father could have wished for more."

Something soft brushed against her foot, and smiling, Cora bent to pick up Starlight. It wasn't as easy as it once had been—he was growing into a cat of magnificent proportions—but since he'd behaved so well today among so many strangers, Cora was willing to pamper him a bit.

"My handsome lad," she crooned, stroking his sleek, velvety head. There were still small bald spots on his ears where the sparks from the fire had burned away his fur, but he wore the scars as proudly as any warrior, and much more happily than the blue silk ribbon around his neck that Cora had made him don for the wedding. "Have you been stealing tidbits from the table, my favorite cat fellow?"

"Mostly he's been paraded about by Diana, who's telling everyone how he made her match with Roxby," said Alex. "Honestly, Cora, I do wish my sister were coming home with us to Appledore. I know that Roxby's exactly the sort of husband Di came here to snag, but I don't like the man and I don't trust him, and I'd feel far happier if she were with me where I could keep her from mischief."

"But Diana loves him," said Cora, "and she's the one who's to wed him, not you. You have to let her go, Alex. No wonder she's had to leave home to find true love, too."

Alex sighed. "Are you always so wise, Cora Margaret?"

"Always," she answered promptly. "In all things."

He chuckled, and drew her closer. "I am so proud of you, my brave and bonnie little wife," he said softly. "Do you know how much I love you, eh?"

"Oh, aye," she said as she turned to kiss him. "But it can never be as much as *I* love *you*. Always and forever, Alex. Mind you remember that, Captain. Always and forever."

And beside them, Starlight blinked slyly, and began to purr in perfect contentment.

Breathtaking romance from

MIRANDA JARRETT

The Captain's Bride

Cranberry Point

Moonlight

Sunrise

Wishing

**Visit the Simon & Schuster
romance Web site:**

www.SimonSaysLove.com

**and sign up for our
romance e-mail updates!**

Keep up on the latest
new romance releases,
author appearances, news, chats,
special offers, and more!
We'll deliver the information
right to your inbox—if it's new,
you'll know about it.

POCKET BOOKS

Sonnet Books
Proudly Presents

Star Bright
MIRANDA JARRETT

Coming in mid-November 2000
from Sonnet Books

The following is a preview of
***STAR BRIGHT*. . . .**

Ashburnham Hall,
Hampshire
1747

From the outside, the letter seemed innocuous enough: a sheet of thick, cream-colored paper, neatly folded, sealed with a blob of red wax, and addressed in a lady's well-bred hand. It stood on its edge, propped between the chocolate pot and the porcelain cup on the silver breakfast tray, demure and unprepossessing and waiting to shatter the blissful perfection of Diana Fairbourne's life.

"Thank you, Mary," said Diana as she hurriedly finished braiding her dark hair into a single thick plait and flipped it back over her shoulder. She plucked a slice of toast from the tray, eating it as she knelt to hunt beneath the bed for her old walking shoes.

"I'll find them for you, miss," volunteered Mary, more than a little shocked to see Diana crawling about on the carpet, and dressed as plainly as any farmer's daughter, too. For a lady and a famous beauty who'd taken fashionable London by storm, Diana showed far too much initiative in making do for herself. No wonder that since arriving at Ashburnham Hall, she'd become the subject of much head shaking and talk in the servants' quarters. "You sit now, and have your breakfast proper."

"But you see I've found them already," said Diana, sitting back on the floor to buckle her shoes on her feet in a way that was quite shamelessly common. "You may go, Mary. I won't need you, truly. I'll be on my way myself in a moment."

"But your breakfast, miss," said Mary, stern with disapproval, her hands clasped at her waist. "You must eat, miss."

"I'll be fine, Mary," said Diana, looking toward the late-summer morning beyond her bedchamber's windows. The dawn wasn't long past, the first pale sunlight drifting in through the curtains, and the hour far too early for anyone other than the servants to be awake in the great house.

Diana grinned as she flung a light shawl over her shoulders. All her life she'd risen early, and not even the fact that in four short weeks she'd marry Ashburnham Hall's master and become the Marchioness of Roxby would make her sleep beyond daybreak. "Madame Lark," the marquess had dubbed her, and promised that once they'd wed, he'd give Diana reason enough to keep to their bed with him and forget her peculiar colonial propensity for early morning rambles.

But Diana had only laughed and kissed him on the cheek. She still could scarcely believe he'd fallen in love with her as quickly as she had with him, or that he'd asked for her hand after only a fortnight's acquaintance, while showing her his collection of Roman intaglios and before she'd even learned his Christian name. He'd called her his destiny, the most romantic declaration she'd ever heard. How could she not love a man who spoke like that?

She was smiling to herself as she reached for another piece of toast to take with her, and saw the letter. The handwriting wasn't familiar, but that meant nothing. Since she'd become betrothed to Roxby, she'd received many invitations and notes of congratulations from people she'd never met. Curious, she slipped her finger beneath the seal to crack it open, and unfolded the single sheet. The message was short, only a handful of words, but more than enough to do what its sender had wished.

Miss Fairbourne,
If you value your Heart & Happiness, you will break off yr. Match with Lord Roxby at once. He keeps a Mistress in London, & loves you Not. Ask him if you Dare, I do not lie.

A Friend who wishes you Well

Twice Diana read the letter to be sure she wasn't imagining it, then read the words through one more time, burning them into her mind, and her heart as well. Of course it couldn't be true. Of course it must be lies. And of course the letter was unsigned. Who would take credit for such vile, troublemaking calumny?

"Are you unwell, miss?" asked Mary with concern. "Not unhappy news, is it?"

"Not at all," said Diana, her fingers trembling as she refolded the letter. She could toss it into the fire, or tear it to tiny pieces, or take it to show Lady Waldegrave, her mother's oldest friend and Diana's companion until she was wed. Or she could do the one thing that the letter's author never expected her to do. "Mary, is his lordship awake?"

"Awake?" repeated Mary with the sudden blankness that practiced servants could muster in an instant. "Nay, miss, his lordship is never awake at this hour."

"Then I shall wake him." With the letter in her hand,

Diana swept from the room, determined not to let suspicion fester and grow a moment longer than was necessary. "His lordship's bedchamber is in the north wing, isn't it?"

"Aye, miss, but you shouldn't—you mustn't—go there!" protested Mary breathlessly, trotting to keep pace with her. " 'Tis not proper, miss, 'tis not right!"

"In a month no one will think anything of it," declared Diana, "or remember that, this once, I went there at all."

"But miss—miss!—his lordship's not there!"

Abruptly Diana stopped. "Not there? Wherever else would he be if not in his own bed?"

An unpleasant possibility, brought on by that dreadful anonymous letter, immediately came to Diana's mind, and just as swiftly she shoved it aside. Roxby loved *her*, and he'd never once given her reason to doubt him.

"His lordship's not at home at present, miss," said the maid uncomfortably. "After you and the other ladies retired last night, miss, he and Lord Stanver decided to go to Robinwood to play faro. On a whim, it was, miss, the way the gentlemen do."

Robinwood was Lord Stanver's estate, and known to be such a gamester's paradise that a faro dealer was as permanent a part of the household staff as a butler or cook. But what Diana considered now was Robinwood's proximity to London, only a half-hour's ride at most from the gates of the house—

But she would *not* think that, not of her Roxby. She was sure there were other ladies and women in his past— he was nearly thirty years old, after all—but she was equally certain that he'd be far too honorable to dare ask for her hand if his heart wasn't free.

Wasn't he?

And her only answer was the rustle of paper as she clutched the letter more tightly in her fingers.

"We expect his lordship's return any minute, miss," said Mary, almost apologetically. "We'll tell him you wish to speak with him directly."

"Please tell him I have gone walking," said Diana sharply, stuffing the letter into her pocket, "and that I shall speak with him as soon as *I* return."

But Diana wasn't even through the door before she regretted both her words and her temper. The letter wasn't Mary's fault, any more than Roxby was guilty simply because some anonymous coward said so. No: the problem instead lay with Diana's own habitual impatience. She tended to charge headlong through life, guided by impulse and so little ladylike caution that, before Roxby, her mother had despaired of her ever staying still long enough to attract a husband.

But Diana had never been good at waiting. She'd always wanted things settled *now*, just as she wanted to hear Roxby himself deny the letter's accusations. That was what she wanted, and what she couldn't have, and what made her stride so swiftly that she was practically running by the time she reached the garden, frustration and ugly doubts driving her footsteps over the neatly raked paths of the rose gardens.

But when she reached the end of the paths, she'd still found no peace, and instead of following the white gravel back to the house, she cut across the open fields where, in the distance, black-faced sheep grazed. The taller grasses brushed against her legs, the hem of her petticoats growing heavy with dew, and the rising sun warmed her shoulders. Still she rushed on without stopping, farther than she'd gone on any other morning, at last coming to the stand of old oaks that marked the end of these tended fields and the beginning of the wood-lands.

She blinked to let her eyes adjust to the shadows, the air cooler here beneath the trees, the ground beneath her feet soft with moss and old leaves. Through the trees, she could make out the glitter of reflecting water, and she remembered Roxby telling her about a long-abandoned mill and pond on his land that he fancied as his "ruin." Holding her arms out for balance, she skipped and slid down the hill to the pond's bank. A stone that she'd accidentally kicked loose rolled ahead of her, bouncing off a tree root to land in the water with a resounding *plop*.

"What the devil are you doing?" roared a man's voice. "Or did you mean to drive every fish away just to plague me?"

"And who, pray, are you to speak to me like that?" Diana shouted in return. She shoved aside the last branches and overgrown vines, determined to see who this impossibly rude man could be.

She didn't have far to look. He sat at the oars of a small boat just off the shore, drifting gently on the still water beyond the rushes. The line from his fishing pole trailed from the boat's side, and at his feet was a basket for keeping the fish with another holding an earthenware jug and his half-eaten breakfast. From the rough belligerence in his voice, she'd expected some gruff countryman, the kind that regarded poaching as an honorable art, and from the man's clothes—grimy leather breeches, a checkered shirt with the throat open, a faded dark linen coat, and a misshapen old black hat—that was exactly what he was.

But though the clothes had been predictable enough, the man inside them wasn't. His features were too strong to be called handsome, his nose a bit crooked from a long-ago break, his jaw pronounced and inclined to stubbornness. Living out-of-doors had browned and weathered his skin, with little lines fanning out from green eyes that seemed to reflect the water's liveliness, and the hair that poked out haphazardly from beneath his hat was light brown, gilded, again, by the sun. His shoulders were broad, his thighs thickly muscled laborer's muscles earned by hard work.

He wasn't handsome at all, not really, especially since Diana's eyes had become so trained to the well-bred Londoner's ideal of handsomeness. But there was a supremely male confidence to him that she couldn't ignore, a determined sort of physical masculinity, almost an arrogance, that reminded her of the men back home—precisely the kind of man that she'd left Massachusetts to avoid.

"Are you finished gawking, then?" he demanded, his green eyes glaring at her as if she were a witch who'd poisoned his well. "Or are you just considering which stone to heave next at me and my fish?"

Diana flushed. "Why must you insist on believing I've purposely spoiled your angling?"

"Because you've given me no reason to believe otherwise," he said, openly appraising her just as she had him. "The way you came crashing through the woods with your guns all a-fire, flailing your arms about and tossing stones—what else am I to believe?"

"I did not throw the stone. I merely dislodged it with my foot and it tumbled into the water before me." She sighed impatiently, pushing her hat back farther from her forehead. She didn't know why she was continuing such a pointless conversation except that she hated to be bettered by anyone, and right now this man clearly held the advantage in the conversation. "Don't you know whose land you're on?"

"I'm not on anyone's *land*," retorted the man, "but I am upon the Marquess of Roxby's water. Not that his high and mighty lordship needs the likes of you defending his property."

She gasped indignantly, then remembered how she was dressed. If she told him she was the future Marchioness of Roxby, he'd laugh out loud.

"You are still trespassing," she said instead. "I could report you to his lordship's gamekeeper. I *should*."

But the man merely stared up at her, his green eyes glinting. "So who the devil fouled your temper this morning, eh? Or do you begin every day picking quarrels with strangers?"

"I should hardly call this a quarrel," she began, then broke off once again. He was right, pox him. Her temper was most definitely fouled on account of that wretched letter in her pocket. "Though I could certainly accuse you of being quarrelsome."

"Aye, you could," he agreed, "and you'd be right. I won't deny it. I am not by nature a peaceable man, and I've started more quarrels than I'll ever remember."

He smiled, a lopsided smile burdened with bitterness, and pulled his fishing line from the water. "But I'm clearing off now anyway. No more fish to be had this day, thanks to you, and besides, I don't want you hauling me before old Roxby's gamekeeper. Why, I'm all a-shiver even thinking of it."

Pointedly he looked away from her, concentrating instead on settling the oars in their locks while Diana fumed. She wasn't accustomed to men talking to her like this—at least any man that wasn't one of her brothers—and she didn't like it, not at all.

But before she could answer, she noticed something odd: the man couldn't row to save his life. Oh, he did well enough with the oar in his left hand, but he'd absolutely no control with the one in his right, the blade first flopping clumsily over the surface of the water, then chopping deep enough to make the boat lurch unsteadily and the man swear with annoyance.

She watched, and smiled sweetly. "You must dip both oars into the water, sir, and keep your elbows close to your body," she noted. "Else your vessel will never go anywhere."

He glared at her from beneath the brim of his hat, challenging, his expression black as a thundercloud. "I suppose a chit like you could do better."

A nearly married marchioness was not a chit, but Diana let her temper simmer inside, and instead widened her smile. "I could indeed."

"The hell you could," he growled. He pulled the oar free of the lock and clumsily thrust it deep into the soft, shallow bottom of the pond, pushing the boat forward that way. With two shoves, he'd reached the bank, bumping up against the moss to where Diana stood.

"Aboard with you, then," he ordered, holding his hand out to her. "Come along. Take the oars, and prove to me you can do what you claim."

"I'll do nothing of the sort," she said as she scuttled backward away from him. "I don't have to obey your orders."

"I'm not asking for obedience," he said impatiently. "I'm asking for proof."

She withdrew further, shaking her head. This was madness; no, this *man* was mad, challenging her like this. If she'd any sense at all, she'd turn around and run and not stop until she'd reached the safety of the house.

"All bluster and empty air, are you?" His green eyes narrowed, scornfully skeptical. "If you don't show me how you can handle this boat, then I'll have to believe you lied about doing better. I'll have to think you don't want to show me because you can't."

That did it. She might be able to do nothing about that cowardly lady who'd written the letter, but she could put this challenging rascal in his place.

"Across the pond to that bank and back," she declared tartly, bunching up her skirts with one hand as she came down the bank to the boat. "More than enough to prove I can row circles around you."

"You've proved nothing yet," he said as he shifted benches, holding the boat steady for her. "Keep low now. I've no wish to be tipped overboard."

"Oh, yes, and be sure to warn me about tiptoeing across the lily pads, too," she answered as she nimbly climbed over the side. She'd been born in a seafaring town on Cape Cod, clambering in and out of boats and ships since she'd been a tiny girl, and she certainly didn't need any advice about keeping low. She centered herself on the bench with her feet against the stretcher, primly tucked her petticoats around her ankles, and with practiced ease set the first oar into its lock.

"I'll need that one, too, if you please," she said, taking the second oar from him. "Otherwise we'll keep making a circle, much the way that you already were."

He grumbled wordlessly, a disdainful growl deep in his throat, and with his left hand pushed the boat free of the bank. The boat was long but narrow, with scarcely space for one man his size, let alone for them both, and as he sat facing her, she was all too aware of how their knees nearly touched.

Chin in, back straight: she'd concentrate on that instead of him. Confidently she drew back the oars, dipped the blades into the water, and pulled. The little boat glided forward, and she pulled again, the rhythm of her rowing easy and sure.

But each time she leaned forward with the oars she also leaned close, closer, to the large man sitting across from her. She couldn't help looking at him because he blocked everything else in her view. Against her will she began noticing more about him, small, intimate things: how his jaw still gleamed faintly from his razor's morning rasp, how the neck of that shirt was open enough to reveal a fascinating patch of curling dark hair on his chest, how his freshly washed shirt smelled of soap and iron-scorch and his own male scent, a scent she'd no right at all to be smelling.

"You've stopped," he said, faintly accusing. "Are you tired already?"

"Not at all," she answered quickly, though she let the boat's momentum carry them forward while the oars trailed idle in her hands and her face stayed safely apart from his chest. "I learned to handle a boat in the ocean, against the waves. To row on this pond is like rowing in a bucket of wash water."

"Then why quit? You promised you'd row to the bank and back, wash water or not."

" 'Tis not that," she said, hedging. Belatedly she pictured what another would see, the two of them so close together in a boat on this isolated pond, and tried to imagine how she'd explain this particular impulsiveness to Roxby. " 'Tis not that at all."

"No?" he asked, his eyes glinting in the shadow of his hat's brim, challenging her yet again. "Then perhaps you're simply afraid of me."

Diana's chin rose defiantly. "I'm not afraid of you, sir. Not with an oar in my hand."

"You'd do it, too, wouldn't you?" he asked, his lopsided

smile now amused but also strangely approving at the same time. "Strike me across the nose like a recalcitrant donkey?"

"If you deserved it." Her brothers had taught her how to defend herself, a necessary skill for a woman in a seaport full of randy sailors. "If you were too forward."

"Ah, well, we cannot have that, can we?" To her surprise, he shifted on the bench, giving her more space. "Row on, then, coxswain, or we'll never make our landfall. Handsomely now, handsomely!"

Once again she dipped the blades into the water, considering not so much what he'd said, but how he'd said it. "You don't speak like a landsman. Have you ever been to sea?"

"Aye," he said, his expression abruptly turning guarded. "But not now."

Close to the bank, she neatly brought the boat around. But now he wasn't noticing; instead he was lost in his own thoughts as he stared out over the water.

"There's no shame in going to sea, at least not to me," she said to fill the silence. She'd rather liked being called a coxswain, and she was sorry he'd turned moody and stopped. "My own family's thick with sailors. That's why I can row. Likely I should've told you that in the beginning."

He sighed gloomily. "Likely you should have, aye. Lucky for me I'd staked no money against you."

"Then you concede?" she asked. "You'll say that I can row better than you?"

"Aye, you do," he growled, shaking his head with undisguised disgust, "as you know perfectly well. Bettered by some chit of a girl. Jesus."

"I'm not an ordinary chit, you know," she said, almost apologetically. Because she'd won, she could afford to be magnanimous. "Another time, and you might well have done better."

"Not in this life," he said, the bitterness returning to his voice. "The damned French have seen to that, haven't they?"

"The French?" she repeated, mystified. Her brothers and father blamed much of their misfortunes upon the French as well, for it seemed the two countries had been at war as long as she could remember. But suddenly she understood what the man was saying, the truth that she'd so blithely, blindly overlooked.

"Your right arm," she said softly. "You were wounded by the French, weren't you? That's why you can't row properly now, isn't it?"

"How kind of you to remark it." Unconsciously he cradled his awkward right arm with his left against his chest, as if to shield it from her concern.

"I am sorry," she said, and she was. She'd seen her share of battle-scarred sailors with missing limbs or shocking disfigurements earned in the king's service, and she hated to think of this man, young as he still was, already crippled for the rest of his life. No wonder he was poaching, too; there'd be precious few opportunities left for a man with only one good arm and hand here in the middle of Hampshire. "I should never have—"

"No pity," he ordered sharply. "I don't want it."

"But I only meant—"

"I know what you meant, and I'd rather you'd strike me with that blasted oar."

"Then perhaps I should, just to be obliging, and to knock some sense into your witless brain, too." The boat bumped against the bank where they'd begun, and she briskly shipped the oars. If he mistook her kindness for pity, then that was his concern, not hers. "Pray hold the boat steady for me, if you please, so I may go ashore."

"Oh, aye, please may I, pretty as pie," he said, goading her as he jabbed one of the oars back into the soft bottom as a makeshift anchor. "Going back to the first man who dared cross you this morning, are you? Eager to bedevil another poor bastard?"

"I am not!" she answered indignantly, wishing she hadn't at that exact moment remembered the letter in her pocket. "I never said I was!"

"You didn't have to," he said, grinning with the triumph she'd thought earlier was hers. "I told you I was quarrelsome by nature, and so are you. You can't help it, lass, any more than I can. And of course it's a man that's provoked you. With a woman like you, it always is, isn't it?"

"You know nothing of me, sir, or of my situation," she said warmly as she scrambled from the boat and up the bank, "nor shall you ever have the opportunity to learn!"

"Go on, coxswain," he called after her. "Give the bastard the righteous hell he deserves. And remember how you're no ordinary chit!"

Look for STAR BRIGHT
by Miranda Jarrett
Coming in November 2000 from Sonnet Books